PRAISE FOR ANNA CAMPBELL

"*The Seduction of Lord Stone* is romantic, emotional, sexy and funny. In fact, everything I have come to expect from Anna Campbell. I'm looking forward to reading the other Dashing Widows' stories." —*RakesandRascals.com*

"With her marvelous combination of humor and poignancy Anna Campbell writes in such a way that every story of hers has a special meaning and remains like a sentimental keepsake with those fortunate enough to read her work!" —*JeneratedReviews.com*

"*Lord Garson's Bride* is a well written and passionate story that touched my heart and sent my emotions on a rollercoaster ride. I particularly recommend this book for fans of convenient marriages, and those who enjoy seeing a deserving character find out that love is lovelier the second time around." —***Roses Are Blue Reviews***

"Campbell immediately hooks readers, then deftly reels them in with a spellbinding love story fueled by an addictive mixture of sharp wit, lush sensuality, and a wealth of well-delineated characters."—***Booklist***, ***starred review, on A Scoundrel by Moonlight***

"With its superbly nuanced characters, impeccably crafted historical setting, and graceful writing shot through with scintillating wit, Campbell's latest lusciously sensual, flawlessly written historical Regency ... will have romance readers sighing happily with satisfaction."—***Booklist, Starred Review, on What a Duke Dares***

"Campbell makes the Regency period pop in the appealing third Sons of Sin novel. Romantic fireworks, the constraints of custom, and witty banter are combined in this sweet and successful story."—*Publishers Weekly on What a Duke Dares*

"Campbell is exceptionally talented, especially with plots that challenge the reader, and emotions and characters that are complex and memorable."—*Sarah Wendell, Smart Bitches Trashy Books, on A Rake's Midnight Kiss*

"A lovely, lovely book that will touch your heart and remind you why you read romance."—*Liz Carlyle, New York Times bestselling author on What a Duke Dares*

"Campbell holds readers captive with her highly intense, emotional, sizzling and dark romances. She instinctually knows how to play on her readers' fantasies to create a romantic, deep-sigh tale."—*RT Book Reviews, Top Pick, on Captive of Sin*

"Don't miss this novel - it speaks to the wild drama of the heart, creating a love story that really does transcend class."—*Eloisa James, New York Times bestselling author, on Tempt the Devil*

"*Seven Nights in A Rogue's Bed* is a lush, sensuous treat. I was enthralled from the first page to the last and still wanted more."—*Laura Lee Guhrke, New York Times bestselling author*

"No one does lovely, dark romance or lovely, dark heroes like Anna Campbell. I love her books."—*Sarah MacLean, New York Times bestselling author*

"It isn't just the sensuality she weaves into her story that makes Campbell a fan favorite, it's also her strong, three-dimensional characters, sharp dialogue and deft plotting. Campbell intuitively knows how to balance the key elements of the genre and give readers an irresistible, memorable read."—*RT Book Reviews, Top Pick, on Midnight's Wild Passion*

"Anna Campbell is an amazing, daring new voice in romance."—*Lorraine Heath, New York Times bestselling author*

"Ms. Campbell's gorgeous writing a true thing of beauty..."—*Joyfully Reviewed*

"She's the mistress of dark, sexy and brooding and takes us into the dens of iniquity with humor and class."—*Bookseller-Publisher Australia*

"Anna Campbell is a master at drawing a reader in from the very first page and keeping them captivated the whole book through. Ms. Campbell's books are all on my keeper shelf and *Midnight's Wild Passion* will join them proudly. *Midnight's Wild Passion* is a smoothly sensual delight that was a joy to read and I cannot wait to revisit Antonia and Nicholas's romance again."—*Joyfully Reviewed*

"Ms. Campbell gives us...the steamy sex scenes, a heroine whose backbone is pure steel and a stupendous tale of lust and love and you too cannot help but fall in love with this tantalizing novel."—*Coffee Time Romance*

"Anna Campbell offers us again, a lush, intimate, seductive read. I am in awe of the way she keeps the focus tight on the hero and heroine, almost achingly so. Nothing else really exists in this world, but the two main characters. Intimate, sensual story with a hero that will take your breath away."—*Historical Romance Books & More*

ALSO BY ANNA CAMPBELL

The Highlander's Lost Lady

Christmas Stories:

The Winter Wife

Her Christmas Earl

A Pirate for Christmas

Mistletoe and the Major

A Match Made in Mistletoe

The Christmas Stranger

Other Books:

These Haunted Hearts

Stranded with the Scottish Earl

LORD GARSON'S BRIDE

THE DASHING WIDOWS BOOK 7

ANNA CAMPBELL

 Serenade Publishing

ISBN: 978-0-6483987-9-0

Cover design: By Hang Le

Print editions published by Serenade Publishing
www.serenadepublishing.com

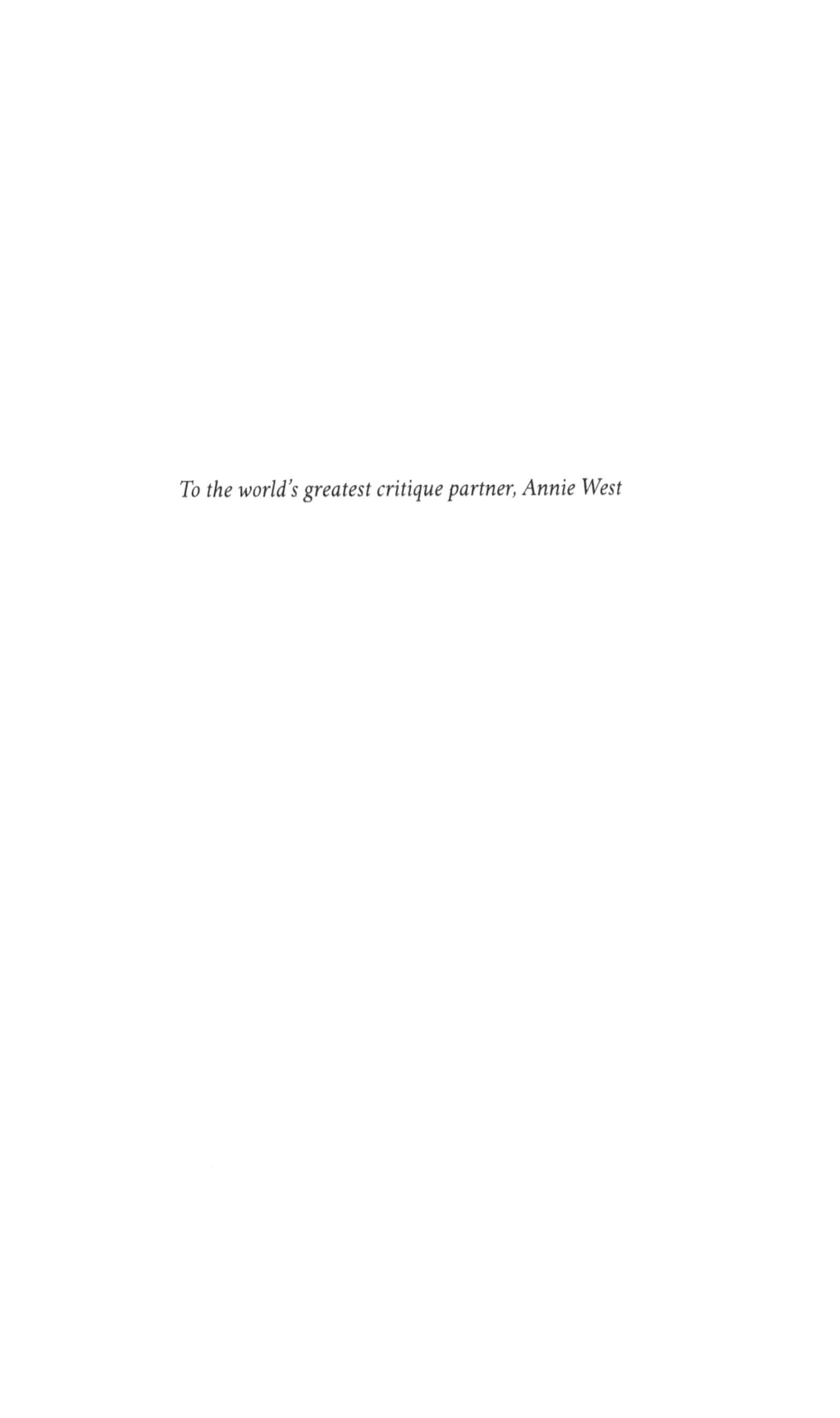

To the world's greatest critique partner, Annie West

CHAPTER ONE

Cavell Court, Dorset, February 1833

"*L*ord Garson has called, my lady."

Her butler's announcement made Lady Jane Norris look up from the huge desk in the library where once her late father, Lord Sefton, had sat to run his estates. Paper littered every surface, as she sorted through the archives. She supposed she could leave this massive task for her cousin Felix, when he took over next month. But a lingering sense of familial obligation had her determined to pass everything to the new earl in good order.

"Garson is here?" she asked, unable to hide her surprise.

Hugh Rutherford, Baron Garson, had known her since she was toddling, although in recent years, he'd rarely visited this isolated manor house in the West Country. She'd last seen him six months ago, when he attended her father's funeral.

"Yes, my lady," Billings said. "Are you at home to visitors this afternoon?"

"I suppose so." Jane cast a rueful glance at her shabby gray frock, with its creases and ink stains. She wasn't dressed to receive one of the ton's darlings. "Did he say what he wanted?"

"I'm afraid not."

She should change into a more suitable gown and tidy her mop of red hair before she greeted her guest. Although she was unhappily aware that whether she combed her hair or not, she remained Lord Sefton's plain, sensible, spinster daughter.

Oh, stop feeling sorry for yourself, Jane Norris. "Would you please show his lordship into the drawing room, Billings, and say I'll be with him presently? And perhaps arrange some refreshments."

Once Billings had gone, instead of dashing upstairs, she stared sightlessly at an account for some bonnets for her mother. Given her mother had been dead nearly twenty years, she could safely throw it away. But she held it in front of her, as her mind raced with conjecture. Garson? Here? Why? It couldn't be a casual call. Nobody was ever just passing. Cavell Court was out of the way, and the roads leading to it were frightful, especially during a bad winter like this one.

With a sigh, Jane rose and smoothed her hair, confined in a loose knot that she feared was more loose than knot. Her father's habit of retaining every scrap of paper that crossed his desk made her run her hands through her hair in frustration.

Once she finished with these papers, she'd completed her last duty at the estate. The task felt like some sort of rite. Felix had been nice enough to let her spend her six months of mourning in the house she'd grown up in. The reprieve gave her a chance to say goodbye to the only home she'd ever known, before she ventured into an unknown future. She also said a final farewell to the father she loved and missed, whatever his faults. For over a decade, she'd acted as his right hand, busy and purposeful. Now the time stretching before her seemed depressingly aimless.

At least Garson's visit might distract her from the constant round of sorrow and worry. Lately she felt like she trudged through an endless mire of toil and exhaustion and grief. Lately? She'd had ten lonely years of shouldering the burdens of the estate and caring for her ill father. No wonder she was so tired, she felt like crying.

When Jane came downstairs again, she was in a clean gown, and her hair was scraped back into a bun. She crossed the hall to the drawing room. The watery sun lit a space crowded with heavy, old-fashioned furniture. Jane suspected the new Lady Sefton would consign most of the house's current furnishings to the bonfire.

Standing in profile to her was Lord Garson, the son of her father's best friend. Six years older than her. Rich. Handsome. Widely praised as the perfect gentleman.

And notorious as the most famous rejected suitor in England.

Three years ago, Garson had been on the point of marrying Morwenna Nash, a naval captain's widow. But Robert Nash turned out to be not as dead as rumor had him, returning to disrupt the ball celebrating Garson's betrothal. When his fiancée reunited with her husband, she left Garson very publicly nursing a broken heart.

Jane stood in the doorway and observed her childhood friend, curious to see the changes in him. He was an attractive man, with regular features and thick, coffee-brown hair. Tall, vigorous, powerful. The world was his oyster, one would imagine.

Except as he stared pensively into the fire, a melancholy air clung to him. The flames played across his chiseled features, highlighting the straight nose and square, determined lines of chin and jaw. And the grim set of his generous mouth.

When they'd spoken at her father's funeral, Jane had been shocked at his appearance—she hadn't seen him for a couple of years, but she'd heard about his romantic disappointment. He'd struck her then as old beyond his years. On this winter afternoon, that impression strengthened.

What a pity that he was so unhappy. She'd always liked him. A kind boy had grown up to be a nice man. He deserved better than to spend his life eating his heart out over a woman he could never have.

Watching him like this without his knowledge, she started to feel awkward, like she intruded on a private matter that was none of her concern. She leveled her shoulders, plastered a smile to her face, and stepped into the room. "Lord Garson, what an unexpected pleasure."

He looked up, and she watched the social mask descend over his features. The brown eyes warmed as he bowed, and the downturned lips curved into a smile. "You used to call me Hugh, Jane. Or does this mean I must call you your ladyship?"

As children, they'd seen each other often. Less often since they'd reached adulthood. Still, he was right.

"Then welcome, Hugh," she said with a curtsy. "I didn't know you were in the neighborhood."

Briefly that impressive jaw hardened, and a muscle flickered in his tanned cheek. He drew himself up to his full height, making Jane feel ridiculously small, although at nine inches over five feet, she wasn't exactly tiny. "I came down to see you."

This visit became more baffling by the minute. "Especially?"

He nodded. "Especially."

Then in an instant, she understood, and gratitude lightened her heavy heart. "How very kind you are. I didn't expect you to remember that I'm leaving Cavell Court."

Billings came in with two footmen and set up the sideboard with cakes and sandwiches. There was ale for Hugh, and tea for Jane. By the time the servants had gone, Hugh was sitting in a leather chair by the fire with his long legs, encased in gleaming Hessians, extended over the faded rug. Jane perched on the window seat with a cup of tea and a cheesecake. She'd miss Mrs. Kelly, the family cook, when she left.

From habit, she added Mrs. Kelly to the long list of everything else she'd miss when she forsook her home. Then she consigned the whole lot to the dark corner, where she locked everything she endured because she had no choice to do otherwise.

When Hugh lifted his tankard for a deep drink, Jane found herself strangely fascinated with the movement of that strong throat as he swallowed. He wore a simple neck cloth, but she noticed that his clothing was more elaborate than was usual for a man in the country. That dark blue coat was a masterpiece of Savile Row tailoring, obvious even to someone as woefully out of touch with fashion as she was. Perhaps after he left her, he intended to go on somewhere else.

"Of course I remembered you had to move out," he said, returning to their earlier conversation. "I wondered about your plans."

She and Hugh had spoken at the funeral, but she'd been lost in a fog of grief, and busy playing hostess to the crowd of mourners besides. There hadn't been occasion for anything beyond what politeness demanded.

"I appreciate you making the effort to check that I'm all right." She slid her teacup onto the windowsill. "But it wasn't necessary. I'll be in Town in a fortnight, staying with my sister Susan and her family."

He put down the tankard and surveyed her out of somber dark eyes. He'd always been thoughtful rather than flashy. But the serious habit seemed to have grown on him over the years. She wondered when he'd last laughed from sheer joy. A long while ago, she'd wager.

"You never had a London season, did you?"

"One was planned, then Papa fell ill." And she'd become nurse and companion and estate manager.

"You'll love the social whirl."

Her lips twisted in self-derision. "Oh, I'm too old for all that nonsense."

"Rot, Jane. You'll find London provides plenty of amusement for a mature woman."

She tried not to mind that he didn't argue with her about her age. However ancient she felt after these last difficult months, she was only twenty-eight. She made herself respond lightly. "I hope so."

His expression was assessing rather than disapproving. "So you're going to live with Susan?"

"No." Jane barely hid a shudder. She struggled to sound enthusiastic about her intentions. "That's only a visit. I hope to find a suitable house in a provincial town. Perhaps Lyme or Weymouth. I'd like to live by the sea. Miss Ashton, my old governess, has agreed to come along to preserve appearances."

This definitely didn't please him. Those thick mahogany brows drew together over his long, straight nose. "You can't be looking forward to that. Within a month, you'll be bored stiff. Why don't you stay in London?"

Because in the years following her mother's death, her father had made a series of unwise investments, and the sum of money Jane had inherited didn't allow for high jinks in the capital. But that was none of Hugh's business. In fact, she was puzzled that he thought he had some right to advise her on her future. Despite long acquaintance, as adults they verged on being strangers.

"I like Dorset," she said.

"You haven't been anywhere else," he said shortly. "Wait until you've seen London and tasted what it has to offer."

Actually she had a suspicion that London just offered more family duty. She loved her sister, but she wasn't blind to Susan's intention to foist the four youngest children onto Jane, while she launched her oldest daughter Lucy into society.

"Perhaps," Jane said neutrally. "I haven't made any final decisions."

"Susan hasn't offered you a permanent home?"

A permanent post as poor relation and uncredited governess, he meant. "Yes, she has. But it's time I tested my independence."

Compassion turned Hugh's eyes a deep velvety brown, so deep Jane felt she could drown in the rich color. Why hadn't she ever noticed what nice eyes he had?

"High time." He paused. "Although I'm hoping after we've spoken, you might choose another path altogether."

She frowned. "I don't understand."

He smiled, although she couldn't feel he put his heart into it. "It's a credit to your modesty that you don't."

Good heavens, what was all this about? It sounded like the prelude to a proposal of marriage. She'd had a few of those over the years, from older gentlemen who noted her devotion to her father and wanted her to look after them with similar dedication in their declining years.

But Hugh was no decrepit old codger. He was in the prime of life.

"Are you well, Hugh?" she asked in concern, studying that tanned face and the large, powerful body.

Well? He appeared almost aggressively fit.

He looked startled and sat up straight in his chair. "Are you worried about my sanity?"

She supposed the question sounded bizarre. "I'm sorry. I was wondering if you needed a nurse."

At least his laugh emerged more naturally than his smile. "Not a nurse, you goose."

He stood and without shifting his attention from her, leaned one brawny arm on the mantelpiece. The room suddenly seemed very small. Jane had never before been quite so aware of his vigorous, masculine energy.

Cavell Court had turned into a female domain, as her father faded and Jane, by necessity, took over the estate. Lord Garson seemed to come from a larger, more charged universe.

She swallowed to banish a ridiculous nervousness and edged back on the window seat until she bumped into the sill behind her. "I thought perhaps you might have a sick relative, if you don't require a nurse for yourself."

The genuine fondness in his expression reminded her how she'd hero-worshipped him when she was a child. "You've been tucked up away from the world too long, Jane. Surely you can guess what I want. I'm trying in my ham-fisted way to express my admiration."

That left her more bewildered than ever. "Your admiration?" she repeated in a shamefully scratchy voice.

"Jane, I'm not here seeking a nurse." His smile was wry as he stared down at her. "I'm here seeking a wife."

CHAPTER TWO

*G*arson's heart sank as he watched shock flood Jane's expression. He'd assumed she'd already have some idea of why he'd called, togged out in his best clothes and requesting a private interview, but her reaction made it clear that his offer came as a bolt from the blue. Not a particularly welcome bolt, at that.

Although she was no beauty, he liked her face. The even features were pleasing, and those wide, shining gray eyes didn't miss much. He remembered that as a girl, she'd had a sly sense of humor and a quirky take on life and its vicissitudes.

But that had been before her father's illness. In recent years, Garson hadn't seen much of her, an admission that now made him feel a little guilty. Studying the drawn face beneath that severely confined mass of dark red hair, he discerned few traces of her former spark.

She didn't have to tell him the price family duty had exacted from her. He could see it in her features. Only her extravagant wealth of hair gave any hint of vitality.

As a younger man, he'd never thought of Jane Norris as anything but the daughter of his father's friend. At least in daylight hours. He'd frequently woken from heated dreams, where he was entwined in skeins of silky red hair, the exact color of Jane's. Dreams that had been unacceptable then, and now struck him as downright perverse, with her sitting before him as neat and self-contained as a bloody nun. Her gray, high-necked dress, unadorned with anything as frivolous as a frill or a ribbon, just confirmed the fiercely virginal impression.

"What a mad idea." In a nervous movement, one white hand rose to her throat. She had pretty hands, he noticed, slender and capable.

His eyebrows arched with a touch of hauteur. By God, she didn't shirk from trampling his vanity. At the very least, he'd assumed she'd find his proposal flattering. In his more optimistic moments, he'd imagined her rushing headlong to accept him. Clearly that optimism was unfounded. "I'm sorry you think so."

She flushed and made an apologetic gesture. At least her blush made her look less like a little ghost. "I beg your pardon. That wasn't polite."

He stepped away from the mantelpiece to approach her window seat. "I'd rather we were honest with each other."

She regarded him doubtfully. "Are you sure?"

"I'll try and cope with anything you throw my way." Despite himself, he smiled. "But won't you tell me why you find the idea of a match so outlandish?"

When she shook her head, he wasn't sure whether she expressed confusion or denial. As she recovered from her astonishment, her voice firmed. "For a start, I've only seen you half a dozen times in the last ten years."

"So I feel like a stranger?"

"Not exactly." Those gray eyes settled on him with such a searching expression that he shifted his booted feet in sudden discomfort. "But you don't feel like a suitor either."

"I'm willing to court you, if that's what you prefer." It wasn't what he preferred. He'd hoped that she'd say yes, he'd have the banns called, they'd marry in a couple of weeks, and the whole inconvenient palaver would be done and dusted with a minimum of fuss.

"I don't know what I prefer, frankly." She spread her hands. "This has come as a surprise."

"Perhaps I should have written before I called."

"I'd still be surprised that you're offering for me. You've never shown any interest before."

"I've always liked you."

"And I've always liked you." She made another helpless gesture. "But that's not grounds for marriage."

He set his jaw stubbornly. "Why not?"

"Because—"

Because there was no love. They both knew that. He went on before she could finish. "A marriage could solve quite a few problems for both of us. I'm thirty-four. It's time I set up my nursery with a sensible, good-hearted woman, willing to make a useful life with me. From your point of view, please forgive me if I trespass on matters that aren't my concern—"

"Which means you're going to," she said sharply.

He ignored her interruption and ventured closer. Would it help to take her hand? A glance at her face told him it wouldn't. With every minute, she looked less downtrodden. She was sitting up so straight, her spine could have doubled as a ship's mast.

"It's no secret that your father made some disastrous investments, and I suspect your portion isn't what it was."

That was why he'd asked about her plans, to confirm that he was right about the unappealing options available to her. She might intend to marry someone else. But she didn't mention an attachment, and surely she would if there was one. It wasn't very worthy, but he'd arrived, hoping she might choose to marry him to escape a bleak future.

Two bright spots of color marked her cheeks, and she glared at him as though she disliked him. "I have enough to live on."

"As long as you retire to some backwater, or you swallow your pride and move in with Susan."

"She's my closest family."

"She's also very happy to take on an unpaid nursemaid." Eight years older than Jane, Susan had always been a little cat with a sharp eye to the main chance. He'd never really taken to her. "Is that the best you can do?"

Jane swallowed and avoided his probing stare as he stood over her. "You're...you're very blunt, my lord."

My lord? Hell, he really had upset her.

He sighed and retreated, cursing himself for a thoughtless bully. What in Hades was wrong with him? The world commended his perfect manners, yet here he was acting the complete boor. "I'm making a muddle of this."

"Could you...could you sit down, so I don't feel like you're about to seize me by the scruff of the neck and give me a good shake?" Her voice trembled, as she fought to maintain her composure.

"Damn it, I meant to woo you, not harangue you," he said ruefully, subsiding into his chair.

Straightaway she looked more at ease, and her bosom rose as she sucked air into her lungs. He couldn't help noticing how very nicely she filled out that unenticing bodice. With difficulty, he dragged his eyes up to her face.

She gave a shaky laugh and smoothed her austere coiffure, not that it needed it. "And I haven't even said no."

"Imagine if you had," he retorted, before he registered what she said. He leaned forward eagerly. "So you will marry me?"

The humor drained from her face, returning her to the wan shadow she'd been when he arrived. His gut tightened in protest at seeing her this beaten down. She looked so weary, he just wanted to pick her up and take her somewhere she'd never suffer again.

What the deuce? That was a more powerful reaction than he'd anticipated. He'd embarked on this course after coldly and calmly weighing his alternatives. Yet here with Jane, his confused feelings were making him stupid.

"Why do you want to marry me?" He heard the effort she made to keep her voice steady. He also noted she didn't answer his question. Was that a good sign or a bad one?

He couldn't tell, although he'd thought he knew her well. Damn it, that familiarity was one of the things that convinced him she'd make a fine wife. Yet looking into the face that he'd never considered anything remarkable, he recognized the presence of mystery.

"I told you."

"Because we both offer a convenient solution to the other's difficulties."

When he heard the tartness lacing her soft voice, Garson hid a grimace. He shifted uncomfortably on his chair. He hadn't handled his premier foray at all well, blast him. Was it too late to regroup?

"It's true. As I said before, I like you."

His lukewarm declaration didn't deserve to move her. And it quite clearly didn't. "You're a rich, attractive man with no obvious vices. You must have your pick of society's unmarried ladies. Women younger than me who can give you babies, and who I'm sure you could come to like without too much trouble."

He noticed that she, too, avoided the word "love." But then, that was the issue that narrowed the list of candidates for his bride to one. Most women expected something stronger than friendship from their future husband.

"Jane, when I saw you at your father's funeral, I thought you'd make me an ideal wife." He was relieved to hear himself sounding calm and measured, the soul of logic. He had no idea what had come over him when he'd first proposed. He'd like to blame the ale, but it was an insipid brew. "I'm not a foolish boy anymore. Nor are you a silly girl. You're a grown woman of good sense. I believe we could make an excellent life together. I pledge my respect and fidelity. You must remember that when I make a promise, I keep it."

"I do remember."

Encouraged, he went on. "Think of the advantages. You'll be mistress of a great house. You'll have money to do whatever you wish. It's the life you were born for, not a hand-to-mouth existence as an indigent spinster in cramped lodgings a hundred miles from the fashionable world. Or would you rather be your sister's dogsbody? You have a choice, Jane. Penury and isolation, or a full, purposeful life as my wife, and the mother of my children."

"I'd like children," she said haltingly.

"You'll make a wonderful mother. You'll make a wonderful baroness. Please say you'll marry me."

Strangely this speech left her looking more troubled than his hectoring. For a long time, she stared down into her lap, then she glanced up, gray eyes somber. "That's a very nice proposal, Hugh."

The tension across his shoulders loosened. She called him Hugh. That meant she relented.

"It's what I should have said when I arrived. I'm sorry I was such a dunderhead. I'm out of the habit of proposing."

She didn't smile. "But then, you have proposed before, haven't you?"

His blood ran cold. Damn and blast, had the gossip about his failed engagement spread as far as this remote estate? What an ass he was. Of course it had. Susan would share all the *on dits* in her letters.

"That was over three years ago," he said stiffly, even as he warned himself about getting all het up again.

Jane sat up straight on her window seat and lifted her chin. Her tone was uncompromising, and her eyes were watchful. "It doesn't matter how long ago it happened, if you're still in love with Morwenna Nash."

CHAPTER THREE

*A*ll expression fled Hugh's face, which was sign enough that she'd touched a nerve. Then Jane met his austere gaze and glimpsed the ocean of hurt seething beneath his polished exterior.

Yes, he was in love with Morwenna Nash. He didn't need to answer her.

With a weariness that struck her as more spiritual than physical, he stood and crossed to look through the next window along from her. "That's not your concern."

Impatience tightened her lips. Apparently he could ask her candid questions, but she wasn't granted the same freedom. Too bad.

"It is, if I'm thinking of marrying you."

He cast her a brief, curious glance. "Are you?"

Was she? Devil if she knew. "The story is she broke your heart, and you've been carrying the willow for her ever since."

He sighed and stared out at the overcast day. "You know," he said softly, as if he spoke to himself and not to Jane, "I'm damned sick of the world only thinking of me as the man Morwenna threw over."

Pity pierced Jane, sharp as a knife. She could understand that he was deathly tired of playing the role of discarded lover, after the dramatic events of three years ago. Up until then, he'd been at the top of the tree, admired and envied. He must have suffered an agony of humiliation over the last few years, aside from any pain he felt because the woman he loved was reunited with her long-lost husband.

"I'm sorry that this is a painful subject." She rose and went to stand beside him. This close, she couldn't mistake his tension. "But if we're contemplating a life together, we need to talk about this."

Still he didn't look at her. "I was a fool to hope you were the only person in England who didn't know."

She couldn't mistake his fierce unhappiness. Could she deal with that if she married him? If she took on the man, she'd have to take on the broken heart, too. A daunting prospect for any bride. "When you were a boy, you were always steadfast in your affections."

"You know the family motto," he said tonelessly. "'Loyalty unto death.'"

A wry smile twisted her lips. "You speak as if that's a bad thing."

He turned in time to catch her expression, and temper sparked in his eyes. "Don't you bloody dare laugh at me."

She raised a hand to touch his arm, then thought better of it. "I'm not."

"I've had enough of that as well."

"Everything was so public."

Her sister's letters had been full of the gossip. When Morwenna's husband returned miraculously from the dead, the reunion had taken place in a ballroom, under the full glare of the world's attention. There had been no way to save Garson's pride, or allow him to make a discreet withdrawal from a romantic triangle that became unbearably crowded.

"The irony is that she never loved me." He leaned one hand on the windowsill. It had started to rain, as if the weather reflected the heavy atmosphere inside the room. The gray light starkly revealed the sorrow in his face. "I always knew that."

"But naturally you hoped."

His mouth turned down in self-derision. "Yes, I hoped."

"After all, her husband had been dead—or at least we all believed he was—for years."

"Five." His voice was bleak. "She has a steadfast heart, too."

A tacit admission that he still loved Morwenna. Not that anyone who saw him now could doubt it. In an odd way, Jane found it admirable that he couldn't turn off his love, despite the lack of any happy ending. Admirable—but not necessarily a positive feature in a future husband.

"I'm so very sorry, Hugh."

"So am I." He straightened and shot her a direct look. "The shambles of my past doesn't change my need to make a life for myself. I've moped long enough. I owe it to the title to marry and have children. There's no use pining for the moon."

Which well and truly put Jane in her mundane place, didn't it? It rankled a little that he saw her only as a broodmare.

Her pique surprised her. Over the last dreary years, she thought she'd forsaken all claims to feminine conceit. Clearly not.

"So you settled for me."

"As I told you—"

"You always liked me," she said flatly, returning to her window seat. All of this was too much to take in. Confused thoughts tumbled over each other, performing chaotic acrobatics in her mind.

"That's something."

"But hardly love's young dream," she said with a hint of bitterness, even as she told her vanity to step back because it had no part to play in this purely pragmatic decision.

"I'd hoped—"

With a touch of irony, she raised her eyebrows. "That I was past the age of wanting hearts and flowers?"

Hugh had the grace to look ashamed. His repentance was charming—she'd forgotten over the years quite what an attractive man he was. Or perhaps she'd never let herself notice before, to protect herself from inevitable disappointment. The women Hugh Rutherford pursued, even before he fell in love with Morwenna, were counted as diamonds of the first water. Jane couldn't compete with that.

He made an apologetic gesture. "Please send me on my way, if you can't hold with more of my blundering."

To her surprise, she raised a hand to stop him. "Don't go rushing off." She struggled to inject a lighter note. "I had no idea you were such an impulsive fellow, Hugh. Please sit down, and let's talk about this."

He eyed her warily, then resumed his seat. He ran his hand through his hair, ruffling it so he looked even more charming, plague take him. Jane hardened herself against his attractions. If this union was going ahead, she needed to keep a cool head. Going gooey-eyed over his handsome face wouldn't help her at all.

Self-deprecating humor deepened the creases around his eyes. "This is turning out to be a blasted unconventional proposal."

"I don't know if I can live without love," she said baldly.

He frowned. "Are you saying if we married, you wouldn't be faithful?"

She shook her head. "Not at all. When I make a promise, I keep it, too. I'm trying to work out whether the absence of love is a strong enough argument against saying yes. After all, I'm twenty-eight, and nobody has yet taken my fancy. Perhaps nobody ever will."

She'd like to share some spark of passion with the man she married. Perhaps for a staid, provincial frump past first youth, that was too much to ask.

"I hate to play devil's advocate, Jane, but your world isn't exactly overflowing with hordes of eligible gentlemen."

"I've had my chances." Even if they were all over fifty, and not in the best of health.

He looked curious, but this time he remembered his manners before he pursued any details. "I'm sure you have. Your devotion to your father's care alone recommends you as a suitable wife."

She hid a wince. Again not a word about her personal appeal. One of today's surprises was the discovery that her romantic younger self still claimed a place inside her respectable bosom.

"What do you want of me, Hugh?"

That impressive jaw set with determination, and his voice

emerged strong and steady. "I want a companion, a mother for my children, a friend. I want a sensible woman who's willing to build a life with me. A woman who respects and likes me, and won't ask for more than I can give her."

His love, he meant.

She crossed the room to stare sightlessly into the fire. One hand began pleating her gray merino skirt as she struggled to decide what to do.

This was a cold bargain, but it had its benefits. She might harbor hidden longings for what she'd never known—love and adventure and excitement. But if she was brutally honest with herself, her chance to experience those things had passed.

At twenty-eight, she was on the shelf, especially now her dowry was so meager. While she might like to think that her alternative to marrying Hugh was some resplendent future, the reality was different. As he'd bluntly pointed out, right now her choices lay in becoming her sister's drudge, or moving to some backwater and sharing her restricted means with a middle-aged chaperone.

Neither prospect filled her with unbridled anticipation.

She'd waited ten years to seek the life she wanted. But she'd left it too late.

Too late. Surely the saddest words in the language.

A sensible woman—how she grew to hate that adjective!—would say yes. As Hugh remarked, Lady Garson would have every worldly advantage. She'd have respect and influence. She'd also be part of a family.

What about love? Doesn't that matter?

Her foolish heart cried out in anguish as it viewed the emotional barrenness extending ahead. But the bleak truth remained that love wasn't on the cards, wherever she went. Surely if she must yearn, it was better to yearn from the comforts of beautiful Beardsley Hall, than from shabby rented rooms in an unfashionable seaside resort.

She glanced up to find Hugh watching her steadily. He showed no sign of anxiety. Why should he? He'd chosen his bride as a practical matter, much as she'd say yes as a practical matter.

If she said yes.

"You claim you want your independence," he said in that reasonable voice. "I can understand that. Especially after running the show here for so long. I can promise I won't be a tyrannical or a demanding husband, and the settlements will ensure a generous allowance."

Jane fiddled with her skirt and mulled over her answer. She knew he wouldn't be demanding. He was an unusually considerate man. Even more to the point, he didn't want her. Not in that way.

A shiver that combined fear with interest rippled through her. She'd tried, not entirely successfully, to reconcile herself to dying a virgin. If she said yes to Hugh, she'd know what it was to have a man in her bed. And a young, virile, good-looking man at that. "When you say demanding…"

Heat flared in the gaze that swept over her in a thorough inspection. She shivered again. Not with revulsion.

"I won't be a cold husband, Jane."

She'd never met Morwenna Nash, but she'd heard the woman was a great beauty. Nobody had ever said that about Jane. Pleasant-looking was about the best compliment she ever garnered.

When she looked at this handsome man who offered her marriage without love, she was woman enough to regret her lack of allure. She shifted under his gaze and wished with a fervor she hadn't felt since she was an adolescent that she was a girl who turned men's heads. Then at least she'd enter into this bargain with some power of her own.

"You want children," she said, heat rising in her cheeks.

"I do. I'll do my best not to make your duties too onerous, but—"

"But that's why you want a wife."

"That's why I want you." He paused and subjected her to another of those scorching stares that seemed to pierce right through to her indecisive heart and stirring carnal impulses. "If the thought of sharing my bed is distasteful, I will understand that you can't accept my proposal."

It was her turn to inspect him. He was an attractive man, inside and out. She tried to imagine that big body rising above hers as he pushed inside her, but inexperience defeated her. No countrywoman remained ignorant of the mechanics of mating. But it was impossible to equate her knowledge with how she'd feel giving herself to Hugh.

Her attention dropped to those large, capable hands, hands that would touch her skin, hold her hips as he thrust into her. That odd, nervous feeling spiked and set her stomach churning.

But she felt no distaste.

Just a good dose of curiosity.

Jane was woefully unworldly. She'd never been to London. Heavens, in the past ten years, she hadn't been past Exeter. But some hitherto unrecognized instinct told her that Hugh Rutherford would prove a skilled lover.

Perhaps this marriage offered more satisfactions than she'd originally counted.

She licked dry lips and made herself meet his eyes. "I'm not...unwilling."

He smiled. "I'm glad to hear that."

Hardly the height of enthusiasm. But he offered her his name to solve a practical problem. His emotions weren't involved.

"If I say yes, how do you see this working?" she asked.

"We'd live at Beardsley Hall and visit London for the season. If you wish, we could travel. Also—"

"No, I mean immediately," she said, although her heart leaped at the idea of seeing new places, new people after her long exile at Cavell Court. While she was sad to leave her home, she couldn't deny that it had become something of a prison. She'd welcome a glimpse of the wider world. "Would we have a big wedding in London? I'm only just out of mourning for Papa."

She caught his quickly hidden dismay at the idea. "If that's what you'd like."

Lucky for him, she couldn't imagine anything worse. Especially as all those curious eyes would compare her to the lovely Morwenna. Not to her advantage. If she accepted this proposal, she'd have to face the fact that not just Hugh, but the entire world would always consider her second best. "What would you like?"

He shrugged as if it hardly mattered. She supposed for him, it didn't. "If you say yes, as I dearly hope you will, I'll call on the vicar here and arrange for the banns to be called. I'll go back to Beardsley and do the same thing up there. On the way, I'll stop in London and ask Lord Stone to be my best man. I'll see the lawyers about the settlements at the same time. In a few weeks, I'll come back here, and we'll marry in the village church. I assume you'd like to have your neighbors at the ceremony to wish you well. After that, we can go to Beardsley for a few weeks, then to London for the season. Or if you like, we could make a wedding trip to France or Italy. Really, it's up to you."

"Italy might be a step too far at first," she said drily, even as she struggled to come to terms with how her constricted life would expand if she said yes.

Hugh would never love her, and she certainly wasn't in love with him. But if they married, she'd assume a great lady's place in the world. It was the role she'd been brought up to fill, and this might be her only chance, now Felix moved into Cavell Court. That alone made Hugh's proposal tempting.

Hugh continued to study her. "Jane, I can guess how lonely you've been these last years."

She'd never appreciated people's pity, but perhaps because Hugh had suffered himself, she didn't prickle up. Her hands spread in an eloquent gesture. "There were times when I felt so alone, I didn't know how I'd make it through the next day."

He stretched out his hand toward her. "Then marry me and be my friend, and you won't be lonely again."

She stared at his hand without moving to take it. Common sense said that accepting his proposal answered most of her problems. But some deeper instinct warned her that marrying a man who was in love with another woman would inevitably lead to a lifetime of unhappiness.

When she didn't immediately agree, he looked disappointed. "Do you want to think about it?"

If she thought about it, her fears, fears that might just be cowardice, would make her choose the safe option. "I'm not convinced that will help," she admitted shakily. "Are you sure you want to marry me?"

A self-derisive smile twisted his lips. "I've been planning my proposal for six months, ever since I saw you being so brave at your father's funeral. Although given my graceless start, you have reason to doubt that."

It hadn't been the sort of proposal she'd dreamed of when she was a girl looking forward to a season and suitors and all the pleasures open to a rich young lady entering society. This wouldn't be the marriage she'd dreamed of then either, with an adoring if unidentified spouse.

But for all that, it seemed to be the marriage she was going to have.

As Hugh had unceremoniously pointed out, her options were limited and unappealing. Marrying him meant she could have children. He'd give her a home to make up for the loss of Cavell Court.

There was no love. But love wasn't likely to result from her descent into genteel poverty either.

Her heart begged her to reconsider any decision that shut off all possibility of love, but her head knew better. Surely when she had children, there would be love, even if not the love between man and woman. Becoming Lady Garson offered advantages that outweighed her unformed misgivings about how she'd feel in the future.

With surprising steadiness, she stood and stepped across to take his hand. As his fingers closed around hers, heat surged up her arm and stirred an unfamiliar and not unpleasant reaction. Perhaps sharing his bed would turn out to be more than a duty, after all.

She summoned a tremulous smile. "I'll be very pleased to marry you, Hugh."

CHAPTER FOUR

*G*arson stood at the altar of St. Mary and All Angels, the squat little Saxon church that served the village of Cavell Stanton. The organ played something he didn't recognize, just as he didn't recognize most of the people in the congregation. He was an only child, and while he had a few aged aunts and cousins, he hadn't asked any of them to make the arduous journey from Derbyshire to Dorset. Nor had he invited his dissolute and sophisticated London friends. They'd been too closely associated with his previous courtship.

"She's late," Silas Nash, Lord Stone, murmured from beside him.

Silas might strike some people as an odd choice for best man. After all, he was Morwenna's brother-in-law. But he remained Garson's closest friend, and despite some awkwardness after that disastrous engagement party, their friendship had eventually settled back into its old amity.

Silas looked tidier than usual, thanks to the attentions of his wife Caroline, who sat in the congregation wearing a spectacular bronze silk gown. The man's shock of light brown hair was almost neat, and he hadn't yet started tugging at his neck cloth to loosen it.

"She'll be here."

Garson wished he felt as confident as he sounded. He'd spent most of the last three weeks in Derbyshire, preparing Beardsley Hall for his bride's arrival. Now he wondered if he should have stayed in Dorset and devoted that time to courting Jane. When she'd accepted his proposal, she'd looked uncertain. This delay in her arrival now hinted that her doubts had only grown during their time apart.

Last night after he'd booked into the frankly inadequate inn, he'd gone up to Cavell Court, intending to soothe any fears Jane harbored about their imminent wedding. But the house had been packed with guests, including her sister Susan and the unruly brood of nieces and nephews. While Jane had seemed pleased to see him, they hadn't managed a private moment to talk.

But as she said, she was a woman of her word. She wouldn't let him down.

He hoped.

"I'm looking forward to meeting her." Silas's hazel eyes were somber with what Garson recognized as concern. Naturally he was bloody concerned. He knew better than most people how deeply his friend had loved Morwenna. Still did, damn it.

Now Garson set his face in a new direction. He meant to make the best of things with the wife he'd chosen. He owed Jane his allegiance, and he intended to live up to the promises he spoke today. Even if it killed him.

"You'll like her," he said. Silas and Caro had reached the inn late last night, after a broken axle interrupted their journey, so he hadn't yet introduced them to his bride. "She's a cracker of a girl."

Jane was a cracker, but that didn't stop his heart from sinking when he heard a rustle and a murmur behind him. The organist burst into a triumphal air. Garson turned to see Jane Norris step into the church with her sister Susan a few paces behind her.

For a dizzying moment, everything blurred, and he saw a slender, dark-haired woman with deep blue eyes walking toward him. Then he blinked and returned to harsh reality.

Except that wasn't fair.

It wasn't Jane's fault that he pined for his lost love, especially when she'd clearly done her best to do him credit today. She'd made a better fist of her appearance than he'd expected. The pale-faced dowd who had accepted his proposal looked almost pretty. She didn't exactly glow with happiness—but then neither of them was under any illusion that this was a love match, thank God.

Her cream dress was bang up to fashion, and it fitted much better than the gray monstrosity from three weeks ago. Her wedding gown clung close enough to hint at a narrow waist and gracefully rounded hips. He'd already noticed her magnificent bosom—he was a man, after all—but on today's evidence, the rest of her was just as fine.

He'd been anticipating the night to come as something of a chore. Now his blood pumped faster at the prospect of unwrapping those luscious curves.

"She's lovely," Silas said beside him.

"She is," he said, and knew he hadn't hidden his surprise when Silas looked troubled.

"You're a lucky bastard."

"Yes, I am," he said, and meant it.

Jane looked up to send him a shy smile. He smiled back.

She wore a lavender bonnet, and as she approached, he saw how the color lent a hint of blue to her gray eyes. There was even some pink in her cheeks.

She wasn't the bride of his heart. But she was certainly a woman to take pride in. She had courage and heart, and she was smart. With good will and hard work, surely he and Jane could create a fulfilling life together. He waited while she passed her bouquet of hothouse flowers, courtesy of Silas's greenhouses, to her sister, then took her hand.

As her fingers trembled in his grasp, his sensual interest stirred anew. He'd never expected to desire his bride, but he garnered some encouraging signs that he might be mistaken.

With an unaccustomed surge of hope, he turned to face the vicar.

So she was married.

Outside the church, Jane took her place in an open carriage bedecked in pretty pink satin ribbons and more of Silas's exotic lilies and orchids. Thank goodness it was only a short ride to the house. The day turned colder, and she could smell snow on the way. Her cashmere shawl, while colorful, wasn't proof against the air. Although perhaps she couldn't entirely blame the bleak weather for the chill settling in her bones.

The carriage creaked as Hugh stepped up to join her. In his severe black, he looked marvelous, the perfect bridegroom. His elegance only fed the nerves seething in her stomach.

Because she was well aware she wasn't the perfect bride.

Too old. Too plain.

If they loved each other, she suspected that wouldn't matter. But they didn't, and she couldn't help feeling completely inadequate.

He was laughing at something Lord Stone said and brushing rice from his broad shoulders. Despite knowing Hugh all her life, today he seemed disturbingly alien. His sheer size. The flash of large white teeth in his tanned face. Something that even in her innocence she recognized as potent masculinity made her shrink into the red leather seat. Until she reminded herself that they were in public and she owed it to Hugh—and herself, by heaven—to appear content with her choice of husband.

As he sat down beside her, he surveyed her from under the curling brim of his hat. "Having a crisis of confidence?"

Her lips twisted. "Can you tell?"

They spoke in low voices, although given the noise from the milling crowd, the coachman would need sharp ears to eavesdrop. Hugh caught her gloved hand and slid closer. She watched how her hand disappeared inside his much larger one. That seemed somehow ominous, symbolic of the way his life was about to swallow up hers.

"Trust me, Jane. I'll do my best to make you happy."

"And I'll do my best, too." If only she could make him happy. Walking up the aisle, she'd been bitterly aware that he'd prefer to have another woman at his side this morning.

That feeling had intensified in the ceremony when he'd kissed her cheek instead of her lips. The contact had lasted a mere instant, but it had burned like ice.

He regarded her with a frown. "You make a beautiful bride."

"Thank you." If he didn't seem so disapproving, it would be easier to sound like she believed him.

"But I'm afraid you're turning the same color as your bonnet."

"The same color..." she said, not following.

He smiled and to her surprise, hooked one powerful arm around her shoulders and drew her against him. "We can't have my bride turning into an icicle before we get to the wedding breakfast."

"It's not far," she said shakily, basking in the delicious heat radiating along her side.

"Too far to shiver all the way."

"But people will see."

The fond note in his rumbling laugh soothed her disquiet. "We just got married, Jane. I'm allowed to cuddle my bride."

Cuddle? That sounded too intimate, when he was merely trying to keep her warm.

Tonight he'd do more than put his arm around her. If she wanted to cower away from him now, how on earth would she survive a night in bed with him?

Except being held so close wasn't uncomfortable at all. It was rather wonderful. Once Hugh's warmth surrounded her, the cold air felt almost piquant. She became aware of all sorts of things she'd never noticed before. The citrus tang of his soap. Beneath the lemon, the spicy scent of his skin. The way her body fitted so neatly to his, as she gave up her quibbles and leaned into him.

He made a sound of satisfaction and tightened his hold.

At Hugh's nod, the coachman set the horses in motion. The clop of hooves, the carriage's soft creak, and the jingle of the harness preserved their privacy.

The well-wishers waved as the carriage drew away from the church. Everybody was happy for Jane. She wished she was. She'd spent most of her life wishing something exciting would happen. Now it had, and she was a mass of jangling nerves.

They trotted up the drive. The way had been cleared of overnight snow, but glistening white banked high on either side, and frost turned the elms lining the avenue into dreamlike sculptures. A pale sun shone through wispy clouds. A hundred people followed, but right now, Jane felt isolated in a cocoon with Hugh.

"This is the beginning of a new life," she said softly. "I wonder what it will bring."

"Happiness and fulfillment, God willing," Hugh said, just as softly. "Today I pledged myself to you, Jane. You're a Rutherford now. 'Loyalty unto death.' From this day forward, it's you and me together against the world."

"That's an odd way to put it," she said, even as she appreciated hearing that she was his priority.

He might never love her, but he took this marriage seriously. He meant to do right by her. She just wished he viewed that as a pleasure, instead of a duty.

But it was too late for second thoughts. She, like Hugh, had to make the best of the vows they'd just made.

He gave a grunt of amusement. "Lately life and I have had a rather combative relationship."

Just like that, Morwenna's ghost intruded. Jane stiffened and tried to pull away, but his hold tightened. "Don't bristle up. I'm sorry I said that."

"No, I'm sorry." She forgot how perceptive he was. "I don't want either of us walking on eggshells."

"But I have no right to ride roughshod over your feelings."

"You've hardly done that," she said, even as she wished Morwenna Nash to the lowest circle of hell, however charming she might be. She wasn't exactly jealous of the other woman. But this taste of how the memory of his lost love would dog her marriage promised trouble.

"I see you've spent the past three weeks worrying if you've made the right decision. I should have stayed. It wasn't fair to leave you alone to organize everything."

She hadn't minded. The pressure of putting the wedding together had distracted her from fretting about leaving Cavell Court, not to mention what she and Hugh would do tonight. She wasn't precisely afraid, but when she thought about sharing his bed, butterflies the size of elephants started dancing in her stomach.

"You needed to arrange everything in Derbyshire. I understood. You wrote." Short, businesslike notes, but at least he hadn't forgotten her, once she was out of sight.

He looked surprised. "Of course I wrote."

"And it's not the easiest journey from Dorset to Derbyshire. You've spent a good deal of the last few weeks on the road." He'd been to London, too. Last night when he arrived, he'd looked tired. But beneath his physical weariness, she'd seen the weight oppressing his spirit.

"Nonetheless I should have courted you," he said stubbornly.

She couldn't agree. A courtship would only underline that he went through the motions, while his heart lay elsewhere. The matter-of-fact arrangement suited her much better.

"There's no need when you've won me already," she said in a flat voice.

"You know, I'm not entirely sure that I have," he said, and his unusually austere tone struck her silent.

CHAPTER FIVE

*J*ane had spent three weeks dreading the wedding breakfast. Too many of the guests knew about Garson's history with Morwenna Nash—it was the kind of scandal the world feasted on, even the world of a small Dorset village —and were aware that Jane was very much her bridegroom's second choice.

But to her surprise, everyone present seemed genuinely pleased for the bridal couple, including Hugh's friends Silas and Caro Nash. Given Silas was Hugh's best man, Jane couldn't avoid him and his wife —much as the more cowardly part of her might like to. When she said she wanted to meet new people, she didn't mean members of Morwenna's family. Or at least not on her wedding day.

She was sipping champagne at Hugh's side when the Nashes approached through the cheerful throng. Jane's stomach knotted with nerves, but she resisted the shameful urge to run away.

"Hugh, isn't it time you introduced your old friends to your lovely wife?" the tall man with the untidy mass of tawny hair asked, clapping her new husband on the back with the familiarity of long acquaintance.

"If you promise to behave," Hugh said with a smile.

"I like that!" the glamorous woman in the stylish bronze taffeta dress protested. "I always behave."

"Only when you feel like it, my darling," Lord Stone said, and Jane couldn't miss how love brightened his eyes when he teased his wife.

The champagne on Jane's tongue suddenly tasted as sour as vinegar. She could never picture Hugh treating her with such overt affection. While she'd entered this marriage with no expectation of love, witnessing the Stones' closeness today of all days was a little too hard to bear. With an unsteady hand, she set the glass down on the marble console table behind her.

Hugh took her hand. He seemed to be doing that a lot today. She almost became used to the warmth that rippled up her arm every time he did it. "Jane, may I present Silas Nash, my best man, and his charming wife, Caroline, Lady Stone?"

She and Lady Stone curtsied, while Lord Stone bowed. They were a striking couple. He had an interesting, quirky face, and she was beautiful, with large blue eyes under elaborately arranged dark hair threaded with diamonds.

"I'm delighted to meet you at last," Jane said, every word a lie.

She knew that she'd have to meet all of Hugh's friends at some stage, and that most, if not all of them were closely associated with Morwenna. But today, she felt too insecure in her new role as Lady Garson to cope with many more reminders of her husband's previous amour.

Jane felt bad about her lack of sincerity, when Lady Stone smiled with an open friendliness she hadn't expected to encounter in Morwenna Nash's sister-in-law. "We've been itching with curiosity to see you, too, Lady Garson, ever since Hugh told us he'd found the woman he wanted to marry. Our very best wishes for your future happiness."

"I second that." Lord Stone's smile was just as warm. "I'm hoping we'll all be great friends."

"Yes, please call me Caro. I'm sure this reprobate won't mind if you call him Silas." The glance Caro bestowed upon her husband was alight with humor. After a dozen years of marriage, the Stones were so obviously in love. The contentment of a life well lived oozed from them like honey from a comb.

Good for them, Jane thought with uncharacteristic bitterness, although she maintained her polite smile. She badly wanted to make a good first impression. "And you must call me Jane."

Out of the corner of her eye, she saw Hugh's shoulders relax. For all his pretense of ease with this meeting, he, too, was aware that past history could make it all go terribly wrong.

"Congratulations again, Garson old chum," Silas said. "I couldn't be happier for you."

Hugh released Jane and shook Silas's hand. Jane couldn't mistake the affection between them. Jane told herself it was her wedding day, and it would be too pathetic to feel like an outsider.

"Thanks, old man. I'm a lucky dog." He almost sounded like he meant it.

Silas glanced at the people hovering to speak to the bride and groom, and his lips turned down in a wry smile. "We won't monopolize you both here, but when you come to London, I hope you'll be a regular visitor, Jane. Caro can't wait to introduce you to her friends. They'll take you about and make sure you find your feet in society."

"How very kind." To Jane's surprise, her response was more sincere than just good manners.

Caro leaned forward and kissed her cheek. "Courage, Jane. Hugh's worth the effort," she whispered before she drew away.

Jane started, wondering whether she'd heard right. That sounded like Caro might be on her side, which was the last thing she'd expected before she met the Nashes. She'd assumed any connections of Garson's lost love would resent her stepping into Morwenna's shoes.

"Th-thank you," she stammered, poise deserting her for an instant until she frantically clawed it back.

Caro's smile was genuinely warm, and she squeezed Jane's hand. "We'll see you in Town."

As Caro kissed Hugh's cheek—did she offer him advice, too?—

Silas took Jane's hand and bowed over it. "Jane, it's been a pleasure. May you and this rapscallion enjoy many blissful years together."

"Thank you, Silas," she said, still reeling at the welcome she'd received from Hugh's friends. Perhaps she'd been borrowing trouble, and London wasn't going to be quite the nightmare she envisioned.

The rest of the wedding breakfast passed in a whirl of good wishes from family and neighbors. As her father's health worsened, she'd largely withdrawn from local society, so she was taken aback at how heartfelt the congratulations were. Saying goodbye to so many familiar faces was difficult. She'd grown up among these people, and she was sorry to leave them.

By the time Jane went upstairs to change into her traveling clothes, she'd almost convinced herself that she might glean a measure of happiness from this match. Meeting the Nashes hadn't been near the ordeal she'd anticipated, and the guests all acted as if she and Hugh embarked on a golden future. Hugh had hardly left her side and hadn't betrayed a moment's dissatisfaction with his choice of bride.

In her pretty pink gown, Susan bustled in front of her. Her sister was always in a rush, which meant she reached her destination ahead of time. But it also meant that she relied on other people to pick up the pieces she left behind.

Jane entered the bedroom she'd slept in all her life. Packed up and ready for Felix's sister, it felt strangely unfamiliar. Her stomach lurched with a resurgence of nerves. Cavell Court was where she'd always belonged, but no longer. Would she ever feel like she belonged with Hugh?

Susan had already fluttered forward to smooth the lavender traveling gown Jane's maid Molly had laid out on the bed. That had been another sad parting. Molly wasn't coming to Derbyshire with Jane. Instead, she stayed behind to marry John, the estate's head groom.

Characteristic impatience filled Susan's face. "Stop looking like a wet hen, Janie, and come over here so I can unlace your dress."

Jane hated the description almost as much as she hated the childish nickname. Still, she made herself smile, although Susan didn't sound like she was joking. "You can't say that to a bride."

"Nevertheless it's true. You should be in alt. Hugh is way above your touch, my girl. Rich. Handsome. Influential."

"And nice," Jane said, disliking the direction of Susan's remarks.

Susan shrugged, clearly unconcerned with Garson's personal qualities. "For a woman at her last prayers, you've done yourself proud. Don't mess it up."

Annoyed, Jane marched across and presented her back to her sister. At least temper chased away her collywobbles. "You make it sound like he's made a very poor bargain indeed."

"He could have picked anyone. Never forget how lucky you are. Remember you were looking forward to years of making do in the back of beyond." Susan's voice took on an unattractive hectoring tone, as she tugged at Jane's laces. "I always thought that was a mad plan, when Frederick and I offered you a home. You're so good with the children, after all."

Ugh. Never in this lifetime. "So I should spend the rest of my days showering my husband in gratitude?" she asked with a touch of acid.

"You could do worse," Susan said equally acidly. "He's saved you from some pretty grim decisions, and let's face it, at your age, you were on the shelf. I can hardly believe you've managed to pull off this coup."

"Stop talking about Hugh as if he's a prize pig in a fair."

"Well, he is," Susan said, hauling the lovely cream dress over Jane's head. Her sister had arrived with both Jane's wedding gown and going away clothes. At the time, Jane had been touched that Susan saved her from appearing a total frump. Those warm feelings cooled by the second, as Susan's frankness trampled her sensitivities.

Carefully Susan laid the silk dress across the bed. She went on before Jane could argue—although the awful fact was that Susan was right. Hugh was a prize, and Jane was miserably aware that she wasn't. Her frail, newborn hopes for her future now seemed foolish to the point of fatuousness.

"Do you know what's going to happen tonight?"

Heat flooded Jane's cheeks. "The estate breeds cattle, sheep and horses. I'm aware of the basics."

"Good." Susan faced her. "Just lie back and let him do what he wants. It's going to hurt the first time."

Dear heaven above. Jane had been struggling not very successfully to avoid stewing over her wedding night. Trust Susan to shift the ordeal front and center.

Except Jane wasn't totally sure it was going to be an ordeal. Or at least she hadn't been until now.

Hugh was kind, and he'd do his best to ease her into her marital duties. Late at night, when she lay exhausted in her bed, she'd pictured Hugh's big hands touching her and Hugh's big body joining with hers, and she hadn't been afraid at all.

"Does it...does it hurt every time?" she asked in a shaky voice.

A smile she'd never seen before curved Susan's cupid's bow lips. With her mass of glossy black hair, flashing dark eyes, and generous figure, she'd always been the beauty of the family. Susan took after their mother, whereas Jane was a Norris through and through.

"It gets better."

That was reassuring. In a way.

"So it does hurt."

"It won't last long. Especially if you lie still and let him get on with it."

By now, Jane was feeling lightheaded with nerves. The last few weeks, she'd been grateful that Hugh had left her alone so she could prepare for the wedding and her departure from the house. Now she wondered if perhaps more time to get used to his company might have been a better idea. If she'd become more comfortable with him in daylight, perhaps she wouldn't be quite so panicked about what happened between them after night fell.

"You're back to looking like a wet hen."

"I wish you'd stop saying that."

"I daresay he won't be too attentive. After all, everyone knows he's in love with Morwenna Nash."

Jane stepped back, even as a great lump of misery coagulated in her empty stomach. "You're full of cheerful tidings today, dear sister."

Susan frowned. "I'm sure I told you the story. He was engaged to her, then—"

"I know what happened." Jane put up her hand. "You don't need to repeat it."

Susan looked abashed. "You always like to know the truth, however harsh. I thought…"

Jane crossed to lift her new lavender dress from the bed with trembling hands. "I'd rather not spend my wedding day dwelling on the woman my husband would prefer to wear his ring."

Except the sad truth was that from the first, the ghost of beautiful Morwenna Nash had haunted today's festivities.

To her surprise, Susan came up and gave her a hug. "I'm sorry. Of course you don't. I hope you and Hugh will be very happy. He's a fine man."

Leaning against her sister, Jane closed her eyes and prayed for courage. Tears prickled behind her eyelids, as she wished circumstances were different. That she married a man she loved and who loved her. That she didn't feel like second best.

And even more futile, that her father hadn't fallen ill and died. That she hadn't had to set aside the hopes of her youth and waste her ardent heart in loneliness and drudgery.

The most pitiful wish of all was that she was as unforgettable as Morwenna. No man would ever break his heart over plain, practical Jane Norris.

After a second, she shifted away from Susan. Giving in to these childish thoughts was doing her no good. "We're crushing the dress."

Susan surveyed her with surprising shrewdness. Her sister could be selfish and flighty, but nobody in the world knew Jane better. However complicated their relationship, they loved each other.

"At least be thankful you don't love him. It would be purgatory to want a man in thrall to another woman. You've always been sensible, Jane, and able to make the best of things. These last years with Papa, you've been marvelous. If you hadn't stepped up, I don't know what would have become of the estate. Hugh is very lucky to have you."

"Even if he doesn't know it," Jane said sourly, although she was surprised and moved at Susan's tribute.

Susan touched her cheek with unaccustomed fondness. "He's a smart fellow. He'll work it out eventually."

"What the devil did Susan say to you?" Hugh asked, as their opulent traveling carriage turned out of the drive and headed north.

Jane stopped staring out at the snowy landscape and stared instead at the man she'd just married. Wearing a disgruntled expression, he sat opposite her in the shadowy interior. Now they were no longer under observation, he didn't have to play the lover by holding her hand or sitting beside her.

"Why?" she asked warily.

"Because you looked quite happy today, until you went upstairs. Since you came down, you've been like a dog whose master just died."

Not much of an improvement over a wet hen. "I'm sad to leave my home."

"And the people you know." Compassion softened his features. "I'm sure this has been a bittersweet occasion for you in many ways."

"The silly thing is I've been preparing for this day for years." She made a helpless gesture. "I always knew that because I'm a girl, I couldn't inherit, but it doesn't make it any easier to let Cavell Court go."

He smiled at her. "At this moment, I'm very happy you're a girl."

"Thank you." She wished she could believe that he meant that, instead of it being another example of his endless kindness.

His dark eyes sharpened. "I suppose Susan criticized your decision to marry me."

"Not at all." Mockery tinged Jane's smile. "She thinks I'm very lucky to have caught you."

He gave a heavy sigh. "And made you feel like a beggar maid on your wedding day. How very considerate of her."

"She loves me."

"Why wouldn't she? Whenever anything unpleasant needs to be done, you step up."

It might be true, but she still didn't like him criticizing her sister. "She couldn't stay down here with Papa. She has a family."

"And I'll wager over these last difficult years, she did nothing to make life easier or more enjoyable for you."

Jane looked at him curiously. "I thought you liked her."

"I do. She's very likable, especially when she's getting her own way."

"That's not fair," Jane said, although in many ways it was. She met his skeptical gaze and sighed in capitulation. "Oh, I know she's spoiled and vain and self-centered, but she's always been the pretty sister, and as a result, people have indulged her far too much. She's used to her wishes being paramount. There's no real harm in her."

"You're worth a hundred of her. You always have been."

"Thank you." Along with shock, unaccustomed warmth flooded her. "You're very nice to say that."

"It's not nice. It's the truth." He made an impatient sound. "More people see that than you think. It's a joke that Susan's convinced you that you're lucky to marry me. Everyone I met at that wedding breakfast told me I was the lucky one."

Jane made a dismissive gesture. "That's what people say at weddings, Hugh. Don't pay too much attention."

His lips flattened as he folded his arms. "Credit me with the sense to see the difference between social flummery and genuine affection. You were always too ready to discount your good points."

She shrugged. "Oh, I'm a steadfast friend and useful in a crisis, and as everyone keeps pointing out, I'm sensible and capable."

"All the worthwhile qualities."

"But none of the glamorous ones."

"You could develop those, you know. It's a matter of confidence and audacity."

She responded with a short laugh, although something about his assessing gaze made her shift uncomfortably on the leather seat. "I almost think you mean that."

He didn't smile back. "I do with all my heart."

"I appreciate you trying to bolster my spirits."

He still didn't smile. "Susan only tried to upset you, because she's jealous that you're stepping out of the shadows at last."

Jane couldn't contain another laugh, although Hugh sounded serious about this nonsense. "Why on earth would she be jealous? She's got everything she wants. She was a winsome child and a beautiful girl. In her first season, she was counted a diamond of the first water, and she made a love match with a dear man, who also happens to be nicely plump in the pocket. Now she has five high-spirited children." Who were spoiled little horrors, but she wasn't going into that now. "Whereas I've been on the shelf for years, and she's well aware you and I aren't in love. No, you're wrong about Susan, but I'm grateful that you're on my side. It's very...husbandly."

His lips flattened, but instead of continuing the argument, he sent her a searching glance. "I'm always on your side, Jane. I hope you know that."

She met that somber, dark brown gaze, and any urge to object dissipated. "Thank you."

As she turned back to the window, she found herself agreeing with Susan. Any woman would be lucky to marry Hugh Rutherford.

CHAPTER SIX

*W*earing a heavy crimson silk dressing gown over his nakedness, Garson knocked at the bedroom door. On the way home after Jane had agreed to marry him, he'd stopped here at the Red Lion in Salisbury and reserved their best set of rooms for his wedding night.

If it was Morwenna waiting for him, he'd be burning with eagerness. But while he wasn't mad with desire, the more he saw of Jane, the more pleased he was with his choice. The prospect of holding his bride in his arms was surprisingly appealing.

He'd always thought of her fondly. She'd been a plucky, open-hearted child, and he admired her devotion to her family. But over the years, he'd forgotten the hint of salt that enlivened her sweetness. And he was avid to discover the secrets of her body. That purple traveling ensemble she wore when they left Cavell Court had clung close enough to remind him of her magnificent figure.

He'd never appreciated the fashion for little dolls like Susan. He preferred a woman with a bit of heft to her. Jane was long of limb, with a superb, deep bosom. She looked like a woman who could give a man a run for his money.

He was about to find out if that was true. When he heard her soft invitation to enter, he felt unexpectedly keen.

Jane was sitting up in bed, looking terrified.

Dear God.

"Jane, are you all right?" He stepped forward, then stopped where he stood when she shrank back against the carved oak headboard and clasped the blankets to her chest.

"Yes," she said in a quavery voice.

"You don't sound it." He smiled, hoping to ease the room's fraught atmosphere.

Her delicate throat moved as she swallowed. That thick white nightgown was the least bridal garment he'd seen in his life. It covered her to the collarbones.

The extravagant tumble of her hair almost made up for all that flannel. He couldn't help staring entranced at the mane of rich red flowing over her shoulders. He'd often pictured her hair unbound, but this abundant beauty stole his breath. His heart began to beat faster, and the call of pleasure inched aside the command of duty.

"I promised I'd do my part," she said in a reedy voice utterly unlike her usual mellow contralto.

He glanced across at the dinner he'd had sent up. He'd assumed she'd want time to rest and gather her thoughts before he came to her. When they reached the inn, he'd noted her exhaustion. She still looked exhausted, and scared out of her wits as well.

"I know you did." Instead of approaching her, he crossed to the tray. "You didn't eat much."

She hadn't eaten anything, from what he could see.

"I wasn't hungry."

Whereas he'd made a hearty meal. It had been a long day, and as the bridegroom, he hadn't had much chance to eat at the wedding breakfast. Nor had Jane, as far as he'd been able to tell.

As he stared unseeing at the array of dishes, he had a horrible premonition that his wife might greet the morrow as virginal as she was now.

A howl of denial jammed in his throat. He was astonished at how piercing his disappointment was. He hadn't had a woman since he'd decided to marry Jane, and he'd looked forward to ending seven months of celibacy.

Cheer up, man. Too early to admit defeat.

First things first. She needed to eat something. The soup had congealed into slop. The stew was cold and unappetizing, too, with a shiny layer of grease surrounding the meat. Bread and cheese might fit the bill.

He put a makeshift meal together. "You need to keep your strength up."

"I thought the man does most of the work."

Despite his grim mood, he laughed. There was that salt again. "I wasn't just thinking about the marital act."

He poured two glasses of wine. The inn sold a fine claret. He'd enjoyed a glass downstairs before coming up to change into his dressing gown.

Garson returned to the bed. He passed Jane the plate and put the glass of wine on the bedside table.

She regarded the food without enthusiasm. "I'm really not hungry."

"Have some wine at least." He sat on the bed, watching her.

She set the food aside on top of the blankets and lifted the glass without drinking. "Will this be easier if I'm foxed?"

"It will be easier if you're relaxed enough not to shatter like glass."

A rueful smile turned her lips downward. Jane's mouth was pink and full, with a perfectly cut upper lip and a lushly curved lower lip. How the devil had he never noticed that before?

"Is it so obvious?"

As obvious as a poke in the eye, but he forbore from saying so. "You're looking a tad wan."

It was a massive understatement. She was whiter than the inn's linen, and in a fine hostelry like the Red Lion, the linen was bleached to within an inch of its life. The only color in the room seemed to be that rich fall of red hair. He refused to believe that a woman with such a brazen wealth of hair had no sensuality in her.

Of course she did. But only careful handling would coax it out.

Jane made an apologetic gesture. "I'm sorry. I thought I'd take our arrangement in my stride, once I got used to the idea. In the last ten years, when awful things happened, I muddled through by girding up my loins and tackling the problems as best I could."

Awful things? Hell, she really wasn't happy about this marriage, was she?

Did he have Susan to blame for this nervousness, or had Jane's uncertainty when he proposed burgeoned into panic during his absence? She'd held herself together through the difficult day, but perhaps he should put that down to pride. "Do girls have loins?"

She shrugged and mustered an unconvincing smile. "You know what I mean."

He did. Better than she probably wanted him to. "You've been so brave, Jane."

Another of those bleak little smiles. "I'm not feeling brave right now."

"Am I really so frightening?"

Fleeting color rose in her cheeks. It faded to leave her paler than before. "I'm making a mess of this, aren't I?"

With a sigh, he collected his glass and shifted to a massive oak chair near the blazing fire. He didn't miss how the line of her shoulders loosened when he moved away.

"No, I am. I shouldn't have abandoned you to fall victim to your fears."

She stared down to where her hands pleated the edge of the sheets. It seemed to be a characteristic habit when she was jittery. "I'm sure it's just fear of the unknown. And I've been so busy since you visited, that I really didn't think much past leaving home after the wedding."

He doubted if that was true, but it allowed him to change the subject to something that might banish the dread from his bride's eyes. Although it was hardly likely to make her smile either.

"I know you found it hard to leave Cavell Court."

His instincts had led him aright. Those fidgeting fingers paused and flattened on the sheet. "I'd feel better if I thought Felix will be a diligent master, but unless he's changed, he'll just use the estate to support the grand life he's always considered his right. Priscilla won't be any sort of moderating influence."

"The new Lady Sefton is as silly as a duckling in a thunderstorm."

This time the smile was a little more sincere. "Two ducklings."

"I'd help if I could," he said, meaning it.

At last she looked at him without flinching. "Thank you. You're very kind."

"I wish you'd stop saying that." He grimaced. "It makes me feel about ninety."

"But you are kind. You always have been. When you were a boy, you were always rescuing puppies and kittens from the local louts."

"Yes, well, I've grown up since then."

She watched him with an unreadable expression. "Have you?"

He frowned. "Don't say you're equating yourself with those scrawny, flea-bitten strays. God give me strength, I told you—you did me a favor marrying me."

"Yes, you did tell me." To his surprise, amusement brightened her face. "I'll wager Beardsley Hall is full to the brim of rescued animals."

He shifted uncomfortably. "No more than most places."

That was true, although not many of the animals were able-bodied. He couldn't resist a creature in distress. Which didn't bloody well mean he'd married Jane because he felt sorry for her.

"There's no need to be embarrassed about it. I always admired your readiness to face a beating to save a fellow creature." She paused. "Although you grew so big so fast, most of the time, you just had to turn up to get your way."

"Good Lord, I was the size of a house before I was sixteen. I used to tread all over your toes when I asked you to dance."

"You just needed to learn how to manage your size. I'm sure you no longer trample your partners' slippers." To his relief, she lifted the wineglass to her lips.

Revisiting childhood memories was helping to blunt the edge of her fear. He also hoped it reminded her that they were far from strangers. She mightn't have thought of him as a lover, but their history together stretched back many years.

"You'll find out for yourself. I'd like to hold a ball at Beardsley to introduce my wife to the neighbors." He went on before she raised any objections. "I know you're going to miss Cavell Court and your friends and neighbors. But we'll make a new, full life in Derbyshire. The estate is prosperous, and we're close enough to Derby for a bit of society. I'm also hoping you'll make the house your own. It's a fine old manor, but it hasn't had a chatelaine since my mother died twelve years ago. It desperately needs a woman's touch."

With every word, Jane looked more cheerful. She was a vital, active woman. She'd enjoy taking the reins at his home.

"I remember." She picked up a piece of bread and cheese. "Not that Beardsley was neglected, but that it was a lovely place. I used to enjoy going there when I was a girl. Do you remember our visits?"

He watched her demolish the humble meal he'd prepared and felt as proud as if he'd defeated Napoleon singlehanded. "I do. With pleasure."

"I'm surprised. You must have thought I was a tiresome little girl."

"You were never tiresome, Jane," he said sincerely, although Susan, even then, had been a nuisance, especially when she was old enough to test her wiles on any males in the vicinity. "I recall you spent a lot of time reading."

"That makes me sound so dull." When she emptied her wineglass, he rose to fill it. She'd relaxed to a point where she didn't cower when he loomed closer. He was damned pleased. He hated to see her afraid of him.

"Not at all. I thought you were frightfully clever."

The disgusted face she made had him laughing. "That's even worse than dull."

"Not at all. I never liked empty-headed poppets." He frowned suddenly. "Do you mind the age difference?"

She looked surprised. "Of course not. Six years to a girl in the schoolroom is a huge gap. But not now we've both grown up. You're in the prime of life, Hugh."

Garson wished to hell he felt like he was. Three dreary years had left him feeling old and jaded. Disappointment had a way of sucking the vitality out of a man.

"I'm glad you think so." Inevitably his glance dropped to her sumptuous bosom. As she settled down, she'd stopped clutching the covers as if to fend off a vile seducer.

His grip on his glass tightened as he itched to unveil the glories concealed beneath that flannel tent. In the candlelight, she became prettier by the moment. The frozen expression had seeped away, and he found himself fascinated by her full lips and the soft, silvery shine of her eyes.

She had beautiful white skin. Was she that perfect pearly shade all over? A hunger to find out flooded him, all the more overwhelming because it was unexpected. He took a mouthful of wine and let its flavor feed his senses. His body stirred with the beginnings of genuine interest.

And there was that hair. In the flickering light, it encompassed every shade of red from garnet to russet. He'd always loved her hair. Jane's beauty was subtle. So subtle it had taken him far too long to recognize its power. Now he did, the night extended ahead, promising a satisfaction he'd never imagined when he'd proposed marriage three weeks ago.

Even better, she no longer looked paralyzed with dread.

CHAPTER SEVEN

*K*eeping his moves easy—he'd worked with enough skittish horses to know that any sudden shifts spooked them—Garson rose and set his half-empty glass on the mantel. He kept his voice even, too. "You looked lovely today."

Jane made a self-deprecating gesture. "Thank you, but that's all because of the dresses Susan brought down from London. I'm afraid in recent years, fashion has passed me by, and all my clothes were dyed for mourning when Papa died."

"I'll take you to London for the season." Had she noticed that he'd edged closer to the bed?

Her expression was a charming mixture of uncertainty and anticipation. "I still don't have anything to wear."

"Every *modiste* in the West End will fight to get their hands on the new Lady Garson."

A faint smile curved her lips. "I would love some nice clothes and the chance to make new friends."

"The world is your oyster, Jane."

Her smile deepened. "I don't like oysters."

"You'll like your new life." He sat on the bed, close enough for his hip to brush hers through the blankets. "I'll do my best to make sure you do."

"Thank you, Hugh," she said softly, without moving away.

"No, thank *you*, Jane." When he took her hand, the silvery eyes widened.

He'd held her hand plenty of times, at least since he'd been hauled in to assist at her dancing lessons when she was a girl. Today, he'd taken her hand in the church. And at the wedding breakfast.

But it felt strange—special—to sit on Jane's bed, cradling her cool fingers in his. He began to rub her hand, brushing his thumb over her wedding ring. The way his large hands encompassed hers was oddly stirring. She was so delightfully feminine and delicate. Knowing she was his wife suddenly seemed a fine thing indeed, by Jove.

"Are you cold?"

She shook her head. "No."

He found himself hoping that was true in every sense. Because with each minute, his impulses toward his bride became more heated. He raised her smooth, white hand to his lips and kissed her knuckles. The scent of lavender teased his nostrils, and underneath, a hint of Jane herself. When his lips glanced across her skin, she bit her lower lip.

"Better?"

She swallowed as she nodded. He was close enough to see the movement of her throat and the rise of her chest as she inhaled. Too quickly. She was becoming uneasy again.

Garson slipped a gentle hand around the back of her neck. To his surprise, his breath caught as he encountered the silky ripple of her hair. Desire kicked his heart into a gallop. Whatever his reasons for proposing, right now he was eager to discover the secrets his shy bride concealed beneath her demure air.

Who would have thought he'd be so mad for little Jane Norris?

Except little Jane Norris was a woman grown. A devilish attractive one at that. What a blasted fool he was, never to have seen that before. Even wrapped up in enough white flannel to sail a clipper to India, she set his blood afire.

The muscles under his fingers were tight, and he began to stroke, warming and softening her into readiness. She didn't try to escape, but she was far from comfortable with this change from conversation to seduction.

"I've wanted to kiss you all day," he murmured.

Her eyes became even wider, so he felt like he drowned in a cool, silver lake. Her pupils dilated to turn her eyes dark. This close, her skin was extraordinary. Against that pure alabaster, the dark auburn eyelashes and brows were striking.

"You kissed me at the church," she said unsteadily.

He had. Briefly.

"I never do my best work in front of an audience."

Her lips quirked. "Is that so?"

"Let me prove it."

She retreated a fraction against the pillows. He felt it. Then she went still, except for a faint tremor running through her. If his hand wasn't resting on her nape, he doubted he'd know she was shaking.

Garson waited for her to speak, perhaps ask for a reprieve, but apart from the ragged saw of air through her parted lips, she remained silent.

It was a step forward, but he was experienced—and perceptive— enough to know that fear outweighed her curiosity. Slowly he tilted forward and cupped the base of her skull to steady her for his kiss.

He placed his lips on hers. She made a sound of shock, and he felt her lean away, but she didn't pull free.

As he'd told her, she'd always been brave.

The thought filled him with powerful tenderness, so when he gently sucked her bottom lip and drew away, his care came from the heart and not strategy. She didn't protest, although her hands clenched in the sheet that covered her to the hips.

His taste of her had been so fleeting, yet a flood of impressions fueled his senses. Her soft mouth. The sweetness of her flavor, enriched with heady notes of claret. The light floral scent, which proved surprisingly alluring.

His hand tightened in her hair and this time, he lingered until her lips fluttered against his. Satisfaction roared through him, and he deepened the kiss, tracing her lips with his tongue. A shudder ran through her, and she pushed back against his hold.

Never had Garson been so conscious of a woman's responses. He counted the changes in Jane across each breath. He was profoundly aware that what happened now determined the shape of the rest of his life.

And hers.

She raised a shaking hand to her lips. The candlelight glinted on her wedding ring. "That was...odd."

He hid a smile. Instinct told him Jane might take it badly if she thought he was laughing at her. "Did you like it?"

"I'm not sure."

"Shall we try again?"

Her gaze was uncertain. "If you like."

Oh, he liked, by God.

This time, he set his hands on either side of her head. When he kissed her, Jane's essence flooded his senses. Her scent made his head swim, and that spectacular hair was a warm tumble over his hands.

He put his arms around her, pulling her across his lap. After what felt like an eon, her lips tentatively moved to answer his. The soft sounds she made conveyed burgeoning pleasure—and a surprise to match his own.

When she caught his shoulders, her touch shuddered through him. He slicked the tip of his tongue across the closed seam of her lips.

Garson broke the kiss long enough to whisper, "Jane, let me into your mouth."

"Into..."

She looked so adorably confused that he felt another rush of aching tenderness. It mixed awkwardly with his rising hunger.

He swooped before she mustered any resistance. His tongue slipped into her mouth, and at last he tasted her fully. When he flicked his tongue against hers, she made another of those astoundingly arousing sounds. When she slid her tongue against his, wild satisfaction flooded him.

As the kiss burst into flame, she gave a husky moan. Another shudder of gratification shook him, as she buried her fingers in his hair and brought him closer.

He angled her until she was flat on her back, and he kneeled over her. The heavy silk of his dressing gown rubbed against his throbbing cock and threatened to make him spill. But devil take it, when he found release, he wanted to be inside his wife.

Still kissing her, Garson placed one hand on her breast and squeezed. Even through the nightdress, he felt the exquisite roundness. The nipple jutted impudently into his palm. He caught the brazen peak between his thumb and forefinger and pinched softly, cursing the nameless bastard who had invented flannel. She gave a muffled squeak against his lips and lurched up toward him in welcome.

Then every damn thing in the whole wide world went wrong.

CHAPTER EIGHT

*J*ane battled to stay enmeshed in sensual bliss. When Hugh first kissed her, the unfamiliarity of what he did left her reeling. Then she reeled because she'd never known anything as intoxicating as the pressure of his lips on hers.

How amazing that a kiss could heat every inch of her. When he began, she just felt disturbed and needy. Then the heat became more specific, weighting her belly and waking a restless craving in the secret hollows of her body.

Barely had she found her balance in this incendiary new universe when he changed the game yet again.

He'd licked her. It sounded so bizarre. But in practice, it was… It was like someone set a blazing torch to dry tinder. That yearning sensation intensified, and her heart pounded hard and heavy, shaking her with every beat.

He kissed and kissed her, as if he fed off her. She lost all contact with the Jane she'd been before and verged on becoming Hugh's creature, quaking and gasping. Natural caution made her retreat from the brink, even as she kissed Hugh back with all the untried passion she'd had no idea existed within her.

Natural caution whispered one unwelcome word. A name. A ghost. A curse.

Morwenna.

Hugh laid her down on the bed and rose over her. Even in her innocence, she couldn't mistake what was about to happen.

She arched up to meet him, struggling to silence that insidious voice. Hugh had married her to have children. She owed him the use of her body. It would be cowardly—and dishonorable—to draw back now.

Morwenna.

Over and over, that name played in her mind, no matter how she fought to block it out.

Hugh's powerful form dominated hers as he shifted closer. She felt utterly consumed in his animal appetite. He was hot and strong, and ready to do his duty.

Duty was another unwelcome word, although surely that was all that held them together.

Jane strained toward him. He didn't appear to notice the desperation creeping into her responses. Or if he did, it didn't make him pause.

One large hand landed on the breast no man had ever touched. She tensed against a liquid surge deep inside her. Was this arousal? When she yielded to her husband, she'd expected something swift but measured. Pain, if Susan was right. An invitation to participate in actions that might seem strange and perhaps repugnant.

She hadn't expected to be swept away into an ocean of temptation. An ocean likely to close over her head and drown her.

He squeezed her breast, and her nipple tightened into a tingling point. Unfamiliar forces battered her from all sides. It was all too much.

She made a distressed sound against his lips and stiffened in his hold.

An instant longer, his hand remained heavy on her breast, before he heaved himself to the side with a guttural groan. His eyes fastened on the ceiling, while she remained on her back and gulped for her first full breath in what felt like hours. Searing tears pricked her eyes. His scent suffocated her. Hot, male musk.

"I'm sorry, Jane." His voice was so gravelly, it emerged as a growl. "I went too far too fast."

She rose on one elbow to study him. His massive chest heaved as he sucked in air. The loose dressing gown allowed shadowy glimpses of dark curls across his chest.

He looked like a ruffled Zeus. Massive. Virile. Omnipotent.

His thick hair was untidy, and one coffee-colored lock tumbled over his noble forehead. In some men that might add a boyish touch. Not in Hugh.

Almost convulsively her gaze ran over him. Now she'd touched him, she knew how strong those shoulders were and how his body covered hers when he lifted himself over her. Even as she told herself to stop, her attention traveled downward. Over his flat stomach to where the part that he would thrust into her rose hard and insistent against his belly. There was hair down there as well. She bit her lip and couldn't help staring, even as she wondered how it was physically possible for something so large to fit inside her.

When she looked up, she realized he'd shifted his attention from the ceiling to her. One slanting eyebrow mocked her imprudent curiosity. A painful blush flooded her cheeks when he tugged the rich crimson silk across his legs, restoring his dignity, if not hers.

Jane flopped back against the bed and stared up at the ceiling. Both she and Hugh seemed to find it of surpassing interest. The tumult in her blood gradually subsided, leaving a bitter residue of shame.

Not at what they'd done, but at her timidity. And her inability to forget that he wished he lay with someone else.

"I'm sorry, too." Her voice was almost inaudible. "I shirked my duty."

His grunt indicated disgust and irritation in equal measure. "I began to hope that there might be more than duty between us."

"You must try again," she said, even as something inside her shrank from the idea. "I promised to be your wife in every sense."

He leaned over her, until she couldn't avoid those searching dark eyes. "I know you did, but it's been a long, difficult day, and I wasn't as…careful as I might have been."

Her lips tightened, as she steeled herself to venture back into that strange world she'd entered tonight for the first time. "You're my husband. You have rights over my body."

Those thick brows lowered over his blade of a nose, and he sat up against the headboard. "Spoken like a right little martyr."

She flinched. "I don't know what you want."

Which wasn't quite true. She'd recognized his increasing interest. If she'd held her nerve, he'd even now be pushing inside her, and she'd be a virgin no more.

He remained displeased. A displeased King of Olympus was a daunting prospect, especially when only a layer of silk covered his nakedness.

"More than I thought I did, it seems. Those kisses got me devilish excited, Jane."

She hid another wince, even as some wanton part of her relished his praise. "I didn't…I didn't know kissing could be like that."

He looked shocked. "You've never been kissed before?"

"Who would I kiss?" Her lips turned down in self-derision as she sat beside him. She felt at too much of a disadvantage lying flat on her back. "Mr. Jones the bailiff? Billings the butler?"

His disbelief didn't fade. "I thought perhaps at some assembly or house party."

"I told you my life has been quiet. Now and again, I went to dinner with the neighbors, but there was never much chance for flirtation."

"Yet you said you'd had a proposal or two."

She gave an unamused laugh. "Old men looking for a nurse and a housekeeper. No flirtation was required."

"What a waste."

She shrugged, while the lonely years of toil and obligation pressed down and threatened to crush her. "A girl can live without kisses."

"She shouldn't have to." He paused. "I liked kissing you, Jane."

Heat rose to her cheeks. "Do we have to talk about this?"

"I'm afraid we do."

When she looked into his eyes, she sought but didn't find anger or resentment. Given how she'd pulled back, she wouldn't blame him for feeling either. "I'm willing to do what I must."

His eyes sharpened on her. "I know you are, but I'd rather you enjoyed this. Especially after those kisses."

She flung out one hand in an annoyed gesture. "Will you stop harping on about kisses?"

"No. Did you like kissing me, Jane?"

Jane wanted her side of the bed to sink through the floor and take her with it. "You know I did."

"That's something we can work on."

He caught her hand. After being in his arms, the heat the contact sparked wasn't as bewildering as it had been. She rapidly reached a point where she liked Hugh to touch her. She thought back to how overwrought she'd been when the world lurched off its axis.

"I'm not sure about any of this, Hugh," she admitted.

"I know you're not." He raised her hand to his lips and kissed it, setting off another wanton quiver. "It's asking too much to think you might be, dear Jane."

She struggled to avoid turning into a puddle of syrup when he called her dear Jane. Turning into a puddle of syrup had been the problem when he kissed her.

She raised her chin. "I made a promise to you—and to God."

"Our marital relations aren't a mountain you must climb."

That was exactly what they felt like. A high, rocky, barren mountain, riven with dangerous cliffs and chasms. When he'd kissed her, she'd felt like she was trapped in a landslide.

His grip on her hand tightened. His hold wasn't reassuring at all, although she supposed he meant it to soothe her fears. "Shall we try again, Jane?"

Dread jolted her. Dread, and a shameful wash of anticipation. She'd never expected Hugh to have this power over her. She was—almost—convinced she didn't like it.

Still, she'd made vows. She hated that she was too spineless to fulfill her marital obligations. But it took an almighty effort to meet that velvety gaze and nod her head. "If you wish," she forced out from a throat as tight as a drum.

A light glinted in his eyes, a light that did nothing to banish the nerves curdling her stomach. "By God, I do wish."

CHAPTER NINE

*H*ugh kneeled over her legs so he could cradle her face between his hands. Jane made herself sit still, although the urge to retreat into the pillows was nigh irresistible. She closed her eyes and trembled in his grasp. Bunching her hands against the sheet, she told herself she could bear this. All she needed to do was keep him from sweeping her away into that terrifying tide of excitement.

He leaned in and brushed his lips across hers. Immediately, she braced against a wave of powerful response that seemed out of kilter with the sweetness of his kiss. He cupped her nape and began a gentle kneading. The temptation to sway forward was overwhelming, but she managed to resist it.

After a few moments, Hugh pulled away. His breath was warm on her face. Another intimacy.

When he didn't speak, she gradually opened her eyes. His expression was rueful. "This isn't going to happen, is it?"

Her guilt spiked. "I won't fight you."

He shook his head, more in disappointment than denial, she thought. "I know you won't."

"Then?"

He let her go and moved away to slump against the pillows beside her. "Do you want this, Jane?"

Did she? The touch of his lips ripping the soul from her body and threatening to turn sensible Jane Norris—Jane Rutherford, now—into someone she didn't recognize? "Do you?"

His grunt held a derisive edge. "More than I ever imagined I would."

Given that until three weeks ago, he'd never expressed a moment's interest in her as anything other than a family friend, that was probably true. She licked her lips, and something feminine inside her responded to his lingering taste. "Perhaps the problem is the kissing."

He looked skeptical, lifting one expressive eyebrow in her direction. "Indeed?"

"Yes," she said, warming to her theory. "If I lie back and you…do what you need to, we can finish quickly and without trouble."

Another grunt of sour amusement. "Like taking a nasty medicine all in one gulp?"

Heat stung her cheeks. He was a little too acute. That had been exactly her idea.

"I don't want to let you down."

"I commend your principles."

Her lips tightened. "Sarcasm isn't helpful."

"No, it's not," he said grimly. "I'll feel let down if my wife takes no pleasure in what I do to her. Do you loathe my touch so much?"

"No," she said aghast, before she could stop herself. "It's just…"

Watching her handsome husband when he spoke of such private matters did strange things to her insides. That heavy, dark gaze set up a quiver in her stomach that reminded her of how lost she'd felt in his kisses.

Hugh sighed and ran his hand through his thick hair. More than ever, he looked like a sulky deity. "You're not yet accustomed to the idea of being my wife."

"I thought I was." Jane looked down to where her hands pleated the sheets. The glint of her wedding ring still caught her by surprise. "You've made a bad bargain."

"I wouldn't say that," he murmured. "But I was unfair, expecting you to make the transition from nurse to wife, without time to adjust to your new life."

"I'm willing to do my part," she said shakily. "Perhaps this time, it would be better if you didn't kiss me."

However mad it seemed, the thought of that vigorous male body pumping into her wasn't nearly so scary as his kisses.

"If you're sure," he said, sounding unconvinced.

She couldn't blame him. No doubt other ladies clamored for his attentions. The thought of those other ladies added a dollop of jealousy to her stew of emotions. Which was a disaster and showed just how dangerous Hugh's kisses were.

Because he was in love with another woman and always would be. If she let that unarguable fact set its claws into her, life would become a nightmare. She couldn't risk developing any possessive feelings about her husband.

"And maybe...maybe you should blow out the candles."

His eyes narrowed on her, as if she posed a logistical problem that he meant to solve. She supposed she must. This turmoil had caught them both unprepared. After all, they'd entered this marriage with the same businesslike approach she'd use to buy a new cow.

Except in this particular deal, she was the cow.

That pragmatism had misled her into thinking that everything between them would be matter-of-fact. Her innocence had betrayed her. Apparently it was difficult to share a man's bed, without crossing the line between friendship and a relationship impossible to define, but more disturbing than she'd ever imagined.

"I don't want shame to contaminate what we do together," he said.

Shame? Was that what she felt? Jane didn't think so. What he'd done had felt outlandish, but she hadn't been disgusted. Even when he'd pushed his tongue into her mouth.

No, it had been exciting. Too exciting.

Instinct insisted that she had to maintain some distance from her husband. When Hugh's mouth claimed hers, that became impossible.

"I think if I can't see you, it will help," she said, hating the squeak in her voice. "Just this time."

"Don't you find me attractive?" he asked, and she cringed at her tactlessness.

What could she say? Any woman would find him attractive, but every ounce of her Norris pride revolted at the idea of yearning after a man who didn't want her.

"You're my husband," she said shakily, and she knew they both noted how she'd evaded his question.

"I am indeed." The sternness returned to his voice.

Hugh left the bed and stalked about the room, blowing out the candles, until only the glow of the fire remained. Jane gulped and told herself she'd only sound more of a fool than she did already if she asked him to bank it. The night was cold, and the big room needed heating.

There was enough light to reveal the offended set of his shoulders and the annoyed briskness of his hands when he tugged at the sash holding his dressing gown closed. Trepidation jammed in her throat, as she waited for him to remove the robe.

He sent her a glance, unreadable in the shadows, but she guessed it was impatient. The dressing gown remained in place, although hanging loose, it hinted at the mysteries beneath in a way that fed both her nerves and her curiosity.

Despite the chill in the air, she flung aside the blankets and lay back. But even as she fortified her courage, she couldn't help the catch of her breath when he stood beside the bed.

His body blocked the firelight, so she couldn't see much more than a big, dark outline. She'd hoped to feel braver if she wasn't watching his every move. It hadn't worked out that way.

"Spread out like a proper little virgin sacrifice," he said flatly.

She didn't try to hide her wince. "You said you wanted to do this."

"I did, when I thought you were willing."

"I've done nothing to deny you." Well, apart from that moment she'd stiffened in his arms, but even then, she hadn't asked him to stop.

"So why do I feel like a villain from a play?"

She bit her lip and avoided answering. "Would you like me to take my nightdress off?"

"Do you want to?"

Not at all. In fact, right now, she wished she'd stuck to her guns and moved to Weymouth for a spinsterish life of good works and afternoon calls. But it was too late to regret her choices.

"I want what you want," she said miserably, curling her fingers into the bedding and biting back a demand for him to get on with it.

"Wrong answer."

Tears blurred her eyes. Jane had no idea what the right answer was. She should have known she'd botch this. Bitterness surged when she recalled the few moments earlier today when illusory hope had lifted her heart.

To her mortification, when she inhaled, her shakiness was clearly audible. She blinked frantically up at the firelit shadows dancing on the ceiling.

"Hell." Hugh ran his hand through his hair again. "I'm a deuced callous brute. Please don't cry, Jane."

"You're not a callous brute," she said thickly.

"Yes, I am." He sat on the edge of the bed but to her relief, didn't try to touch her.

"I've failed you." Her voice was scratchy, as she fought back the urge to howl like an abandoned baby.

"No, you haven't. I expected too much."

"You're being nice, when really you shouldn't be. This hasn't been the wedding night you wanted."

Something about the shape of his body in the darkness reassured her that right now he had no designs on her. Gingerly she sat up and rested against the headboard.

"It's had a few compensations," he said drily.

Now that it seemed she was safe—which was a telling word to choose to describe her failure as a bride—what he said made her recall his kisses. She'd been so frightened and overcome. But in retrospect, the power of what she'd felt set off another of those heated ripples.

Surely she couldn't be regretting that he'd stopped. At the time, all she'd wanted was for it to be over.

Well, perhaps not all she'd wanted.

Because now that the passionate stranger was gone, replaced by the cordial companion she knew, she could admit that she'd been afraid of the pleasure, not that Hugh would hurt her.

"Shall I lie down again?" she asked, although the charged atmosphere had receded.

He shook his head. "We have all our lives ahead, Jane. Perhaps this isn't the beginning we'd choose, but we have good will and friendship." He paused. "We have, haven't we?"

"Of course."

He caught her hand and lifted it to his lips again. Stupid, now he'd given her a reprieve, to suffer a pang of longing at the contact.

He lowered her hand. "Then that's enough for now."

Even through her relief, she didn't believe that. However much he loved Morwenna, for a brief space tonight, he'd desired his wife. But she was wise enough not to argue.

"Yes," she said, her voice reedy.

He released her and stood. "I'll sleep in the dressing room, and we'll talk tomorrow."

Even more stupidly, she regretted that he let her go. Henwitted as the notion was, she couldn't help thinking that nothing could hurt her when Hugh held her hand. She'd felt like that, even as a little girl.

She licked dry lips. "You can...you can stay if you like."

His snort was dismissive. "Definitely not a good idea, Jane."

"The...the bed in there won't be as comfortable as this one."

Why on earth was she pushing this? She wanted a chance to find her feet in this marriage before he touched her again, and Hugh appeared willing to give that to her. She should just shut up and let him go.

"I wouldn't say that," he said drily.

"Oh," she said, feeling useless and awkward. And guilty. "I'm so sorry, Hugh."

"Please stop apologizing. It's not the end of the world."

Right now it seemed like it. Had her stupid jitters destroyed any hope of making a success of her marriage? The silence extended, turned heavy with so much she'd like to say, but couldn't.

I wish you weren't in love with another woman.

I wish we could start with a clean slate.

I wish I wasn't your second-best bride.

Hugh bent his head in an oddly courtly gesture. "Good night, Jane. I'll see you in the morning."

"Good night, Hugh," she whispered, watching him leave the room. The slump of his shoulders reeked of defeat. He, too, must wonder where they went from here.

She felt a mad urge to call him back. But what would be the point? He wanted a passion that promised oblivion, and she wanted something much more prosaic. Somewhere they'd have to find a meeting place. There were those children he planned on having, after all.

Even once he'd gone, Jane sat staring after him. Although Hugh had done his best all day to hide it, she had no doubt that he regretted that she wasn't his beloved Morwenna. She harked back to his honesty about his lost love when he'd proposed. Part of her wished that he'd deigned to lie. Even just a little.

Plague take her. She needed to stop moping. She'd vowed that she wouldn't torture herself over Morwenna. She'd also vowed—publicly and before God—that she'd be a good wife to Hugh. On both counts, she'd fallen short.

"You can do better, Jane," she said aloud, but the bracing command didn't help to raise her spirits. Instead she felt inadequate and unfair.

And as she stared into the darkness, mostly she just felt...lonely.

CHAPTER TEN

*G*arson shifted yet again to try and find a comfortable position on the cramped bed in the dressing room. The cot was meant for a servant who traveled with the people sleeping in the main chamber. A valet or a maid. Not a huge brute like him. And definitely not a bridegroom who had every right to be enjoying his bride.

He bit back another curse and rolled over so that his feet stuck off the end. Tugging the blanket high about his shoulders didn't help much against the cold night.

He could have stayed next door, but he didn't trust himself to lie beside Jane without taking her. Shuddering, he recalled her spread out across the bed like a doll. The only color had been that magnificent fall of deep red hair, almost black in the firelight.

He'd be no gentleman to insist on his way, when she was so obviously afraid. But the sight of her arrayed for his use had made his cock stand hard and eager.

Damn it, he didn't want his wife's first experience of a man to be a matter of duty and discomfort. Especially as when he kissed her, he'd glimpsed something altogether sweeter.

Garson had approached his wedding night with no great anticipation, but when Jane had been so beguiling, a storm of desire had swept him up. All the more powerful for being unexpected.

Then, like a fool, he'd taken her responses for granted and frightened her. Now he lay alone and wakeful and bloody frustrated, a whole room away.

Had he scared her to a point where he'd never again awaken her passions? There were women who couldn't or wouldn't respond to a man. Was Jane like that? Surely not. She'd always been reserved. A shy little girl had grown up to become a self-contained woman. But he'd never believed her self-effacement signaled a lack of warmth, just a natural reticence and a lack of confidence, encouraged by that witch Susan who monopolized any available attention.

No, he'd wager every acre of his estate that Jane wasn't cold, just uncertain and innocent. She needed careful handling, when so far, all he'd done was lumber around like a drunken yokel.

Despite his discomfort, a reminiscent smile tilted his lips. His wedding night might have proven a dismal failure, but he saw the promise of better things to come.

He just needed to overcome his wife's fears and make her want him.

Much against expectations, Jane slept deeply and late. After all that turmoil, she'd been convinced that she'd see the dawn. But when she opened her eyes, the morning was well advanced. Sheer exhaustion had triumphed over turbulent emotions and a troubled spirit.

As one of the inn's maids helped her dress, last night's events took on a dreamlike quality. It was hard to believe that Hugh had kissed her to the verge of madness. But when she entered the sitting room and found her husband in his shirtsleeves, reading the London papers, her stomach lurched and her heart started to race. She couldn't help remembering how he'd touched her.

Studying the man she'd married, she acknowledged that Caro Nash was right. Hugh was worth the effort.

He sat turned away from her, his armchair in a pool of winter sunshine. In profile like this, he looked like a knight in an old engraving.

Last night, he'd been a knight, too. In the light of day, she could appreciate his extraordinary chivalry. He hadn't shouted at her. He'd even seemed to understand her quibbles. And he'd left her to sleep alone.

He lowered the broadsheet and met her apprehensive regard. To her surprise, he smiled. A proper smile. She knew him well enough to recognize the difference.

"Good morning, Jane. How did you sleep?"

Not sure how to respond, she shifted from one foot to the other. She was as uncomfortable as she'd be if he'd used her body last night. "Good morning," she said shakily.

She'd wondered whether he'd be angry, now he'd had time to stew on how she'd reneged on their arrangement. But he seemed just the same as always. Easygoing. Polite. Considerate.

He folded away the paper and rose to cross the floor toward her. He extended his hand and without thinking, she accepted it. More warmth and that inescapable ripple of awareness. Awareness deepened by her recollection of how she'd felt lashed tight in his arms.

Something that looked like masculine interest flickered in his dark eyes. She blushed.

As if it was the most natural thing in the world—which she supposed it was, given they were married—he brushed his lips across her cheek. "You're looking lovely."

It was a chaste salute. Not like last night's hungry kisses. But her blush deepened, and her stomach gave another of those odd lurches. Her knees wobbled, and she tightened her hold on his hand.

"Th-thank you," she stammered, and didn't think to argue with his compliment. Although she'd changed into one of her plain, unfashionable gowns ready for travel, and her mirror told her that the strain of the last days showed on her face.

In a daze, she let him lead her to a table set for breakfast. For two.

She cast him a curious glance under her lashes. "Did you wait for me?"

How pitiful that this seemed such a concession on his part. Nobody had ever adjusted their habits to fit in with her before.

"Naturally." Still holding her hand, Hugh took the seat cornerwise. She was staring at him like a moonling, when a pair of servants, including the maid who had helped her dress, arrived with their meal.

When Mary bestowed a misty-eyed glance on the newlyweds holding hands over the breakfast table, Jane blushed again. Which must only make her look more bridal.

Once she and Hugh were alone again, she made herself face him. "I promise I'll do better."

He paused in serving her some breakfast and shot her a searching look that pierced to her bones. "No, the fault was all mine."

He slid a plate piled high with eggs and bacon and sausages in front of her, then he served himself. Jane stared glumly down at her breakfast. "You know that's not true."

"Yes, it is. But I have a plan to fix things."

Startled, she glanced up. "You have?"

"Once we've had breakfast, I'll tell you about it."

"Can't you tell me now?"

His lips twitched into a smile. Looking at his mouth made her think of his kisses. Her blood thickened and beat so hard that she almost missed what he said next.

"I'll tell you when you've eaten something. You're fading away before my eyes."

"Hardly," she said. "You fed me last night."

"A mere snack."

"I'm not five years old anymore, Hugh," she said with a hint of vinegar.

The smile widened. "I'm well aware of that, my lady." His voice deepened into sincerity. "Yesterday, I promised to cherish you. I know for years, it's been Jane Norris as the lone warrior, fighting her own battles. But it doesn't have to stay that way."

She stiffened in her chair and fought back an absurd desire to cry.

She hadn't known Hugh guessed so much about her life at Cavell Court. Because that was exactly how it had been.

"Curse you." Her voice was scratchy. "What am I supposed to say to that?"

His eyes softened to the brown velvet that always tangled her heart into a knot. "'Yes, Hugh. I intend to eat all my breakfast.'"

She hoped he didn't hear the crack in her laugh. But to her surprise once she took her first mouthful, she was hungry. Her husband had no qualms about devouring his meal. Their difficult first night together clearly didn't prey upon him the way it did on her.

Of course it didn't. He might be disappointed that he'd missed the chance to plant a child in her womb, but otherwise, nothing of great significance had happened.

Stop it, Jane. You'll go mad if you think like that. You've made your bed. Now you must lie on it.

With Hugh.

This morning, that prospect didn't seem quite as intimidating as it had yesterday.

She'd entered this room eaten up with embarrassment and remorse. But Hugh's relaxed manner gradually made her view last night's events not as high tragedy, but as a step on the way to establishing their life together. A scene in a domestic comedy, perhaps.

Garson watched Jane pick up her coffee and wander across to the open window overlooking the bustling street. It was market day, and Salisbury was crowded. The cacophony from outside rose to their room.

She craned to see something below her, then laughed.

"You should do that more often," Garson said from the table.

Her face alight with amusement, she turned to him. "What?"

"Laugh."

The sparkle faded from her eyes. "Life has been deadly serious lately."

"I know." He hated to think of the toll the last years had taken on her.

In her drab, gray dress, she should look like the little mouse who had accepted his proposal. Except she hadn't been a mouse then either, had she? Despite her grief, the woman at Cavell Court had carried an indefinable air of authority.

The list of his damn fool assumptions grew by the day.

Jane was plain and unassuming? No, she was pretty and intriguing.

He only wanted his wife because he needed a child? Tell that to the poor sap mad for her last night.

Most galling of all to his self-satisfaction was the asinine idea that seducing his new bride would pose no problems. With bleak amusement, he looked back on his simplistic expectations. He'd assumed marriage would require no major changes to his habits. A mere day after his wedding, and he already foresaw a host of complications. Not least his hunger for the bride he'd chosen purely for his own convenience.

Jane proved to be many things. So far, convenient wasn't one of them.

He needed to change his definition of his wife from ordinary and cooperative, to fascinating and troublesome and devilish appealing. No wonder he was floundering. He cringed as he admitted that he'd planned to buy a workhorse, and instead found himself in charge of a Thoroughbred.

Curious to discover what caught her attention, Garson rose to stand beside her at the diamond-paned window. When she didn't shrink away, it felt like a victory. Earlier, she'd looked ready to bolt. His attempt to lower the room's emotional temperature seemed to be succeeding.

"What's happening out there?"

She pointed to where a brindle mongrel raced through the market with a string of sausages dangling from its mouth. A fat man in a blood-stained apron, clearly the butcher, lumbered after the dog, but the animal was going to get away with his thievery. "It's so interesting to have all this activity going on around us."

As Garson surveyed the frankly provincial gathering, a vague idea solidified. "You'd like to see more of the world?"

"Very much." Jane turned away from the hubbub below to study him. "In recent years, I've been no further than the cattle sales in Exeter. I couldn't leave Papa for long periods. You've wed a woeful rustic."

How lonely her life had been. Pure drudgery. Her delight in Salisbury's limited entertainments was proof of that. His plans firmed. "I've been thinking about what we should do."

When the ease drained from her expression, he damned his unintentionally ambiguous statement. Her wariness was familiar from last night. "Oh?"

The tight little syllable made him want to curse, although a display of temper wouldn't advance his case. "I meant our wedding trip."

Of course he'd thought about last night, too. But he needed extreme care to negotiate his way through that thorny subject.

Her shoulders lowered, but her eyes remained watchful. "Aren't we going north to Beardsley?"

He'd intended to rush her back to his estate, but now he reconsidered. Last night, she'd obviously felt completely overcome. Taking her to a new home where she'd feel even more at a disadvantage didn't seem the wisest move.

Perhaps if they lingered on neutral ground, she might reconcile herself to becoming his wife more easily.

"I was wondering if you'd like a holiday first. This part of the country offers plenty of attractions, and the inn is good. We could stay a few days, take in the sights."

"Stonehenge is only a couple of miles away. It seems a pity to miss it." She looked thoughtful. "Are you sure? You seemed so eager to go back to Derbyshire."

He had been, when he'd thought Jane would fit into his life like a doll packed inside a box. "I'd enjoy a short honeymoon."

She looked strained once more. The connotations of a honeymoon clearly remained unappealing.

By God, he intended to change that before too long.

"It's not the best weather," she said.

"We'll manage. If you like the idea."

She considered briefly, then nodded. "I do. Thank you."

Garson stepped closer and noticed her subtle shift away. He had so much work to do to make up for being such a dunderheaded oaf last night. "Then I'd like to go to London."

"London?"

He took her hand. She never objected to that. "We could buy you some new dresses and go to a few parties. The season is starting, so I can introduce my lovely bride to society."

"If you think so."

He'd expected her to applaud his suggestion, but she seemed hesitant. "If you want to avoid society and just take in the sights, that's fine, too. We're newly married. People will grant us some privacy."

Jane shot him a mocking glance. "As if we'll be allowed to hide away. All your friends must be dying of curiosity about the woman you married."

She was right. "Will you mind?"

"I'll have to face them some time," she said. "Probably better sooner rather than later."

"Good girl." He stared hard at her. "There's something else we need to face, you know."

"What happened last night," she muttered, withdrawing her hand. Her reluctance to broach this subject couldn't be clearer, if she'd shouted it from the rooftops.

"Yes. Can you bear to talk about it?"

"If we must."

He studied this woman who proved more complex—and more interesting—by the minute. "What happened, Jane? Tell me, so there are no misunderstandings."

He liked it when she blushed. The pink rising under her clear white skin made her look about sixteen. "I hadn't expected..."

He waited patiently, although he guessed what was to come.

Jane bit her lips and cast him a nervous glance before she looked out the window again. He'd wager that this time, she didn't see much on the busy street. "Must I say?"

He decided to help her. "You felt desire, and it scared you."

When she looked back, her gray eyes were troubled. "Of course."

"It's good that you desire your husband."

"Not when…" She bit her lip again, then went on in a rush. "Not when we're strangers."

Garson bit back a curse, although he'd diagnosed the issues pretty accurately. The question of how to solve them remained. "You've known me all your life, Jane."

"But not like…this."

No, not like this. His hunger had shocked him, and he was a sophisticated man. Jane was a complete innocent. No wonder she'd recoiled from a fire that threatened to rage out of control.

"I'd like to make a bargain."

The wary look remained. "Oh?"

"Yes, another bargain." Despite the fraught atmosphere, he hid a smile. "One that I hope you'll like better than the one we made three weeks ago."

"I don't dislike that bargain." She sounded as if she faced the hangman. Avoiding his eyes, she plucked at her skirts. "I just had a…a failure of nerve."

"I rushed you into this."

"You're sorry that you married me?" She looked stricken. "I can't blame you. I'm acting like such a ninnyhammer."

"Oh, sweetheart, no," he said urgently, catching those busy fingers. "I'm pleased as Punch with my choice of bride."

Typical of Jane, she didn't look convinced. "You're just being kind."

Garson squeezed her hand. "On my honor, I mean it. Now I have to convince you that you've made the right choice."

"It's too late to change my mind."

He winced theatrically. "That sounds bad."

"No, I mean that I intend to make the best of our situation." She raised her chin. "I won't be difficult tonight."

"Damn it, Jane," he bit out, resenting the stony purpose in her tone.

She pulled her hand free. "I don't understand what you expect," she said sadly. "I thought I did when you proposed. But everything has changed."

Because he'd discovered he wanted her. He believed that if he was careful and clever and lucky, he could make her want him back. Good God, she'd wanted him last night. Otherwise she wouldn't be so skittish now.

"Is that necessarily a bad thing?"

She faced him, slender and gallant in the sunlight pouring through the window. "It is, if I can't give you what you need."

"That's true for my part as well. I don't want you unhappy."

She made a helpless gesture. "So here we are, full of good intentions, but with no way to fulfill them."

Ah, at last his moment arrived. "That's not true. What you need is time to get to know me, as a husband, not a friend. In short, Jane, I aim to give you a proper courtship."

CHAPTER ELEVEN

"*B*ut we're married." Baffled, Jane frowned. "Courtship after the fact seems redundant."

Why in heaven's name was she raising any objections? Hugh suggested a delay in marital relations. Last night, this would have felt like rescue. Today, perhaps not so much.

The hint of tenderness in his smile set her wayward heart wobbling. "We've done everything else in a topsy-turvy fashion, so why not this as well? You need to get used to being my wife."

She sank into an armchair near the fire. "A reprieve?"

When he sighed, she realized she'd been less than tactful. Again.

"If you like." Hugh returned to the chair where he'd sat reading the paper. "The decision about what happens next is yours. I'll only come to your bed when you ask me."

"What on earth…" Surprise made her stutter. While she should like the sound of this arrangement, she wasn't sure that she did. "But my fears might grow."

He leaned forward and linked his hands between his knees. "I hope they won't."

"It will be like waiting for an ax to fall."

"For me or for you?"

"For me."

To her surprise, he burst out laughing. "Don't mind my feelings."

She shot him an unimpressed glance. "You know what I mean."

"Unfortunately I do." His humor faded, and he sat back, gaze unwavering. "Which makes the rest of what I want to say even more important."

"Oh?" she asked suspiciously.

His lips twisted. "This won't be any common courtship."

"Given I'm your wife, it could hardly be that." She spread her hands. "You've already read the last chapter of this book, Hugh. The hero and heroine get together at the end."

The gleam in his eyes stirred an echo of last night's wanton feelings. "But how do they get together? I'm hoping for a blissful happy ever after."

Not likely when he loved someone else. She surged to her feet, a protest rising to her lips. Then she reminded herself how accommodating he was being, given he'd spent his wedding night alone in the dressing room.

"How do we manage that?" Jane only just stopped herself from finishing that question with "impossible goal." She had to give Hugh points for trying, when every rule of law and custom said he didn't have to.

He folded his arms. "I want to teach you to enjoy my touch."

A shiver ran through her, not entirely dread. "Oh?"

His eyebrows arched at her instinctive withdrawal, but he went on as though they discussed some mundane subject. A walk in the gardens, or cards after dinner. "If you know that I won't take things to their end, you may learn to appreciate the preliminaries."

She doubted it. Oh, not that she would enjoy his touch. She'd enjoy it far too much. But that he could lull her into a state where her fears disappeared and she tumbled into his arms as easily as a ripe apple fell from a tree. Last night's experience indicated otherwise.

"What about kisses?"

"Ah," he said slowly. "Kisses are different."

She stepped closer to the fire, although she wasn't cold. "I suppose you want to kiss me whenever the fancy takes you."

"I'd like that." When she struggled to hide her dismay, a knowing smile curled his lips. "But I'll ration myself to one a day."

"How very...restrained," she said shakily. "A good night kiss?"

He shrugged. "Or good morning. I reserve the right to choose my moment."

"I...see." Although she really didn't.

She appreciated him trying to smooth her way. To a certain extent. Touching and kisses still seemed more threatening than claiming her body in a quick physical act. But she could see that he sought more from her in bed than dumb obedience.

The problem—or one of them—was that last night, she'd had a hint of what "more" might mean. It had terrified the life out of her.

"I hope, with time, you'll learn to trust me."

"I do trust you."

His glance was skeptical. "Not really."

His doubts were justified. "I thought I did."

"Your body tells me you don't." He stood and joined her beside the fire. "I give you my word of honor that you'll sleep alone until you invite me to join you."

"I invited you last night."

"Out of duty."

"I owe you my duty."

"But I want your desire."

What should she do? A wooing might be nice. She couldn't hope to be the woman he really wanted, but just because she was his second choice, did that mean they must settle for second best in everything?

"Jane?" he asked softly.

"What if it doesn't work?" Her eyes narrowed as she studied his expression. "You're sure it will work, aren't you?"

His shrug was unconvincing. "I live in hope."

More than hope, Jane was sure. Every line of his body betrayed self-confidence.

Why shouldn't Hugh be confident? He was an attractive man,

experienced in the ways of women. They both knew that before panic set in, she'd been mad for him.

"Do we have a deal?"

On the surface, what did she have to lose? But a deeper, barely formulated disquiet niggled. She had an unshakable premonition that Hugh's kind, generous offer—he was a kind, generous man—foretold disaster.

Oh, grow a backbone, Jane Norris.

He already had the right to do everything he asked for, whether she agreed or not. As he said, at least this arrangement restored some agency to her. Over the last two days, she'd felt like a leaf swept away in a flooding river.

She snatched a breath and nodded. "Yes, we do." She paused. "Thank you. You've been very understanding."

"It's my pleasure, Jane." He subjected her to a thorough inspection.

As the silence extended, she sidled from one foot to the other. "You're making me feel like a side of beef in a butcher's window," she muttered. "And as if you're wondering whether I'm worth the extra penny in the pound."

He laughed. "I'd never choose such an unflattering description. I'm just deciding when I'll take today's kiss."

Oh, dear Lord. She wasn't prepared for the arrangement to begin straightaway. "Perhaps we should get it out of the way."

Laughter lit his eyes, even as she wanted to kick herself. She kept putting her foot in her mouth. Yet before this, she'd never have said she was particularly maladroit in social situations.

Curse Hugh. It was all his fault.

"That's an idea." His deep voice wrapped around her like a warm blanket and made her blood pump slow and thick.

He cupped her jaw. To her shame, she jumped like a startled rabbit. Inevitably she recalled how she'd felt last night, plastered against that broad, powerful chest. Her heart took a dizzying swoop down, then up, until it lodged in her throat.

"Jane, Jane, meet me halfway," he said, in that same alluring tone.

She stared into dark eyes glowing with interest. She'd never imagined Hugh Rutherford looking at her like this. Like she was a bonbon, and he was a man with a very sweet tooth.

Jane wasn't sure she liked it. Life was simpler when he was her amiable childhood friend, rather than her ardent suitor.

"I'll try," she said shakily, overwhelmingly conscious of his hand on her face.

"I hope so," he said, without a hint of rebuke, although surely it was a rebuke. "Or this won't succeed at all."

Lightly his thumb stroked the corner of her lips, making them tingle. His brilliant eyes filled her vision, and the room receded. She swayed, and Hugh caught her by the waist, setting off another sizzle of heat.

"Breathe, Jane," he whispered.

Oh, what a goose she was. She parted her lips and gulped air into her starved lungs. Her sight cleared, and her legs no longer felt likely to collapse beneath her.

"You're quite lovely," he murmured, as if speaking to himself and not her. His fierce concentration on her mouth turned her knees to jelly all over again. "Why didn't I ever notice?"

She wanted to say it was his turn to be tactless. But she wasn't miffed. Instead, she felt that he found a beauty in her that nobody else ever had. The stab of grateful pleasure made her want to cry. After so long being overlooked and neglected, Hugh's admiration felt like rain falling on a desert.

Blinking at the mist in front of her eyes, she dredged up a croaky response. "I don't suppose you ever looked before."

"Which makes me a blind fool," he retorted, with the self-deprecating humor she'd always liked.

Standing in his hold, her body softened. It was a queer feeling, as if her very bones molded to his hands. This close, she caught his scent. Lemon soap. Healthy male.

Did he loom closer? Or did she lean in, drawn like a tide to his attraction? He flattened his hand across the small of her back and angled her in his direction, still keeping up that teasing caress on her face.

Her breath emerged in uneven gasps. Her head swam with conflicting impulses. To run. To stay. To please. To protest.

What on earth had made her think that marriage would prove an uncomplicated partnership? Fate must be snickering at her naivety. Right now, she'd never felt more at sea.

His focus sharpened on her. Every drop of moisture dried from her mouth. When she licked parched lips, he muffled a groan.

She tilted her face up. Curiosity outweighed any lingering reluctance. Last night his kisses had undermined her sense of herself. Had that been a trick of circumstance, or something more indelible? She closed her eyes and silently told him to get on with it. A hum of anticipation escaped her.

"Shall I kiss you now, or save it for later?" He still sounded like a man choosing a bonbon from a gift box.

Jane barely resisted crying out, "Pick me, pick me!" Why the devil was he talking, when those lips could be doing so many other enjoyable things? "Hugh," she grumbled.

"You know, I'm famous for my patience…"

Patience? What drivel was this? She strained closer.

Abruptly he released her. Her eyes snapped open, and she staggered. He stood several feet away, looking like the man she'd known all her life. Calm. Sensible. Genial.

"You're not going to…" she stammered, struggling to find her balance.

"I'll save my treat for later."

"When later?" She sounded mortifyingly disgruntled.

His soft laugh tantalized her. "You'll see."

A putrid stew of frustration roiled in her stomach, and she had a nasty suspicion that he'd just made a fool of her. At that instant, she understood how well founded her fears about accepting his proposal had been. Hugh wielded such power already. What command would he hold over her emotions, once they were husband and wife in the fullest sense?

CHAPTER TWELVE

*A*s he escorted his bride around Salisbury, Garson felt considerably happier with the world. Snow lay on the ground, but something in the air promised better weather for tomorrow when he planned to take Jane to Stonehenge. He looked forward to that. In a closed carriage, a man could get up to no end of mischief.

The day might be milder, but it was still February. With her slender arm in his grasp, his wife's nearness lured him like a blazing hearth in a cold room.

As he'd hoped, allowing Jane some say over what happened eased the constant hum of tension between them. Perhaps even gave him reason to hope that she wouldn't prolong his ordeal. He'd noted her disappointment when he'd put off kissing her.

But as the afternoon wore on, a new tension began to stretch between them. He, familiar with desire, recognized the way two people in thrall to each other craved physical contact. Jane just went quiet, where earlier she'd been delightfully chatty.

"It's very bare." Jane surveyed the cathedral's cavernous interior. "I'd imagined something a little more…"

He drew her into a dimly lit side chapel. "Ornate? Spectacular? Mysterious?"

With a slight roughness—and he was never rough with a lady—he pushed her up against the cold marble tomb that housed the earthly remains of some long-dead archbishop. A reminder, should he need it, not to waste his chances on this earthly plane.

Jane gasped as her back hit the cold stone. She observed him from under the brim of the dark blue bonnet that matched her fashionable pelisse. "What are you doing, Hugh?"

As he swept off his hat, he glanced around. This late in the winter day, little light penetrated the high, clear windows, but enough to reveal that the cathedral was almost empty. There was nobody in this side aisle, although evensong was due to begin soon.

He placed one hand beside Jane's head, hemming her in with his body. "I'm going to touch you."

"For shame." Her reproof contradicted the flaring excitement in her eyes. "This is a church."

Despite her disapproval, she didn't try to escape. He shifted close enough to catch a drift of floral scent. Last night, that fragrance had fueled his arousal. After he left her, it had haunted his restless dreams.

He set his hat on the tomb behind her head. "And nicely private."

"That's blasphemous."

"We got married in a church."

When Jane's lips twitched, he cursed himself for limiting himself to only one kiss a day. "That reasoning is self-serving, and you know it."

"I need to put my hands on you."

Her alarmed squeak evoked a reaction more profane than sacred. He leaned in, until his lips touched her delicate earlobe. "Is that a yes?"

After a shuddering exhalation, her answer was a whisper. "Don't do anything too brazen."

A soft huff of laughter escaped him. "I'll try my best."

With manufactured casualness, he tugged off his gloves and shoved them into his pocket. He reached out to flick open the top buttons on her pelisse, one of the garments Susan had brought from

London. The stylish dark blue merino parted to reveal a high-necked gray gown.

"You don't make it easy for a fellow, sweetheart."

"Next time, tell me I need to dress for a ravishing," Jane responded with that hint of tartness he liked.

Garson trailed one hand down her throat until his fingers rested against the pulse skittering at the base of her neck. "So I can ravish you?" he asked idly, although the question wasn't idle at all.

No surprise when she shook her head. "Purely a figure of speech."

"Pity."

Beneath his fingers, her skin was warm and smooth. His excitement mounted, although so far, he hadn't done anything that might upset any saints loitering in the shadows.

Jane studied him steadily, although he felt her trembling. "Do you tire of the game already, Hugh?"

He retraced his path up her throat. With so little skin revealed, touching what he could see felt like the height of depravity. He really had to get her some new clothes. Gowns to display that spectacular figure. Gowns that fastened up the front, for a husband's convenience. The urge to touch her breasts was a physical ache.

"No, I'm looking forward to more of it." His lips quirked. "Although if you want to be quick about your surrender, I'll like that even better."

"I'm sure," she retorted.

The temptation was too much. When he kissed the side of her neck, she gave a voluptuous shudder. He lowered the arm he'd braced against the marble and slipped it around her waist.

"Oh, that's wicked," she gasped, as he scraped his teeth across a nerve. "Can I touch you?"

Lord above, what he'd give to have her touch him properly. But she was still shy, and last night proved the danger of racing ahead too fast. "By heaven, yes."

When tentative hands hooked over his shoulders, his heart battered his ribs. God help him, he'd brought her in here for a bit of light flirtation, another foray in their sensual battle of wills. Now, so swiftly, he was lost in a fog of desire.

"That's good." He set his lips to the luscious curve where her neck met her shoulder.

She tilted her head to give him better access. This close, the floral scent was richer, earthier. He felt drunk on Jane.

Garson was likely to embarrass himself. A rag of common sense insisted that he couldn't tup his wife in a church. As if to confirm that thought, the organ started to play softly from the loft high above them. He hauled Jane around the tomb and into the gloomiest corner of the chapel.

"Hugh?" she asked uncertainly.

With a massive exercise of will, he pulled away. "We should go."

She looked troubled. "You sound...angry."

He struggled to find a reassuring smile, but her expression told him it didn't work. "No."

For a heart-pounding interval, he crushed her into him. Even through layers of winter clothing, he was sharply conscious of the lithe, graceful body in his arms. Then he released her, grabbed his hat, took her hand, and headed outside into air hardly less icy than the air inside the cathedral.

He drew a bracing breath and fought to return to reality. The short day faded into night. The first stars winked in a clear sky. Smoke from a thousand fireplaces tinged the air. Bells pealed from the spire, summoning worshippers for evensong. Muffled figures hurried across the cathedral close to attend the service.

The wild rush of Garson's heart gradually slowed. "I'm sorry, Jane," he said, as they approached the ornate gates leading back to town. "I shouldn't have started that. Not there."

"The archbishop wouldn't have approved."

Her mocking tone took him by surprise. He dropped her hand and stopped to stare at her. More surprise when he saw how rosy and winsome she looked. "You didn't mind?"

"I've led a very secluded life." She made an apologetic gesture. "Letting a handsome devil manhandle me in a cathedral is the most exciting thing I've ever done."

Damn it, it was probably the most exciting thing he'd ever done as well—and he hadn't led a secluded life. This time, his smile felt completely natural. Although he feared it might be too wolfish to count as reassuring.

"I thought you'd want my gizzards for garters."

Amusement flirted with her lips. "Not today."

He stared after her as she wandered ahead, trying to wrap his mind around the fact that his nefarious plan already seemed to be working. God bless cold chapels and warm women.

CHAPTER THIRTEEN

*I*n their rooms at the inn, Garson and his wife sat up late, revisiting childhood memories over an excellent meal. He congratulated himself on his choice of bride. Jane was interesting, funny, intelligent. He could hardly believe that he only now recognized her manifold physical attractions. In short, she promised to be the perfect wife.

If only she'd take him to her bed.

After those incendiary moments in the cathedral, he hadn't tried to coax her any further down the path of surrender. But he'd touched her lightly, fleetingly, often. A meeting of fingers when he passed her a dish. A caress across the warm curve of her nape when he wandered over to stoke the fire.

Now Garson rose from the dinner table and extended his hand. "Shall I escort you to your chamber, my lady?"

She regarded him doubtfully. "It's all of three steps."

For dinner, she'd changed into a dark green dress that wasn't quite as nun-like as the one she'd worn this afternoon. His gaze drifted across her scooped décolletage. Ridiculous to be so titillated by that modest display of white skin. "I'd hate a bear or a wolf to snatch you up."

She smiled at his absurdities. All evening, she'd been more relaxed. Perhaps she became accustomed to his company. Perhaps she'd had an extra glass of claret.

"I have a feeling the only wolf here is the one talking to me."

Smart girl. "Unfair. I've been the perfect gentleman."

She stood and accepted his hand with an ease that underlined the progress he'd made. "Yes, you have." She paused and cast him a shy glance. "Thank you, Hugh. It's been a lovely day. One of the loveliest I've had in a long time."

His fingers tightened as he drew her toward the bedroom door. "Shall I call for a maid, or will you bear with your husband unlacing your gown?"

"You don't need to play my servant."

He shrugged. "I'm happy to help."

And by God, the chance to get her out of those depressing clothes was an incentive to any man with blood in his veins, even if helping her undress was the only concession he was likely to win from her right now.

He waited for her to say no. She was no fool, and she must guess that strategy prompted his offer. But after a moment, she nodded. "Then, thank you. I don't feel like dealing with a stranger."

Satisfaction filled him. He'd been promoted. Several times yesterday, she'd called him a stranger. Yet tonight he wasn't.

He opened the door for her to precede him into the bedroom. To a man facing exile to the dressing room, it seemed packed with forbidden luxuries. A blazing fire. A large, comfortable bed. A lovely woman he'd dearly love to swive into next Tuesday.

Garson reminded himself that this was a seduction, not a siege. An avalanche of pleasure to come would repay an ounce of patience now.

At least he bloody well hoped so.

Jane stopped in front of the cheval mirror and glanced over her shoulder. A come-hither look? Or was that wishful thinking?

He stepped up behind her and laid his hands on her straight shoulders. She didn't jump when he touched her. More progress.

For a long moment, he stared at their reflection. A large man towered over an auburn-haired woman, whose eyes betrayed a longing he suspected she didn't recognize. Something about the way they stood said they belonged together. He puzzled over how their wedding vows could establish this visible bond.

"We look like a couple."

"I almost feel married," she said softly.

Smiling, he kissed her nape. He both felt her shiver and saw it in the mirror.

He ran his hands down her arms and up again, fighting the urge to rip the dress away and uncover the treasures beneath. But as the day with his wife played out, he'd noted more than just a growing acceptance of his presence. He'd seen a nascent trust. If he broke the truce now and took what he wanted—by the devil, how he wanted—he'd be back where he was last night.

Learning to be a husband was a long, hard road.

"Hard" being the word.

"Hugh?"

The sound of his name wrenched him back to the present. Waiting for Jane's capitulation was torture worthy of the Spanish Inquisition.

All thumbs, he plucked at the laces down the back of her gown. She remained silent under his attentions, although he could hear her erratic breathing. This was the closest he'd yet come to his wife's nakedness. Last night's flannel nightgown had been thick enough to repulse a cavalry charge.

Under the dark green wool, he discovered pale skin and a graceful back. What he'd give to slide the pins from her rich red hair, until it cascaded around his hands.

Eventually, even his fumbling fingers completed their task. "Shall I undo your corset, too?"

He winced to hear the crack in his voice. It must be something about marriage. He'd never been this mad for a mistress, even as a randy boy let loose on society—and society's women—for the first time.

"N-no." Her answer echoed his unsteadiness. "I can manage."

The girl in the glass was flushed, and her eyes shone with a beguiling mixture of reticence and curiosity. She clasped her bodice to her bosom to save her modesty. The urge rose to send her modesty to the devil, but he conquered it.

"Pity," he bit out, setting his hands on her hips.

In the mirror, she stared at him, as if afraid he meant to jump on her.

And as if afraid he might not.

"I'll...I'll see you in the morning."

He tilted an eyebrow in her direction. "Haven't you forgotten something?"

Apprehension tightened her features, a sign that any trust remained frail. "You said the decision about...about what happened was mine."

"It is." He studied her face, wishing he could banish her doubts with a snap of his fingers. Because he'd never been more certain of anything as he was that when they came together, they would shake the heavens. "But you promised me a kiss."

"You already kissed me." Dark red brows contracted in confusion. "In the cathedral, and just now."

This time, the wolf definitely owned his smile. He looked like he wanted to devour her. "My dear, those don't count."

"That doesn't seem fair," she protested, although when her attention fell to his lips, a spark of interest lit her eyes.

No wonder she'd been so relaxed over dinner. She thought she'd fulfilled the day's obligations.

"Are you really so unwilling?"

"N-no," she said shakily, turning to face him. "I'm not unwilling."

It was hardly a ringing endorsement. But not a denial either. Garson decided to take what he could get. He caught the hands clutching her sagging bodice. The dress slipped lower. Jane still wore corset and petticoats, so she wasn't near to naked. Not near enough, in his opinion. But the sight of the slope of her breasts rising above the plain white linen of her undergarments slammed through him like a punch.

He kept a grip on tactics—just. He'd kiss her then leave, to prove she could trust him.

Then tomorrow? Well, tomorrow, who knew what might happen? Jane had already set aside so many of her defenses.

She noticed the direction of his gaze, and her hands tugged against his hold as she tried to cover herself. "You're looking…"

"Yes?"

"Like you want to do something wicked."

His lips curved in appreciation. "I do."

When consternation widened her eyes, he relented. "But tonight, I'll just kiss you."

"Your kisses are wicked."

"I'm glad you think so." Garson raised her hands and brushed his lips across them.

She exhaled with an audible sigh, and her eyes fluttered shut. One hand flattened across her back, and the other angled her chin up. The touch of his mouth drew a soft gasp from her. She reached blindly for his shoulder.

When he didn't pursue his advantage, she opened dazed eyes, smoky with confusion and dawning desire. "Is that it?"

"The arrangement was one kiss."

She stepped back. "I imagined…"

More of those ravenous kisses from last night, he'd wager. But right now, his purpose was to gain her cooperation. Even if tasting her made him want to return again and again, until she forgot the very meaning of the word no. "You're safe."

When she looked disgruntled, he almost smiled.

"That's very…good of you." She didn't sound particularly grateful either.

"Unless you'd like me to stay?"

"By stay, you mean…"

Garson nodded. "Oh, yes. I've chosen this path for your benefit. For myself, I'd be overjoyed to share your bed sooner rather than later." Then a confession that had been unthinkable last week. Two days ago, even. "This delay is pure agony."

Astonishment widened her eyes further, although she must know by now that she put him in a fever. "Surely not."

"Surely so," he said with grim amusement. "Are you asking me to come to your bed?"

Her gaze dropped, and those slender hands began to fiddle with her skirt.

The silence was answer enough.

He was sleeping alone. Not that he was surprised. She'd ventured a long way toward him, but it was only a day since he'd made a mess of their wedding night. This wasn't the outcome he preferred, but he was wise enough to accept it as the outcome that was inevitable.

"I'll see you in the morning, Jane. If it's fine, we might take the carriage out to Stonehenge."

"Very well," she said half-heartedly. He was delighted—amidst his frustration—to notice her dismay that there was only one kiss.

His plan to lure her into his arms was succeeding, although God knew how he'd sleep. Even that one quick kiss made him as hard as a bloody truncheon. "Sleep well."

"Good night."

Garson bowed and left the room before he changed his mind. Once he was on the other side of the door, he slumped against the wall. A groan escaped as he bent his head. Keeping his hands off his lovely bride was excruciating. He hoped to hell that Jane didn't intend to test his good intentions for long, or he feared for his sanity.

He ran a shaky hand through his hair. Hell, there had been a few moments tonight when he hadn't been sure that honor would outweigh desire. When he'd unlaced her. When he'd seen her lush breasts pressing against her thin shift. When he'd restricted himself to a single kiss.

He groaned again. He was so on edge, even a feather bed would torture him. Let alone his narrow cot in the dressing room.

But he'd survive.

And he had cause for hope. Oh, yes, the frost melted from lovely Jane. Soon she'd be his.

For the sake of his mental health, she'd better be.

It was only as Garson lay with his feet dangling over the end of the bed and his eyes wide open staring at the dark ceiling that he realized the most astonishing fact about a day packed with revelations.

He hadn't thought about Morwenna Nash once.

CHAPTER FOURTEEN

The promised excursion to Stonehenge had to wait an extra day. Unseasonably clement weather melted the snow, but turned the roads to impassable mud. Today the sun was shining, and it was dry enough to travel to the ancient monument. Jane and Hugh had spent a fascinating afternoon imagining ancient rites among the stones.

Now she and her puzzling, increasingly compelling husband headed back to Salisbury in their luxurious carriage. Hugh sat beside her and stared out the window. The way he held her hand and played with her fingers stirred her senses into a ferment.

Not that she needed encouragement.

Yesterday in Salisbury, she'd been surprised when he didn't push her much past where he had the day before. Not as far. Thinking about their encounter in the cathedral two days ago made her pulses race. What a fine scandal they'd have sparked, if a deacon had stumbled across them in each other's arms. She'd have died of mortification.

Except the fear of discovery had added a thrilling charge to what they did in that empty chapel.

Last night's kiss had repeated the previous day's chaste salute.

Even so, when he'd asked if he could stay, it had been difficult to say no.

So why had she?

Perhaps because she was still afraid, if not nearly as afraid as she had been.

Perhaps because she was enjoying that he took the time to woo her. Nobody in her life had devoted this amount of attention to her. She discovered she rather liked it.

Over the last few days, Hugh looked at her like a starving man eyed a loaf of bread. Oh, what indecent feelings those hard, intent eyes stirred. After last night's kiss, and today when he'd taken her arm to help her over a fallen stone or across a slippery patch of grass, she'd felt his tension. She'd quivered with wicked anticipation and wondered if he might break his promise to wait.

"What are you thinking about, Jane?" Hugh asked softly.

She emerged from her confused thoughts to find him studying her. That fierce brown stare pierced her like an arrow. An arrow aimed at all her tender, female places.

She wanted to say "you," but her courage failed. Although what she said instead was probably worse. "Kisses."

"Mine, I hope."

She blushed, but couldn't look away. "Who else's?"

"Are you still frightened, Jane?"

Yes. No.

Yes.

"You've been very patient."

"I wouldn't say that." His gaze seemed to drink in every detail of her face. It was a heady experience. One she feared she could come to crave, the way an opium eater craved his poison.

Yes, she was still afraid. But she hurtled toward a point where fear ceased to matter.

"I would."

A silence fell, then he spoke in a considering tone that made every nerve in her body zing with anticipation. "You know, Salisbury is more than an hour away, and we have privacy all the way. This might be the ideal opportunity to further your education."

Just like that, a throbbing heat set up between her legs. Dear Lord have mercy, and so far all he'd done was hold her hand, even if he did speak sin. "Is that what you're doing?"

"In part. You shy away because a man's touch is unfamiliar."

"Becoming less so," she said drily.

They'd been married four days, and she was still a virgin. She found that almost impossible to credit. Her havering must exasperate Hugh. Although right now he looked interested rather than annoyed. A patient man indeed.

"I'm pleased to hear it." He settled into his corner and sent his long legs in their buff breeches sprawling diagonally across the well between the seats. She'd never been so conscious of another person's physical presence.

"You...haven't touched me all day."

His gaze turned smoldering. "Yes, I have."

Yes, he had. "You know what I mean."

He didn't smile. "Do you want me to touch you, Jane?"

Her cheeks heated. "Yes."

The word emerged as a thread of sound, but the moment he heard it, he went on the alert, all languor abandoned. "I'm delighted. Because I want to touch you."

He didn't mean holding her hand, either. Excitement swelled in her core at the thought of those big hands on her breasts. Her nipples tightened, and her soft exhalation was audible even over the creaking coach.

"What shall I do?" she asked.

He released her hand and laid his arm along the back of the seat. "Take off your pelisse. I'll keep you warm."

Right now, the rush of blood in her veins was doing that more than adequately. Under his unwavering gaze and with hardly any embarrassing fumbling, she released the buttons on her winter coat and slid it off.

"And now?"

He pulled the blinds down, plunging them into shadow. "Shift across and sit on my lap."

Gingerly, balancing herself against the swaying carriage, she wriggled over and perched on his knee.

His thick dark lashes lowered as he inspected her gown. "Why, Jane, I do believe you're wearing a dress that fastens up the front. Can it be you had dalliance in mind?"

She blushed again. "Given what happened in the cathedral, I didn't want you to tear it."

"Very…sensible of you."

"You married me because I'm sensible," she said, regretting the sourness that crept into her answer.

He didn't seem to hear it. Instead his gaze remained fixed on the way her breasts molded against the front of her dress. The ache in her nipples intensified, and she shifted on the seat. The itch between her legs had become familiar. As had the needy weight in the pit of her stomach.

"You've proven to be so much more," he said. "I'm a lucky fellow."

Given he hadn't yet had her, she couldn't believe he really felt like that, but she'd learned enough in the last few days to let the comment pass. Right now, she didn't want to distract him from putting his hands on her.

Which was why she'd worn this gown. As he'd guessed straight-away. There was nothing slow about Hugh Rutherford.

The carriage hit a rut, and she bumped against his thighs. Those strong hands—hands that, in her restless dreams, did so many brazen things to her—closed on her waist. It would be easy to fall off his lap, but she knew Hugh would keep her safe. Somewhere since their wedding, she'd learned to trust her husband.

The shock of that revelation kept her silent, as his touch softened and the male part of him hardened. So close to him, she couldn't miss his swift arousal.

"Now, how to manage this," he said in a musing tone. "I think perhaps… That's right. Turn your back to me and tuck your head into my shoulder."

Battling the moving carriage and propping her hand against the firm width of his chest, she wriggled some more until her cheek pressed against his neck. She rested upon him, buttocks nestled against his rod in a most improper manner. Once that might have frightened her, but now it just heightened her need.

"That's good," he murmured. "Now straddle my knees."

"Like I'm riding astride?" She remained overwhelmingly conscious of the hard flesh rising against her bottom.

"Yes." His arms closed around her as she shifted. His groan vibrated in her ears.

"Am I hurting you?"

They were so closely entwined that she felt as much as heard his grunt of derisive amusement. "No more than usual."

"Hugh…"

As the carriage dipped into another hollow, she automatically closed her legs around his and dug her fingers into his forearms. This pose permitted no modesty. Her skirts were generous enough—just—to accommodate her, but the constant lurching intensified the empty ache inside her. Through layers of petticoats, she felt the strength of his thighs against her sex. She might as well be naked.

He firmed his hold. "You know how to make it better."

She did. But she wasn't yet ready to change from bride to wife. This courtship made her feel powerful and desirable, and not like plain, practical Jane Norris at all.

"Perhaps not in a carriage."

"A man can hope."

"One day his hope may even be fulfilled," she said with an attempt at humor, but the words emerged in breathy fits and starts and sounded like a promise. Between her legs, she became embarrassingly damp. She squirmed to escape the tormenting friction of his thighs, but that only made it worse.

Or better.

"You're shaking," he whispered, although there was nobody but the two of them to hear.

"I'm not afraid," she said, which wasn't entirely true.

"I'm glad." He pressed a kiss to the side of her neck, and the blazing response speared down to the liquid heat between her legs, making her gasp and curl her fingers into his arms.

"Hold onto the strap."

She obeyed with alacrity, then waited in a lather of anticipation as he unfastened the buttons down the front of her dress. With every touch, his hands brushed her breasts, making her skin tighten in yearning.

When her bodice parted, he made a soft sound of appreciation. By now, her nipples were so hard, they hurt. She glanced down and saw how abandoned she looked, with her dress undone and the beaded pink peaks pressing against her linen shift.

"Pretty." His hands drifted across the skin above the plain scoop of her shift. Her trembling intensified, as she waited in an agony of longing for him to touch her nipples. But for the moment, he seemed content to stroke her with apparent idleness.

She'd almost believe that, if she couldn't feel him hard and insistent behind her, if the rattle of his breathing didn't proclaim burgeoning hunger.

By the time he pushed her shift down to uncover her, she was shaking like a daisy in the wind. When his hand closed around her left breast, she stifled a whimper. Dear heaven, she felt ready to burst into flame.

"You take my breath away," he murmured and pressed his palm to her nipple. Instead of offering relief, his touch made her burn. He pinched and rolled the peak between his fingers. This time, she couldn't control her whimper.

His other hand found her right breast. She bit her lip and turned her face into his neck. His tangy scent flooded her senses, became another part of the storm of sensations buffeting her from all directions. She pushed back so that his insistent weight pressed into her rump. He gave an incoherent growl and released her breasts to tangle his hands in the skirts cascading over his legs.

When he eased her skirts higher, she braced against him. He'd prepared her so well, luring her to the brink of desire and beyond.

The prospect of his hands between her legs rolled through her like thunder.

Still he teased her. His hand traced a seemingly erratic path. Touching her knees. Venturing under the loose lawn of her drawers to caress her thighs. Returning to her knees.

When long, knowing fingers stroked the sensitive skin behind her knee, she trembled with delight. Who knew such a prosaic part of her body could provide such pleasure? She burned to touch him in return, but in the speeding carriage, she didn't dare release her hold on the strap or lift the hand she spread against the seat for balance.

"Please."

Her broken plea achieved the last thing she wanted. He stopped touching her.

"Please what, Jane?" he murmured into her hair, his hand resting at her waist.

"You know." If he didn't soon answer the throbbing demand inside her, she'd start screaming like a banshee.

"Tell me." He hooked his hand across her hip, settling her more securely. But she reached a stage where Hugh's touch through layers of dress and petticoats wasn't enough. He spread his other hand beside hers. She merely needed to shift her fingers an inch to make contact. But shyness made her hesitate.

"You're cruel," she forced out, through a throat so constricted she feared she might strangle.

"I've had three days of hell since you banished me from your bed," he grated out. She'd never heard Hugh sound like this, as though he might shatter. "Who's the cruel one?"

"So this is revenge?" She hardly knew what she said.

"No, it's torture. For me and for you."

Licking dry lips, she pressed harder into his shoulder. She cursed the neck cloth and high collar that denied her the taste of his skin.

"You can't stop now," she gasped, as a jolt of the carriage rubbed his rod against her.

"No, by God, I can't. But I want you to be brave enough to tell me what you want."

"It's not proper." She cringed at the spineless response.

He gave a short, grim laugh. "No, it's not. Proper isn't the word to say, when your breasts are bobbing against my hands and your skirts are up around your waist."

His frankness should make her blush, but she'd traveled way past embarrassment. Instead his words made her shake. "You really won't relent?"

"I really won't."

"T-touch me," she said, but her courage faltered and her voice emerged as a feeble sigh.

"I didn't hear you."

He had, the villain. With them jammed so close, she heard his every unsteady breath. He'd definitely hear anything she said to him.

She licked her lips and spoke more strongly. "I said touch me."

"Where?"

"Must I say it?"

"Yes."

"You're a devil."

"Right now, I feel like I'm roasting in hell."

Jane tried to get the words out, but a boulder blocked her throat. She tightened her grip on the strap and clenched her thighs against his legs, as if firming her seat on a horse. Her hand lifted off the seat and caught his wrist. Actions might speak louder than words.

She lifted his hand to her lips and kissed his knuckles.

"Jane..." he said in a shaken voice.

"Let me show you what I want." She brought his hand between her legs, pushing up her skirts and letting him feel her soaked drawers. Finally she found the nerve to speak. "Touch me here."

He cupped his hand over her mound. "You're wet."

After four days with Hugh, the welling surge was familiar, but it still made her self-conscious. To think, she'd imagined her embarrassment had passed.

"I can't help it," she muttered.

"It means you want me."

She released his hand to clutch at his strong male thigh. "You know I do."

He squeezed her soft flesh, then stroked her. She made a choked sound, when his finger circled a place that set off a volley of pleasurable explosions.

"You're so hot and ready," he said with such satisfaction in his voice, she almost laughed.

"You sound pleased with yourself."

"I am. I hope you'll be pleased with me, too."

He rubbed that hidden place, and she whimpered, all urge to laugh abandoning her. She thought she'd wanted him before, but now every muscle contracted in agony. Behind her, he was as taut as a bowstring. That seeking finger stopped tormenting her, just as she rose toward some unknown ending.

Before she could protest, she felt a subtle stretching as one long finger penetrated her.

"Hugh," she gasped, instinctively flinching away. But with a large male body at her back, there was nowhere to go.

"You'll like this," he murmured, cupping one bare breast.

All these wild responses left her shaken and bewildered. "It's wicked."

"But good." When he teased her nipple, she softened around his predatory finger.

He pulled out, only to use two fingers on her. This time, her body accepted him more readily, and when his thumb teased that sensitive place in time with the glide of his fingers, she sank into a sensual fog where nothing existed but Hugh and what he did to her.

That strange spiraling feeling stirred again, tension coiling tighter and tighter with every shift of his hand. Her breath emerged in jagged gasps, and the hand on his leg curled into talons, digging into taut muscle.

"Don't fight it, Jane," he murmured into her ear.

Even as she strained toward something she didn't understand, her old terror of losing herself to passion flickered to life. But the clamor for relief drowned that small voice of caution. She shivered and squirmed against Hugh's chest. Still the mysterious outcome hovered out of reach.

Tears pricked her eyes, and shallow inhalations left her lungs short of air.

Then abruptly, the unbearable tension snapped on a flash of light, flinging her free into a shuddering, clenching, brilliant release. This was like flying high in the sky over a new world. She cried out and soared toward the sun.

CHAPTER FIFTEEN

*G*arson gritted his teeth together so hard that they threatened to crack. The pain in his jaw saved him from losing himself.

The pain in his jaw almost made him forget the pain in his balls.

It would be so simple to…

He lashed one arm around Jane, as she dissolved into her first climax. The rich scent of satisfied female intoxicated him, and the broken music of her moans threatened his barely held control.

She surrendered to her crisis with voluptuous ease, then slumped back against him with an exhausted exhalation. The tug of her muscles on his fingers as he withdrew was an almost irresistible invitation to take the next step. Even though it worsened his plight, he lifted his hips so the thick length of his dick pressed into her rump.

After a long, sweet interval, she shifted to drape her legs over the seat and rest her cheek on his shoulder. At last he could see her face. Her cheeks were flushed, and her lips were swollen and red. Tendrils of dark auburn hair coiled across her bosom.

Jane's breasts were exquisite, white as milk with two perfect pink nipples. Her skirts bunched around her thighs, revealing long, shapely legs. He could hardly reconcile the composed lady who had accepted his proposal with this vision of earthy sensuality.

Slowly she opened her eyes, lashes fluttering on her cheeks. A sigh parted her lips, giving him a glimpse of small white teeth.

"Hugh…" She sounded almost surprised to see him.

His lips quirked, although he remained stretched on an agonizing rack of frustrated desire. He'd loved seeing her attain her peak. He'd loved that he'd been privileged to introduce Jane to physical pleasure. Hell, a few days ago, she'd never even been kissed.

But he was only human. The need to thrust inside his wife was an agonizing imperative. He was excruciatingly aware of each bump of the carriage and how close she was to naked.

"You expected someone else?" He pulled his handkerchief from his pocket and wiped his fingers, when his deepest impulse was to inhale her scent until his head swam.

"No," she answered seriously, as if the silly question deserved an answer. He saw she hadn't yet returned to prosaic reality. She gave him a dreamy smile and touched his jaw. "That was lovely. Thank you."

The last time he'd lured her to the brink of surrender, she'd raised her defenses immediately afterward. But now lying across his lap, she looked sweet and satiated and languid.

Garson leaned down before he remembered the stupid rules. Rules? More like a prison sentence. He had nobody but himself to blame. He'd shoved his hands into the shackles by his own free will.

"Damn it, I want to kiss you." He wanted to do a hell of a lot more than that.

She tilted her face up. "Then why don't you?"

"Because I've kissed you already today, and I made a promise. I must have been insane, when I came up with these blasted nitwitted conditions."

Her low laugh made the hairs on his skin rise. "I'm willing to reward good behavior."

He took a second to register what she'd said. "Truly?"

"Truly."

Before he could swoop in to kiss her, she slid her hand behind his neck and drew him down. Her kiss was breathtakingly playful, a rain of teasing contacts. He groaned and opened his mouth over her, drinking her in. Then regretfully he retreated.

She frowned. "Is something wrong?"

Apart from a case of blue balls likely to prove fatal? "We can't be far from Salisbury."

Jane looked bewildered, then he watched reality smash through pleasure's lingering spell. The misty light left her eyes, and she looked horrified as she glanced down at her bare breasts and splayed legs. "Oh, my dear heaven, I'm half-naked."

"Yes, and what a glorious sight you are."

She scrambled off his knees, shaking hands hauling the edges of her bodice closed. "You ravished me in a carriage."

He didn't appreciate the tone of accusation. "Not quite."

Jane settled on the seat facing him. Only a couple of feet distant, but she still felt too far away. "As good as."

Tell that to my dick, he wanted to retort. "Don't be embarrassed."

She sucked in an audible breath and hitched at her shift and corset, to his regret restoring her modesty. His hands fisted against the leather seat as he resisted the urge to drag her back into his arms.

A shy glance from gray eyes. "Actually I'm not as…embarrassed as I should be."

"I'm glad."

"Why didn't you…"

He passed her his handkerchief. "Go ahead and finish it?"

Her expression turned troubled. "Yes."

"I'm caught by my own clever plan." Garson tried not to watch as she quickly cleaned herself up. Even while she did her best to preserve her dignity, the sight was too arousing, too intimate for a man on the verge of losing control. "With the trip ending in an hour, I knew I'd have to rein myself in. I never thought you'd let me take things so far."

She set the handkerchief on the seat beside her and began to fumble with the fastenings of her dress. "You did rein yourself in."

He ran his hand through his hair. God give him strength. That sounded like a complaint.

"You only had to say the word." He sighed and shifted to sit beside her. "Let me do that."

"Yes, Hugh," she said with uncharacteristic docility and dropped her hands so he could do up her bodice.

Grinding his teeth, he struggled not to touch her skin. Wheels rattling on cobbles warned him they were back in Salisbury. They'd reach the Red Lion any moment.

Garson set her bonnet on her head and did his best to tuck her hair under it. As she tipped her face up and gave him a soft smile, the horses drew to a stop. "Thank you for looking after me."

He almost growled. He was still far from tranquil. Fiddling with her clothing and messing about with handfuls of that warm silky hair didn't help.

"Of course I'm looking after you." He grabbed the crumpled handkerchief and shoved it into his pocket. "You're my bloody wife, aren't you?"

A mysterious smile touched her lips. "You know, I think I just might be," she said in a low voice.

Before he had a chance to ponder that startling statement, the ostler opened the carriage door, and Garson had to pretend that he was a civilized man and not a ravening beast, slavering to tumble his bride.

Jane emerged from the bedroom to find the parlor table set for one. She surveyed the silver and glassware arrayed across the oak surface, and a great lump of foreboding settled in her stomach.

Had she done something wrong this afternoon? Had she been too eager?

Surely not. Hugh had wanted her so much, he'd been shaking.

She'd felt reckless and eager. She wanted to feel that way again.

Her instincts told her that she stood at the threshold of indescribable pleasure. Perhaps it was time to abandon caution and step inside.

With a shuddery breath, she recalled those extraordinary moments in the carriage. Her hand crept toward the breasts he'd caressed to such devastating effect. Oh, what his hands had done to her after that. Just now when she'd run the damp flannel over her body, wicked images had flooded her mind, and she'd blushed, even though she was alone.

The maid came in with a laden tray and set it on the sideboard. She turned and curtsied. "Good evening, Lady Garson."

"Good evening, Mary. Do you know where his lordship is?"

The expression in the girl's eyes looked like pity. "I saw him heading out for a walk, my lady."

Clearly Mary thought the bridegroom already tired of his wife and went in search of diversion.

Had he? No, it couldn't be true. Jane refused to accept Hugh could touch her like that, then rush out to pump his frustrations into some doxy. Call her naïve, but she just couldn't believe it.

Jane glanced out the window to avoid the maid's sharp eyes. While she and Hugh had been doing outrageous things in his luxurious carriage, the weather had closed in. "It's snowing."

"He mentioned wanting some fresh air." The girl began to set out the dishes, then paused to place something else on the table.

"What's that?"

"He left you a note, my lady."

That sounded more like him. "What about his supper?"

"He said he'd have something downstairs when he came in. He also said he might be late."

What in heaven's name was going on? Although one thing was clear. She'd provided Mary with enough entertainment for one evening. "You may go."

"Shall I come back to help you to undress?" With a curiously gloating light in her eyes, the girl plastered a humble expression onto her pretty face. Jane cringed to realize that everyone at the inn must know that she and her husband didn't share a bed. The clean sheets were evidence enough.

"I'll ring if I need you," she said firmly.

"Very good, my lady." The girl's curtsy conveyed a hint of insolence.

Nasty little minx. Although she always simpered at Hugh.

Once Jane was alone, she ripped open the note. But it proved irritatingly uninformative.

I'll see you in the morning. Sleep well. H

Sighing, Jane set the sheet of paper down and stared blindly across the room. Since the wedding, she and Hugh had been together every day. Perhaps he wanted some time to himself. The fact that she enjoyed his company didn't mean he felt the same about her. She'd been so lonely at Cavell Court—the recent attentions of an attractive, intelligent man had shown her how lonely. Hugh on the other hand had always led a full, engaged existence.

Oh, dear, had she bored him? Was that why he left her alone? She'd seen no sign that she had, but his perfect manners meant he'd do his best to hide any dissatisfaction.

"Stop panicking," she muttered. "He's gone for a walk. It's not the end of the world."

But while she'd come into the parlor famished after a day in the fresh air, not to mention that exquisite hour in the carriage, now she contemplated her rapidly cooling dinner and wondered if she could swallow even a morsel.

CHAPTER SIXTEEN

A distant thud wrenched Jane from a restless dream where she was running across the treeless wilderness of Salisbury Plain toward Stonehenge. But the monument kept receding, and she never got closer, no matter how she tried.

She opened her eyes to thick darkness. The lack of noise from the street told her it must be late.

There was another thud, and a muffled curse.

She was up out of bed and wrapped in a shawl before she was really awake. Cold air on bare toes banished the last of her drowsiness, and she slid her feet into some slippers before she rushed into the parlor.

Nobody was there. The banked fire gave off enough light to show that Mary had cleared away Jane's untouched dinner.

Only as she stood in the empty room did she think how foolish this was. If burglars had broken in, she wasn't exactly dressed to deal with them. She was defenseless, unless she intended to smother them in flannel.

Another bump from behind the door to the dressing room. And something that sounded like a groan.

It was Hugh. He didn't sound well.

Before she could question the wisdom of bearding him in his den, she was at the door and knocking. "Hugh, are you all right?"

After a pause long enough to make her frantic with worry, he answered.

"Jane, go to bed." His deep voice was slurred.

She didn't retreat. "Are you ill?"

"No, I'm not ill. Go away."

"I'm coming in." She stifled a twinge of hurt at his curt dismissal. "You sound awful."

"Damn it, don't—"

She pushed the door open to find him standing in the center of a narrow, windowless room, not much bigger than a cupboard.

"...come in." In the flickering light of a single candle, he glared at her.

She studied him with concern. He looked disheveled and uncertain on his feet. Had he caught a chill, staying out so late on a freezing night? "I heard you fall."

"I lost my balance. There's nothing going on. Go back to bed."

He sounded grumpy. That in itself worried her. Hugh was almost always even-tempered. Even on their wedding night, he'd remained polite and pleasant. Mostly.

"Not until I'm sure you're all right."

Those thick coffee-colored brows contracted in a fearsome scowl. "I'm all right."

"You don't sound it."

"I'm tired." Actually now she looked, he appeared utterly exhausted and beneath his truculence, heartsick. His prickly temper stemmed from something deeper than a simple late night.

Oh, no, was he desperately unhappy with their marriage? After the last few days, she'd hoped they started to find a way to go on together.

Inevitably, the specter of Morwenna Nash rose. Why wouldn't Hugh be unhappy? He was in love with another woman.

Which didn't mean Jane intended to leave him alone and sick and wretched. "Let me help you undress."

"That's the worst suggestion you've made yet," he snapped. Or at least she guessed he meant to snap, but the words didn't emerge with the usual crisp clarity.

"You're dead on your feet."

"Go away, Jane." He was swaying and seemed to have trouble focusing.

She ignored him and stepped forward to take his arm. He looked likely to collapse.

The moment she came close enough to touch him, she knew exactly what was the matter. "Ugh."

Unsuccessfully, he tried to pull away. "I told you your wifely concern was wasted."

She winced at the bitter emphasis he placed on "wifely." "You're drunk."

"I am indeed." He blinked owlishly at her. The stench of brandy was a miasma around him. "Now go away, and let me sleep it off. I'm no fit company for a lady."

"No, you're not." Good heavens, she hadn't heard Lord Garson was a drunkard.

"Save the nagging for the morning." He tugged at his crumpled, dirty neck cloth. "I know I deserve it."

"I have no intention of nagging," she said coldly.

"Pleased to hear it," he sniped back. "Clearly I've got myself a wife in a million. If only she could bring herself to be my wife."

Ouch. That was pointed. "I hate to think I've driven you to drink."

"I'm in no state to bandy words with you," he said, although she hadn't been joking.

"You're not getting anywhere with that." She stepped in front of him and brushed his hands aside. "Here, let me."

After a few quick movements, she'd unknotted the neck cloth and thrown it over the only chair. The room was so small, it didn't take much of a throw.

"I can look after myself," he grumbled.

"I doubt it," she said, sliding his creased coat from his powerful shoulders. This close, alcohol fumes made her dizzy, but she didn't pick up any hint of cheap scent. It was no proof he hadn't been with another woman, but something told her he'd sought refuge in liquor not lechery.

"Jane, you are a pain," he chanted, although he put up with her ministrations. "A pain who drives me insane."

"Not kind, when I'm being so helpful," she said drily, turning to lay the coat across the back of the wooden chair. It seemed he was ready to bandy words after all. "And if you rhyme Jane with plain, I'll strangle you with your neck cloth."

She turned back to find him bracing one hand against the wall. He shook his head, his abundant brown hair tumbling over his high forehead. "Not plain at all. Pretty. But that doesn't rhyme with Jane."

She smothered a spurt of pleasure. The oaf had no idea what he was saying. "No, it doesn't."

"But I can fix that."

"How?" She unbuttoned his silk waistcoat, slid it off, and tossed it over his coat. In this confined space, his big, brawny body, clad only in white shirt and buff breeches, seemed even more impressive than when he dressed like a gentleman. "By calling me Jitty?"

He shook his head again. "Jane, you are a pain who drives me insane. But you're pretty as a sunset in Spain."

"I appreciate the thought." When she reached to help him with his shirt, her shawl slipped to the floor. "Lift your arms."

She expected another objection, but he stood docile as she pulled the shirt over his head. He even bent down so she could reach. "Jane, whose kisses taste like sugarcane. Will you kiss me, Jane?"

"No."

"Pity."

A shirtless Hugh really was a magnificent sight, even half seas over with drink. Dark hair curled across his chest and arrowed down over his flat stomach in a way even an innocent like her found tempting.

He'd be more comfortable out of his breeches. Too bad.

"Sit on the bed, and I'll take off your boots."

When he didn't obey, Jane placed her hands flat on his chest and pushed.

It was like watching a mighty tree topple. For a moment, he

teetered, then he went down. At the last minute, he twisted to save himself from knocking his head against the wall. The bed gave a loud creak, and he stretched his legs out across the bare wooden floor. His feet nearly touched the opposite wall.

He stared up at the ceiling and spoke in a slurred, singsong voice. "I can't kiss Jane, and that's a strain."

She hid a smile and went down on her knees before him. "Make room for me."

When he didn't cooperate, she shifted his legs up with no particular gentleness. Bracing her back against the wall, she pulled off his boots. To her astonishment, she was enjoying herself. There was something heady about having this great, handsome galoot under her sway.

He'd gone quiet, and she wondered if he'd fallen asleep. But when she looked up, he was leaning on his elbows and his gaze clung to the jiggle of her bosom under her nightgown.

When he tilted forward and cupped her breasts, a smile of beatific appreciation curved his lips. "Jane, Jane, who has a big brain."

Her nipples beaded as he squeezed. Even drunk, he remembered how to touch a woman. "That's not my brain," she managed to say.

He raised heavy eyes to meet hers. "Give us a kiss, wife," he said without releasing her.

For a moment, she considered saying yes. But he wasn't in his right mind—"Jane drives me insane"—and he must be getting cold, sitting half-naked in this icy room.

She managed to extricate herself and stand up. "Tomorrow."

He groaned and slumped full length onto the bed, prompting another alarming creak. "Jane does refrain."

"She does."

At last, she paid attention to what he lay on. She'd never been into this room. If she'd thought about it, she would have assumed his bed was as comfortable as hers. Which turned out to be wrong.

His large feet protruded over the end, and he looked awkward, even as he closed his eyes and settled onto the thin mattress. He fumbled to drag the blankets up, but they hardly covered him. Dear heaven, it was the middle of winter. Over the last three nights, he must have frozen. While next door she'd been cuddled up under goose-down quilts.

Guilt assailed her. No wonder he looked tired. She leaned in. "Wake up, Hugh."

Long dark eyelashes fluttered, and she found herself staring into bleary brown eyes. "Why?"

"You can't sleep here."

"Nowhere else to go." He rolled over and presented her with one shoulder. "Wife won't have me."

Jane suffered another twinge of guilt. "You can come back to the bedroom."

She set one hand on his back, then snatched it away. Perhaps too much touching wasn't wise. It would be so easy to give in to him, but not now when he was drunk.

He rolled over with a speed that startled her, given his inebriation. The hand that closed around her wrist seemed to belong to a sober man, too. "What did you say?"

Jane licked dry lips and fought to steady her voice. She wondered if he noted her racing pulse. "You can't be comfortable in here. It's cold, and the bed's too short. You can sleep with me." She paused, although the disappointment in his face told her that he understood what she was offering—and what she wasn't. "Just sleep."

He let her go and turned on his side away from her again. "I'd rather stay here."

"Don't be a child, Hugh," she said impatiently.

"You said you wouldn't nag."

"I changed my mind." She caught his hand and tugged with no result. She tugged harder. And again, until she was panting.

Hugh shifted onto his back and surveyed her with weary displeasure. "Don't be a henwit, Jane. You can't shift thirteen stone of unwilling chap."

"I can try." She braced her feet against the floor and tugged again. With as little success.

"You'll hurt yourself."

"Or you could cooperate." She narrowed her eyes. "And you can stop staring at my…bosom."

His eyebrows arched in a supercilious expression. He looked less drunk by the minute. "When I made that damned fool arrangement with you, I never said I wouldn't look. Or is this a new rule?"

She flattened her lips and let him go. "I'm trying to be sensible."

"No, you're trying to torture me."

"No, I'm not," she said hotly, picking up her shawl and knotting it around her neck.

"That's a shame. Because you could win a cup for that."

That hurt. She bit back a cross response and grabbed the edge of the threadbare blankets. "Move over."

He sat up and regarded her balefully. "What the hell are you doing?"

"I'm going to keep you warm. I don't want to be a widow before I'm a wife."

"I'm as tough as old boots."

Actually even their short—and chaste—marriage proved that wasn't the case. Oh, physically he could take on all comers, but she'd learned that his feelings weren't nearly as impervious to pain as he'd like them to be.

But it was late, and she had enough trouble on her hands already, without arguing the finer points of his nature. "It's my fault you're sleeping in the cold."

"I get by. Anyway there's no room."

"If you lie on your side and squeeze up against the wall, there is."

He didn't look convinced. "You're playing with fire, Jane."

"I trust to your honor."

"An inebriated man has no honor."

She didn't believe that either. "Hugh, I'm sleeping next to you. We can do it on this inconvenient contraption, or we can do it in the other room where we'll both be comfortable."

"Speak for yourself." He groaned and set his feet flat on the floor. "You *are* a pain, Jane."

Jane stepped back. His voice was so full of rueful affection, that she didn't even mind him calling her a pain. She extended her hand. "I'm glad you saw sense."

"You won't be so smug, if I have a dream about snuggling up to my dear little bride, and you wake up to find me heaving about on top of you."

She gave another of those delicious shivers. Right now, that didn't sound nearly as threatening as he imagined. But this wasn't the moment. She wanted him fully conscious when he claimed her.

Soon...

"You're so tired that the second your head hits the pillow, you'll start snoring."

He still looked discontented, but he took her hand and stood. "I wouldn't bet on it, sweetheart."

The endearment was all irony, so it shouldn't make her melt. But she couldn't help smiling, as she collected the candle and led him into the bedroom.

Immediately the fire in the grate made her feel warmer. She let Hugh go, blew out the candle, and made for the bed. After a hesitation, he followed. Without meeting her eyes, he lay down about a foot away.

For a long moment, they remained unspeaking and flat on their backs. Then with another of those heavy sighs, Hugh reached out to wrap an arm around her and haul her across into the shelter of his body. Jane released the breath she'd been holding and curled against his side. Closing her eyes, she drifted to sleep, warm and strangely happy.

CHAPTER SEVENTEEN

*A*s Garson swam up from the murky depths of troubled sleep, the first thing he knew was that some buffoon was using the inside of his skull as kettle drums. The second thing—so close upon the first that it was almost the front runner—was that a soft, round breast filled his left hand.

This didn't make immediate sense, but the percussionist's enthusiasm beggared connected thought. Without opening his eyes, he gave a soft grunt of satisfaction and squeezed.

The woman in his arms responded with a sleepy sigh and pushed back so her rump pressed into his stirring cock. Despite his headache, he recognized that this was an unusually promising beginning to the day. But long and bitter experience counseled against opening his eyes.

For more than three years, Garson had dreamed that a lovely woman lay beside him, only to wake to odious reality. During most of that time, the woman had ruler-straight black hair and eyes the color of the Cornish sea. Over the last few days, though, his fantasies had undergone a change in casting.

Devil take him, when had that happened? Suddenly, even through his pounding head, it seemed important to get this straight.

He didn't mistake his current companion for his lost love. Nor did he imagine that he was dreaming. His wife's physical presence, warm and drowsing, was too vivid to be anything but real.

His eyes cracked open to darkness, although instinct told him dawn wasn't far off. Inhaling Jane's rich scent, he buried his face in her hair. The temptation to take this closeness to the next level rose, along with his unruly dick.

After all, the deal was that if she invited him to her bed, he could claim his husbandly rights. While patches of last night were deuced fuzzy in his recollection, he vaguely remembered her insisting that he joined her.

But his mouth tasted like the floor of a stable, and he badly needed a wash, and he wasn't sure whether his wife was merely acting the Good Samaritan. Much as he wanted Jane, the risk of shattering the fragile trust they'd built over the last days was unacceptable.

While his conscience mightn't have woken when he did, it was vocal now. What a bloody fool he'd been last night. He hadn't been so bosky since his wild days at Oxford. He'd hoped he'd learned more sense since then.

Clearly not.

Half seas over as he still was, he was in no fit state to do Jane justice. After that incendiary and damned frustrating drive yesterday, he'd felt sick with self-pity. One drink in the shabby pub he'd stumbled into near the river had turned into another. And another. Before he knew it, the pub was closing, the world was reeling, and he was staggering home through dark streets to seek his lumpy bed.

Except when he'd got back, Jane had rescued him from his prison cell. More, she'd treated him with a tolerant affection he hadn't deserved.

She was a jewel among women, his Jane.

Garson should get up, go back to the dressing room, wash, shave, dig out some clothes that didn't stink of smoke and drink. But his late night weighed on him, it was cozy where he was, and he had his wife in his embrace. He'd get up in a few minutes, but right now he couldn't summon the will to leave.

She was a luscious bundle, his Jane. Who knew that she'd fit so nicely into the space next to his heart? Who knew that he'd ever think of Jane Norris as *his* Jane?

When Jane woke, it was late and she was alone—and disappointed that she was. A few times during the night she'd stirred, restless to be sharing a bed with someone for the first time. But there was something delightful about having a large male body pressed tight to her back and powerful male arms holding her close. She'd hoped Hugh might wake her with more kisses, like the kisses he'd given her yesterday. She'd even harbored a cowardly wish that events might pursue their course and save her from having to say the words inviting him to take her.

But it seemed if she wanted him, she had to tell him.

She set her hand where he'd lain. Ice cold. He must have been up for a while. She glanced around the room, but nothing hinted that Jane Norris had slept with a man. Even if she remained as pure as ever.

Almost. Heated reminiscence rippled through her, as she recalled the shocking, delightful things Hugh had done in the coach yesterday. Wickedly, she wondered what other marvels her husband could show her.

Obeying a sudden impulse, she rolled over and buried her head in his pillow. Immediately she inhaled Hugh's rich scent. She'd know that scent anywhere. In the carnal sense, she mightn't yet be his wife, but somewhere she'd crossed a barrier. He was no longer just her childhood friend, but closer to her than anyone else in the world.

Garson's wife appeared in the doorway, neat as usual, beautiful hair constrained in a formal knot. How his fingers itched to release that glorious mane. He'd only once seen it unbound, on their calamitous wedding night. But even in a parlous state after yesterday's overindul-gence, he feared that if he started with undoing her hair, he'd move to undoing other things. Who knew where they'd end up?

He laid down his newspaper and summoned a smile, even as he winced at the bright light. "Good morning, Jane."

Sunlight poured through the mullioned windows and added a touch of summer to the pleasant parlor. The light caught russet high-lights in her hair, reminding him of the passion concealed under that demure manner. A passion he prayed she'd soon share with him.

He wanted to cross the room and take her in his arms. But he was uncomfortably aware that he'd been less than gallant last night, and some good behavior was called for.

"Good morning, Hugh," she said with a faint blush. "How are you feeling?"

"Better than I should." He rose from his armchair and pulled a dining chair out for her. The vestiges of a headache lingered, but several cups of the Red Lion's strong coffee kept the worst aftereffects at bay. "I'll ring for breakfast."

"Thank you," she said, sitting down.

While the servants set up their meal then left, Garson composed an apology. But before he could speak, Jane gestured toward his full plate with her teacup. "That's more than I thought you'd want. I expect you have a beast of a head."

He heard no hint of criticism. "You're used to seeing the effects of drunkenness?"

"I had to deal with the farmhands after the harvest. I may not have enjoyed much sophisticated society recently, but running the estate meant I saw plenty of real life."

"I sometimes forget how capable you are." He went back to his sirloin and potatoes. "You've had to take on so much, Jane, and I admire you for doing it with such pluck and efficiency."

Her blush deepened, which was odd. She usually only blushed when he complimented her looks. Although she looked very pretty this morning, even in that gray rag of a dress.

"Thank you. I didn't have much choice."

"You still did a fine job in a difficult situation. I take my hat off to you."

She set down her cup and began to butter her roll. "I enjoyed restoring the estate to prosperity, although I needed more capital to make a big difference. Papa lost interest in Cavell Court long before he fell sick."

"It must have been hard work, though, and not what you'd been raised to do."

"I already knew quite a lot. Because I was the plain sister, Papa saw no harm in it, when I went to the cattle sales with him or helped the steward with the accounts."

Garson bit back a protest at the word "plain," even if he'd once been guilty of thinking it. He still marveled that he'd missed her potential. After all, he was accounted a man with an eye for a pretty woman. That day in Dorset, he'd been in such a blue funk about contracting a loveless marriage. He'd been too het up to see that once Jane recovered her spirits, she'd be something special. Until now, he'd always believed Morwenna was the loveliest woman he'd ever seen, but his wife, pink-cheeked and sweet as she was right now, gave his true love a run for her money.

The idea felt vaguely disloyal and made him shift uncomfortably. Not that Morwenna gave a fig for what he thought, he bitterly admitted. "I hope in time you'll come to think of Beardsley Hall as your home."

Jane's shy smile raked across his heart. "Thank you."

"When was your last visit?" He should remember. But then he'd had no idea Lord Sefton's quiet, bookish daughter would grow up to become his bride.

"Papa brought the family up for a hunting party when I was twelve."

"Was I away at university?"

"No, you were there, but you and your friends were far too top lofty to pay attention to annoying little girls."

He laughed at her mocking tone. "Top lofty at eighteen? I doubt my conceit was justified."

The twitch of her lips sparked a sudden urge to kiss her. Except if he did, he wouldn't want to stop. He was well aware that while last night had stretched their bargain almost to breaking, he was still bound to his promise that he'd kiss her only once a day.

"At eighteen, you were considerably more on your dignity than you are now."

He suspected it was true. "I'm sorry I was a snotty-nosed little toad, Jane."

"You were never little." The twitch blossomed into a full smile. "Even at that age, you were a young Hercules."

He stared at her, grappling with his wife having the temerity to call him a toad, if not in so many words. Then he burst out laughing. "I suppose I deserve that."

"Actually you were very kind." She touched his hand. "You always have been a kind man, Hugh."

He caught her before she could withdraw. "So I didn't break your tender heart?"

"Oh, you did that. You were my hero, and it was pretty clear that I was getting under your feet. But to be fair to you, I was absurdly shy and silly."

"Never." He raised her hand and kissed it. Her fingers fluttered in his, but she didn't try to pull away.

"I'm still shy," she said softly.

He took the words as a warning—or perhaps an apology. "I know, sweetheart. But never silly."

The endearment made her gaze fall. "I can be silly."

"So can I." It was time to apologize for his drunken blunderings. "I'm sorry I was such a damned lout last night."

This time, Jane's smile conveyed secret amusement. "You weren't so bad."

"Still I owe you better than rolling home drunk as a wheelbarrow, then stumbling around in a stupor and waking you up."

To his regret, she withdrew her hand and poured him some more coffee. He noted that she made it as he liked, with a dash of milk and no sugar. This honeymoon that was no honeymoon at all drove him mad with frustration, but it had its benefits. They grew easier in each other's company, and more accustomed to each other's habits.

"You were rather charming."

Not so he recalled. "Was I?"

"Yes. Until last night, I didn't know you had a whimsical bone in your body."

Whimsical? Was that a good thing? He didn't think so. "You're truly not angry?"

She sipped her tea. "No."

Her forbearance had him rushing into explanations. "I didn't set out to get foxed. But after that drive back from Stonehenge, I had to clear my head."

She arched her eyebrows. "So you drank?"

"It sounds asinine, I know." He shifted awkwardly. "I assure you that I'm a man of regular habits. I don't make a practice of staggering about in my cups."

"I'm glad to hear it," she said, still with a trace of irony.

He frowned. "Jane, are you teasing me?"

That luscious mouth pursed in thought, but when she met his eyes, he caught a flash of laughter. "Only a little."

He was unable to resist, although usually he strategized when to take his kiss. He surged across the table and snatched her up. Her breath escaped in a startled oof, and her lips moved against his with an innocent enthusiasm that reminded him of their first kiss.

But not for long. Despite the awkward position, caught between her chair and the table, she twisted her body into his. Her arms slid around his neck, as she stretched up to kiss him back.

When her soft mouth opened, his tongue dipped inside. He made a deep sound of satisfaction and kicked the chair out of the way. Vaguely through the blood hammering in his head, he heard the thud as it tipped over.

Linking his hands loosely around her waist, he drew back to look down into her face. He loved to see her all flushed and ruffled, and at a loss for the self-possession she'd cultivated as mistress of Cavell Court. "You're so lovely, Jane."

"Thank you." For once, she didn't argue. "Kissing must be good for the complexion."

He gave a grunt of laughter. "There should be more of it, then. Purely for therapeutic reasons, of course."

"Of course," she said drily, arms still around his neck.

Garson wanted more, but there was something to be said for loitering in a patch of sunlight and flirting with a comely wench. And he had plans for the day ahead. "You have a treat in store, wife."

He liked calling Jane his wife. The evocative word planted all sorts of pleasantly masculine feelings in his chest. Pride. Possession. A surprisingly powerful affection. With every day, he liked her more. Good God, she didn't even nag a fellow when he toddled home, soused as a sailor. She was a good sport, his bride, and nowhere near as prim and prune-faced as he'd feared she might have become over the hard, lonely years. She'd be a wonderful mother. Heat percolated in his veins as he imagined making those children.

Her eyes turned the color of the sea on a day of sunlight and rain. Her soft expression hinted that she grew fond of him, too. "A treat?"

"Yes, I'm going to show you around Pembroke's place at Wilton. It's only a few miles out of town, and I think you'll like it."

"I daresay I will. Are the family in residence?"

"No, they're in London, but his lordship's given us the run of the house. Even asked if we want to move in for the rest of our honeymoon."

"That was generous."

"I thought so. I got his letter yesterday in reply to my request to see over the house."

"I'm sure the accommodations will be an improvement on the dressing room. I didn't know that your room was so Spartan. Do you want to shift to Wilton?"

He suspected even in the Earl of Pembroke's best chamber, he'd be uncomfortable. Hunger for his wife kept him awake at night, not his mean little bed. "Do you?"

When Jane glanced around the parlor, a light entered her eyes. He couldn't remember paying such close attention to anyone before, even

Morwenna. But he'd conducted his first courtship under the full blaze of society's gaze. He and Morwenna hadn't spent much time alone and unobserved.

"You know, it might be selfish, but I like our rooms here."

"Good." He didn't want to move into a cavernous barn of a place, no matter how elegant. He wanted to sleep closer to Jane, not further away.

"I might get some ideas for decorating Beardsley Hall."

He rolled his eyes with theatrical disgust. "I see we'll be talking cushions and wallpaper."

She gave a laugh. "Chin up, sir. It's all for the greater good."

"Just don't expect me to proffer any opinion on frills and furbelows."

"Heaven forbid," she said, with more of that delightful dryness.

And Garson decided that he didn't at all mind the idea of looking at cushions and wallpaper, as long as his lovely wife kept teasing him so fondly.

CHAPTER EIGHTEEN

*I*t was late. Dinner had long since been cleared away, and Garson and Jane shared the oak settle before the fire. He finished his port and set the empty glass on the table. After an active day, he was pleasantly weary. Jane had been eager to see as much of Wilton House as she could and had even hauled him across the wintry grounds to visit the famous Palladian Bridge.

"What are you thinking about?" she asked softly from beside him.

It was the kind of question lovers asked. Anyone looking at them would assume they shared a bed. They sat hip to hip, and he absently stroked her hand as he stared into the flames.

Since this morning's impulsive kiss, he hadn't gone past holding her hand. A change was in the air, but he still feared pushing Jane too far too fast—as he had their first night—and tearing the filigree net drawing them inexorably together. A woman's trust was both fragile and exquisite.

"I'm thinking how you'll love Italy."

"I'll be so wide-eyed, I'll drive you mad, I suspect."

He gave a soft huff of laughter. "I'll bear up."

"Such a hero."

"You have no idea."

"You certainly bore up today when I made such a fuss about all the treasures we saw. What a lovely house."

"Yes, I've always liked it."

"It's been the nicest day." To his surprise, she turned her hand and laced her fingers through his. "Thank you."

"It was my pleasure." Another surprise. It had been his pleasure. Showing Jane around Wilton House had been fun.

She drew her hand away. "And now it's time for bed," she said softly.

Although her announcement heralded nothing more than the sleep of the innocent, his blood heated. He gave his masculine instincts a stern order to step back. There was no reason to get excited. He didn't even have a kiss to anticipate. "What would you like to do in the morning?"

"Let's see what the weather brings." She rose and smoothed her skirts. Another dreary dress. He couldn't wait to see his Jane in some real color. "Are you coming?"

Devil take her. These damned ambiguous remarks asked for trouble. "I'll see you tomorrow."

Her fine russet brows drew together. "Aren't you going to…sleep with me?"

There was no point telling his dick that she really did mean sleep. He ground his teeth and prayed for patience. Surely by now, Jane knew that teasing him like this verged on cruelty. How his debauched friends would fall around laughing, if they found out Hugh Rutherford's bride was still a virgin five days after his wedding.

"No, I'm damn well not."

His tetchy answer made her jerk back. "Don't you want to?"

"You know I bloody want to." Garson lurched to his feet, the evening's peace shattering as if it had never existed. "I might have held you in my arms pure as an angel last night, but nothing this side of heaven can make me do that again."

The somber gray gaze settled on him, as he struggled to control his temper. She was too inexperienced to understand what she put him through. When she licked her lips, Garson swallowed a groan. This was agony.

"I'm not asking you to do that again, Hugh," she said calmly. She raised her chin. "I'm asking you to make me your wife."

For what felt like an age, Hugh stared at her as if he didn't understand. Once she spoke the words, she'd expected him to sweep her into his arms and through to the bedroom. Preferably kissing her, so she didn't have to think too hard about what was about to happen.

"Are you sure?" His growl wasn't reassuring, and he still didn't touch her.

"I was." Irritation fought its way up through an ocean of bewilderment. "You've been trying to bed me for days. I can't believe you're dithering like an old woman deciding on green tea or black."

To her relief, a spark of humor lit his dark eyes. "Green tea or black?"

"Yes," she said steadily. To her vast relief, he no longer looked like she'd struck him with an ax. "Fussing and fretting and asking for something, then deciding you don't want it after all."

The spark in his eyes flared into a blaze. As that glittering gaze focused on her, she gave a long, sensuous shiver, and her heart performed acrobatics.

"I want it." He took a pace toward her. "By God, I want it."

She licked her lips again, and for the first time said the words that had been true since their wedding night. Powerful words, expressing a powerful feeling. That very power had once turned her to ice. But no longer.

"And I want you."

At last, he seized her in his arms. "My beautiful wife, you make me so happy."

By now, she should be used to his kisses, but perhaps because this kiss wasn't an end unto itself, but the beginning of a passionate journey, it felt different. Hungrily she kissed him back, twining her arms about him and pressing as close as she could.

He turned around, almost waltzing her into the bedroom where last night, she'd slept in his arms. Tonight she'd lie in his arms again, but she suspected there wouldn't be much sleep involved. He set her on her feet near the bed.

With greedy hands, she ripped at his neck cloth and cast it away. "I wanted to tell you first thing this morning."

He shrugged his coat off his shoulders and tore at the buttons on his cream brocade waistcoat. "I wasn't fit for you then."

She knocked his hands out of the way and pushed the waistcoat off, letting it drop to the floor with his coat. "What about now?"

He kissed her as if he starved. When he raised his head, the light in his eyes made her shiver again. What a long way she'd come in these few days. This unabashed passion would have sent the girl who married him fleeing for the hills.

"I'm burning up with wanting you." He kicked off his shoes and grasped her shoulders to turn her round so fast, her head swam. "Why are you wearing so many damned clothes?"

"Because I like to make your life difficult," she said, wondering who this smart-mouthed wench was. It certainly wasn't prim Jane Norris.

"Then congratulations, it's working," he grunted, tearing at her laces so roughly that her body jerked. "That bloody maid should be shot for trussing you up like a Christmas goose."

Jane was panting, and her hands opened and closed at her sides as she fought the urge to tell him to forget about undressing her and just throw her on her back. "Tear it," she said in a strained voice.

He didn't query the command. The sound of rending fabric, and air brushed across the bare skin of her back and shoulders. She wriggled to pull the long sleeves down and twisted her hips until the ruined gray gown puddled at her feet.

"Shall I tear the corset, too?"

"No, I'll unhook it from the front." She turned to face him, as her shaking hands unfastened her plain corset and dropped it to the floor.

Hugh looked like a man on the brink of disintegration. How she loved that what happened between them was so important to him. She watched hungrily as he tugged his shirt over his head and sent it flying into the corner. That magnificent chest was just as breathtaking as she remembered from last night.

This time, she didn't have to hold back from touching him. She ran seeking hands down those ridges of hard muscle. His trousers didn't do much to hide the hardest part of all. The way he responded to her had once been terrifying. No longer.

He caught her by the waist, grabbing handfuls of linen shift, and hauled her closer until her breasts met his chest. She stroked his powerful back, feeling the subtle shift of muscle under her palms. More ruthless kisses that left her shaking with excitement. The heat of his mouth, his blatant need, made the blood pound between her legs. Dark, irresistible desire churned in her belly, as her body turned hot and liquid.

On their wedding night, she'd started to feel like this, as though she lost her footing in a raging sea. It had scared her into running away. She'd felt like this when he'd touched her in the carriage, and she'd discovered that these intoxicating responses were the gateway to blazing sensation.

Tonight instead of recoiling from the flames, she flung herself forward, seeking immolation.

With a groan, Hugh tore his lips from hers and scraped his teeth down the sensitive skin of her neck. A dizzy, quivery feeling gushed through her, and her knees turned to water.

"Oh," she gasped, tilting her hips toward his erect rod. He groaned again and bit her neck. The faint sting sharpened her arousal. As her body convulsed, she dug her fingernails into his back.

He rubbed her loose shift up and down her bottom, creating a teasing friction. Then he edged a few inches away and tugged the shift over her head. That left her wearing filmy white drawers, black satin shoes, and white stockings gartered at the knee. She wasn't naked, quite, but she felt like she was.

Hugh's eyes flared as they focused on her breasts. Her nipples, already tight and aching, hardened to the brink of pain. Her hands fluttered toward her chest, before she deliberately forced them back to her sides. It took courage to face him without concealment, but she refused to be frightened. Fear had already stolen too much time.

His gaze lifted to meet hers. What she found there moved her to the depths of her soul. His expression held endless wonder.

"You're a goddess, Jane." The awe in his voice clutched at her heart. "I've wanted to see you like this for so long." The humor she loved creased the skin around his eyes. "Or perhaps more like this."

Trembling, she waited for him to touch her breasts, but instead, he drew one pin from her upswept hair, then another. A long tress snaked down over her shoulder to curl over her bare breast.

"Shall I let my hair down?" she asked huskily.

He still looked like he witnessed a miracle. The power she pretended to possess became real power. She might be inexperienced, but with Hugh spellbound in her presence, she was his equal.

"No, let me," he said gruffly. "I've dreamed of your hair."

He'd dreamed of her? The discovery pierced like a knife. That insistent demand between her legs heightened, made her feel hollow and hungry. Only Hugh could fill her emptiness. Only Hugh could feed her craving.

He undid her hair, taking his time to untangle each lock until the red mane tumbled around her shoulders. The silky drift of hair across her nipples added a new level of sensation. As he took out each pin, he murmured praise. A nonsense litany. *Lovely. Beautiful. Pretty. Soft. Shining.*

The way he absorbed every detail made her feel precious. She felt like he was the first person who truly saw her. His unwavering concentration on her was extraordinarily powerful. Absurd tears pricked at her eyes. His passion was a mighty force indeed, but this quiet tenderness threatened to shatter her.

When he turned his attention to her breasts, a moan broke from her lips. He stroked and squeezed her until she quivered. "Please…"

A smile hovered about his lips as he cupped her breasts. Through the rising fever, she saw what he was doing. "You're teasing me, you devil."

"And myself." He raised eyes so dark, they were almost black. The desire she saw in his face made her heart somersault. Desire that had built over days of dancing closer, then away, then closer once more.

The dance ended now. Her heart thumped so hard, each beat made her shake. She set her hands on his shoulders and leaned forward. "Kiss me there."

Another flare of heat in his eyes before he bent his ruffled dark head to take one nipple between his lips. She'd reached such a pitch of arousal that the kiss felt like a whiplash. Heat flashed through her, and a broken cry escaped. She jerked, when he flicked his tongue against the exquisitely sensitive tip, then drew hard.

Feverishly his hands traveled across her back, then shaped her bottom. Her drawers sagged and through the storm of pleasure, she realized he'd untied them. The next time he touched her, he stroked bare skin.

Panting, he raised his head from her breast. Adamant hands curved under her bottom and hitched her off her feet and up, until her mound crushed against him. She shuddered as she met his hot flesh through the fine wool of his trousers.

Jane cried out again, her secret places clenching on absence instead of him. This yearning became torture. He groaned and bumped forward, building her arousal. She grabbed his shoulders and wrapped her legs around him, so the pressure shifted to between her thighs. As her sex jammed into him, a wave of searing pleasure tightened every nerve.

"Please, Hugh..." she begged incoherently.

"Soon," he groaned and still carrying her, he walked toward the bed. It was only a few feet, but with her curled around him, each step created exquisite torment. By the time he swept back the covers and laid her on the sheets, she was gasping and quaking. He set her down as if she was likely to break with the slightest bump.

Hugh quickly slid her stockings and shoes off, then stepped back to rip off his trousers. When Jane saw him naked, the breath crammed in her throat. He was splendid. Massive and powerful, like some mighty force of nature. She remembered how on their wedding night, she'd thought he looked like Zeus. She hadn't been far wrong.

The moisture dried from her mouth and stopped her speaking. Or perhaps his male beauty struck her speechless. She took a couple of tries before she managed a few words. "Hugh, we've waited long enough."

He set one knee on the bed and straddled her. The last time she'd been under him, she'd panicked. This time, she stared up into eyes the color of strong coffee and held his arms to keep him exactly where he was.

To her surprise, she was smiling. "Don't wait anymore."

CHAPTER NINETEEN

Through the blood thundering in his temples, Garson heard Jane invite him to take her. His heart gave a great cymbal crash of triumph. At last, she would be his.

Kissing her, he caught her legs and spread them to cradle his hips. Paradise was so close.

How lovely she was as she lay beneath him, her beautiful hair arrayed like a mantle and picking up a thousand shades from the flickering candlelight, ruby to palest gold. Her scent was more intoxicating than the richest brandy, and he felt as drunk as he had last night. He ran one hand down her body, following the sinuous line of flank and waist and hip, and finally touched her there, where he wanted so badly to be.

When he explored the mysterious, satiny folds, she jerked in response. He nipped at her lower lip and stroked the small pearl of flesh, until she was shuddering and whimpering.

He slid a finger into her, enthralled by the way her body tightened in welcome. Then two fingers, delicately stretching her. He didn't want to hurt her when they joined together, but he feared given his size, that pain was inevitable.

She raised her knees and angled upward in silent invitation. God help him, he couldn't wait any longer. In silent apology for the discomfort to come, he kissed her again.

His hips tautened, and he pushed. Slippery heat. The sweet resistance of untried muscles. The sting of fingernails digging into the skin of his back.

He rose on his elbows to watch Jane's face. She was flushed, and her lips were red after those fierce kisses. Her features were tight with strain.

"Are you all right?" he asked, not sure what he'd do if she wasn't. Taking this slowly already threatened to snap him in two.

"Hugh, I want you." She arched up to place a clumsy kiss on his lips. "Do what you must."

Her movement edged him further inside her and set off a volley of fireworks behind his eyes. On a long, resonant groan, he plunged forward.

She gave a muffled cry and stiffened. Then as he lay gasping in her embrace, she tilted her hips, miraculously taking him deeper. He snatched in some air and squeezed his eyes shut. With every ounce of gratitude overflowing from his soul, he thanked whatever powers had brought him to this moment.

Perhaps because Jane was his wife and this closeness staked his right to the future, perhaps because he'd worked so hard to win her, perhaps because she was just so damned marvelous, these profound feelings were beyond anything he'd ever known. Before now, sex had been a pleasure, a diversion, an appetite. Never before had congress with a woman shaken his world to its foundations.

Jane breathed in ragged spurts. He remained unmoving until her tension loosened. When she began to stroke his back, he opened his eyes. "Can you bear more?"

Her gaze widened, and her wriggle threatened to blast his head off. His control hung by the frailest thread, but he'd be damned if he brought his wife this far, only to disappoint her at the end.

"More?" she whispered, as if the concept beggared imagination.

Garson answered with a slow withdrawal, reveling in the way she clung to every inch. When he rose on his elbows and pushed forward again, she accepted him more easily. "Does this hurt?"

"It did."

At his wince, she touched his cheek with a tenderness that added a poignant edge to his desire. "A little. At first."

Ridiculous that Jane's attempt to comfort him should move him so powerfully, when he was the one who had caused her pain. The awful truth was he couldn't even say he was sorry, because this union gave him nothing but pleasure. "No longer?"

She shifted fractionally, detonating more fiery explosions in his head. "I think I'll like it."

His huff of laughter took him deeper into her body. She was so hot and tight. He'd set out to possess her, but instead she possessed him. It was a glorious sensation.

"Shall we make sure?"

Her hand drifted so sweetly down his face that his heart stumbled. "Yes, please."

When they kissed, her lips conveyed that same sweetness. He fought against the nearly irresistible urge to rush to climax. Never had he basked in such an extraordinary mixture of gentleness and passion. "Am I squashing you?"

"In a nice way."

Passion clamored for its due. As the next kiss flared into hunger, the rise of her hips snapped the last chains of his restraint. He moved purposefully, claiming her with every thrust.

With a luxuriant caress, she slid her hands down his arms. "I can't tell you how wonderful it feels when you move inside me," she said huskily. "If I'd known, I'd have leaped into your arms that first night."

His withdrawal was slow. "You like this?"

"So much." Her long sigh of enjoyment vibrated to his bones. Her eyes fluttered shut, and she tilted her head back as if relishing every shift of his body in hers.

"And this?" With steady purpose, he pushed forward. Her body flowered to greet him, and her low, keening sound conveyed sump-

tuous enjoyment. When she undulated against him, he nearly deto-
nated into a thousand smoking shards.

"Do it again."

"With pleasure," he growled. He'd never meant anything more
sincerely.

"Goody," she said, like a child presented with a birthday treat. He
couldn't contain a gasp of laughter.

"Oh," she said with surprise. "When you laugh, I can feel it.
It's…nice."

Her artless delight in what they did filled him with wonder. And
hunger for more of her. With a guttural groan, he began to move,
going full and hard, crushing her into the mattress. Her fingers turned
into talons on his back, and she gripped him with every thrust. The
need for her to find fulfillment before he lost himself warred with a
ferocious craving to pump every last ounce of passion into her.

He heard her breath catch, then a sobbing crescendo. "Let it
happen," he bit out, as his crisis built toward its release. "Remember
the carriage."

"I loved what happened…in the carriage." The words emerged in
bursts.

She clenched around him. He ran his teeth down her neck. She
cried out, tightening like a fist. Need rocketed beyond his control. As
Jane quaked through her pleasure, the irresistible surge started in the
soles of Garson's feet, rolled up through his legs, and flooded like
flame into his balls.

His hot seed spurted into her, and he made a guttural sound of
release. Jane cried out and dug her nails into his shoulders, clinging to
him as they tumbled headlong into raging fire.

CHAPTER TWENTY

"Our arrival in Town is no longer a secret." With a mixture of bewilderment and anticipation, Jane set down her teacup and surveyed the pile of invitations that had arrived in the morning post.

They formed a tottering pile on the mahogany table in her sitting room, where she and Hugh had just finished breakfast. During the three days they'd been in London, she and her husband had taken their meals here. It had the advantage of being closer to the bedroom than the elaborate dining room downstairs.

"We don't have to answer them." Hugh sent her a lazy smile from the leather couch beside the blazing fire. He wore only his crimson silk dressing gown and a loose pair of cotton trousers.

"That's not polite." She shot him a cross glance, although he looked so beguiling, lounging around like a lascivious pasha, that really she just wanted to haul him straight back to bed. They weren't long up, although it was getting on for noon. To a countrywoman like her, that seemed disgustingly late.

Here she was sitting at the table, still in her peignoir, with her hair flowing about her. She'd soon recognized that her hair exerted a strange power over Hugh, and it was easier to leave it unbound if they were at home. Which they mostly were. He'd offered to take her to Astley's Circus, and the Tower of London, and the British Museum, but so far all they'd managed was a stroll in Hyde Park that had quickly turned into a torrid kissing session in a secluded glade. She hadn't yet seen the sights he'd promised to show her. Not that she minded. She basked in Hugh's insatiable appetite for her. The woman who had once shrunk from physical pleasure was becoming a dedicated voluptuary.

To a point where she resented any time she spent away from him. Susan had called yesterday and badgered Jane into visiting her *modiste*, when all she'd wanted was to remain in the enchanted world she and Hugh created together.

"I told you society gives newlyweds some privacy," he said with a careless gesture.

"It's all very well to say that, but we'll have to emerge some time, and I need help to get through all this as a credit to you." She watched as Mathers, the butler, cleared away the breakfast dishes.

"If you want to be a good wife, come and sit on my lap," Hugh purred.

When she caught Mathers' swiftly hidden smile, she blushed. She'd noted that Hugh's staff at Half Moon Street held him in great affection. An affection they seemed willing to extend to the new Lady Garson.

Once Mathers had gone, she stood and leveled a disapproving stare at her indolent husband. "You're scandalizing the servants."

He still looked at her as if he'd happily snap her up between his straight white teeth and swallow her in one bite. Her heart began to dance a wild tarantella. She knew what that look meant. By heaven, she should. After that extraordinary night when she'd abandoned her fears, they hadn't left their room at the inn for three days. An eventful trip to London had followed, and since then, they'd enjoyed three heady days cloistered inside this lovely house.

"They're delighted to see me happy again," he said, echoing her thoughts.

"Well, you're scandalizing me," she retorted, although once she'd locked the door, she crossed the room to curl up on his lap as he'd asked. She slid one arm around his neck and rested her cheek on his chest. Her fingers tangled in the crisp curls at his nape.

"Do I make you happy, Jane?" he asked softly.

She glanced up at him. "You know you do."

That was true, as long as she didn't spend too much time pondering the emotions underlying her delight. Right now, large parts of her life were marked "Here be dragons."

He smiled and swooped in to capture a kiss. Since the wedding, she'd become a connoisseur of Hugh's kisses. There were light kisses, over in a second, as if he marked his place in a book he intended to return to later. There were the kisses that conveyed his current satisfaction with the world and his place in it. There were the slow, seductive kisses, where he coaxed her into some reckless act that once would have shocked her into next week. Then when he joined his body to hers, there were the long, open-mouthed, passionate kisses. While he was inside her, nothing else in the world existed, except him and her and the heat melding them together.

This latest kiss expressed his pleasure in her, with a touch of "If you're interested, we could go back to bed." She was interested—he turned her into a shameless baggage. But she and Hugh weren't long upright, and she wanted to talk to him about his plans.

Then they could go back to bed.

"I never knew I could feel like this," she murmured.

"Let me check just how you feel."

"Hugh…" she said in confusion, then laughed with relief, as his hands began to explore her body.

"Hmmm. Soft." He squeezed her breast, unconstrained under the silky nightdress. Before they'd left Salisbury, he'd sent Mary to the best haberdasher in town to buy some undergarments and night-dresses suitable for a bride. Jane hadn't set eyes on her white flannel in days. She had a suspicion Hugh might have thrown it away.

"Hugh," she said in a completely different tone, when his long fingers teased her nipple.

"Would I say that's hard?"

"I don't know. Would you?" she asked drily and sneaked a hand down to where he rose boldly against her hip. "If it's not, I know something that is."

"Hussy," he said unsteadily, as she curled her fingers around him. His hand left her breast and tangled in the fall of her hair. "That paragon Jane Norris wouldn't approve of such lechery."

"Jane Norris, alas, is no more," she said in mock sorrow. "Jane Rutherford has taken her place, and I fear that she has no morals at all."

She had an inkling that might be true. The girl she'd once been would never treat a man's body as her personal playground.

"May dear Jane Norris rest in peace," he intoned solemnly. "And I'll make sure that Jane Rutherford doesn't rest at all."

"So far that's been true," she retorted, sliding her fist up the rigid column of flesh and relishing how it swelled in her hold. "You know, we really do need to talk."

His deep chuckle vibrated in his chest and under her cheek. She loved being close to him like this, wrapped in his warmth and strength. He made her feel that nothing could ever hurt her. "Now?"

"Perhaps later."

"That's the right answer." With gentle insistence, he slid her off his lap and onto the seat. Her legs sprawled across the rich red and blue Turkey carpet.

He kneeled before her and pushed up her skirts, until blue silk and cream lace frothed about her thighs. With an intent expression, he caught her knees and pushed them apart. "You're blushing."

Her hands fluttered nervously, before they settled above her breasts. "Perhaps I'm not as wicked as I thought."

As his gaze fastened on the shadowy space between her legs, unabashed greed curved his mouth. "We'll soon fix that."

She guessed he meant to touch her there. He'd done that before, but in the course of making love. Her blush turned to fire. He must be able to see everything. It was difficult to resist covering herself.

Her heart was skittering, and that familiar heavy feeling set up in the pit of her stomach. His scrutiny of her sex made her tremble with need.

Hugh's smile widened, as he took hold of her legs and tugged her forward. Peignoir and nightdress hitched up, so her bare bottom met the leather sofa. She gave a startled gasp, then another as he bent his head and…kissed her there.

"Hugh!" she cried, lacing one hand in his soft, thick hair.

The intimate contact was over in an instant, but the heat of his lips still sizzled like a lightning bolt. This game between them was new, and she felt uncertain.

"Trust me," he said softly. He remained so close to her cleft that his breath teased the yearning flesh. "You'll like it."

His first kiss hinted that she probably would, but that didn't make it right. "Do you want to do this?"

When he lifted his head, she met heavy-lidded eyes. She knew that look, too. His answer came as no surprise. "Oh, yes. I've wanted this since our first night, but I feared it might shock you."

"It would. It has." Her answer sounded more like a husky invitation than a protest.

"Should I stop?"

The week of debauchery hadn't totally banished her shyness. What he wanted was perverse. No respectable lady would allow it. But the woman who had discovered a world of miraculous pleasure in her husband's arms was eager for this new adventure.

As the silence extended, she watched disappointment flicker in those rich coffee eyes. He sat back and started to rise. "I ask too much."

She was incorrigible. The angels must despair of her. She caught his hand before it slid off her bare knee. "Don't stop," she whispered.

His eyes flared. "Really?"

"Really." She hoped she sounded braver than she felt.

Now he had permission, Hugh acted with a purpose that stoked her anticipation. He shoved her nightwear up to reveal her mound. When he placed another kiss, longer this time, on the feathery auburn curls at the apex of her thighs, every hollow in her body turned liquid.

The evocative scent of her need tinged the air, mixing with traces of coffee, fresh rolls, and bacon lingering from breakfast. Jane wondered if she'd feel quite so abandoned doing this by candlelight. Something about bright morning sunlight pouring through the sash windows made Hugh's intentions seem even more outrageous.

Except as he stroked his hands up and down her pale thighs and lowered his disheveled head between her legs, she moved past amazement to curiosity. When he touched her there, his hands made magic. She couldn't help wondering what his clever mouth might do.

His tongue traced a hot line along her cleft, making her cry out and bury her hands in his hair. Heat roared through her and made her quake.

He did it again, and this time he lingered to torment the source of her delight. Her belly cramped in ecstasy, and her spine turned to water. She lolled against the couch as her legs splayed on either side of him.

She closed her eyes, so sight couldn't distract her from the rich symphony of pleasure. Another cascading response, when his tongue penetrated her body. Her hands turned to claws, pulling his hair as she broke through into climax.

Hugh's deep growls told her that he was enjoying himself. His mouth and tongue and teeth tormented her, licking and sucking and biting until she saw stars.

Jane floated back to earth and lifted eyelids that felt as heavy as bricks, to find him watching her with a gloating expression. She shivered again, when he wiped one large hand across his glistening lips. What a thrill to know that he'd feasted on her.

"Oh, Hugh…" she said in a broken voice and caught his hand. She brought it to her lips, smelling her own excitement on his fingers. Another wave of reaction clenched her belly. "You give me so much pleasure."

She was exhausted after that quaking reaction, but his flashing smile, all male arrogance and straight white teeth, said he wanted more. "I haven't finished with you yet."

He rose and shrugged off the crimson dressing gown. When he

kissed her, she tasted her juices on his lips. The knowledge made her desire spike.

With a couple of impatient movements, he discarded the loose trousers. Her gaze settled between his thighs, and hunger roared through her. Along with shock at her own wickedness. She couldn't help wondering if her mouth could give him the same pleasure he'd just shown her.

Hugh scooped her up into his arms and carried her through to the bedroom, still shadowy with drawn velvet curtains. Carefully he placed her on the rumpled sheets they'd crawled out of a mere hour ago.

"I'm guessing we're not going to see the Tower of London today," she said, as he came down over her to pepper kisses across her neck and shoulders, revealed under the loose nightgown. He gave a soft grunt of laughter and ran his teeth down the nerve in her neck. He knew that drove her mad.

With a groan, he flopped onto his back beside her. "I feel like the Tower of London right now."

His joke prompted a horrified giggle, although she couldn't deny that his erect rod was impressive. "I shouldn't laugh."

"No, you shouldn't." He cast her a narrow-eyed look. "You should be struck silent with awe."

"You're a lunatic, Hugh." Shyness wasn't strong enough to contain her wayward impulse. She slid down to kiss that hard flesh.

He lurched back against the headboard. "Bloody hell!"

She sat up and regarded him in consternation. "Was that awful?"

"Jane..."

"I liked what you did to me before." She still couldn't read his expression. Had her boldness repulsed him? "I wondered..."

His Adam's apple bobbed as he swallowed, and a hectic flush marked his pronounced cheekbones. "If I'd like something similar?"

She was so embarrassed, she wanted to disappear. "Yes," she said in a small voice. "Clearly I was wrong."

He swallowed again. "Ladies don't..."

If her cheeks got any hotter, she'd go up in flames. Given how mortified she felt right now, that almost seemed preferable to facing Hugh's censure. "I hope you'll forgive me."

Nervously she licked her lips. Did she detect a trace of him? Her forbidden kiss had been so quick, surely she only imagined a faint hint of musk and salt.

Hugh's eyes flared. "Forgive you?"

He still seemed to have trouble speaking, which was strange when the kiss was over in a blink.

"Yes." She licked her lips again.

He groaned and closed his eyes. "If you keep doing that, I won't be responsible for the consequences."

Relief flooded her. He still wanted her. Although she should have guessed that. The Tower of London looked more like granite than ever.

"I might enjoy the consequences," she said breathlessly. "I'm sorry if what I did disgusted you."

He opened his eyes and stared at her in disbelief. "You can't think I'm feeling disgust."

"Aren't you?"

His laugh was cracked. "Good God, the thought of you taking me in your mouth is a fantasy I never thought would come true."

"You said ladies don't…"

"I assumed you'd find the idea utterly revolting. After all, you were delicately reared."

She crossed her legs and settled beside his hip. "I'm beginning to think I'm not so delicate after all. Do you mind?"

When he rolled his eyes, she wanted to laugh. "What do you think?"

She frowned. "So you're saying you'd like me to kiss you…there?"

"If you can bear it."

A smile curled her lips. "Actually I find the idea…intriguing."

Hugh surged up and wrapped his arms around her. He kissed her hard and long. By the time he finally lifted his head, she was dizzy. "I don't deserve you, Jane. The day you married me, you turned me into the luckiest cove in England."

She stared up into his brilliant eyes and saw he meant it. How odd. How unexpected. How wonderful. "Even after I put you through all that torture in Salisbury?"

His lips twitched, and he kissed her quickly. Jane's wits had just started to settle. Now they were in a spin again.

"If you take me in your mouth, I'll forgive you anything."

Jane laughed at his outrageousness, even as a deep well of feminine longing softened her insides. He wanted her to pleasure him like this, she couldn't doubt it. She ran one hand along his jaw, feeling the smooth skin. He'd shaved before breakfast. When he'd turned to her in the dawn, his whiskers had added a bristly spice to his kisses.

She squirmed out of his hold and inched down his body, pausing on the way to kiss his hair-roughened chest. "I'll remember that."

CHAPTER TWENTY-ONE

*S*urely Garson must be dreaming when his fastidious wife stared at his dick as though it was indeed a famous monument. Despite his lurid fantasies, he'd never imagined Jane would be bold enough to perform this brazen act.

He'd been hard for what felt like hours. Dear God, she had him in a perpetual fever, even before this latest offer to rocket him to heaven. He'd expected his hunger to lose its edge, once he'd possessed her. But ever since that astonishing night of transcendent passion in Salisbury, his appetite had only increased with feeding. He became a complete satyr. Jane just had to look at him sideways, and he was ready to jump on her.

When he'd called himself the luckiest cove in England, he hadn't exaggerated. Hell, right now, he felt like the luckiest cove in the whole world. He wouldn't change places with the King himself.

Partly to combat the temptation to grab her, he stretched out flat and folded his arms behind his head. Protracted and excruciating torture lay ahead.

He could hardly wait.

Tentatively, she reached out to curl her fingers around his aching cock. The blast of heat that jolted him almost made him explode, and he bit back a groan. Over the last week, she'd become less shy about touching him, but he always sent blasphemous thanks to heaven when she stroked him like this.

Her expression was solemn, as if she solved some intellectual problem. The pretty blue nightdress and peignoir floated around her, adding a tantalizing touch of modesty. He loved her naked, but there was something delicious about the promise of nakedness to come.

Determination lit her silvery eyes, and she shifted to straddle his legs. Then with a languor that promised to shatter him, she leaned forward. A curtain of glossy auburn tumbled forward. Her loose garments gaped at the neck, providing heart-stopping glimpses of her lovely breasts.

This was the first time Jane had taken the lead. She was an eager participant in everything they did—even if sometimes he had to coax her into playing—but she let him set the agenda. Not this time. The change in their roles fed his excitement.

Anticipation flooded him, as he waited in an agony of suspense for what she did next.

What she did next threatened to blast him into a pile of smoking ashes.

Slowly, so slowly he could hardly endure it, she lowered her head. His cock jerked when the humid heat of her breath drifted across the sensitive head. She glanced up, a flash of bright silver that sliced through him like a blade. Then soft pink lips brushed the tip.

"Hell's bells." Surely his very blood must boil away to nothing.

She kissed him again, then every angel in heaven sang hallelujah when she dipped to take him into her mouth. A fusillade of responses zapped through him, turning him to stone. The hardest part of all basked in wet, sultry heat. The craving to raise his hips, make her take more, was nigh irresistible. Where would his beautiful wife lead him, now he let her steer the course of this encounter?

She flicked her tongue against him and tightened her grip. Then stopped and raised her head. He grabbed the headboard with shaking hands to save himself from seizing her and pushing her down. She *was* going to kill him.

"Don't stop," he choked out.

A frown wrinkled her brow. "You don't seem to be enjoying it."

Even through his urgency, he couldn't contain a grunt of grim laughter. "If I enjoy it any more, I'll burn to a crisp."

Relief filled her face. "Am I doing it right? I want you to like it."

How could he veer so close to flying apart in a million flaming fragments, yet still want to laugh? He wasn't used to this barrage of emotions. Jane had this extraordinary ability to engage his senses and his feelings at the same time.

Now despite the pounding need to put his cock into her mouth, his most powerful response was tenderness. This combination of uncertainty and daring was so true to his wife.

"I'll like it." Even if he knew that she'd subject him to the torments of the damned before she was done. "Whatever you do."

He cupped her cheek and rubbed his thumb over her lower lip, feeling the lush cushion of flesh give under the gentle pressure. Best to avoid picturing those lips closing around him. Otherwise he'd lose himself here and now.

Jane turned her head and drew his thumb into her mouth, rousing inevitable thoughts of what else Garson wanted her to do. When her tongue rasped against his skin, heat sizzled through him and he gritted his teeth to contain a guttural groan. Then all the air escaped him in a whoosh as she sucked.

Damnation, he'd never survive this. He closed his eyes and snatched for air until he stopped seeing colored lights behind his eyelids. The pressure relaxed, and he struggled for control. "By God, Jane, do that again."

He opened his eyes to meet a speculative expression. She pulled his hand away from her mouth, pausing to kiss his knuckles with one of those heart-arresting gestures of affection that he should be used to by now, but somehow wasn't.

Her smile set his heart slamming against his ribs. "I'd rather do something else."

His reeling mind struggled to encompass what she meant. She turned him into a thick-witted ox. Then even the few wits he still possessed evaporated in a searing conflagration, as she lowered her head and took him fully into her mouth.

Suction. Pressure. Heat.

Garson groaned and twined his fingers in the soft mass of her hair, as he battled to hold himself back. Although perhaps next time they did this, he'd convince her to let him come in her mouth. After today, who knew what fresh sins he could tempt her to sample?

She drew harder, and he bit back a profanity. Her fist slid to the base of his dick, so that between her mouth and her hand, exquisite pressure encompassed his length. Excruciating pleasure tightened his balls. All he could hear was the saw of his breath and the evocative sounds her mouth made as it moved on him with succulent greed.

With a shaking hand, he pushed back the fall of her hair so he could see her face. Her features were set with concentration. As she took to her task with a diligence that threatened to incinerate him, her rump rose impudently into the air. The thin silk nightdress molded to her bottom, revealing every lavish curve.

At first, she was beguilingly clumsy, but soon she found the rhythm, sliding up and down his shaft. Her tongue circled his tip, and her hand cupped his balls. With every second, he verged nearer to spurting into her mouth.

"Hell, Jane, I'm too close," he growled in a voice he didn't recognize. "Come here."

She sat back and licked her lips in unabashed appreciation. The sight smashed through him like a cannonade. He needed to be inside her now. Her earlier clumsiness was nothing compared to his quaking desperation when he hauled her up.

"For pity's sake, take me." Blatant need thickened his command before he pressed his eager mouth to hers.

CHAPTER TWENTY-TWO

*J*ane rose on her knees, breaking the kiss, and regarded Hugh with dazed eyes. His rich taste lingered on her tongue. How she'd relished having him at her mercy, as she'd licked and sucked him until he shook. She'd loved the physical intimacy, as she claimed him in a way she never had before. What they did in bed was wonderful, but lying beneath him, she'd always felt the possessed, not the possessor.

"Like this?" Her voice sounded rusty, and she swallowed to loosen a tight throat.

A muscle jerked in his lean cheek, and he bumped his hips up between her legs. "Ride me, darling."

Who was she to argue? She kissed him, but didn't linger. He was too close to the brink. She gathered her silky skirts in one hand, so she could watch as she lowered onto him. Below the pale plain of her belly, her dark red curls glistened. She was slick and ready.

His rod was large and engorged, and straight as a ruler. The head shone with moisture. Thick veins made her think of a mighty tree. A thrill ripped through her, as she recalled her tongue tracing those veins.

She shifted to find the right spot, then held him steady with one hand as she sank down. The stretching sensation was different from their other joinings because of the angle. As her internal muscles clenched, she gasped and bit her lip.

When her body closed over the head, Hugh jerked and released another of those long, hoarse groans. She stared into his face. His eyes were closed, and his jaw was set so hard that she feared it must crack. He shook as if he had a fever.

She let her skirts fall about her thighs and placed her hands flat on his powerful chest, feeling the soft friction of hair against her palms. Inhaling air that tasted of male musk, she descended. To her surprise and pleasure, he slid into her with splendid ease.

She moaned and wriggled to take him deeper. He became completely hers. To prove it, she squeezed. When he bucked, a gush of heat welcomed him. Astonished at the swiftness of her response, she felt the fluttering beginnings of a climax.

Hugh watched her. "You like this."

It wasn't a question. "Very much."

She tightened her thighs and rose, relishing the stroke against the sleek inner walls of her body. The fluttering heightened to irresistible demand.

"Come for me, Jane," he crooned.

She tensed tighter than a fist. "I don't want this to be over."

"We can do it again."

"I'm starting to feel overdressed." With no finesse at all, she tore the silk and lace garments over her head and pitched them to the floor.

"You're magnificent," he grated out, and she squirmed as his large hands caressed her breasts.

Jane rose and fell, then again, circling her hips. She delighted in how every time she shifted, Hugh moved, too, finding new places to stimulate. The seeking, frantic need became an unstoppable tide, and this time she swam with the rising wave of transcendent oblivion. With her next undulation, the crisis struck. She cried out as the world dissolved into luminous rapture.

As she shuddered over him, his hands slid from her breasts to her hips, holding her as she convulsed. His fingers dug into her bare bottom, and he brought her down hard. A long groan of surrender rang in her ears, as he flooded her with his essence.

Floating down from her peak, she felt the tension ease from his thighs and belly. The part of him that had delivered that unearthly experience softened. Without breaking their union, she flattened herself against his chest. He was panting, and the fresh scent of his sweat was sharp in her nostrils.

He kneaded her buttocks and gave a last, exhausted twitch inside her. "That was...extraordinary," he said, breath emerging in jagged gasps.

She placed a kiss above his laboring heart as his powerful arms closed around her. "I like being your wife."

The words were inadequate, but how could she express the joy she'd found? She needed to out-Shakespeare Shakespeare to do justice to the lovely things Hugh did to her.

And she did to him.

"I like being married to you, too," he said, sleep roughening his voice. She snuggled closer and shut her eyes.

Another day gone, and still Jane hadn't seen anything of the capital. Unless she counted a thorough inspection of her private Tower of London.

"Why are you smiling?" Hugh was standing at the sitting room window, watching dusk descend on the street. Or he had been watching the street. Now those gleaming dark eyes focused on her.

"Don't you dare look at me like that," she said, even as burgeoning female interest had her shifting on the chair. She'd found a place near the fire where she pretended to read an old Water Scott. The adventures of Quentin Durward couldn't compete with her memories of what she and Hugh had done to pass the last hours.

He tried and failed to look innocent. "Like what?"

"You know."

His lips twitched. "Like I want to take you back to bed?"

"Yes."

"Well, I do."

She blushed, although given what she'd done today, she surely lost any right to maidenly modesty. "We only got dressed an hour ago."

His expression conveyed a world of devilry. "I've decided dressing is a complete waste of time. Tomorrow we won't bother."

The silly, flirtatious conversation made her want him even more. Before they'd married, she'd had limited contact with grown-up Hugh, and he'd always impressed her as a serious, thoughtful man. This vein of whimsical humor was a surprise—and irresistible. As was his innate sensuality. She'd entered into this marriage prepared for a pragmatic arrangement, not this voyage of sexual discovery.

"I'd like to keep my clothes on until after dinner," she said lightly. "For the servants' sake, if nothing else."

He sighed and approached to drop a kiss on her sensitive nape. Goosebumps rose all over her body. "You're no fun, Jane."

Once she might assume he meant that, but she'd learned to recognize when he was teasing. "That's not what you said an hour ago."

His laugh held a note of appreciation. He drew a chair across, so he could sit close enough to take her book away. "Any good?"

Her lips quirked. "I wouldn't have a clue."

He set the book on the carpet. "So what were you smiling about?"

She lowered her lashes. "The Tower of London."

For a moment he looked thunderstruck, then he burst into delighted laughter. By the time he'd settled down, she'd risen to pour them both some claret.

"Thank you." As he accepted the wine, the brush of his fingers was a caress. He slouched back and studied her, the glass dangling from one large hand. "I thought you went dress shopping with Susan."

As she resumed her seat, she cast a rueful glance at her gray gown. "I did."

"By God, I hope you made a pauper of me."

A self-derisive laugh escaped her. "Far from it. I didn't find much that I liked."

He looked disappointed. She could imagine he was nearly as sick of her uninspiring wardrobe as she was. "Didn't you order anything?"

She shrugged without enthusiasm and took a sip of her wine. "An evening gown." And wished she hadn't. The yellow taffeta with busy black trim made her look like a wasp. "And two day dresses."

His lips lengthened in disapproval. "Susan got a little too insistent, did she?"

Jane ignored that, although it was true. Her sister had rejected anything Jane leaned toward ordering as too fast for a young matron. "I'll try again. I don't want to let you down."

The prospect of the knowing smiles when Lord Garson's frump of a bride appeared in public made her pride cringe. She might know she was second best, but that didn't mean she had to look like she was.

Oh, dear, she'd been so happy. Now bitter reality battered at the door and barged inside without an invitation to make itself at home. She much preferred the sugar-spun fantasy where her husband thought only of her and was overcome with joy that he'd chosen her.

"You're a credit to me, whatever you do, Jane."

Jane only just resisted saying how kind he was. He didn't like hearing that, even if it was true.

She made an apologetic gesture. "I thought of getting some new dresses before the wedding, but the village seamstress is as woefully ignorant of current modes as I am. I decided I'd wait until we got to Beardsley Hall and ask the local ladies where they buy their clothes. Then plans changed, and we came to London instead."

"It's hardly an insurmountable problem, sweetheart." Hugh set his glass on a side table and took her hand. "We're at the heart of a world-wide empire, and I have plenty of money. I'm sure we can lay our hands on a few bits and pieces to bring you up to scratch."

She summoned a smile and told herself that he didn't mean anything when he called her sweetheart. "I'll ask Susan if she wants to come shopping again."

"I've got a better idea." When he looked so pleased with himself, like a little boy who had done his Latin translation to his tutor's satisfaction, her heart gave a strange lurch. Briefly the room reeled around her and all she saw was Hugh's face.

"Oh?" The odd reaction receded, but left her unsettled.

"I'll ask Caro to help you. Or perhaps Helena. She's Silas's sister and married to Lord West. Helena's always up to the minute. Most stylish woman I know."

Jane ripped her hand free and began to pleat her plain skirts. "That won't be suitable."

Hugh frowned, his self-satisfaction fading. "I thought you liked Caro. You seemed to get along at the wedding."

"Of course I liked her." Jane bit her lip and didn't look at him. "She's very nice. So is Lord Stone."

"I see."

When the silence extended, she made herself glance at him. His austere expression told her he did indeed see.

"I know these people are your friends," she said miserably.

To her surprise, he reached out to still the busy fingers that turned her unimpressive gown into a creased mess. "They could become your friends, too."

Wondering how she could leap from elation to such confused awkwardness in the space of half an hour, she swallowed. She made herself speak the fatal name. "Morwenna is married to Silas and Helena's brother."

She braced for anger, but the eyes that studied her were thoughtful instead of condemning. "We live in a small world, Jane. You'll have to lock yourself away in a cellar, if you intend to avoid everyone connected with Morwenna. You must have known when we came to London that you'd bump up against reminders of my previous engagement."

She'd known. She wasn't a fool. But that didn't mean she had to become bosom bows with people so closely connected with her rival.

Shock shuddered through her. *Her rival?* What nonsense was that? With a shaking hand, she set her glass on the table near her elbow.

Morwenna had already won this particular race, whether she

wanted to come in first or not. Jane was perpetually assigned to last place. A fact that grew more depressing by the day.

Hugh's voice deepened with the compassion that was such an essential part of his nature. "I know this is difficult, but there are advantages to facing your fears." A smile lightened his somber expression. "As I'm sure I don't have to tell you."

He referred to what a namby-pamby twit she'd been on their wedding night. "I suppose so," she said reluctantly.

"You're afraid of talk, I can understand that. If I could, I'd spare you the gossip."

He was wrong. She was more afraid of her handsome husband making sheep's eyes at his lost love, while he forgot he had a wife with a call on his loyalty.

When she remained quiet, he went on. "You know, the best way to counter rumors is to hold your head high and prove you don't care a snap of the fingers for what people say. If you're so untroubled by the old scandal that you're ready to make friends with Morwenna's family, the wagging tongues will have nothing to spread poison about. If you set up a silly feud with the Nashes and their circle, it will only fan the tattle."

She wished he'd release her hand, so she could go back to fiddling with her skirt. "That's easy for you to say," she said, hating how sulky she sounded.

"Not really."

Something in his tone made her rise above her worries and really look at him. A tightness around his eyes hinted that he was equally reluctant to brave the arena of public opinion with his bride. What an idiot she was. Of course he was. And it was worse for him because he loved Morwenna.

While she wasn't quite ready to surrender, what he said made sense. "I'll do my best," she mumbled.

"That's my girl."

Despite her unhappiness, his approval made her heart swell. "Is Morwenna in Town?"

He shook his head. "She rarely comes to London. She and her husband live on an estate in Devon that once belonged to Silas."

Jane suddenly felt ashamed of herself. Hugh must loathe speaking of his failed romance. She twined her fingers in his and mustered a smile as false as his composure in the face of irreparable loss. "I'm sorry, Hugh. I'm being silly. I'll be very happy to ask Caro to help me."

CHAPTER TWENTY-THREE

Jane was still on edge two days later, when Hugh escorted her to Lord Stone's elegant house in Berkeley Square. Despite Silas and Caro being so kind to her at the wedding, she didn't feel near ready to face a multitude of Morwenna's friends and family.

Nor did the wasp dress do much to bolster her confidence for her first London party. It had arrived from the *modiste* yesterday, along with its slightly less offensive companions, and was even worse than she remembered.

Looking in her mirror before leaving Half Moon Street, she heartily wished she'd never bought it. But Susan had insisted that the style was all the crack, and as the afternoon wore on, her sister had become increasingly annoyed when Jane vetoed all her suggestions. In the end, Jane had chosen three gowns not because she liked them, but to placate Susan.

The problem was that when one attended an intimate dinner in Mayfair, one needed to wear an evening gown. The wasp dress was the only candidate. Which meant she did what she'd done so often in her life. She put aside what she'd prefer and made do with what she had.

But, oh, how fervently she wished she met Hugh's sophisticated friends looking her best.

"Are you ready?" Hugh asked in an undertone, taking her gloved hand to help her from the carriage. He was tall and handsome in formal black. His sartorial perfection only made her more miserably aware that she looked a complete antidote.

Jane bit back, "As I'll ever be," and struggled to sound as if she wasn't terrified. "Yes, I am."

He cast her a skeptical glance but bless him, didn't argue. As they mounted the stone steps to the open door, he squeezed her fingers in encouragement.

They paused in the hallway to remove their outer wear. To her husband's credit, while his first glimpse of her garish gown made him blink, he maintained his composure. He took her arm, and followed the butler into a sumptuous drawing room.

"Lord and Lady Garson, my lady," the butler intoned from the doorway.

Jane entered a room crammed wall to wall with people, and the urge to run away rose like vomit. She squared her shoulders and stiffened knees that threatened to fold. She owed it to Hugh to perform creditably tonight. For heaven's sake, she owed it to herself. As Hugh's grip tightened in reassurance, she fixed a smile on her face.

"Jane, how lovely to see you again." Caro advanced with her hands outstretched in welcome. Jane found herself hugged and kissed on the cheek, as if she was a friend and not an interloper at all. "I've been itching to call, but Silas said I couldn't intrude upon your honeymoon."

"And good evening to you, too, Caro," Hugh said drily, as he bowed.

The lovely brunette released Jane and cast Hugh a laughing glance. "You must know all eyes are on Jane tonight. You're merely background scenery."

Silas came up to kiss Jane's cheek. "Courage," he whispered. "It's years since anybody here has bitten a visitor."

Jane stifled a shocked laugh and finally dragged some air into her lungs. What a difference a breath made. The hordes infesting the room shrank to a mere six people.

Caro and Silas she already knew. Curiously she looked at the other guests. A pretty blonde woman sat on a chaise longue beside a mountain of a man with black hair. A stylish, dark-haired lady with a commanding nose occupied a chair under the window. Standing beside her was a tall, elegant gentleman with thick gray hair that seemed incongruous on someone who couldn't be much more than forty.

As expected, they were all beautifully presented. If only Susan's *modiste* had offered her a gown like the black-haired lady's teal blue silk, Jane would have had no difficulty making a hole in Hugh's fortune. At least the faces turned toward her expressed friendly interest—despite the wasp dress and Hugh's history with Morwenna. She began to feel less like a freak, although after two weeks alone with Hugh, she was unsettled to be in company again.

Caro drew her forward, while Silas and Hugh retreated to the corner beside the fireplace. "Let me introduce you to everyone."

"It's very kind of you to invite me," Jane said, meaning it. Her smile became more natural.

Caro made a dismissive sound. "Hugh is one of Silas's best friends —and anyway, I liked you at the wedding. I thought it might be nice if you met some people at a small gathering, before you have to face society *en masse*. I know how daunting that can be."

"You liar, Caro. You wouldn't have a clue." With a mocking laugh, the dark lady rose. She was tall and slender, and Jane didn't think she'd ever coveted anything in her life the way she coveted that spectacular gown. "When you came out of mourning, you were champing at the bit to queen it over the beau monde. Wild horses couldn't have dragged you back to rural obscurity." She turned to Jane. "I'm Helena, Silas's sister. This is my husband, West."

Jane had a moment to reflect that Helena and Silas looked nothing alike, as the striking, gray-haired man bowed over her hand. "Lady Garson, I'm delighted to welcome you to London."

"Thank you, my lord." Jane curtsied.

The blonde approached. Her pale green gown was more under-stated than Helena's teal, but just as becoming. She took Jane's hand and leaned in to kiss her cheek. "I'm Fenella Townsend, and I hope we'll be friends."

The greeting's warmth left Jane floundering. "I hope so, too," she stammered.

She caught a glint of approval in Hugh's eye. Her panic receded another few inches.

Fenella gestured the huge man forward. "This is my husband Anthony."

The man held Jane's hand. "It's grand to meet you at last, lass."

The thick Yorkshire accent took Jane aback. Then she realized that this must be Lord Kenwick, reputedly the richest man in England. News of his rise in the world had penetrated even as far as deepest Dorset. He and the ethereal Fenella seemed an odd pairing, Beauty and the Beast.

"I didn't know you and Fen were back from Italy," Hugh said, striding forward to shake Anthony's hand with unfettered pleasure.

"We got in on Tuesday."

"Good trip?"

"Aye, very. I closed a right jammy deal with the Genoans, and Fen hustled me around every mucky lump of broken masonry between Pompeii and the Alps." He didn't sound like he minded, Jane noted. "We ran into Sally and Charles in Venice."

"They're away more than they're home these days," Silas said.

Jane let the conversation flow around her, grateful that while discussion centered on travel and absent friends, she ceased to be the focus of attention. She soon found herself sipping a glass of sherry and sharing the chaise longue with Fenella Townsend.

"The new names and faces must be overwhelming," Fenella said, her blue eyes sympathetic. "Eventually you'll sort everyone out, but it's all right to feel at sea at first. We're all so happy that Hugh has married you. I can see just looking at him, how good you've been for him."

"Thank you," Jane said, glancing across the room to where Hugh and West were talking about horseracing.

Hugh had told her a little about his friends before she met them. He moved in influential circles. The Kenwicks formed the center of a worldwide network of power and business. The Wests were renowned horse breeders, with several Derby winners in their stables. Silas was a respected botanist and President of the Royal Society, while Caro busied herself with a brood of four children and charity work.

"How did you meet? When Caro wrote to us in Italy to say Hugh was getting married, it came as a bolt from the blue. He's such a dark horse."

Jane made herself smile. It wasn't quite the effort it had been when she'd first arrived. "His proposal came as a bolt from the blue to me, too."

"A whirlwind romance," Fenella said with unabashed delight.

If only, Jane thought with a touch of bitterness. But she owed it to Hugh to keep the details of their pragmatic bargain to herself. "He's known me from the cradle. Our fathers were best friends."

"Childhood sweethearts, then?"

Jane blushed with mortification. Not sweethearts in any sense. "Not at all. When the families got together, he thought I was a complete pest."

Hugh caught her answer and crossed to stand beside her and rest his hand on her shoulder. His touch steadied her, lent a tinge of warmth to her blood. She'd need to get used to people asking questions—and most of the curiosity wouldn't be as benevolent as Fenella's.

"Jane, that's not true. I never thought you were a pest."

Her laugh was mocking. "What about that time I stole your favorite fishing pole and broke it? Or when you had to climb the tallest oak at Cavell Court to save me from falling?"

"Well, perhaps you were occasionally a pest." The affection in his smile reminded her that while they mightn't be in love, they were genuinely fond of each other. That meant a lot. "But you improved as you got older."

"You didn't," she retorted.

"I say!" He looked startled. "That's a bit rough."

Her smile widened. "You were always an extremely nice boy, much kinder to a little girl with a bad case of hero worship than she deserved. And you've grown up to be an extremely nice man. See? No improvement needed."

His face softened, and he kissed her briefly. "You little tease."

The kiss was over in a second, but it left her lips tingling. Her blush flared hotter when she noticed all eyes on them. She caught flickers of astonishment and pleasure and relief, and the atmosphere in the room eased noticeably.

"That's just lovely," Caro said, breaking the surprised silence. "I can imagine Hugh was a nice boy. You'll have to tell us more."

"Let's bring in some champagne and toast the happy couple, Hunter." Silas nodded to the butler circling the room with the decanter. "This sherry is filthy stuff."

By the time the ladies rose from the dining table to leave the gentlemen to their port, Garson was elated with how well the evening progressed. Jane had arrived so unsure—he couldn't blame her, everyone at the dinner was intimately connected with the old scandal of his broken engagement. She knew she was on trial as Morwenna's substitute. Even worse, she'd let that witch Susan talk her into buying that ghastly yellow dress. Being awake to Susan's penchant for the limelight, while her sister faded into the background, Hugh suspected the lapse in taste had been deliberate.

Marriage had transformed Jane from a downtrodden drudge to the vibrant woman she'd always been at heart. With the right clothes, she'd sparkle like the jewel she was. If Hugh saw that change, Susan certainly would, and she wouldn't like it.

But even in that expensive, unbecoming rag, Jane's natural charm shone through. At first, his friends welcomed her for his sake. But by the time dessert was served, they liked her for her funny, quirky self.

He was dashed glad. His friends' interest would be nothing, compared to the full glare of society's scrutiny. Jane would now have Caro, Fen and Helena to defend her against the cats.

As if he read Garson's thoughts—he probably had—Silas set down his port and regarded him searchingly across the shining width of the mahogany table. "That's a fine girl you nabbed for yourself there, Garson."

"Yes, she is," Garson said, and found himself smiling. He was so damned proud of how Jane held her head up tonight. "Better than I deserve."

He waited for his friends to make some joking rejoinder about his general unworthiness, but none of the three did. Instead West settled serious green eyes upon him. "Nice to see you getting on with your life at last."

"Hear, hear," Silas said, refilling Garson's glass.

"Grand that you've rejoined the human race," Anthony chimed in.

The reminder of his public humiliation and hardly less public sorrow over losing Morwenna stung. Although of course, everyone here knew how wretched these last years had been for him.

"It was time to marry," he said, as the simplest explanation for a complex series of decisions and events.

"Time to stop looking like a bilious piglet," West muttered loudly enough for Garson to hear.

Garson scowled at his friend, although much as he disliked the description, he had a queasy feeling it held an element of truth.

"A bilious piglet's a bit strong," Silas protested, but before Garson could feel too grateful, he went on. "Society's ladies found Garson's pining very romantic. Not a one of them didn't want to take his weary head to her bosom and anoint him with her tears."

Garson shuddered. That was definitely true. It was one of the reasons he'd asked Jane to marry him, instead of some London belle. The picture Silas and West conjured up struck him as worse than looking like a bilious piglet. "You're getting bloody poetic in your old age, chum."

Derisive amusement twisted Silas's lips. "Every time I heard one of them sigh after you, it made me feel dashed poetic, too. I thought Byron had to be back from the dead, until I looked around and saw it was just you."

"Byron without the unsavory bits, so even better," Anthony added in his bass rumble.

"Ugh," Garson said, too pleased with how the night had turned out to take real offense at the jibes.

"Anyway, jolly glad to see you've found love again," West said, sounding uncharacteristically sincere. "We've all hated to see you so unhappy, Hugh."

Astounded, Garson regarded his three friends as if they'd lost their minds. Even without West breaking the habit of a lifetime and using his Christian name, he couldn't mistake how worried they'd been about him. He only just bit back an angry denial of their asinine assumptions.

He could hardly credit this sentimental claptrap. They'd been cronies for years, in some cases since childhood. These men knew that he was as stubborn as a mule, once his affection was engaged. They also all knew that he'd been head over heels with Robert Nash's lovely widow—even if in the end she turned out to be no widow at all. For God's sake, Garson mightn't have told Silas in so many words that he made a marriage of convenience, but his friend had known the truth when he stood up as best man in Dorset.

Over the last three years, Garson had come to loathe his steadfast heart. But loathing didn't change its ways. He'd sworn his devotion to Morwenna. He'd go to his grave loving her.

It was his curse. It was his destiny.

He'd believed his closest friends understood that. But clearly they were as susceptible to the lure of a happy ending as any other romantic fool. These three men loved their wives. That good fortune deceived them into taking an overly rosy view of every marriage.

Garson's hand tightened on his port, and he raised his glass to drink before he set it down with an angry bump. Damned love. Who needed it? Certainly not him, by heaven.

Love had given him nothing but humiliation and misery. If he'd fallen out of love with Morwenna, which he hadn't, he had no wish to fall in love with anyone else, even his delectable wife. He and Jane were doing very well. He certainly wasn't going to spoil things by convincing himself he was in love again.

The mere idea made his guts curdle. The fine port tasted sour on his tongue.

Only loyalty to Jane made him force a smile to his lips and raise the glass. After all, if his friends suffered the delusion that he'd married for love, not duty, what did it matter? "I'd like to offer a toast to our lovely wives, gentlemen."

CHAPTER TWENTY-FOUR

*D*espite finding Hugh's friends much less daunting than she'd feared, Jane was uneasy about coping with Caro, Helena, and Fenella on her own. It wasn't just that she felt like an outsider in a group of women who were such close and long-term friends. She was afraid that now the men had gone, the ladies might bring up the one name that had hovered, resonant because unspoken, all evening.

Damn it, she didn't want to talk about Morwenna. In fact, she'd be overjoyed if the unknown but clearly peerless Mrs. Nash sank into a bog, never to be seen again.

Even as these thoughts arose, she knew they were unworthy. But that didn't mean she intended to spend her first night out in London, listening to how wonderful Morwenna was and how she'd broken Hugh's heart.

Once everyone found their places around the fire, she pre-empted the conversation before it could veer toward Hugh's lost love. "Helena, I'd love to know the name of your *modiste*. I adore that dress, and I'll need a new wardrobe if Hugh's planning to join the social whirl."

Helena smiled at Jane from where she sat on the sofa near the window. She was drinking port, while Fenella had served tea to everyone else. Jane suffered a moment's curiosity as to why Caro didn't play hostess in her own home, but didn't know these women well enough to ask. "It's natural that he wants to show off his new bride."

How Jane wished she merited showing off. Then she reminded herself that she'd renounced self-pity. Since she'd discovered her husband was mad for her, her confidence had advanced in leaps and bounds. It was forgivable to feel a little wobbly here, because of Morwenna's ghost and because she hated what she was wearing, but now was the time to put her nerves away.

"Then I need something better than this." She glanced down at the wasp dress, which created a vile clash with her chair's orange and green striped upholstery. "My sister Susan says it's the last word in style, but I don't think it suits me at all."

"Your sister is Lady Bacon, isn't she?" Caro asked from her place beside Helena on the sofa. She tactfully avoided remarking on the dress, Jane noted.

Helena frowned. "I remember your sister made a great splash when she was introduced to London."

Wry fondness curved Jane's lips. "She's always been the beauty in the family."

"I wouldn't say that's true, Jane." Fenella subjected her to a thorough inspection. "You're lovely, although in a very different style. No wonder Garson is so besotted."

Jane stifled a snort of derisive laughter. Her husband might want her, but nobody in their right mind would believe his feelings extended past that. Still, Fenella was generous to try to make her feel better.

"You are pretty," Caro said, saving Jane from summoning a response to Fenella's remark that combined discretion and truth. An impossible task, she couldn't help thinking. "But a different color might work better, if you don't mind my saying."

"I don't mind at all." Jane only just stopped herself from declaring that she could pass as an insect. "I already told you I don't like this dress."

"It's not the color." Helena also studied her, an almost scientific light in her bright, black eyes. "With your spectacular hair, that golden yellow could be wonderful. The trimming is too fussy. By the way, whoever told you to put topazes with that ensemble was a genius."

Jane felt a warm glow. It was the first time she'd worn any of the Garson jewels. This morning, Hugh had produced several sets for her to choose from, including an elaborate diamond and emerald parure that must be worth a king's ransom. But her instinct was to select something simpler for a quiet dinner among friends, no matter how significant this occasion might be for her. She'd almost gone for a magnificent string of pearls, but had decided against them, perhaps because pearls were linked to tears.

Her marriage didn't need anything more working against it.

"Please, I'm happy to take any advice you can give me."

"I'll do better than that," Helena said. "If you're free tomorrow, I'll take you to my *modiste*, then my milliner."

Caro smiled. "That's a major compliment, Jane. Helena doesn't hand out fashion advice willy-nilly."

Helena cast her friend a dismissive glance. "As if you need my advice."

"I'd take it if you gave it," Caro retorted. "The way you dress always makes me green with envy."

"Green's not your color."

"Ha ha," Caro said with good-natured sarcasm. "If you were any sharper, you'd cut yourself."

"They're very fond of each other, Jane," Fenella said gently. "Pay no attention to their bickering. It's a sign they feel comfortable with you. Out in public, Caro and Helena behave themselves. Mostly."

"We're the best of friends," Caro said, standing and drifting across to the fire.

Jane could see that. There was a bond between all three women that she could almost touch. She felt a surge of envy. She'd never had a close woman friend. Susan was too much older—and much as Jane hated to admit it, too self-centered. How odd to realize that the nearest she'd ever come to this sort of relationship was her marriage. Although given the complications of desire and Hugh's love for Morwenna, she wouldn't precisely call that a friendship either.

"Who made the dresses for your season?" Helena asked.

"I didn't have a season," Jane admitted.

"Why on earth not?" Caro flung one hand out, her delicate cup narrowly missing the edge of the marble mantelpiece. Perhaps Jane had her answer as to why tranquil Fenella presided over the tea tray. "Your sister did."

"Yes, well, things were different for Susan."

"Why?"

"Caro, Jane's only just met us," Fenella said in soft reproof. "Perhaps she doesn't want to give us her life story."

Caro made an unimpressed sound. "That's how you find out about people. You ask questions."

"Indeed, but people don't have to answer."

"I'm sure Jane can tell me that herself, if she feels that way." She paused. "Anyway, I haven't just met her. I went to her wedding."

Despite feeling uncomfortable at the interest in her life, Jane couldn't contain a giggle when Helena rolled her eyes. "In that case, there should be no secrets between you."

"There was a season planned for me," Jane said, surprised that she didn't mind talking about this with people she'd just met. "But my father fell ill, and I had to stay home to care for him. I've spent the last ten years buried in darkest Dorset. The local farmers don't give a fig if my gowns are the *dernier cri*. They just want to talk to someone who knows how to run the estate."

"Didn't you long for London?" Caro asked. "When my first husband was alive, I was mired in the depths of the country, and I nearly went mad."

"Needs must." Jane set her cup on a side table. How unexpected to discover that this sparkling, sophisticated creature had been trapped, too. "Someone had to take the reins. In the early days, we hoped my father might recover, but it wasn't to be."

"Jane, I'm sorry," Fenella said. "It sounds like you've had a sad time of it."

She smothered a pang of grief for her father and the way he'd let himself fade away. After her mother's death, his life had started to unravel, ending in a long, wasting illness. When she was a child, he'd been a vital, fulfilled man. "Managing the estate was interesting, and I was glad to be useful."

"But it wasn't much fun, I'll wager," Helena said.

"Fun? No, that's not exactly how I'd describe it."

"Now Garson has brought you to London, and you've fallen into our clutches," Caro said with another reckless swoop of the teacup. "Nobody knows how to have fun better than a Dashing Widow."

"A Dashing Widow?"

"That's what we called ourselves when we came out of mourning for our first husbands." With delicate precision, Fenella placed her cup on the tray. It still seemed unlikely that she was married to huge, bluff Anthony Townsend. "We decided we were sick of moping about, and it was time to take society by storm. None of us had the least notion of marrying again."

"No, we were positively set against the idea," Helena said, with a sardonic twist of her lips. "My first husband was a rake and a wastrel. I swore I'd never put myself at a man's mercy again."

"And while my first husband was a good, steady, reliable man, he only thought about farming. I was so bored, cooped up in muddy Lincolnshire with him, I went into a decline," Caro said. "When I finished my year of mourning, my plan was to dance and flirt, and take lovers, and live for giddy pleasure. Marriage meant going back to prison."

"Yet you both married—and you seem very happy," Jane said.

"We're happy, all right." The formidable Helena looked almost sentimental. "And we were much luckier with our choices, the second time around."

"Luck?" Caro said. "Luck had nothing to do with it. We were clever enough to know Silas and West were the ones for us."

"Even if it took you far too long to see that," Helena said. "I thought unrequited love would finish my poor brother off, before you finally agreed to take him on. His hangdog looks were becoming unbearable. If self-pity didn't kill him, I vow I would have."

"I didn't marry Silas just to save you a bit of annoyance," Caro retorted.

A smile of surprising sweetness curved Helena's lips. "No, you married him because you love him too much to live without him. I married West for the same reason."

"Love is a sneaky devil," Caro said. "Fen, you'd better speak up, or Jane will imagine you don't love Anthony."

Jane was well aware of Fenella's reticence while Caro and Helena shared their surprising stories. On first meeting, she'd assumed these women had always had the world at their feet. Now reading between the lines, she saw that they'd all had their battles to fight before attaining their present contentment.

"Of course I love Anthony," Fenella said impatiently. "He gave me a new lease of life."

Jane knew what it was like to shrink from exposing fragile feelings to the light. "You don't have to tell me, Fenella, if it's difficult for you."

Fenella's smile contained an ocean of sadness. "My story is quite different from Caro and Hel's. As girls, they wed men unworthy of them. I didn't. My first husband Henry died a hero at Waterloo. Losing him broke my heart, so I was determined to retire from the world and live only for my son Brandon. I was sure I'd never love again."

"But we dragged you back into the world," Caro said.

"Yes, you did."

"And Anthony dragged you back to life. I can still remember how astounded we were, when you announced that you intended to marry him, despite only knowing him for a couple of weeks."

Fenella's smile turned brilliant, and with a shock, Jane saw that she was as besotted with her big brute of a husband as Caro and Helena were with theirs. "I fell in love at first sight, but because the feeling was so different from what I had with Henry, it took me a little while to recognize what had happened. In many ways, Henry and Anthony are poles apart. For all his bravery as a soldier, Henry was gentle and self-effacing. Whereas Anthony is..."

"A force of nature," Helena said promptly.

"He is at that." When Fenella looked like a cat at a cream pot, Jane laughed.

She couldn't help contrasting Fenella's situation with her own. Fenella was proof that it was possible to love again. Did this mean that one day Hugh's devotion to Morwenna might waver? Was Jane being a jealous cow, to wish that it would?

"So you see, Jane, we're all victims to love's vagaries," Caro said. "All our plans went awry, and we ended up leading lives we'd never imagined."

That was true about Jane's plans, too. She'd never pictured becoming Lady Garson. And while she'd foresworn love when she married Hugh, she couldn't quash a pang of envy at the happiness her new friends had found in their marriages.

CHAPTER TWENTY-FIVE

*J*ane was very quiet in the carriage on the way home. Garson sat beside her and held her gloved hand, but he felt like she was a thousand miles away.

"They liked you," he said. "Every fellow there fell over himself to congratulate me on my good fortune."

No exaggeration, until he reached a point where if one more person mentioned his love for his new wife, he'd start smashing furniture. He was disappointed in his friends. Not with the way they'd recognized Jane's obvious qualities—he'd never worried about that. But that they'd fallen so quickly for the easy lie that he'd forgotten Morwenna.

Especially Silas. If anyone in the world knew what it had cost Garson to step back when Robert Nash returned to claim his wife, Silas had. Yet this evening, Silas had led the chorus praising the glories of married love, as if he preached to a man converted.

This evening also exposed how Garson's dogged and hopeless adoration for Silas's sister-in-law had made things awkward for his cronies. He'd always guessed it had, but the extent of his friends' relief now he'd married Jane demonstrated quite how bad the problem had been.

Well, a pox on all of them. A man of honor didn't change his heart, the way he changed his coat. He loved Morwenna and always would.

None of which helped him make a future with the wife he increasingly liked and endlessly wanted. When he plunged deep into Jane's body and she gripped him tight inside her, the rest of the world vanished into smoke. He felt whole in a way he felt with nobody else. If it didn't feel so good, he might almost be worried.

"Jane, did you hear me?"

"Yes." She shot him an unreadable glance, before staring out the window at the rows of tall, white houses. "You said they liked me."

"I thought you'd be pleased. You were in enough of a tizz beforehand."

"Yes, I was, wasn't I?" The carriage's outside lamps illuminated a faint smile. "I'm sorry everything is such an effort. I'll find my feet eventually."

Her measured response worried him, although she was only repeating back to him what he'd said to her a hundred times. "You've had a lot to come to terms with. Anyone would be flummoxed." He paused. "In fact, you fitted in beautifully. They liked you."

"Yes, so you said." She turned away from the window and faced him. "Stop worrying, Hugh. I'll be all right. Helena's taking me shopping tomorrow."

He had a nasty feeling that his clumsy masculine brain had missed something. Something important. "That's excellent."

"She's very stylish."

Helena was. She'd never have chosen that unbecoming yellow and black gown. But his wife had managed so well, even her dreadful frock hadn't mattered in the end. Jane had acted as if it shouldn't matter, and it hadn't.

"I didn't have to come to your rescue." He was rather ashamed of his pique that she'd managed without his help. He didn't want a clinging vine for a helpmeet, but he'd have liked to play her hero.

A frown wrinkled her brow. "Your friends were very kind to me."

"It wasn't kindness. They liked you." Even Garson started to think he sounded like a parrot.

"And I liked them. Caro suggested we all go to Lady Oldham's ball on Thursday."

"Thursday?" Devil take it, Thursday was only two days away.

"You sound put out. Surely we're in London for me to make my debut."

"That's right," he said, wondering why the idea of introducing her to the ton suddenly made him so uncomfortable.

Was he afraid she'd make a fool of herself? Given how well she'd gone over tonight, that would be silly. Was he afraid she'd make a fool of him? Not in the slightest. Any man who appeared with Jane as his companion could only benefit from the association.

So there was no reason to delay her entry into the fashionable world. She'd been isolated and alone for too long. It was more than time for her to spread her wings, meet new people, experience new things.

And he didn't resent that. Not really.

But as he considered this evening and Thursday's ball, and undoubtedly the balls and dinners and musicales and ridottos and Venetian breakfasts and God knew what else to come, his heart sank into his boots. Because his wife would no longer be purely his. During the last few weeks, he and Jane had existed in a luminous bubble, where they were everything to each other. Now society would claim her, and that precious intimacy would of necessity change.

"We don't have to go, if you don't want to."

In her subdued voice, he heard the echo of a thousand previous occasions when she'd wanted something and hadn't ended up getting it. Like the season her sister had been given and she hadn't. "Do you want to go?"

"Yes, I think I would. The evening will be easier if your friends are there."

It was true. "Your friends now, I hope."

She made a dismissive gesture. "I'm too new to the group to make that claim, but they're very fond of you. I daresay they'd like to lend their countenance to your wife's first steps into society." She paused. "And as you said, once people see that I've found favor with the

Nashes and their circle, it might scotch any gossip. If I'm on good terms with Morwenna's family, people won't find it so titillating."

Garson hid a wince. He always felt uncomfortable when Jane talked about his lost love, although he never detected a trace of jealousy in her tone. Most brides would resent his loyalty to another woman. Not Jane.

But that's why you married her, isn't it?

He tried to ignore the snide little voice. But it stubbornly persisted.

You married Jane because she wouldn't make emotional demands and insist you mend your broken heart. You married Jane because you knew she'd make the best of a bad lot.

Was he a bad lot? He hated to think he might be.

"Hugh?" she asked. "Are you all right?"

"Why wouldn't I be?" he said impatiently, even as he couldn't help recognizing how selfish he'd been when he proposed to Jane. He'd known he caught her at a disadvantage when she was about to become homeless. Now she was committed to a life without love.

After Morwenna left him, he'd resigned himself to a loveless future. But Jane was a warm, vibrant creature who deserved better than a husband who could never give her his heart.

A just man would give her leave to take a lover. Later. After she'd produced a couple of children. She deserved the freedom to fall in love, as surely she must. And men would fall in love with her. She'd whirl through London's ballrooms, convincing every damn rake in town—as she'd convinced him—that the new Lady Garson was a prize indeed.

She should seek some happiness for herself, once she'd done her duty by her husband. Gritting his teeth, he forced himself to picture her in the arms of some faceless cad. He made himself imagine her kissing the blockhead, taking off her clothes, lying naked in the sod's bed, spreading her legs for the bastard.

He shifted abruptly on the leather seat and bit back a savage curse.

His wife might have a right to stray, but devil take it, he'd do everything in his power to keep her to himself.

Therein lay his dilemma. Until now he'd always believed he was a reasonable man, and that reasonable man pointed out that he wasn't being fair. Just because he'd been unlucky in love, that was no reason to condemn his wife to an emotional desert.

Bugger it.

"Hugh, are you sure you're all right?"

"I said I was." His frustration with the conundrum made him snap.

"If you don't want to go to the Oldhams', we don't have to." She pulled her hand free of his, and in his blue-deviled state that seemed the first step toward forsaking him altogether. "It's not as if we're short of invitations."

Invitations meant meeting men. And who knew which of those men might turn out to be the swine Jane fell in love with? Garson wanted to bundle her up in his arms, so she could never wander.

The worst of this was he'd brought it on himself. He could have stuck to his original plan to take her straight to Beardsley Hall.

Although there were men in Derbyshire, too. Neighbors and visitors, and guests of his neighbors. Not to mention the men she'd meet on trips into Derby or Matlock or York. The anonymous blackguard who stole her away mightn't be in London at all. It wasn't as if the provinces had put a ban on attractive coves with an eye for another man's wife.

Danger lurked everywhere for a lady with an unattached heart.

Garson had entered this marriage, planning for a trouble-free future. A meek wife. Obedient children. Freedom to nurse his romantic disappointment, without anyone demanding what he was unable to give.

Instead he found himself confused and bad tempered. Obsessed with his wife. Jealous as a starving dog eyeing the only bone in the village. And hating himself for being such a blockhead.

Garson had a depressing suspicion that his mixed reaction to tonight's success was only going to worsen as this visit to London progressed. He sucked in a breath that tasted rancid with self-pity and tried to sound like the affable man the world believed him to be. "Let's go to the Oldhams'. You'll enjoy it. It's always a highlight of the season."

A highlight of the season, and a one-way voyage to Hell.

CHAPTER TWENTY-SIX

*J*ane was still puzzling over Hugh's odd humor, when she and Helena set out on the next day's promised shopping trip. He'd seemed happy at Caro's dinner, and she'd even caught a gleam of pride in his eyes when he saw her fitting in so well with his friends. Then on the short drive home, he'd been irritable and distracted.

She'd taken too long to notice the change in his mood, because she'd been brooding over what she'd learned about the Dashing Widows, particularly Fenella's story about finding love after a crippling loss. She found Fenella's courage inspiring and wished she could talk to Hugh about it. But he'd think she was trying to nudge him into forsaking his allegiance to Morwenna.

The humiliating truth was that he'd be right.

She'd wondered if somehow she'd blundered at the dinner, but when they got home, he rushed her upstairs and barely got her behind a closed door before he started pulling her clothes off. His passion had contained an edge that was breathtakingly exciting. No leisurely, sensual exploration, but fireworks and overwhelming pleasure, and the two of them collapsing in exhaustion once they were done.

He'd turned to her twice more, once in the early hours, then just as the sun came up, he'd taken his time to drive her mad with need before he took her on a journey to the stars. That encounter had extended into the morning. Afterward they'd both tumbled into a deep sleep. She'd had to hurry to be ready for Helena at two.

Now with weariness and satisfaction weighting her limbs, she had trouble concentrating on what her new friend said. Her new friends. Fenella had joined them at Madame Lisette's, where Jane had spent the last hour, struggling to differentiate between hundreds of fashion plates, each more beautiful than the last.

Jane had been grateful to see Fenella. Not only was she the least intimidating Dashing Widow, she wasn't Morwenna Nash's sister-in-law.

Fenella laughed, as with unflagging enthusiasm, Helena opened yet another album. "You're making the poor girl dizzy, Hel. You're used to wading through all these choices. Jane isn't."

Helena looked up in surprise, then laughed as well when she saw Jane's expression. "Do you feel like you're drowning?"

"Yes," Jane said faintly, stepping back from a table littered with albums and magazines and falling into a chair upholstered in pink velvet. Madame Lisette, a petite bird-like Frenchwoman, loved pink. The shop was festooned in every shade of that color.

"And each time she comes up for air, you push her head under again," Fenella said.

"*Zut,* I am too excited at the chance to make milady Garson *un succès fou.*" With a decisive snap, the *modiste* closed the large book she was poring over on the other side of the table. "Would you like to see *tout* and choose for yourself? Or would you like milady West *et moi* to guide you through this forest?"

Jane gave a tired laugh. "I put myself in your hands, Madame."

"And mine," Helena said.

Fenella placed a reassuring hand on her shoulder. "I'm here for moral support, if these two get too bossy."

Madame Lisette gestured for Jane to stand up—Jane had already noted that the Frenchwoman treated her clients with scant deference. "In that case, let's look at you."

"Trust Madame, Jane. She's a genius," Helena said. "I owe all my social cachet to her brilliance."

"*C'est vrai*," Madame Lisette said, her gaze running over Jane as if assessing every inch. "That is a *très jolie* dress, but too young and too staid for a milady in the first stare of fashion."

Helena pushed Jane in front of a cheval mirror, as Madame continued her inspection. Reflected back, Jane saw a tall girl with red hair and uncertain eyes. She wore the ensemble she'd put on after her wedding, one of the two dresses Susan had brought down from London. The soft lavender was a flattering color on her pale skin and suitable for someone coming out of mourning.

But when she compared it to Fenella's blue walking dress or Helena's figure-hugging aubergine merino, she saw what Madame meant. The dress was pretty, certainly prettier than her other clothes, but dull.

"Milady has a superb figure. Clever cutting will show that off. And good skin—but you need strong colors, like crimson and fuchsia and peacock blue."

"I'm not…" Jane began, afraid that she'd end up looking like a fairground monkey.

Madame ignored her and produced a tape measure from her pocket. "That bosom. *Ooh la la*. A woman with such a bosom shouldn't dress like a nun."

Helena laughed at Jane's nonplused expression. "Well, she's right."

"And that hair. True Titian red. *Magnifique. Quelle couleur.* Not a lady in London has hair to rival this."

The delight in Madame's face made Jane feel jittery, even as she soaked up the praise. She'd come to accept that Hugh liked how she looked, but it had never occurred to her that anyone else might share her husband's eccentric tastes in feminine beauty.

"You're too kind," Jane said.

Madame made a very French sound of contempt and waved away

Jane's thanks. "Kind? *Non, non, non.* I am honest. The English never give praise to what they should and always with the tucking away of their pleasure in their own beauty. You are lovely, milady. I know it. Your friends here know it. Undoubtedly, your husband, the so 'andsome Lord Garson, knows it. Put yourself into my hands, and soon the whole world will know it. There will be no more hiding your light under a thicket."

"Bushel," Helena said.

Madame scowled. "Bushel? Thicket? *Zut!* What do I care? What I care about is making this retiring violet the tiger lily she was born to be—and turning her into the toast of London."

Jane stifled a hysterical giggle. Dealing with Madame Lisette was like trying to hold a firecracker in her hand. Before this, her experience of London *modistes* was confined to Susan's Mrs. Haines, who had exuded a grandmotherly air as she'd measured Jane up.

Then she gave you clothes worthy of a grandmother, a nasty little voice reminded her.

"Do you want to be the toast of London, Jane?" Fenella asked.

"*Naturellement* she does," Madame retorted.

Jane looked around this elegant, if overwhelmingly pink room, then she glanced at Fenella and Helena. There was no doubt that they were confident of their place in the world.

She wanted to feel that same confidence. Perhaps she should begin by emulating how they looked. "You know," she said thoughtfully, "I daresay I might."

"*Brava*, milady," Madame Lisette said and gestured to the two assistants watching procedures from a distance that it was time to move. "*Enfin*, let's get to work."

"I hope you were serious about not stinting on my wardrobe," Jane said to Garson as they sat in the Wests' box at the Theatre Royal.

The first act of the silly comedy had come to an end. If he was on his own, he'd go home. But Jane had never been to the theatre before, and while he might take little pleasure in the performance, he took great pleasure in her enjoyment.

He smiled, touched by her transparent delight in her new clothes. "If everything is as becoming as this dress, it's worth it, even if I have to throw the dining table into the fire for heat next winter."

"Helena kept ordering things. And Fenella said I should just go along with her."

"One should always listen to Fenella," he said drily.

Jane nodded, taking his comment seriously. "I'm finding that's true."

They were alone in the box. When the interval began, Helena and West had left to talk to the Kinglakes, who were just back from Italy. Garson had tipped the footman outside to keep any curious intruders at bay. As he and Jane were still officially newlyweds, the request should be respected.

Or at least he hoped it would.

The gossip mills were surely grinding at full speed with the news that Lord Garson had finally chosen a bride. The fact that nobody knew the lady in question would only stoke the fever of curiosity. He doubted Jane had noticed the stares—she was too in alt with her new dress and the novelty of a night out in London to see much beyond her immediate company—but he had.

He passed Jane a glass of champagne from the tray the footman had brought in before he took up guard duty. She accepted it and took a sip, as she looked around the sumptuous red and gold interior. "I'm glad we came. I got home completely exhausted this afternoon—you have no idea how tiring it is to stand still for hours while someone pins and measures and fusses. But I'd hate to have missed this."

"I commend your efforts," he said. "That gown is worthy of Helena."

With an awed expression, Jane stroked the silk skirts belling around her. The gown was in a deep shade of forest green that added a jade tinge to her sparkling eyes.

She was so happy and excited. How her restricted circumstances in Dorset must have chafed. With her wearing the height of fashion and her magnificent hair scooped up in a devilishly attractive style that seemed all loose curls, it was as if at last he saw her. How on earth had he dared to call this vivid woman a mouse?

Jane Norris wasn't born to fade away in some backwater. She was born to reign like a queen. She hadn't recognized it yet, although she was visibly pleased and surprised at the difference becoming clothes could make. But he'd noted enough glances toward their box to know that Jane's days of obscurity were numbered.

The change sparked a fleeting sadness. He had fond memories of the shy girl he'd married. But he couldn't begrudge her the coming success. It was like watching a butterfly emerge from its cocoon and unfurl wings in all the beautiful colors of the world.

"Madame Lisette made this dress up this afternoon as a special favor so I'd have something nice to wear to the theatre. Oh, Hugh, you should see my ball gown for tomorrow night. I intend to dazzle."

"You do," he said with perfect sincerity. He smiled at her. Whatever else he felt about her transformation, he was dashed glad that those nun-like frocks were a thing of the past. "There's not a woman here who can hold a candle to you."

She took his hand. Once she'd been reluctant to touch him. No more. "You're being kind again."

"Not at all," he said. "Just don't tell Helena what I said."

Her lips twitched as she released his hand and picked up her champagne. "She's been kind to me, too. And West has requested a waltz at the Oldhams'."

Hugh gave a mock growl. "Well, save me the other one and the supper dance. I don't want to be the sort of husband who can't get near his wife in a crush."

He and Jane hadn't danced together since those awkward childhood lessons. The prospect of twirling around a ballroom with his lovely wife in his arms was deuced appealing.

She gave a snort of laughter. "You're such a wag. You'll probably have to dance with me all night to save me wilting away with the wall-flowers."

"I promise to come to your rescue if you can't find a partner, darling," he said, knowing that outcome wasn't likely. He had a sudden memory of how cranky he'd been about Jane becoming the focus of masculine attention. But he couldn't wish her first ball to be a disappointment. That would be too petty.

"Is that the done thing, to dance with the same man over and over? I'm woefully out of practice, but before Papa fell ill, I occasionally went to the assemblies in Lyme. A girl was compromised if she danced with the same partner more than twice."

He laughed. "That doesn't count with husbands, sweetheart. The world knows I've well and truly compromised you." Under the cover of the back of her chair, he trailed his hand down her spine and briefly cupped the lush roundness of her rump. She shivered with sensuous enjoyment as he slowly drew away. He'd like to do more but damn it, they were in public. "Just in case you're not sure about that, shall I compromise you again when I get you home?"

"Yes, please." She leaned forward, eyes alight. "Would it cause a scandal if I kissed you?"

"Do I care?"

"Behave yourself, you two," Helena said from behind them. Garson had been so focused on Jane, he hadn't heard the door click open as the Wests returned.

"Killjoy," he muttered, but he sat back and drank some more champagne. "How are the Kinglakes?"

"Avid with curiosity about Jane. They were most put out that you introduced her to us first. I've asked Sally to tea on Friday, Jane. Would you like to come? Sally's great fun, and she'll have plenty to talk about, as they've just spent the winter in Rome."

"Are there any Caravaggios left south of the Alps, or did Charles buy them all?" Garson asked.

West smiled. "I gather the Kinglake art collection has a number of impressive new additions."

Garson turned to Jane. "Charles Kinglake has a famous art collection. We must go and see their new pictures while we're in Town."

"And Charles asked if Jane will save him a contredanse at the ball."

"That's a relief," Jane said. "I was afraid nobody would dance with me. Now I have Hugh and West and Sir Charles."

Helena's snort was dismissive. "My dear, don't waste time worrying about sitting on the sidelines. When the beau monde get a look at you in that red dress, you'll need a whip to beat off the eager partners."

CHAPTER TWENTY-SEVEN

*H*elena's remark proved prophetic.

From the moment Jane set foot in the Oldhams' lavishly decorated ballroom, she felt like the heroine in a fairy story. At the theatre, she'd caught a glimpse of the ton *en fête*, but nothing prepared her for the sophisticated, stylish, glittering crowd jammed into this huge white and gold space. She entered a magical place, where violins played sweet music, the scent of lilies and orchids filled the air, and jewels sparkled like legendary treasures.

She'd been grateful to Helena for introducing her to Madame Lisette. But on this, her first foray into high society, she came to understand quite what a massive favor her friend had done her. The deep red dress clung to her body in a way that had made her self-conscious in the shop. She'd protested at how low it was cut across her bosom, but the others had talked her out of choosing something more modest. Her courage had received its reward when Hugh's eyes lit up at the sight of her before they left Half Moon Street. For a few fraught seconds, she'd wondered if he meant to escort her to the ball, or whisk her upstairs into bed.

The red should clash horribly with her hair, but even Jane recognized that the color was superb on her. It made her look like a sensually confident woman, instead of a frightened girl. It made her look the way she felt when she lay in Hugh's arms and until this moment, had never felt anywhere else.

Still, Cinderella must have been nervous before that fateful ball. So was Jane. She couldn't help contrasting herself with the drab, careworn creature she'd been at Cavell Court. That sad woman would never put on such a flamboyant gown and set out to stake her proper place in the world.

Butterflies swooped and dipped in her stomach when she ventured into the ballroom at Hugh's side. Then she lifted her chin and summoned all her pride. She was Cedric Norris's daughter, with a bloodline going back to the Norman Conquest. She was Hugh Rutherford's wife. She had every right to join this daunting new milieu.

Even without her new friends' warnings, she'd known that she'd be the cynosure of all eyes. Not only was she a new face, and the daughter of an earl, but she was also Lord Garson's bride. It was soon apparent that the denizens of this brilliant world held Hugh in high esteem. The woman he chose was of abiding interest, not just because of the old scandal with Morwenna, but because people were genuinely fond of him. Everyone she met expressed the warmest good wishes for her happiness.

Sooner than she'd dreamed was possible, her terror subsided, and she started to enjoy herself. All night, gentlemen besieged the new Lady Garson, vying to dance with her. She'd thought Hugh was being kind, when he reserved two dances ahead of time, but soon she was glad he had. Because flattering as it was to have all these elegant fellows clamoring for her attention, the only man in this throng who meant a jot to her was her husband.

Now at last it was time for the supper dance. She thanked her most recent partner, Sir Charles Kinglake, and turned to watch Hugh approach, tall and striking in his somber black. To her mind, her husband was the handsomest man here, with his classic features and chiseled jaw. His face reflected his character and goodness. Her heart did one of those strange little somersaults, as she reminded herself she was married to this superb man.

He smiled with the mixture of tenderness and affection that always turned her brain to custard. Her heart stopped flipping like a landed trout. In fact, it stopped altogether. The chatter and music and frenetic activity receded into a strange, echoing silence, so when her heart stumbled back to life, all she heard was the throb of blood in her ears.

"Has my wife got time to dance with her poor, neglected husband?" he asked, holding out one white-gloved hand.

"I might be able to fit you in," she said lightly, curling her fingers around his.

When Sir Charles bowed, the candles cast a sheen over his coffee-colored hair. "Garson, I haven't had a chance to congratulate you on your marriage and wish you both well. Lady Garson is utterly delightful."

"Thank you, Sir Charles." To her surprise, she didn't sound flustered. In fact, she sounded as though she was accustomed to spectacular gentlemen calling her delightful.

She had a brief recollection of the dull, lonely life she'd planned for herself after her father's death. Instead of respectable and stultifying spinsterhood in some shabby seaside resort, here she was at the heart of society, being treated like a princess and making wonderful new friends. What a lot she owed to Hugh. He really was her knight in shining armor.

"Thank you, Charles," Hugh said. "I'm a very lucky man."

He even sounded like he meant it. Feeling like a shaken champagne bottle, with happiness fizzing up ready to spill over, Jane let Hugh lead her onto the dance floor. The orchestra played the introduction to a cotillion. She wished it was a waltz, then reminded herself she and Hugh would waltz later.

She'd whirled the evening away with a stream of partners, but she reached a stage where she hungered for her husband's nearness. In the last few weeks, his touch had become an addiction.

As they took their places in the square, she stared up into his eyes and saw them darken with intent. "Are you desperate to dance, or may I take you out for a walk on the terrace?"

Susan had told her about enough balls for her to understand that "walk" was a euphemism for "privacy." How delicious. She smiled at Hugh. "Did you read my mind?"

"It happens with married couples. My parents never needed to finish a sentence."

"How very...economical," she said drily, while the idea of such intimacy squeezed her susceptible heart.

Hugh bustled her through the French doors before she had a chance to offer her excuses to the other dancers. The night outside was mild for March, but still cold enough to discourage guests from lingering. Flaming torches lined up along the balustrade, turning the large garden below into a region of mysterious shadows.

Jane laughed as Hugh tugged her toward an alcove around the corner of the building and out of sight of the ballroom. He rushed her across the flagstones so fast, she felt like her red satin slippers barely skimmed the ground. "Where's the fire?"

He hauled her into the darkness. "If I told you, I'd shock you," he muttered, as he backed her into the wall.

The saw of her breath betrayed her excitement, then she forgot to breathe altogether when Hugh's mouth crashed down onto hers. Searing heat stole all thought, and after a startled hesitation, she kissed him back. With a rumbling growl of satisfaction, he set to driving her mad.

By the time he pulled away, her knees felt like wet string. She sagged against the cold stone behind her and gazed up at him. In the darkness, she could make out his high cheekbones and that determined jaw.

"I should take you back inside." He leaned his forehead against hers. "You must be freezing."

The places he didn't touch were cold. Where he touched, her blood pumped hot. "Let's stay a moment longer."

He wrapped his arms around her and pulled her into his body. "Is that better?"

She felt surrounded with Hugh. "Yes."

They stood without speaking, and her soul fluttered down to lie easy in a way it hadn't all night. Gradually she became aware of sounds apart from the music and laughter from inside. The rustle of leaves in the breeze. The tinkle of a distant fountain. The call of a night bird.

"I've missed you," he muttered. "A pox on all those blockheads who insist on dancing with you."

His mocking self-pity was amusing, but even nicer was the note of sincerity beneath the humor. "Do you mean that?"

"I do, although there's some consolation in knowing you're coming home with me." He firmed his grip until her breasts squashed into his chest. He was crushing her lovely dress, but she didn't mind. "Are you enjoying your triumph, my darling?"

She loved it when he called her his darling. It made her all gooey, like toffee toasted in a fire. "Oh, yes. Your friends have been so kind to me." She pulled away and pressed one hand to the ruby and diamond necklace she wore. "Thank you again for my present. I love it."

Before they left Half Moon Street, Hugh had come into the bedroom just as the new maid Peggy finished dressing Jane's hair. He'd been carrying a flat leather case, which he'd presented to Jane after Peggy had gone. What she'd found inside had robbed her of words. A glittering array of gems, fashioned into a necklace, a bracelet, earrings, and pins for her hair. She'd blinked back tears of poignant emotion, as she'd stared down at his magnificent gift, and wondered just why she was crying. Even now, with Hugh's big, strong body sheltering her from the cold, the memory of her overpowering and puzzling reaction to his present lingered.

"On this special night, I wanted you to wear something bought just for you," he said, as he rested his chin on her hair and tightened his embrace against the cold. "You're welcome to use any of the family jewels, but I hope you'll treasure my small tribute to how happy you've made me."

"Oh, Hugh..." she said, lost for words, and feeling like crying again. Which was stupid when she should be ecstatically happy.

She'd long ago accepted that he was a romantic—only a dyed-in-the-wool romantic would pine so long for a lost love. And presenting her with that extravagant gift had been a romantic gesture, however unromantic their dealings might be. Yet some instinct made her keep that revelation about his character to herself. She didn't want his past sorrows intruding on her evening. More selfishly, she didn't want to shift his focus to Morwenna in a moment when his thoughts were all for his wife.

"I haven't bought you nearly enough presents. Clearly it's a lack I need to make up for."

"Every man should have a hobby." Although her sentimental heart still overflowed, she mustered a light tone. "If you want to shower me with baubles, I approve."

"I thought you might," he retorted. "We'll need an extra carriage for all your finery when we head back to Derbyshire."

"When do you plan to go?"

"Whenever you like. But I thought you might want to enjoy the season first."

She rested one hand on his shoulder. "I do, but I'm also looking forward to starting our real life."

"I am, too, but we can spend a few weeks being frivolous. It's time you had some fun, Jane. Let me—" He stopped abruptly and shifted closer, taking them both deeper into the shadows.

"Here you are, George. I've been searching all over for you." The woman's voice was warm with tolerant affection.

"Just sneaked out for a cigar, my love," the man said. "I'll be inside to dance with you any moment." The couple were out of sight around the corner, although within earshot of where Hugh and Jane stood.

"Well, you'd better hurry. The supper dance is nearly over."

Jane caught the faint tang of tobacco on the air. She hoped to heaven the man had just arrived. The thought of anyone eavesdropping on her conversation with Hugh made her cringe.

"You've danced with me a thousand times since we married. Surely the thrill is gone."

"Never," the woman said with a touch of irony.

Jane buried her face in the front of Hugh's crisp white shirt, as his hold tightened in reassurance. She didn't fancy the idea of being caught kissing in the shadows like a naughty maidservant. Although at least the man she kissed was her husband.

"It's Lord and Lady Frame," Hugh whispered.

The man's voice had sounded familiar and Jane realized she'd promised him a quadrille later in the evening. He was a bluff, middle-aged man, and she'd rather liked him when they were introduced. Right now, she wished him to Hades. And his wife, too.

"Perhaps they'll move on," Hugh murmured. "It's too cold to hang about."

No such luck. "It's so hot in the ballroom, I almost appreciate this brisk air," Lady Frame said.

Lord Frame gave a grunt of amusement. "Brisk? It's colder than a witch's tit."

"Then why the devil are you out here?"

"My darling, we've been married twenty years. You must know that when a chap needs a puff, he'll brave any weather." He paused. "Can I interest you?"

"George, think of the scandal if anyone sees me."

"There's nobody around, Delia."

A silence fell, presumably while Lady Frame shared her husband's cigar. How Jane wished they'd be convivial somewhere else. Hugh's nearness kept the worst of the chill at bay, but her feet threatened to freeze to the paving.

"What do you think of the bride?" Lord Frame asked after a few moments. "Before tonight, everybody was saying she must be the greatest fright in Christendom. Garson seemed determined to hide her away from society, which only fueled the rumors. But it turns out she's a comely wee thing."

Jane felt Hugh go rigid against her. She placed a placatory hand on his cheek and shook her head. She didn't want him to rush out to defend her honor and draw attention to their rendezvous.

The woman laughed. "Not so wee. She just looks that way because Garson's such a big brute."

"Not to mention a lucky dog."

"That he is," her husband breathed in Jane's ear, making her skin tingle with awareness.

"A fitting rival to the beauteous Morwenna," George went on. "And the bride's clearly done him good. He doesn't look nearly as hagridden as he did a month ago. He's been like a parson at an orgy, ever since the spectacular Mrs. Nash threw him over in favor of her husband."

Like the fall of an ax, Jane felt the exact moment Hugh's arms dropped from around her. He was as taut as a violin string. The sound of Morwenna's name shattered the atmosphere of delicious conspiracy between them.

It also shattered the shell of deluded happiness that had lasted all night. All week. She'd been acting like a giddy girl, madly in love with her new husband. She'd been acting like she was Hugh's first choice and not a glorified broodmare, here to provide him with an heir.

An heir that might already be growing in her womb. After all, nobody could accuse Hugh of shirking his duty, when it came to begetting the next generation of Rutherfords.

Feeling suddenly awkward, she lifted her hands from his shoulders and placed them over her stomach. Not to shelter the place where a baby might lie, but because her insides curdled with nausea.

The awful thing was she had only herself to blame for her current misery. Hugh had never tried to deceive her about their marriage.

"Yes, she's pretty, and that's a beautiful dress she's wearing. Someone clever has been giving her advice about how to make her mark in society." Pity infused Lady Frame's voice. "But I feel sorry for her. I think a lot of people do. Everyone knows how mad he was for Morwenna, and I doubt he's changed his affections. I saw his face the night Robert Nash came back. I've never seen a man so heartbroken."

"What a sentimentalist you are, Delia. Men love the woman who shares their bed."

"George, I despair of you, I really do," she said. "After all our happy years together, that's the best you can do?"

"I'm a simple creature, my dear. Most fellows are." He paused, then went on in a low voice. "And you've always filled my bed to my complete satisfaction, so never doubt that I love you."

"And I suppose I love you," she said ruefully. "Not that you deserve it. Now pass me that cigar."

Another silence fell. In an agony of awkwardness, Jane waited for the couple to go back inside. She was cold and wretched, and she wanted to get away from Hugh, before he guessed quite how rattled she was. Amidst the ballroom's bustle, she might have a chance of hiding her unhappiness.

"Time to do the pretty, my love," Lord Frame said. "May I have this dance?"

"What's left of it."

"I think they've gone," Hugh whispered after a minute or so.

When he placed his hands on Jane's waist, she struggled not to stiffen. She had no right to resent her husband's love for another woman, especially when he'd given her so much over the last days. Sensual pleasure. Companionship. The beginnings of a contentment she'd never expected.

He'd given her too much. If he hadn't encouraged such physical and emotional intimacy, she wouldn't at this moment feel like drowning herself in one of the Oldhams' fountains.

"Shall we take up where we left off?"

She gave him credit for sounding almost normal. But she couldn't forget how he'd frozen in her arms at the mention of his beloved. What a woman Morwenna Nash must be, Jane thought with uncharacteristic spite. Clearly once she sank her claws into a man, he never broke free.

And she, too, had to try and sound as if nothing important had happened. As in any real sense, it hadn't. The whole world, including Jane, knew her husband loved Morwenna. She might have briefly forgotten that salient fact, but she and Hugh remained bound together until death did them part.

"We've been outside long enough." She struggled to smooth the edge off her tone. "This isn't the weather for an al fresco tryst. Lovely as it was." She just about choked on the last four words, although the sad truth was it had been lovely. Up to a point.

"I'm sorry, Jane. Of course I'll take you inside. You're so cold, you're shaking."

It wasn't the air that made her shake, but she went along with the lie. "I'll meet you back here in June."

"That's a deal." He leaned in, clearly intending to kiss her.

Despite all her stern words to herself, she tensed. How could she bear to feel his lips on hers, when his heart remained chock full of another woman? She told herself she would come to terms with this. She must.

But she needed a little time.

At the last minute, she turned her head so his kiss glanced across her cheek.

She hoped he wouldn't notice, or if he did, he'd think the evasion was accidental. But she felt him go as still as a stone, then slowly straighten.

"Let's get you into the ballroom before you turn into an icicle." He sounded like the polite man who had proposed to her, not like the passionate lover who shared her bed with such enthusiasm.

Jane told herself that was a good thing. She could maintain some emotional distance from the first man. It was so much more difficult to maintain any detachment from the second one. She'd just had a salutary reminder that if she didn't keep a corner of her soul for herself, she headed for devastation.

"I'll warm up, once I'm dancing again," she said, her voice heavy with unshed tears. She shouldn't resent Lady Frame's pity, but she did, how she did. Especially when the woman had only spoken the unpalatable truth.

Hugh took her arm. "Don't forget you promised me the next waltz."

"I can hardly wait." Although right now, pretending to the world—and Hugh—that she was in alt to be his partner seemed an impossible goal.

They crossed the terrace toward the ballroom. Supper must have started. She couldn't hear any music, and the ballroom only contained a few people, compared to the vociferous multitudes earlier.

As she was about to step inside, Hugh drew her back.

"What is it?" she asked, feeling likely to shatter, but still battling to behave like the carefree creature who had sneaked out into the moonlight to steal a few kisses.

He looked deadly serious, his dark eyes searching. He didn't look like the lighthearted man who had swept her into his arms half an hour ago either. "I meant it when I said you make me happy."

She tightened her throat against a sob. This was her night. The new Lady Garson had triumphed, however crushed vulnerable Jane Rutherford might feel. She couldn't face his friends with tears in her eyes. There had already been more than enough gossip about her husband and his romantic entanglements. And the thought of anyone else saying they felt sorry for her made her want to retch.

It took her a moment to remember she still had the right to touch him. She raised a tentative hand to his cheek and dredged up what she prayed was a reassuring smile. His skin was warm through her delicate satin glove.

"Thank you, Hugh." She guessed he was waiting for her to proclaim a reciprocal happiness, but the words jammed unspoken in her throat.

He placed his hand over hers and pressed it into his face. "You do make me happy."

His tone sounded as if he countered some argument, when she hadn't said a word to disagree. In its way, what he said was probably even true. He'd certainly enjoyed her body, and she couldn't mistake his pride in her tonight.

He waited for a response, but she remained silent, staring up at him as if she'd never seen him before.

In a way, she hadn't. Odd how those moments in the darkness had forced her to take a clear view of her situation at last. She swiftly slid her hand away from his face and buried it in her skirts.

"Shall we go down to supper?" he asked, his gaze still concerned.

"Yes," she said, wishing her answer wasn't a muffled croak. She turned away, before he read too much in her face. A fortnight of marriage had taught her to beware his powers of perception.

He offered his arm, and they went inside the ballroom. Jane squared her shoulders. So what if people were talking about her husband's devotion to another woman? Nothing new in that.

But something had changed. Something momentous.

Because this evening, Jane had done more than act like a giddy girl in love, silly as that might be. When she'd listened to the Frames talking about her, she'd soon realized that she'd gone disastrously past what she'd promised her husband when she married him.

God help her, no acting was involved anymore. The giddy girl had fallen in love with a man who would never love her back.

And she didn't know how she could endure it.

CHAPTER TWENTY-EIGHT

*I*t somehow made matters worse that the first people Jane saw in the supper room were Susan and Frederick. She'd caught a glimpse of her sister through the crush earlier and meant to seek her out, but her procession of eager partners had kept her busy since then.

Jane didn't want to deal with her sister right now. Susan had a bad habit of saying "I told you so." The fact that she'd predicted unhappiness for this marriage made her a far from ideal companion tonight.

But the room was crowded, and Susan and Frederick's table had two spare seats. Jane gestured toward the corner. "Susan's over there, and she has space."

She glimpsed Anthony signaling for them to squeeze in on a table with him and Fenella, but Susan had caught her eye now and it was too late.

"Whatever she says to you, don't listen. You've made a splash, and you'll be the talk of the Town tomorrow," Hugh said under his breath, as he approached his new in-laws with a reluctance Jane hoped was visible only to her. "I'll wager she's pea green with envy that her mousy little sister has turned into a peacock. She'll tell you your dress is too daring, and your hair is too wild, and you're a shame to the Norrises."

Jane had a sinking feeling he was right. Susan had always reserved the older sister's privilege to criticize the younger. As they approached, Frederick stood with every appearance of pleasure on his unremarkable face. She'd always liked her sister's husband, although his good nature meant Susan and her horrid children bullied him unmercifully.

"I wasn't a mouse," she said, more for form's sake than because she meant it.

"Not for the want of trying," Hugh muttered, before he turned to Frederick with what she'd come to think of as his social smile. It went no deeper than the surface of his eyes, whereas when he really smiled, he revealed every inch of his generous soul.

"Good evening, Bacon. Nice crowd here." He bowed to Susan. "Susan, you're looking a picture."

Susan simpered at him from where she sat in the corner. "Thank you, Hugh. Are you and Janie planning to stay in Town? I thought you were going to Derbyshire."

Jane had learned enough of fashion, even in the short time she'd spent with the Dashing Widows as her guides, to recognize that while her sister's rose sarsenet gown was becoming, it lacked the extra touch that lent Helena's clothes such panache. The same touch Madame Lisette had given to the dresses Jane had ordered from her.

"Plans change," Hugh said evenly. "I thought Jane might enjoy some society, after so long at Cavell Court doing her family duty."

A puzzled frown crossed Susan's face, as if she wasn't sure whether he reprimanded her. Jane, who knew very well he did, kissed her sister's cheek, getting a lungful of gardenia scent for her trouble. "Good evening, Susan. How are the children?"

Luckily that launched a good twenty minutes of monologue. Lucy apparently promised to be the belle of the season, even if a head cold kept her from tonight's ball. A litany of her niece's conquests kept sisterly advice at bay long enough for Jane to dig deep into her courage and find the poise her pride insisted upon.

Susan's voice formed a background to her turbulent thoughts. She was in love with her husband. She'd been in love with him since their days in Salisbury. But she'd been too inexperienced to understand that in awakening her passions, Hugh had also captured her heart.

What a fool she was to assume she could resist him. How could he fail to win her love? He was everything she admired. Good. Considerate. Understanding. Ardent. Intelligent. Strong. It would be a miracle, if she hadn't tumbled head over heels in love with him.

Hugh was the perfect man for her. Except for one glaring flaw. He was in love with another woman. She could almost commend his steadfast loyalty to his beloved.

Almost.

But she wasn't that much of a saint. Morwenna must be a paragon. The woman had to be special to earn the unswerving devotion of such an exceptional man as Hugh Rutherford. But right now, Jane would love to claw out Morwenna's no doubt sparkling eyes and tell her to let Hugh go, so he could love again.

Stupid fantasies. No doubt even if Jane blinded her out of spite, Morwenna would retain her iron grip on Hugh's heart.

"Janie, did you hear me?"

She'd drifted off and missed the end of Susan's tale of a duke dancing with Lucy at Almack's last night. "I beg your pardon. I wasn't listening. The evening's been overwhelming. You know how quiet my life was at Cavell Court."

"I do indeed." Susan cast a glance at the empty seats at the table. Hugh and Frederick had gone in search of more champagne, so the two sisters had a moment's privacy. More was the pity. "You're not eating very much. Are you expecting a happy event?"

Jane blinked at her sister and bit back the self-pitying retort that she never expected to be happy again. She refused to let that be true, by heaven. "We're engaged to go to the opera tomorrow night with Charles and Sally Kinglake."

Susan made an impatient sound. "Don't be such a goose. Are you going to have a baby? I vow I couldn't keep down even a morsel, when I was carrying dear Lucy."

A baby? With everything else that had happened in the last hour, the idea was too momentous for her to consider.

"No, I don't think so." She swallowed a surge of nausea, as she looked down at the untouched delicacies on her plate. "We've been married little more than a fortnight. It's too early to tell."

Susan looked unimpressed. "You might have anticipated your vows."

"Susan," Jane protested, genuinely shocked.

Her sister shrugged and reached to transfer the lobster patties from Jane's plate to hers. "I would have, just to make sure of him. Hugh's one of those chivalrous types. He'd never abandon you, once he took your cherry." Her tone sharpened. "Don't look at me like that. You two haven't sat around for the last two weeks, doing nothing but hold hands."

Jane blushed, which she supposed was answer enough.

Susan went on. "I'm so glad we have the chance for a quiet word."

Here it comes, thought Jane, her bruised heart sinking even lower.

Her sister didn't disappoint her. "Where on earth did you get that dress? It's not respectable, Janie. You're new to London. You don't want a reputation."

Didn't she? She'd been careful all her life, but tonight she'd glimpsed a more adventurous path. "Lady West took me to her *modiste*. She seemed to think this gown was in the current mode."

"That explains it." Susan glanced around. Jane guessed she was checking if Hugh was within earshot. "Lady West is spoken of as an original. Why, she's considered quite the bluestocking, and corresponds with all sorts of men on mathematical subjects. Or at least that's the story."

Jane frowned. Susan implied Helena was conducting intrigues, where it had been immediately obvious to her that she was madly in love with her husband. "I like her. She and West are good friends of Hugh's. I won't hear anything against her."

This animated defense startled Susan. Usually for the sake of peace, Jane pretended to heed her sister's advice. "I'm only telling you this for your own good. You've started running with a fast crowd, who are likely to lead you astray. They already have. Papa would be appalled to see you dressed like a harlot, with your bosom on show for all the world to see. You put me to the blush, Janie, you really do."

Jane cast a glance down at her chest. The gown was more dashing than she usually wore but nowhere near unacceptable. As Hugh so unflatteringly remarked, she'd dressed like a blasted nun before she married him. "Susan, why are you trying to spoil my pleasure in my first ball?"

"I…" Susan spluttered, but Jane spoke over her, in a way she never had before.

"You know how humdrum my life has been for the last ten years."

"Don't be silly. You loved living in Dorset."

"No, it suited you to think that." Jane's eyes narrowed on her sister. "But don't you think I regretted missing out on having a season like yours? Don't you think I longed for company my own age, and new and interesting people to talk to?"

Susan looked increasingly uncomfortable. "You never said anything."

"What was the point? Someone had to take charge at Cavell Court." Aware that they were in public, Jane kept her voice low, but the strength of her feelings vibrated through every word. It was fortunate that the noise in the packed room masked this increasingly contentious discussion. "Now I'm married, and I have a wonderful husband, and the chance to do the things I've always wanted to. I'm twenty-eight, not sixteen. I won't be lectured about my clothes, or my friends, or my behavior."

Susan's face flushed, and temper flashed in her dark eyes. "I was only trying to help."

"Well, I appreciate it," Jane said, without meaning a word. "But you can leave me to make my own way in society."

Susan glanced past Jane's shoulder to someone behind her. "You should keep better control of your wife, Hugh, or she'll bring the whole family into disrepute. This unseemly rag she has on is only the start of it. You mark my words."

Jane wondered how long he'd been standing there. "Rubbish," he snapped. "Jane's a credit to the Norris name, and a credit to me as her husband. Susan, your sister is going to become a power in the world."

Anger thinned Susan's lips to a tiny red line. "I wash my hands of both of you." She looked up at Frederick, who Jane realized hovered beside Hugh. Poor Frederick. It was his fate to be overlooked. "Take me home, Frederick. I find I have a headache."

Under his receding brown hairline, Frederick's eyes were bewildered. He extended a glass of champagne toward Susan as she stood up. "But, my love, you asked me to get this for you."

"I don't want it. We are leaving." She snatched the glass away from him and slammed it down on the table so hard, champagne sloshed over the top. Jane was grateful they were in a corner and out of general view. As it was, she caught a curious glance from Caro a few tables away. She sent her new friend a subtle shake of the head to discourage her from coming over.

Jane stood. "Susan, don't be silly."

"Silly, am I?" She puffed up to her full five foot two and shot Jane a searing glare. "Let's see if you still say that, when your name has become a byword for depravity."

"It's only a dress."

"It's the thin edge of the wedge. I can see it in your eyes, that you're not the same girl you were."

"That's a good thing," Jane said bravely, but Susan swept over her comment as if she hadn't spoken.

"I forecast trouble ahead. All this attention has turned your head. You'll get yourself involved in a scandal, and we'll all be dragged in after you. Remember what I've said, when your niece can't find a husband, because no decent man will marry into a family that includes a wayward creature like Jane Norris."

"Jane Rutherford," Hugh said coldly. He bowed briefly to Frederick, who looked like he'd sell his soul to be anywhere else but here. "Bacon, Susan's right. It's time you took her home."

Hugh stood beside Jane and took her hand. "Are you all right?"

Feeling as if she'd been caught in a violent thunderstorm, Jane watched Susan sweep from the room. How could a night that began so auspiciously deteriorate into this mess?

"Yes." She paused. "No."

"Susan completely overreacted. She had no right to say what she did."

"Perhaps not."

"Definitely not. I would have stepped in earlier, but you were fighting your corner without my help."

She drew a shaky breath. "A lot of what I said has been festering for a long time."

"Would you like to go home?"

Go home like a whipped dog with its tail between its legs? Go home where she'd be alone with Hugh, and helpless to know what to do with this unwelcome, engulfing love that flooded every cell of her body? Go home where she'd have time and space to think about the emotional wilderness stretching ahead of her?

"Good Lord, no," she said decisively. "I want to stay here and dance the night away."

He looked startled. "You seemed a little...peaky when we came into supper. I don't mind leaving, if you'd rather."

She tilted her chin at a jaunty angle and stuck a smile to her face. Peaky? She refused to be so pathetic. People might feel sorry for her now. They wouldn't by the time the night ended, devil take them.

"We have a waltz coming up, and I'm promised to Silas for the contredanse after supper," she said with a wholly manufactured brightness. "I want to drink that champagne you brought. I want us to be the last to leave. Tomorrow, I want to dance again, then every night until we have to go to Derbyshire."

CHAPTER TWENTY-NINE

*J*n the coach on the way back from the Oldhams' ball, Hugh regarded Jane with a troubled frown. She sat beside him, hands lying limply in her lap and her attention focused on the street. He'd tried to take her hand when they left the ball, but she'd avoided him by making a great show of fiddling with her cloak.

Something was wrong. He'd wager every penny on it.

He thought back to those torrid, interrupted moments on the terrace. Until then, everything about the ball had been a grand success. His wife had shone bright as a star in her daring red dress. He'd witnessed the ton's astonishment when this radiant stranger entered their midst, then curiosity, and finally acceptance and approval.

Before they went outside, she'd glowed with the inner fire that illuminated everything she did when her heart and soul were engaged. After they'd come inside, she'd still sparkled like a jewel. But the brilliance had turned feverish.

Not that anyone else noticed. Jane had arrived at the Oldhams' as a complete unknown. Hugh took her home as a wild success. Gossip, most of it cruel, about the new Lady Garson had clearly filled the capital's drawing rooms for weeks. After tonight, people would continue to talk about Jane, but in tones of envy and admiration.

"Are you upset because you had a fight with Susan?"

"I'm not upset." Her voice was cool, and she didn't look away from the window.

Hell, he wished he believed her. "It was time she heard a few home truths."

"She'll get over it."

He wasn't so sure, but he'd felt like cheering when Jane stood up for herself. Especially when she'd described him as a wonderful husband.

If it wasn't the clash with her sister that troubled her, it must be what the Frames said. He recalled that odd, rather awful moment when she'd turned her head to avoid his kiss. "I'm sorry you overheard that nonsense when we were outside, Jane. People love their tattle."

She turned to look at him. Because the ride was short, the lamps inside the carriage remained unlit. Now with the dimness hiding the subtle shifts in her expression, he regretted that.

"Of course they do, Hugh." She sounded calm and sensible, the way she'd sounded when he proposed. "It's not like Lady Frame said anything we didn't already know."

"I'm sure if anyone felt sorry for you at the start of the night, nobody feels sorry for you now."

To his surprise, she responded with a huff of derisive laughter. At the ball, she'd laughed frequently, dazzling her partners. When Hugh had whirled her around the floor in the promised waltz, she'd been incandescent with gaiety. He hadn't believed it was real then. He still didn't.

"Now I'm out in society, people will realize I'm not a complete antidote. At least I hope I'm not. Or is that fishing for compliments?"

It was an attempt to stop him asking probing questions, that's what it was, but he accepted her unspoken request to keep the conversation superficial. "What a pity you broke my favorite fishing pole so many years ago. I'd forgotten all about that, until you mentioned it at Caro and Silas's. Did you enjoy your first ball?"

"Very much. Thank you for taking me." She shifted on her seat to face him. "I'm sure I was so wide-eyed that it must have been a complete bore for you."

"Quite the contrary. I had a superb time." At least he had until supper. "Apart from having to put up with all those men ogling my wife."

She shrugged, and he saw she truly hadn't registered the scale of the success she'd made. "I suspect novelty explains that. Novelty, and the fact that I polished up into something quite acceptable. After all their hard work, Madame Lisette and Helena would be disappointed if I didn't."

"Madame Lisette and Helena be damned." Annoyance edged his tone. "You were the loveliest woman in that ballroom, Jane, because you're so vital and alive and, yes, beautiful. Your new clothes only bring out what was there all the time, even in Dorset."

She made a fluttery gesture. "You're being kind again."

He was getting bloody sick of hearing that. Particularly when something in her relentlessly cheery tone hinted that for once she didn't see his kindness as an altogether positive trait. He leaned forward and kissed her, not just because he wanted to—although he always did—but to confirm his suspicion that something was amiss.

At the touch of his lips, she stiffened, reminding him of the woman who had shrunk from him on their wedding night. What the hell? He was about to retreat, when she started to kiss him back with a desperation he could taste. She twined her arms around his neck as if she held on for dear life, the way she'd cling to a branch in a flooded river to stop being swept away.

But there was no flooded river, and no chance that she was going anywhere but home with him.

Troubled anew, he pulled back and caught her wrists, bringing them down to her lap. "Jane, something's wrong. Please tell me."

A reverberant silence fell, long enough to send his imagination into a spin. Had something horrible happened at the ball that he didn't know about?

Then she took a shuddering breath and leaned forward to place a clumsy kiss on the corner of his mouth. "What could be wrong? I've just been fêted at my first ball. I finally told my sister to mind her own business. Now I'm going home with my lovely husband. I'm the happiest girl in London."

Doing it too brown, Jane. "You don't sound like the happiest girl in London."

Although she sounded like she tried to be. The amount of effort she put into the act betrayed her.

Her smile flashed in the darkness. "It's late. I'm tired. Truly, it's been a lovely night, Hugh. Stop fretting."

He caught her hands. "Perhaps we should stay home tomorrow and forget the opera."

She shook her head, the rubies and diamonds in her hair catching the light from a passing street lamp. "Oh, no, I want to go to everything we're invited to. I told you—I plan to be out every night."

He heard that same desperation he'd tasted in her kiss, but for pity's sake, he'd asked every way he knew for her to tell him what worried her. Perhaps the wise husband would wait until she was ready to confide in him. He always strove to be a wise husband.

Well, most of the time.

The carriage pulled up outside the tall, white façade of Rutherford House, and a footman ran forward to open the door. It was only when they were inside that Hugh finally got a proper look at Jane's face. She did appear tired, fine drawn with strain and something that looked very like unhappiness.

The wise husband would not pry. Especially when his attempts to help had so far met with nothing but unconvincing denials of any trouble.

"I'm sorry that a few unpleasant moments spoiled your evening," he said as they went upstairs. She held his arm, walking in step with him so their hips brushed. Why did he still feel she was on the other side of the world?

"Don't be silly, Hugh. It was beyond my wildest dreams." She sounded so bright, he winced as if he stared into the sun.

But the wise husband knew that he'd get no answer as to why his lovely wife seemed brittle enough to shatter, after the night when society had fallen at her feet.

∼

"Will that be all, my lady?" Peggy asked, collecting Jane's extravagant red gown from the bed and folding it over her arm. She'd already locked away the jewels. "Or would you like me to stay and brush out your hair?"

Jane met her glassy gray eyes in her mirror and prayed that the girl left quickly. Maintaining the illusion that she was on top of the world had given her a pounding headache. "No, I'll do that. You find your bed. I'm sorry I kept you up so late."

The girl looked startled, before she resumed the demeanor of the perfect servant. "Lud, my lady, that's what a lady's maid does."

Jane made herself smile. "Perhaps, but I appreciate it. I suspect there will be many more late nights to come."

Peggy sent her a proper smile, and the Irish accent she tried to suppress tinged her answer. "I don't mind at all. It's a privilege serving such a nice lady—and one who promises to become the toast of London. On my day off, I can lord it over the other girls."

"That's splendid." Jane summoned a smile. "Good night, Peggy."

The girl curtsied and left the toast of London to stare into her reflection and wish with a fervor only bolstered by its futility, that she was in Sidmouth with her old governess. She'd trade every one of tonight's extravagant compliments to be looking forward to nothing more exciting than a walk by the seaside.

As Hugh came through the door connecting the baroness's rooms to the baron's, Jane picked up her brush. His chamber contained a large, luxurious bed that he was yet to use. They always slept together in this room.

"Let me do that for you," he said quietly. The familiar red dressing gown covered his nakedness, and he, too, looked tired and a little downhearted.

"Thank you," she said, extending the brush toward him. If brushing her hair delayed the moment when they went to bed, he could brush her hair until Doomsday.

It wasn't that she didn't want him. It was that she doubted her ability to conceal her newly discovered love when he touched her and kissed her and joined his body with hers. Right now, she felt too raw and vulnerable to survive having her deepest feelings exposed to the light.

Without doubt, Hugh would be kind, but secretly horrified that his wife had so egregiously broken their agreement.

Then he'd start to be careful of her, because he'd hate to hurt her. She'd know it and want to die of mortification. One of the things she enjoyed about their desire was how natural it felt. She had a queasy feeling that their warm, laughing intimacy would prove the first casualty of tonight's unwelcome revelations.

Still, Jane wasn't going to give up without a fight. Perhaps if she pretended nothing was wrong, she'd convince Hugh that she was happy. Perhaps if she pretended nothing was wrong, soon nothing would be wrong.

So she made herself smile at her husband as he brushed her hair. In the mirror, she watched the strain fade from his expression as he took his time, until her hair formed a shining cloak around her shoulders. He seemed content not to speak, which suited her. The less she said, the less likely she was to betray her fragile new feelings.

His hand brushed her cream velvet robe from one shoulder, and he bent to kiss the skin he revealed. The heat of his mouth made her shiver with need, more poignant tonight than it had ever been.

"Come to bed?" he murmured.

"Of course."

He kissed her neck, until she was shaking. Raising her hand to stroke his rumpled, dark brown hair, she watched her face change in the mirror. She looked completely in Hugh's thrall.

She looked like she was in love.

That would never do. This marriage was too new to bear the heavy burden of her unrequited love. She tipped her head to give him better access to the sensitive skin beneath her ear. He slid his hands under the velvet to cup her breasts through her sheer silk nightdress.

When his thumbs brushed her nipples, she gasped and arched against him, feeling his impatient need against her back. She untied the belt of her robe and pushed it away. Against the white nightdress, the beaded peaks of her nipples were clearly visible. He groaned and pushed her breasts together. "I want you so much, Jane."

Jane caught his hands and pressed them closer to her breasts. "Don't tarry, Hugh."

And wondered if he heard the stilted note in her plea.

CHAPTER THIRTY

*L*ate the next morning, Garson woke alone in Jane's big bed. Memories of their passionate union after the Oldhams' ball rushed through him, exciting but not altogether reassuring.

Devil if he could put his finger on what troubled his wife. He'd hoped Jane would forget her strange mood when he took her in his arms. But while he'd thoroughly enjoyed what they'd done, he'd sensed an absence, even during the incandescent moments when she shuddered into climax and cried out his name with the husky abandon that always made him feel like a king.

He doubted he'd notice the distance with any other woman. But over the last days, he'd basked in a physical and, yes, emotional intimacy with his wife that was unique in his experience. Clearly marriage changed things in the bedroom.

So even with Jane stretched out beneath him and moaning with rapture, he'd known that she wasn't the same as she'd been the previous morning.

His nebulous disquiet heightened when he entered the sitting room and found Jane sitting at the table, heavy-eyed and pale-faced. She stared down into a cup of tea that smelled of ginger. The downward curve of her lips struck him like a blow.

He crossed the room to kiss her. Her lips moved beneath his with no reluctance, but no eagerness either. Worried, he pulled back and took his chair, noting the half-finished roll on her plate.

"Jane, are you well?" he asked, with more urgency than the conventional question usually warranted.

"Hugh, I've got something to tell you," she said in a flat voice.

Hell, perhaps she really was ill. Fear slammed through him like a speeding carriage and stole his breath. Last night, she'd dazzled the fashionable throng. It was impossible to find any trace of that brilliant creature in this subdued woman.

Shaking, he grabbed the hand that lay on the table near her plate. "What is it? What's wrong?"

Then staggering under another blow, he added up what he saw. The tired girl, the herbal tea, the lack of interest in breakfast. Elation made him sit up in his chair, and his grip on her hand tightened. "My darling, are you with child?"

It was all Garson hoped for. His wife by his side. A family. A future to look forward to, after years of wandering in a world where all happiness had died.

Just as quickly as his hopes rose, she dashed them to earth again. As she pulled her hand free, she was already shaking her head.

"No," she said unsteadily. "The opposite, in fact. I...I'm definitely not pregnant. I found out this morning."

That would explain her dejected air. Garson should have paid more attention when he came in, before he leaped to conclusions. "I'm sorry, Jane."

"So am I. I know how much you want a child."

He shrugged, even as he struggled to overcome his disappointment. "I'm not worried. We're having such fun trying."

Her smile was perfunctory. "You're very kind."

Kind again? He came to loathe that small word. "No, I'm not. But we've only been married a few weeks. I'd be surprised if you conceived so quickly." Despite him doing his damnedest to plant a child inside her.

Jane began to pleat the tablecloth. "Will you mind very much if I sleep alone the next couple of nights?"

Denial slammed through him, and something that felt very like hurt. "Alone?"

She avoided his eyes and stared down at the crumpled linen. "We won't be able to…"

Perhaps not. But exile to a cold, lonely bed awoke unwelcome memories of his early days in Salisbury. Even if his comfortable room here bore no resemblance to that airless cupboard at the Red Lion.

He realized with another shock that as long as Jane was beside him, he didn't care where he slept. If she wasn't there, the softest bed in Christendom felt like the cold, hard ground.

"I could still hold you in my arms." He hoped he didn't sound as needy as he felt.

She shook her head again. "That would be nice, but when this happens, I'm a restless sleeper. You really would be happier in your own bed."

He damn well wouldn't. But he could see she'd rather he left her to herself. "If you're sure."

She managed another shaky smile, and he had a sick feeling that she wasn't far off crying. The lack of a baby had really rattled her. He'd had no idea she was this eager to be a mother. For himself, he was so wrapped up in forging the bond between them, he could wait. Hell, for a couple of years if he had to.

"Thank you. It's only a few days."

He had a bleak premonition that those few days would feel like an eternity.

"You look like you wagered the family fortune on a three-legged horse." Silas stood in the doorway of Anthony Townsend's library and surveyed Garson with disapproval. "What the devil are you doing, skulking in here?"

Garson paused in pouring a brandy to shoot his old friend a glare of cordial dislike. "Go to hell, Silas."

Instead of getting the message that Garson wanted to be alone, Silas stepped in and closed the door, muffling the sound of music and laughter from the ballroom. Lord and Lady Kenwick were hosting their annual ball, and the extravagant house was infested with every blue-blooded blockhead and hussy in London. The same crowd of nitwits Garson had seen each night for the last six weeks. Since the Oldhams' ball, his wife had thrown herself into the London season with an élan that beggared Garson's enthusiasm for company. He looked back on those days when he and Jane had stayed holed up in Rutherford House with a nostalgia so powerful, it verged on painful.

He wouldn't mind as much, if he wasn't convinced that Jane's eagerness to dazzle society was firmly grounded in her wish to avoid time alone with her husband. Heaven forbid they should have a chance for a serious conversation where she might actually tell him why she'd changed toward him.

"You should be out there, fending off all the rakes and roués vying to capture Jane's attention," Silas said.

Garson stiffened all over like a hunting dog scenting a fox. "She doesn't take any of that seriously."

"Harslett is pursuing her with great purpose."

Harslett was handsome, rich, and bloody charming. The bastard. "There's nothing in it."

"How do you know?" Silas tilted one tawny eyebrow in his direction. "By the way, can I have one of those?"

Reluctantly Garson poured Silas a brandy and passed it across. At least on this God-awful night, there was the small consolation that Anthony Townsend's liquor was top notch. "Only if you drink it quickly and slouch back to where you came from."

Ignoring the command, Silas walked round to flop into one of the leather chairs in front of the fire. "By God, you really are blue-deviled, old man. Tell Uncle Silas what troubles your noble heart."

As he slumped into the chair opposite, Garson scowled at the tall man with the mass of untidy, light brown hair. "Shut up and go away, Silas."

"It wouldn't be British to leave you on your own, hunkered down like a bear in a cave."

Garson hardly heard his friend's good-natured jibe. "Is Harslett really pestering Jane?"

He didn't ask the question that really worried him. Did Jane encourage the chase? The most obvious answer to why she'd withdrawn from him was that she was attracted to another man. He'd feared such an outcome since the night he'd taken her to dinner at Silas and Caro's.

"You married a beautiful woman, Garson, old man. Other fellows trying to poach on your territory is an occupational hazard." Silas frowned as Garson downed his brandy, and the facetiousness vanished. "Dash it, Hugh, you think I'm serious. Jane isn't the sort to stray. If that's what's worrying you, you need to see for yourself. Sulking in here isn't doing you any favors."

"I'm not sulking," Garson said, resenting the childish description, and resenting even more that his reply really did make him sound childish.

Silas studied him with the penetrating intelligence that made him one of the world's greatest botanists. "What would you call it, then?"

With a bang, Garson set down his empty brandy glass. "Can't a man seek a moment's privacy, without every fool and his dog nagging at him?"

As usual, Silas proved remarkably difficult to offend. He leaned back in his chair and extended his long legs in their black trousers toward the fire. He looked completely at home, whereas Garson felt like a scientific specimen under Silas's microscope.

"Not when he retreats to his burrow in the middle of one of the season's most anticipated balls." He still spoke in that deuced reasonable tone. "Not when he's been slinking around like a sick cat for the last month or so."

"Do you think anyone else has noticed?" he asked, although he'd had no intention of admitting that Silas was right.

Silas shrugged. "You know what the ton is like, always ready to sniff out trouble, even when there is none."

Damn, damn, damn. He'd hoped his turmoil and confusion went unremarked. "There is no trouble," he said, knowing he fought a losing battle.

"Glad to hear it," Silas said peacefully, emptying his brandy glass.

"Really there's no trouble."

"What trouble could there be?" Silas's lips twitched. If the sod laughed openly, he'd earn himself a punch on that beak of a nose.

"Exactly."

To Garson's relief, silence descended. Silas rose and filled both brandy glasses before returning to his seat. Garson didn't touch his second drink, although he'd come in here, desperate for something to help him through the rest of this hellish evening.

After what felt like a long time, Garson finally spoke. "Marriage is harder than I expected it to be."

Silas, to his credit, didn't look smug—although Garson knew very well that his friend had manipulated him into confessing his worries. "Worth it in the end, though, especially with a good woman."

"Jane's a good woman."

"I know. Are you unhappy that she's become such a success?"

"She was such a quiet little thing when I married her."

"She's just kicking up her heels. I remember when Caro came out of mourning—she'd have danced all day and all night, if she could. She was making up for the time she'd wasted."

As always when Silas spoke of his wife, love warmed his voice. Hugh stifled a pang of envy for his friend's domestic contentment. "Jane's life has been so restricted until now. I can't blame her for wanting to squeeze everything she can out of her first season."

He wondered if he was alone in noting the desperation behind her endless flurry of activity. As if pausing for even a moment's reflection threatened annihilation.

"But that's not what you signed up for."

A grunt of unamused laughter escaped Garson. "Looking back, what I signed up for strikes me as completely unrealistic."

"The marriage of convenience isn't convenient after all?"

"No." Garson was well aware that the world's opinion was divided about his marriage. Some people were convinced he'd married Jane, while still in love with Morwenna. The more sentimental—bone-headed—members of the beau monde believed he loved his wife and made a new start.

"You appeared delighted with your choice when you came to dinner back in March. I know this started as a practical solution for both of you, but when I saw you together, I hoped that you might have fallen in love with your wife. That night, you certainly acted like you had."

He shot Silas a dark look. "You should know better than that. Love was never part of the arrangement."

"I'm sorry to hear that. You seemed so comfortable together."

"We were." He noted the past tense and felt like smashing something.

"Tell me—just what were you expecting, when you married Jane?"

Garson shrugged, although he felt anything but casual about his wife. "I'd pictured something like a friendship, with a bit of bed sport thrown in to spice things up."

"But that's not what you got?"

He thought he had. At first. But what intimate details could he share without betraying his wife? That was another unexpected result of married life—the way he and Jane had become a unit. Now his first loyalty was to her.

Anyway, he wasn't even sure he was capable of defining the problem. Most people would say he had damn all to complain about. In bed, Jane was endlessly cooperative. When she was indisposed, she slept alone, but she invited him into her chamber readily enough afterward. If she held something back from him, something she'd once shared, the difference was so subtle that he'd be hard placed to describe it.

Perhaps it was that these days, she never initiated their encounters. He craved the return of the woman whose sensual curiosity prompted her to take him into her mouth. She'd taken him into her mouth since, but always at his request.

And there were no more jokes about the Tower of London. There were no more jokes at all. Damn it, he missed the laughter they'd shared more than he missed anything else.

He'd feel a fool trying to explain these hazy impressions to a friend, even if he was inclined to share such private matters.

"I don't think she's happy she married me," he said in a low voice. Putting the oppressive truth into words twisted his gut into tangles of misery.

Silas looked thoughtful. "Are you talking to each other? I mean, really talking."

"We talk," Garson said. Although he knew what Silas was asking, and the answer was no, they weren't. After his wedding, he'd spent a fortnight discovering an intriguing woman. But these days, the gates to true intimacy slammed shut in his face.

And left him outside on the empty road, starving and cold.

"Good," Silas said. "Because if I've learned anything in all my years of marriage, it's that a woman's mind is a labyrinth where a man gets lost if he's not careful. You need to find out what's worrying Jane and fix it, if you want to have a prayer of making her happy."

Garson gave a heavy sigh and set aside his brandy. Liquor wasn't going to soothe his wretchedness. "I've asked her what's wrong, and she says everything's fine."

"Bugger."

When Silas looked really worried, cold terror settled in Garson's belly. "What?"

"Fine is the worst thing she could say. If she says everything's fine, it most definitely isn't."

"Perhaps I should take her up to Derbyshire. All this gallivanting might be the problem."

"Don't be a damned coward. Sit down with her and don't get up until she's told you what's upsetting her."

That was good advice if only she stopped flitting about long enough for him to catch her.

"I hate feeling so inadequate. I hate to think she regrets marrying me." Garson spread his hands in bewilderment. "This isn't what I wanted."

Silas's glance was unimpressed. "What you wanted when you married her didn't do her justice. Damn it, it didn't do you justice either. It was a blasted cold bargain."

"There's nothing cold about how I feel about Jane," Hugh snapped, bristling at the criticism, even if he deserved it. "That's part of the problem."

Silas's smile held too much pity for Garson's liking. "Having a yen for your wife is a good thing."

The damnable truth was that, despite their estrangement, Garson still wanted her all the time. He resented being at the mercy of his animal impulses. "Maybe."

"You'll work it out." Silas tried to sound encouraging. "All marriages require compromise. It's early days yet."

"Any other platitudes you want to share?" Garson asked grumpily.

"No." The pity in Silas's expression deepened. "Because I see my good advice is falling on barren ground. I wish you well, my friend. You'll muddle through. We all do in the end."

Hugh gave a noncommittal grunt and stared moodily into the fire. He'd muddle through, all right. But the devil knew where he and his beautiful wife would be once he did.

CHAPTER THIRTY-ONE

*J*ane watched Hugh and Silas return to the ballroom. Her husband always danced the second waltz with her, and whenever he did, it only sharpened her heartbreak. Every time he touched her, she thought she must crack with the force of the titanic feelings she struggled to contain.

She'd spent her life longing for a London season. Now here she was, popular beyond her wildest dreams, and she hated every moment of it.

Because the man she loved didn't love her.

She suspected Hugh was as unhappy as she was. The stiff set to his broad shoulders hinted that his casual manner was as artificial as her endless sparkle. She supposed she could ask him, but these days they only spoke about trivial matters. That was her fault, she admitted. She couldn't risk a deeper discussion, for fear that she might reveal too much.

But the strain of keeping up a constant façade was telling on her. The pretense—to Hugh and to the world—that she was blissfully happy was draining every ounce of vitality. She felt like she was nothing but a dried-out husk. How much longer could she continue? Pride was all that sustained her, and it grew more tattered by the day.

Hugh bowed to her. "My dance, I believe."

"I wondered if you remembered." She took his arm and let him lead her onto the crowded floor. "I looked for you and couldn't find you."

They turned to face each other. He looked exceedingly handsome in his evening clothes, the crisp black and white setting off his chiseled features. Somehow that just made Jane feel worse. He was so fine inside and out, and having to live without his love was a constant torment.

"I'll always remember you," he said. The gentle words only increased the weight of misery pressing down on her heart. He cared about her, she knew he did. But it wasn't enough. "I was talking to Silas in the library."

She sniffed and tried to sound teasing. "And drinking Anthony's brandy."

He smiled, but compared to the smiles he'd once given her, this was a mechanical effort. "It's too good to pass up."

The violins took up a lilting melody. Hugh's arm curled around her waist, and his gloved hand caught hers. She set her other hand on his shoulder and started to move in time with him.

Once, his touch had been paradise. No more. It only reminded Jane of what she couldn't have. Oh, how she hated her stupid heart for wanting more than he could give her. She wished she could rip it out and go on without it.

Still, she must endure. They were in public, and she owed Hugh an appearance of amity. She lifted her head and fixed a smile to her lips. Most nights by the time she went home, her jaw ached with smiling, when all she wanted to do was crawl away into the dark and cry.

Jane tried to lose herself in the swirling movement, to recapture some of their earlier ease, but it was impossible. She was too aware of his hands on her and how he cursed the fate that placed his wife in his arms and not Morwenna.

"You're very quiet," he said, after a while.

Her feet naturally followed his, without her having to think about it. After all, he'd been her first dance partner. Warily she glanced up at him. "I'm a little weary."

A little weary? The effort of hiding her feelings, not to mention all the late nights, and the endless tossing and turning when she finally got to bed, left her feeling like a wrung-out rag.

"Jane," he said, and the edge in his voice alerted her that for once, this wouldn't be some polite banality, "would you like to go up to Derbyshire? There's nothing to keep us in London. Not really. You haven't seen the house in years, and it's beautiful there with spring coming on." He paused, then went on with an urgent sincerity that made her heart cramp. "We could spend some time alone together, away from all this flummery."

Oh, God, give her strength. The last thing she wanted was to be alone with Hugh. But on the other hand, she was reaching her limits as the queen of society.

She swallowed to moisten a dry mouth and said in a low tone, "Let me think about it."

"Please do." His grip on her waist tightened. "I want to have you to myself again. I want what we found in Salisbury."

"We've still got that," she said, knowing it was a lie. "You share my bed every night."

And she could hardly bear it. Because the desire between them, however powerful, was a mere counterfeit of what she really wanted.

She could never have what she really wanted.

He frowned, and regret sliced her heart when she saw his disappointment. "Yes," he said, not sounding convinced. "Think about Derbyshire. A few weeks in the country would do you good."

While she was convinced that a few weeks in the country would dissolve the threadbare truce that kept her marriage together.

But Hugh was right. The way they went on was untenable. She rapidly ran short of both pride and endurance. Something had to change—and if change meant utter destruction, right now, she almost welcomed that.

Her touch on the back of his neck was tender with unspoken love, all the more poignant for being forbidden. "Yes, let's talk about it tomorrow."

"Lady Garson, your ladyship."

As Jane stepped into Fenella's airy morning room a couple of days after the Kenwicks' ball, she found her friend playing with her children, Henry and Emily. A tan and white beagle puppy gamboled toward her with a high-pitched yelp and a madly wagging tail.

"I do beg your pardon, Fen." Clearly she'd interrupted some private family time. Flustered, she turned away, eager to leave. "You're busy this afternoon. I can come back another day."

Fenella rose from her chair, the book she'd been reading to her seven-year-old daughter dangling from one hand. Dark-haired Emily had inherited her dynamic father's striking looks, whereas Henry had his mother's classic features and golden coloring.

"No, Jane, come in." The blonde woman raised her free hand to smooth the stray strands of hair escaping her simple knot. Jane had never seen Fen less than perfectly turned out, but today her pink muslin gown was crushed and showed traces of puppy paws and a nursery tea. She gestured to the toys scattered across the priceless Aubusson carpet. "As you can probably tell, we weren't expecting company, but it's always lovely to see you."

"I was just passing, and I thought I'd call in." Not true. She'd set out, hoping to catch Fenella on her own. She liked all her new friends, but she felt a particular affinity with Fenella. Perhaps because unlike her stubborn clodpoll of a husband, Fenella had learned to love again. Or perhaps because Fenella's quiet strength was something she desperately needed right now, as she struggled to find a way forward in her marriage. "I didn't mean to intrude. I'll see you this evening at the Jamesons' musicale." She struggled to sound enthusiastic about yet another party.

"No, please stay. The children will play in here, and we can go through to the drawing room." She sent nine-year-old Henry a minatory glance. "The first sign of a quarrel between you two, and it's back to the schoolroom and Latin translation. And don't let Milo chew the furniture, or your father will hit the roof."

"Papa likes Milo," Emily said, darting forward to pick up the squirming puppy and clutch him close to her chest.

"He won't, if every chair in the house is only fit for firewood," Fen said sternly, then turned to Jane with a brilliant smile. "Jane, take me away from this madhouse."

Jane soon found herself clutching a cup of tea and sitting beside Fen on a green brocade sofa. She looked around the pretty room and struggled not to sound too envious. "This is such a happy house. You can feel it."

"Thank you." Fen smiled and nibbled at a sugar biscuit. Jane's biscuit balanced on the edge of her saucer. She hadn't touched it. Lately food stuck in her throat. Her glamorous new dresses all hung too loose on her. "When I married Anthony, everyone except my closest friends was convinced it was the mismatch of the century, especially as we'd only known each other a few weeks. It's been nice to prove all the old biddies wrong."

"You're lucky," Jane said, staring down into her cup.

"Yes, we are." Fenella's emphatic tone was surprising, coming from someone who looked as fragile as a Meissen shepherdess. "People predicted disaster for Anthony and me, just as they predicted it for you and Garson."

Jane's eyes flashed up in shock. "We trot along all right."

Fen looked skeptical, as she took the cup and saucer. "Give me that. You're just playing with it. I'm really glad you came to me today, Jane. I've wanted to talk to you for weeks, and it's hopeless trying to find a private moment at any of the crushes we've attended." To Jane's relief, she began to sound a little less militant. "Am I wrong in thinking you need a friend?"

Jane hadn't arrived with any plans to confide her troubles. She'd just felt a craving for some undemanding company to distract her from endless brooding on her hopeless and destructive love.

"I believe we're friends," she said cautiously. The ton was a hotbed of gossip. Much as she liked Fenella, she wasn't in a hurry to spill her secrets.

As if she read her mind, Fen sent her a straight look. "You can tell me to mind my own business. Usually I do. Interfering is much more in Caro or Helena's line. Anyway, I expect I can guess most of the trouble."

Jane frowned. "I didn't say there was trouble."

Fen's glance was unimpressed. "You don't have to. If you lose any more weight, poor Hugh will have to buy you a whole new wardrobe, and you work too hard showing everyone you're having a good time to actually be having a good time. You look more brittle than that delicious sugar biscuit—which I might point out you didn't deign to taste."

"You...you're very frank." Jane stood up, her knees shaky. This attack wasn't what she'd sought. "I can see I shouldn't have come."

"Don't go. Please." Fen caught her hand, before she could turn away. "You think I'm rushing in where angels fear to tread. But I hate knowing you're unhappy."

Jane was so close to breaking, the friendly gesture had her blinking back tears. "Is it obvious?"

"No, not at all. Most people wouldn't have a clue." She tugged Jane's hand. "Sit down. Have some more tea."

"I've spent my whole life hungering for some excitement," she said, subsiding back onto the couch. "I envied Susan so much because she had a season, while I missed out."

"Now you're a grand success." Fenella paused. "Yet it doesn't matter a fig, because you're in love with a man who loves someone else."

Jane's breath caught on an audible gasp. "I can't talk about this."

"You should. It would do you good. You can trust me, you know. I'd give anything to see Garson settled. He's had a rum time of it and behaved like a complete hero throughout."

"And all he has to show for his gallantry is a broken heart and a loveless marriage," Jane said bitterly, before she thought to stop herself.

Fen's eyes were searching. "Are you sure it's loveless?"

"Well, I love him," she admitted. Just saying the words aloud to someone, even if it wasn't Hugh, felt like shifting a boulder off her soul.

Fen smiled. "Of course you do. But isn't there any chance he loves you?"

"When he proposed, he told me that he'd always love Morwenna Nash."

The name she'd come to hate hurtled into the conversation with a crash.

"My dear, I'm sorry." Fenella's lovely face glowed with compassion. "When I met you, he was obviously in alt that he'd married you. You seemed so perfect together."

Jane shrugged, unable to force any words past the jagged lump in her throat. She and Hugh were perfect together, but he remained too mired in past disappointment to see that. Honestly, sometimes she wanted to bang that noble head against a wall until he saw sense.

She swallowed, then swallowed again, before she could ask the question that had tormented her since her marriage. "Please, can you tell me what she's like? Nobody ever says. They just speak her name, then pause as if they're in the presence of something holy."

"You poor thing." Fenella looked appalled. "Your imagination must be running wild."

"It's like fighting a ghost," she said in a reedy voice.

Fenella squeezed her hand. "We all got into the habit of protecting Morwenna, after the news that Robert had died in a skirmish at sea. They were so in love, and she couldn't move past her grief."

"You did."

Fenella sighed. "It took me a lot of years to start living again. You don't shake real love off in an instant."

"No." Jane was discovering that, much as she wished it were otherwise.

What a lot of misplaced love the world contained. Morwenna longing for Robert. Hugh longing for Morwenna. Fenella longing for her first husband. Jane longing for Hugh. It was like a childhood game of chase, if one ignored the broken hearts littering the playground.

"We were all delighted, when she and Hugh became engaged. He's a good man and perceptive enough not to push her too far too fast."

Hugh *was* a good man. Jane braced to ask the question that she'd never been brave enough to ask her husband. "Do you know if Hugh and Morwenna were lovers?"

Fenella pondered before she answered. "I don't believe so. In fact, I'm almost sure not."

Jane shouldn't be relieved to hear that. After all, the problem was his spiritual connection with his beloved, not anything physical they'd done. But nonetheless she was pleased.

Fenella went on. "That's part of the problem. Garson never got to know Morwenna as a real woman with all the normal imperfections."

"In his mind, she's like an exquisite painting."

"Yes. That makes it frightfully hard to live up to her image, I'm sure. And he's such a knight in shining armor. Morwenna's tragic loss made her doubly appealing, even if she wasn't so beautiful."

Of course Morwenna was beautiful. Fairytale princesses awaiting rescue from their towers always were.

"He's always collected lame ducks, right from when he was a boy." Jane sighed. "You could say I'm another lame duck. When he proposed, my father had died, and I was facing some unappealing choices after my cousin inherited my home."

"You're a very different woman from Morwenna, Jane."

"Which doesn't help."

"Nonsense. Hugh and Morwenna weren't meant to be. Morwenna never stopped loving Robert, and now they're together and blissfully happy. Hugh has no hope of winning her back, even if honor permitted. You're here. She isn't."

Jane's lips turned down. "I'm here with all my faults."

"All your warmth and gaiety and beauty."

She shook her head. "It's not enough."

"Have you asked him if he still loves her?"

"No." She shuddered at the idea. "I'm afraid to mention her name."

"That only makes her more powerful," Fenella said sharply. "I love Morwenna dearly, but she's not superhuman."

Jane shook her head again and pulled free of Fenella's comforting hand. "In Hugh's heart, she is superhuman. I can't bear it." Her voice broke on the last words, and she turned away toward the windows. She didn't want Fen to see how close she was to breaking down.

"Jane?" Fenella asked, in sudden concern. "Are you all right?"

Jane fumbled for her handkerchief and dried the few stubborn tears she couldn't stanch. She turned back to Fen. "It's impossible, living with a man who loves someone else. Every moment feels like a punch in the face."

"Oh, my dear…"

She stood on unsteady legs and stepped away from the sofa. If Fenella touched her in sympathy now, she really would lose control. If she did, she'd cry into next month. "I don't know what to do."

Fenella's delicate features hardened in determination. "First, you must find out if you need to keep fighting this battle. Hugh feels something for you. That's clear to everyone who cares about him. I'd hoped it was love—or at least its beginnings. But you say not, and you're in a better position to know."

"Love wasn't part of our arrangement," Jane said bleakly.

Fen made a dismissive sound. "Arrangements change as circumstances do. Believe me, when I met Anthony, the last thing I wanted was a new husband."

Jane considered Fenella's remark. Was she torturing herself over a phantom? "You're right. All this silence only gives Morwenna more space in my marriage."

"You won't believe me, but if you met her, I think you'd like her. Most people do."

Jane doubted it, although she was well aware that the real Morwenna wasn't the same as the idealized Morwenna who set such a wedge between her and her husband. "I'd probably scratch her eyes out."

Fen gave a huff of laughter. "Then it's a good thing she rarely comes to Town."

Jane hardly listened. "What do I do if I ask him, and he says he can never love me?"

That was the likely outcome, she knew.

"Then you have some thinking to do." Fenella stood up next to Jane and placed her hand on her arm. "If you need a friend to talk to or some neutral territory to make your decision, I'm always here. Remember you're not alone in this, Jane. You have somewhere to go."

Curse it, she was going to start crying again. Jane blinked back prickling tears and forced a wobbly smile to her lips. "Thank you, Fen. I don't deserve your kindness."

"Of course you do." Fen smiled back, but concern clouded her blue eyes. "I'd give anything to see you and Garson resolve your problems."

CHAPTER THIRTY-TWO

When Garson emerged from the bedroom the morning after the Jamesons' dull musicale, he was puzzled to see Jane in the sitting room. Over recent weeks, he'd mostly breakfasted alone, then taken a long ride in Hyde Park. His wife's late rising made perfect sense, given the hectic life she led. But he couldn't help thinking that she lingered in bed to avoid him.

The sight of her lifted his mood. Perhaps she waited to tell him that she wanted to go to Derbyshire. He'd come to loathe London, which was strange as he'd always loved it before these last weeks. The prospect of a few quiet months at Beardsley Hall beckoned like heaven. But he'd be damned before he abandoned Jane to her admirers, while her husband limped away like a beaten hound. He and Jane left together, or they stayed to finish this purgatory of a season.

"Good morning," he said, hoping against hope that he was right about Derbyshire.

He tightened the belt of his dressing gown, then sat and poured himself a cup of strong coffee to clear a thick head. Although last night when he got home, he hadn't done much beyond go to sleep. If Jane had shown the slightest interest in bed sport, he'd have responded with alacrity. But he was sick to the stomach of making all the running.

"Good morning, Hugh," she said without smiling.

She wore a pretty light blue gown, and behind her, the window was open on a lovely day. Spring had arrived since they'd come to London. Unfortunately the bright sunlight revealed Jane looking tired and drawn. His spirits fell as swiftly as they'd risen. This wasn't a woman anticipating a rural idyll.

Although he supposed in its way, her subdued manner was an improvement. Lately she'd been as glittering at home as she was in society. It wore him out. He couldn't imagine that maintaining the relentless cheerfulness was any easier on her. Especially as he knew damn well that it was all an act.

He hated to see her looking as downcast as she did this morning, though. As he'd grudgingly admitted to Silas at Anthony and Fenella's ball, he was conscious that so far, he made an utter hash of his marriage.

"Have you had breakfast?" he asked, seeing the crumbled roll on her plate. Lately, she didn't eat enough to keep a sparrow alive. It hadn't missed his notice that the blue dress hung more loosely than it had last time he'd seen her wear it.

"Yes, thank you." Her perfect politeness reminded him of the large-eyed little girl she'd been, getting under his feet and suffering a bad case of hero worship. Devil take it, these days he'd give his right arm to be her hero again. He had a disagreeable suspicion that he'd proven a vast disappointment as a husband.

"I wondered if you could spare me a few minutes this morning," Jane said, as though she addressed a stranger. "There's something I'd like to talk about."

He scowled at her. "You're my bloody wife, Jane, not a tenant in arrears with the rent. You don't need to make an appointment to see me."

Garson regretted his outburst the moment he made it. He regretted it even more when she flinched as though he'd hit her. "I'm sorry, Hugh. We've both been out and about so much, I thought I should check if you'll be here."

"Out and about" really meant staying out of each other's way. How in hell had all the passion and laughter they'd shared led to this point? "No, I'm sorry. Would you like to talk now?"

Jane began to pleat her napkin. When she fiddled with the table linen, it was always a sign that she was troubled. "No, I'll see you in the library, once you're dressed and ready for the day."

"This sounds serious," he said, trying to make her smile.

The gray eyes she raised to his were as dull as a cloudy sky. "Yes, I rather think it is."

Shaken, he watched as she stood and left the room without another word.

He stared after her in consternation. What in Hades was going on? Was she about to confess some wrongdoing? Silas had mentioned Harslett pursuing her. Was that by way of a warning?

Surely not. Jane wanted him. He'd wager his whole fortune that she did.

But did that mean she couldn't want another man as well?

The thought of his wife in someone else's arms made his empty stomach churn. He'd feared this, almost expected it. But not this soon. They'd only been married two months. She couldn't have tired of him already.

Couldn't she? Something was wrong. Had been wrong for weeks. Like a blockhead, he'd hoped the trouble would blow over. Now he couldn't mistake the ax poised over his head, ready to fall.

His hand slammed down on the table, setting the china rattling and a knife bouncing to the floor. Be damned if he'd give up without a fight.

~

Within half an hour, Garson was downstairs. Only to find his wife already waiting in the library.

His gut knotting with inchoate dread, he paused in the doorway to study her. As she sat on the couch and stared into the fire, her expression was desolate. This wasn't the glamorous beauty who set society in a spin. She looked, in fact, like a better dressed version of the wan creature he'd called on in Dorset. His gut gave up twisting. Instead, it constricted with creeping, freezing fear.

He'd promised to make Jane happy. Given what he saw now when she believed herself unobserved, he'd abjectly failed. Guilt rose until it tasted like bile on his tongue, and he shifted on his feet.

The movement alerted her to his presence, and she looked up. "Hugh, you're early."

"So are you," he said, grimly noting that she didn't even try to smile.

He checked her hands, but they weren't doing their nervous dance. Jane was still and composed—and that suddenly seemed the most worrying aspect of all. He stepped into the room and closed the door behind him. He was so on edge that the click of the latch rang like a death knell in his ears.

He moved to sit beside her, but she stopped him with a curiously truncated gesture. "No. Please. Sit...sit over there."

With bad grace, he shifted to where she indicated. The chair was a few feet away, yet he felt like she exiled him to Siberia in the depths of winter. Only when he sat did he realize that the light streaming through the window lit him like he was on a stage and left Jane in the shadows.

"What the devil is going on, Jane?" His roiling panic flared into annoyance. He folded his arms and scowled at her. "You look like you're about to make a dreadful confession."

Her mouth flattened in dismal acknowledgment. "I am."

That rancid feeling in his gut turned nastier than ever. She didn't look like she was joking.

"Is it someone else?" To his shame, he sounded like he suffocated.

Jane's eyes were like mirrors. The pause before her answer shredded his heart into ragged gobbets. Until this moment, he hadn't really believed she'd taken a lover. Yet why the hell wouldn't she? It was clear that her husband didn't make her happy.

His raging bitterness almost made him miss her soft response. "I suppose it is."

Garson's world turned black as pitch, and the blood in his ears pounded like an angry ocean. "Jane?" he asked through the gathering storm.

He wasn't even angry—yet—the hurt was too grievous. He started to rise on unsteady legs, but she made another of those keep off gestures, and he slumped back into his chair.

"Hugh, if I ask you a question, will you answer me honestly?"

He felt disoriented, awaiting a disclosure, not this calm inquiry. Despite everything, he just couldn't believe that she'd gone to another man's bed. "I've always been honest with you."

He hoped to hell it was true.

Another of those bitter little twists of her lips. "Yes, you have."

A longer pause that felt like the silence before an execution. When her question came, it was from such an unexpected direction, it left him at a loss.

"Are you still in love with Morwenna Nash?"

He lurched to his feet. "What in Hades..."

The temper that flashed in her eyes was the first sign that Jane wasn't as self-possessed as she strove to appear. "Please answer me."

"Has someone been talking?" His brows lowered, and he glared at her. "I warned you there would be gossip."

Her gaze remained uncompromising. "Answer my question."

Garson ground his teeth. He hated talking about Morwenna and his old engagement. To date, the greatest failure in his life. Although his marriage promised to become a fiasco on an even grander scale.

"I told you when I asked you to marry me..."

Jane rose abruptly and stepped forward into the light. He bit back an appalled exclamation. She looked strained to the point of breaking, her features bleached white beneath the deep red banner of her piled-up hair. "Yes, you did. But a lot has happened since then. I wondered if you'd changed."

"I don't change," he said flatly, even as with reluctance, he visited the shrine in his heart where a beautiful black-haired woman would always reign. Did he love Morwenna? Of course he did. "'Loyalty unto death,' remember?"

Jane's expression didn't alter. She still looked like she faced the gallows. But somehow he knew that a light inside her had flickered into darkness. She twined her hands together at her waist, so tightly that her knuckles turned bloodless. "That's what I thought."

Gradually he found his feet in this bizarre conversation, and his brain began to link the facts together. He should be relieved she wasn't confessing to taking a lover—by God, he was. But he found no consolation otherwise. "What's all this about, Jane?"

She lowered her shoulders and met his eyes. The misery he read there made him flinch. "I thought perhaps if you didn't love Morwenna anymore, there might be a chance you could come to love me."

He recoiled as if she'd cursed him. His foreboding, building over weeks, gathered into a great crashing wave of denial. He bloody well didn't want to hear what came next, although he had a queasy feeling he already knew what that would be. "That's damned—"

"Because I've gone and done a really stupid thing, Hugh." She went on as if he hadn't interrupted. Then she spoke the words that forever dissolved the fragile, spun sugar confection of their life together. "I've broken every promise I ever made. I've fallen in love with you."

CHAPTER THIRTY-THREE

*J*ane observed Hugh's appalled reaction to her stumbling confession without surprise. Which didn't stop a great tattered rift splitting open across her heart. It was the nature of love to hope, even when nothing justified that hope. But she couldn't mistake his horror at hearing of her feelings for him.

Because he'd loathe hurting her, he swiftly masked his immediate rejection. Compassion softened his handsome features, and he stepped forward and reached out for her. "Jane, I'm so sorry."

She stumbled away, bumping into the wall behind her. "No, don't touch me."

He flinched, but at least he lowered his hands to his sides. "I said when I married you that…love wasn't on the table."

Her stomach clenched to hear the way he could barely pronounce the word "love" in her presence.

"Yes, you did." It was an effort to keep her voice steady. Her eyes were dry enough to sting. She felt as desiccated and lifeless as desert sand.

He made a bewildered gesture. "Are you sure?"

"Don't insult me," she said sharply.

"It's just—"

"It would be so much easier if I didn't love you, I know." She swallowed to relax a throat tight enough to hurt. "I've spent weeks telling myself the same thing. But it's no use."

He paused before he spoke, and she saw he started to connect the clues to how she'd changed. "This is why you've been...distant."

During these last weeks, they'd come together over and over, but he was right. Now she had something precious and fragile to protect, caution smothered all generosity and openness. And without generosity and openness, the joy they'd found in each other had swiftly shriveled away. "Yes."

"What can I do? I hate to think of you being unhappy."

She dredged up the courage to speak the truth. "You could love me back."

In all this vile, agonizing morning, the vilest, most agonizing moment was this, when his face inexorably closed against her. "That's not possible."

She spread her hands and spoke urgently, knowing she wasted the effort. "We could be so happy together, Hugh, if you let go of your hopeless longing. We get on well. We want each other. We have a similar view on the world. Together we can build a fulfilled life, a family, a future where we grow old together in deepening affection and respect."

"Nothing stops us from having those things, Jane." Hugh looked dreadful, stricken and broken, but she gave him credit for trying. "You know how fond I am of you."

She bit back a whimper. "Fond" was a brutal punch to her solar plexus. "We can't have those things if I love you, and you love someone else."

His hands bunched at his sides. "You're asking too much."

"No, I'm not." Her voice hardened. "My fault is that I didn't ask for enough in the beginning."

Anger darkened his features. "Are you saying I cheated you?"

He had. He still did. But she saw he'd never understand.

"I was wrong to believe that I could live without love."

His face contorted. "Why?" he asked savagely. "If I can bear it, why can't you?"

His bitterness made her want to sink into the floor. "Hugh…"

But what could she say? They were trapped in mutual misery, both stuck with inconvenient, immovable loves that would sour the rest of their days.

Breathing unsteadily, he swung away to flatten his hands on the desk. He hunched his shoulders and hung his ruffled dark head. It broke her heart to see him looking so defeated. Unthinking she stepped forward to offer comfort, but stopped before she touched him.

"Jane, I'm sorry this has happened." His voice was so deep, it vibrated in her bones.

"So am I." She wished to heaven she could change. There was no point wishing Hugh would. This fraught interview demonstrated that he was as bewitched as ever.

A weighty silence crashed down. Eventually he raised his head and turned to face her. "We must go on."

She shook her head. After seeing Fenella, she'd reached some painful decisions. Confessing her feelings to Hugh was only the beginning, and she suspected far from the hardest part.

"I can't live like this."

He jerked back as if she'd hit him, and she saw him finally turn his mind to what these weeks had been like for her. "I'm sorry."

"You keep saying that."

"What else can I say?"

I love you, Jane. She shoved aside the futile wish. "I've put you in an impossible position."

"I'll do my best not to hurt you."

"That will hurt me more than carelessness," she said sharply. "We can't spend every minute guarding our words and actions."

"Then what do you suggest?" Impatience lengthened his mouth. "You seem to forget that we're tied together for life."

Her turn to wince. He made that sound like a death sentence— which she supposed it was. It was certainly death to anything that felt like gladness or hope. "I don't forget," she said flatly. "I suggest...a separation."

He swore on a deep growl. "By God almighty, you won't leave me."

She'd known he wouldn't like her idea. If only because once again, he'd be caught up in a scandal. London's most famous rejected suitor suffered another rejection, this time from his wife. Any man's pride would revolt at the prospect.

"We can arrange it so we avoid gossip." She paused. Since arriving in London, she'd come to know this world he inhabited better than that. "Or mostly."

"Good Lord, girl, I don't give a rat's arse about talk." A muscle jerked in his cheek. "Let the rattlepates wag their tongues into the next century. I only care that you don't want to stay with me."

She didn't believe him, but she appreciated his attempt to save her pride, if not his own. "I'll retire to the country. That's nothing note-worthy. Plenty of men come to London without their wives."

"Do they indeed?" His voice struck her like a whip. "And what the devil do you do when I go home to Beardsley? Hare back to London like we're playing some stupid children's game?"

She bore up under his anger. After all, from his point of view, she'd spoiled everything. He must want to strangle her. Worse, the news of her love struck him completely unprepared, while she'd had time to winnow their limited choices.

"I won't be at Beardsley Hall." The thought of living somewhere redolent of Hugh's presence, even when he wasn't there, made her stomach heave.

"So where are you going? To Susan? To Felix?"

"After our last quarrel, I'm not sure Susan would have me. And the last thing Felix wants is his cousin moving back to the estate she once ran."

"You seem to be out of options, don't you?" Given he so rarely used sarcasm, this cut to the quick. "You'll have to stay with me, much as you despise the idea."

"Hugh, you'll be better off if I leave you." She struggled to steady her voice. "Think about it. Life's been bad enough these last weeks. It will only get worse. Already, what's happening between us is breaking my heart and driving you to distraction."

Tears edged Jane's shaky inhalation. Last night when she'd rehearsed this scene in her mind, everything had proceeded much more smoothly. She'd laid out her position, and Hugh had responded like the reasonable man he was. If he said he couldn't love her, they'd calmly and sensibly discuss a divided future.

She'd never imagined she'd have to deal with a wounded lion. She knew that Hugh didn't love her before she asked the question. As expected, he'd made his rebuff more than clear, but that didn't stop him snarling at her for wanting to leave and all but roaring his pain aloud.

"Being without you will drive me to distraction," he said, his beautiful voice harsh.

If only she could believe that. "I don't expect you to stay faithful."

Saying the words nearly killed her. While for all the good they did toward placating him, she might as well have saved herself the trouble.

His anger, barely suppressed, flared again. "Well, that's bloody marvelous, isn't it? I have my wife's permission to become an adulterer. What a treasure I unearthed when I married you, Jane."

When he'd said that before, he sounded like he meant it. Hearing this distorted version shrank her heart to a tiny pebble. She extended a shaking hand to clutch at the back of the sofa. Unless she held onto something solid, she'd crumple into a heap.

"Stop it," she said through stiff lips. "You're not helping."

"And you'd really like me to be helpful," he jeered, folding his arms. "Tell me the rest of this brilliant scheme. I'm all ears."

She struggled for composure. "If you'll still pay my pin money, I can revive my original plan and find cheap lodgings somewhere."

Her suggestion, well meant as it was, made him angrier. It seemed everything she said only made him angrier.

"Tea and good works, and tucked up in bed by nine every night? After taking London by storm, you expect to be happy with that?"

Jane's lips tightened against the urge to cry. Her instincts screamed that if she betrayed any weakness, she'd never escape him. "I don't expect to be happy."

Narrowing his eyes, he stepped closer and held out his hands. His tone softened, and his expression turned pleading instead of belligerent. "Then, don't go, Jane. I won't have my wife rotting away in genteel poverty, just because I didn't have the sense to keep her. I can't bear to think of you eking out your days all alone in some mean little room."

Oh, dear God, this was worse than his rage. "Hugh, I can't stay," she said huskily, praying she could resist him. "You must see that."

He prowled near enough to catch her hands. His touch always had such power. Now it shuddered through her like an earthquake. Soon this touch that had brought her alive would only be a memory. Without it, she feared she'd die of longing.

"You've fretted yourself into a state," he said, his rage gone as if it had never existed. This was the voice of the man who had given her pleasure night after night. "I know you're upset and confused. But we've only been married a few weeks. Don't throw away everything we have, for the sake of a chimera. Let me show you that what we've built can be the foundation for a lifetime of happiness."

Devil take him, he was so persuasive. The alluring voice. The firm grip on her hands. The affection warming his expression. For an instant, she wondered if she was being a fool. Perhaps she should settle for what he offered. A share in Hugh's life might be better than nothing at all.

Hugh's head lowered and drawn like iron filings to a magnet, she leaned toward him. Anticipation rippled through her, softened her hard-won resistance. He was about to kiss her.

He loved Morwenna.

Heaven help her, if she didn't break free now, she'd never find the will to leave. Suffering would eat her away, the way maggots ate at rotten meat. The last few weeks, she'd nearly gone mad, thirsting after what she could never have. As she'd told him, she had no expectation of happiness in the years to come, but if she didn't have to see him every day, perhaps somewhere in the distant future she might find a measure of peace.

"No..." she sighed, before she went rigid and wrenched free. Her voice sharpened. "No. I can't live with you, knowing you're in love with someone else."

His jaw firmed. "I can't change my heart."

"I can't either." She stiffened her shoulders and met his eyes, as she gathered the dogged determination that had carried her this far. "I'm leaving today, Hugh."

"Today?" Shock tightened the skin on his face and turned his features ashen, giving her a hint of how he'd look as an old man. "You've already gone behind my back and chosen your hideaway? Damn you, that was quick work. So nothing I can say will change your mind about going?"

He was back to sounding angry. But she'd reached a pitch of anguish where she just wanted this over with. "No," she said miserably.

"Damn you, Jane, that was shabby."

It had been, but she didn't see that she'd had any choice. "I need somewhere to go."

"Where?" One large hand made a sweeping gesture, as if he brushed away the whole blasted mess. "You know I'll be worried sick about you. However upset and fed up you are, that would be cruel. And you're never cruel."

Determined not to cry in front of him, Jane bit her lip until she tasted blood. The urge to relent hovered so close to the surface. While she was convinced that leaving Hugh offered her only hope, a large part of her wanted to say she'd take any crumbs he deigned to give her. Even though she knew she'd starve to death on such short rations.

"Fenella and Anthony are letting me use the dower house at the Beeches, while I decide what I do next," she said in a faint voice.

"The devil they are." His anger reached another level, the new quietness of his tone indicating just how furious he was. "You've told them about us?"

She knew he'd feel betrayed. "I needed help, and I couldn't think of anyone else to turn to."

"You could have turned to me, Jane," he said, and the infinity of pain in his words sliced at her like razors.

She struggled to continue. "Fenella won't gossip, you know that. She's told Anthony I need a short rest from the social whirl."

"He'll think you're bloody pregnant," Hugh said sourly.

Which brought up another delicate, but essential matter. She'd rather discuss this when her husband was his even-tempered self. But she couldn't think when that would be. After today, there was no hope of resurrecting the easy friendship that she'd cherished.

What a trail of destruction their marriage had wreaked. How she wished she'd said no when Hugh proposed. She almost had. She'd feared she ventured into a world of pitfalls beyond her imagining.

She'd been right.

Which was no consolation, when she stood here with her heart in jagged pieces. "I'm not pregnant."

"I know."

"Or at least I think I'm not." She stiffened her spine, until she feared it must crack. "I'll write and let you know."

"Big of you."

She ignored that. Right now she needed to concentrate on getting the words out, before she lost her nerve. "I promised you an heir."

Impatience darkened his face. "Not very likely when we're leading separate lives, is it?"

Stupidly she felt herself blush. "The Beeches isn't far outside Winchester. It's not an impossible distance from London."

"You're offering to let me keep my marital privileges?" His eyes flared, although she saw he remained suspicious of this sudden concession. "Damned sporting of you, Jane. In that case, stay here. That would make more sense."

Jane shook her head. "No." She straightened her shoulders and braced for more anger. "I mean...I mean that I'll stay in Hampshire and lie with you once a month, until you plant a child in my womb."

"I see." The corrosive cynicism returned to his expression. "And if the baby's a girl?"

What if it was always girls? What if there was no child at all? She shoved away her fears that this plan was bound to fail. "Then the arrangement continues until I have a son."

He clearly also thought it was bound to fail. "This is madness."

"Perhaps." It was the best she could do, while keeping any chance of staying sane. She cheated Hugh of a wife. She couldn't deprive him of the heir he desperately wanted, too.

His eyebrows arched in haughty disdain. "What about all that tomfoolery about loathing my company?"

She shuddered. This was the worst of it. She'd hoped she wouldn't have to explain her intentions in so many words.

"I'm not planning a...seduction, Hugh. Your visits will be purely utilitarian."

Jane saw the precise moment he understood. His eyes went glassy and dead, and he wrenched back as if she disgusted him.

It might be better if she did, she thought bleakly.

"I...see."

She knew he did. And he'd never forgive her.

Hugh went on with corrosive bitterness. "You're back to offering me what you offered me on our wedding night. No pleasure, no real connection, just a quick swiving to get the job done."

She hid a wince at his frankness. "Yes."

"I didn't accept this then. What the devil makes you think I'll accept it now?"

"Because it's the only offer I'm making," she said flatly, desperately wishing this was over.

His lips curled in an unamused smile that made her shudder. "You've been busy working everything out. I'm impressed."

She flinched under his biting tone. "I believe it's for the best."

"That's apparent." Although it was still morning, he strode to the sideboard and poured a large brandy. Only the faint clink of the decanter on the glass hinted that his hands trembled.

"I hope one day you'll understand," she said weakly.

His glare conveyed the contempt that sniveling remark deserved. He raised his glass in her direction. "To you, my dear wife, and to future understanding."

Tears ranged so close to the surface that her eyes burned, although she saw far too clearly how profoundly she'd wounded him. She'd never imagined he cared this much.

Oh, Jane guessed that his pride would smart when she left him. But something about his desolation as he swallowed the brandy in one gulp and slammed the glass down on the mahogany hinted that his pain stabbed deeper than masculine ego. She ventured toward him, although what comfort could she offer, other than giving up her plan to escape this impossible situation?

With a bow cold enough to make her shiver, he retreated out of reach. "I wish you a safe journey to Hampshire, madam, and I'll hold myself at your disposal for when you require my services."

She'd never thought kind, generous Hugh Rutherford could sound like that, as though he intended every word to pierce her skin. She swallowed an agonized whimper and backed toward the door.

It was time to go. She'd already done more than enough damage. For the first time, she let the aching depth of her love fill her voice. "Goodbye, Hugh. May heaven keep you."

Jane didn't wait for his reply. She couldn't bear to witness his suffering. Nor could she any longer maintain her pretense of strength.

Blindly she turned and on trembling legs, stumbled from the library.

CHAPTER THIRTY-FOUR

Garson rode up to the pretty Queen Anne dower house on the Townsends' country estate outside Winchester. Around him, spring flourished. Tender green covered the trees. Birds sang their hearts out. A gentle breeze whispered promises of summer to come.

Unfortunately he was in no mood to hear. For him, life was all freezing winter.

A sour brew of self-hatred, trepidation, and, much as he resented it, uncontrollable longing stewed in his belly as he dismounted from Lysander's back onto the gravel drive. No groom emerged to take his horse, but the door at the top of the short flight of limestone steps opened to reveal his wife.

His heart crashed against his ribs, winding him. Every other turbulent emotion died away to nothing, as overpowering sorrow closed his throat. He hadn't seen Jane in a month, not since the day she'd told him she loved him, then packed her bags and left. He'd missed her like the very devil.

So many times, he'd nearly broken the rules she'd set and pursued her. Then he recalled her stark expression as she'd claimed she could only hope to find happiness away from him, and he'd resisted the impulse. He'd done her more than enough damage—and she didn't deserve any of it.

What sin had she committed? She'd fallen in love. He better than anyone knew that love made its own rules.

As she came down the steps toward him, his pulse broke into a headlong gallop. He hadn't expected her to seem like a stranger, but she did. A lovely, distant stranger in a pretty yellow dress he hadn't seen before. A red-headed woman with a composed air that caught him off balance. He'd wondered—hoped—that their separation weighed as heavily on her as it did on him.

Not very worthy, perhaps, to want his wife to suffer. But he'd endured a hell of guilt and rage and remorse since she'd gone. Not to mention a gnawing sexual frustration that threatened to make him claw at the wallpaper.

If she was happy, then it was more than likely she'd never come back to him. He couldn't face that possibility.

"Good afternoon, Hugh."

Her serenity grated on nerves already stretched to breaking. It just felt so wrong that they should come together in these circumstances. The raging storm of loneliness and hurt inside him felt ready to explode like lit gunpowder, while she sounded the way she had when they were nothing more to each other than childhood friends.

"Don't you have any bloody servants?" He'd arrived, determined to uphold his good intentions. Those good intentions outlasted that cool greeting by precisely five seconds. "It's damn shabby of Fen and Anthony to leave you to fend for yourself."

In fact, everything about the Townsends' interference was damned shabby. What right did they have to meddle in a man's private business? He had a nasty suspicion that Fenella had fostered Jane's plans to leave him.

Much too soon after Jane's departure, before any scar tissue had grown over his wounds, he'd fronted the Townsends and accused them of butting in. Harsh words had been exchanged, and as a result, a coldness had arisen between him and people he'd always considered good friends.

Not that he cared much. Compared to the loss of Jane, what did his quarrel with Anthony and Fenella matter?

Now he noted that his surliness didn't rattle this woman who was much closer to prim Jane Norris than that passionate creature, Jane Rutherford. "I sent them away. I thought you'd prefer privacy for your visit."

Admitting she was right didn't improve his humor. "My summons, you mean," he snarled.

Because he wasn't angry about the absence of servants. Or about her measured reaction to his arrival. He wasn't even angry because he had to ride all this way to bed his wife. Once. Then ride home again, even more frustrated—if that was possible. In any right universe, Jane would sleep beside him every night, and he'd exercise his husbandly privileges whenever the impulse took him.

He was angry because she'd gone away, and he had a horrid feeling that she was never going to come back.

His hand crept up to cover the inside pocket where he'd shoved the letter she'd sent to invite him here. When he'd first read it, he'd wanted to burn it. But somehow it had ended up nestled next to his heart instead. Damn it, he didn't know why he even kept it. It was no billet-doux.

My Lord...

She didn't even address him as Hugh, curse her.

As I have no happy news of a forthcoming event to share, I will expect you this week. Perhaps Tuesday afternoon? If this arrangement meets with your approval, I will await you then. If not, I am at your disposal any other day you wish to nominate.

Yours respectfully

Jane.

No expression of affection. Not even an inquiry after his bloody health. He'd received more effusive letters from his tailor.

He'd wondered if letting his wife spend these weeks away from him might convince her that she was better off returning to him. But so far, the yawning chasm between them seemed even wider than it had in London. She'd drawn herself up behind walls that he couldn't assail, and that fact made him want to roar his fury and despair to the skies.

"Hugh, you seem out of sorts." Jane's regard was impressively steady. "Would you prefer to postpone our meeting?"

"I've been traveling for three days," he retorted. "No, I don't want to postpone our meeting."

"So long? When I came down, I managed the trip in a day."

"I stayed overnight in Winchester," he said coldly, even as a humiliating schoolboy flush heated his cheeks.

That chilly little note had been his first contact from his wife since her departure. He'd been so desperate to see her, he'd set out far too early on Sunday, then remembered she'd said Tuesday. If he turned up on Monday, he risked alienating her altogether. He'd stopped at a flea-bitten inn about thirty miles from London, then last night, he'd had to cool his heels in Winchester until it was time to leave for his appointment.

"Oh," she said, clearly puzzled.

"I didn't want to arrive too exhausted to perform," he responded nastily.

Part of him stood back, appalled at his churlish manners. He'd always been lauded as the perfect gentleman. Even when Morwenna left him, he'd behaved well. Right now, not even his best friend would accuse him of behaving well.

Hell, given how Silas had sided with the Townsends over this farrago, his best friend would call him an unmitigated boor. Jane had always had this ability to pierce through his civilized shell to the primitive man beneath.

"I see," she said, blushing, too. "I'll take you to the stables, and you can look after your horse."

The poignant reminder of her sweet innocence as his bride only made him feel worse. He struggled against his urge to seize her up in his arms and kiss her until she admitted that she'd been wrong to leave him.

"Thank you."

She cast him an uncertain glance, as if she didn't trust his courtesy.

Who could blame her? He noticed, too, how she kept her distance, as they went around the back of the house to the stable yard. She'd studiously avoided all physical contact when she greeted him. No handshake. Definitely no kiss.

The memory of kissing that lush, pink mouth slammed through him like a cannonball. Even straight and stern as they were now, those lips were as alluring as ever. He stumbled on the cobblestones, dragging on the reins and making Lysander toss his head in protest.

"Are you all right, Hugh?"

In silent apology, he patted Lysander's glossy ebony flank. "I just missed a step, that's all."

They entered the stables. A pretty chestnut mare poked her head over a stall gate and whickered a welcome.

"Nice horse," he said to break the oppressive silence.

Jane paused to rub the chestnut's nose and whisper some nonsense. Garson was in such a bad way, he felt jealous that a horse could make his wife smile. It was a talent far beyond his meager powers.

Guilt emerged dominant from the roiling stew of emotions in his gut. He'd promised to make her happy and instead, he'd broken her heart.

"Fenella and Anthony lent her to me." She leveled a troubled gaze on him. "Fenella said you didn't appreciate them offering me their help."

As he led Lysander into a stall, Garson bit back a torrent of heated invective. "I was annoyed that they encouraged you to leave me."

The understatement of the year.

"They didn't. Don't blame Fenella and Anthony for our problems. You and I both know things couldn't continue as they had."

His belly knotted with anguished denial, as he began to unsaddle Lysander. Jane sounded so certain that the decision to abandon him had been hers alone, and that she'd been right to make it. Perhaps she was. Even his jaded eyes saw that she looked in better form than she had in London. Still lovely, of course, but the brittle air had vanished.

Whereas every time he glanced in a mirror lately, he felt like he'd aged another ten years.

Living with him had clearly come close to destroying her. How he wished he could change that. But he had a sick feeling that it was too late to make amends.

"When you're finished, come back to the house," she said. "The first door on the left off the landing leads to your room."

Garson paused in unbuckling the girth and straightened to stare at her in shock. "My room?"

Had he mistaken what Jane offered him today? Was she inviting him to stay? His battered heart swelled with excruciating hope.

She retreated a pace. "I thought you might like to wash and have something to eat before..."

Bugger and blast. Hadn't he learned by now that hope was always a mistake? "Before I do my duty?"

Damn it, there was no dignity in playing the deserted husband. This was worse than those days after Morwenna left him. But then, Morwenna had never worked herself into every facet of his life the way Jane had.

To do his wife credit, she responded calmly enough to his barbed question. "Yes. I'll be waiting in the next room. When you're ready, come to me."

"You've got it all worked out, I see," he bit out.

She didn't wince. Her self-control started to worry him. In his more optimistic moments, he'd wondered whether seeing him after these weeks apart might weaken her resolution. After all, she claimed to love him. Surely she'd missed him, even just a little bit.

But he found no chink in this woman's armor, no hint of indecision that offered him a chance to lure her back.

And despite repudiating her love, he ached for her return. He'd spent every day of the last month feeling like someone had taken a saw and amputated a leg or an arm. Yet now, in Jane's presence, however unsatisfactory their meeting, he felt whole again.

Odd but undeniable.

"Next time, we can organize things differently, if you like," she said with more of that deuced detachment, as if she discussed an afternoon walk instead of how she'd give herself to him. "Perhaps you'd prefer it if I came to your inn."

"I'd prefer it if you came home," he growled, heaving the saddle off Lysander's back and setting it on the wooden barrier dividing the stalls.

"You know that's not possible," she said, and be damned if he heard any trace of regret in her tone.

"I know nothing of the kind." Before she could argue, he went on. "Shall we dine afterward?"

There were already oats and water in the stall, so he took up the saddle cloth and began to rub Lysander down. Not that the short ride from Winchester had tired the magnificent brute.

"Hugh, I thought you understood," Jane said, eyeing him as if he might cut up rough. "After you've…finished, you have to leave."

"What?" he asked, baffled. "When do we talk?"

She met his gaze, her eyes opaque. "We don't."

Garson dropped the saddle cloth and stared at her in consternation. "I want to know how you are."

Her lips firmed. "I'm well."

Good for her. "I'm not."

"I'm sorry to hear that."

She didn't bloody sound it. He wasn't angry now. He was sad and lonely, and deathly afraid that he'd blundered about and ruined something that could have been marvelous. "Is this really what you want?"

Her delicate jaw set with the stubbornness that he'd learned, to his cost, could match his. "I'm not going through my reasons again."

"Come home to me, Jane. Forget this nonsense." He abandoned pride to admit the shameful truth. "I miss you."

Her pale features were so set, they could be carved from alabaster. "Have you changed?"

He knew what she wanted to know, but nonetheless he tried to weasel out of answering her. "I'll never take you for granted again."

She wasn't fooled. "You know what I'm asking."

He did. She wanted to know if he was still in love with Morwenna.

He considered lying, but in the end, that assessing gray stare undid him and his threadbare strategems. "I haven't changed," he said miserably.

"I thought not," she said in a carefully neutral tone and turned to leave the stable. "I'll see you upstairs."

"You know," he said in a harder voice, sick to his stomach of playing the villain in this scene, "a monumental attack of the sulks isn't likely to persuade me to love you."

Jane stopped without turning. Her shoulders were straight as a ruler, but the white nape of her neck under the weight of coiled red hair was strangely vulnerable. God above, how he wanted her. He damn near died of wanting her.

"I'm not trying to manipulate you into caring for me, Hugh," she said in a quiet voice. "You can't make someone love you, as you should know better than anyone."

He hid a wince. The jibe was low, but justified.

She went on before he could dig himself any deeper into a hole. "If I'm to go on, I have to find a small corner of sanity."

By driving me mad, he wanted to say, but didn't. Feeling awkward and useless, he watched her walk out of the shadowy stables and into the bright sunlight.

CHAPTER THIRTY-FIVE

*J*ane sat in a low-backed chair beside the bedroom's unlit fire, waiting for her husband and praying she could do what she must.

Meeting Hugh again cast her into such confusion. She'd missed him so much. She'd missed his presence in her bed. More, she'd missed his company. His sly humor, and sweet teasing, and kind understanding.

When she first saw him today, she'd had a job concealing her dismay. He looked ill, pale and strained. The deep lines running from his nose to his mouth added a forbidding sternness to his features.

The urge rose to enfold him in her arms and tell him everything would be all right.

She was glad she'd resisted. After almost a month at the Beeches, she started to feel her life was her own. Years as her father's nurse, six months as a grieving daughter, then the whirlwind of her marriage had left her fragmented and on edge. The estate's quiet beauty knitted together a few of the holes in her soul.

Five minutes in her husband's company, despite his uncharacteristic testiness, wrecked her artificial calm and hard-won contentment as if they had never existed. Proof of his power over her. Proof also that she couldn't go back to playing his second-best bride. It would annihilate her. Condemning herself to a future where the man she loved was a few feet away while endlessly out of reach would be purgatory.

A soft knock on the door indicated Hugh was outside. She beat back a poignant memory of all those nights in Salisbury when he'd slept in her bed. "Come in," she said in a shaky voice.

He opened the door. She'd feared he might be naked, but he kept his breeches on and his white shirt hung loose around his hips. His long, elegant feet were bare.

When he saw her in her corner, he frowned. "You're dressed."

Clearly he didn't approve. She bolstered her courage and made herself stop pleating her skirts. If only she didn't have to do this. But she owed him a child.

"I'm not wearing any drawers." She hoped he didn't hear how her voice squeaked.

"Very efficient." This bitterness was new since she'd left him. He'd taken her desertion so badly, much worse than she'd ever expected.

He crossed the room and took her hands. She started at the contact, as she'd started on their wedding night.

She waited for this sardonic stranger to treat her roughly. When he'd arrived, he'd been in a foul mood. But when he drew her up to stand before him, he was gentle.

"You're not even going to let your hair down?" he asked softly.

She stared into his unforgettable face. The eyelids lowered over his brown eyes in a way that was familiar from a hundred seductions. If he touched her as if he cared, when they both knew he didn't, the travesty of what they did together would become unbearable.

"This is...this act is for you to get a child, Hugh." Just as he no longer sounded like he had a grudge against the world, she sounded tremulous and unsure. Like a bride again.

He raised her hands and set a kiss on each set of knuckles. Her wedding ring glinted in the dim light. "Must it be just that?"

Longing swept through her like wildfire. His tenderness posed such a danger. This was how she'd tumbled into this impossible love in the first place. He acted like she was the only woman in the world when it was all lies.

"Yes, it must." Stiffening, she tried to withdraw. "You're not a cruel man, Hugh. Do what you need to, then leave me to find what peace I can."

He didn't let her go. That muscle flickered in his cheek, although his voice remained steady. "Until next month, when we have to go through all this again. Give it up, Jane. Come back to me. You haven't stopped wanting me. I'd wager on it."

Yes, she wanted him. She loved him. He wasn't the only one with a loyal heart, damn him. "Wanting isn't enough, Hugh."

"Make it enough."

"No."

His lips tightened, and the lines on his face deepened into furrows. "Then let's get this over with."

It was what she'd asked for, so his terse response shouldn't make her flinch. She didn't realize he meant to kiss her, until it was almost too late. She jerked her head, and his lips slid across her cheek. Even that clumsy kiss made every hair on her body stand up in charged response.

"No kissing," she said indistinctly.

She waited for a protest, but he curved one hand around her neck and tilted her chin so he could nibble a trail down her throat. Despite everything, Jane couldn't contain a whimper of pleasure.

"This...this isn't necessary," she forced out. "I'll lie on the bed, and you can do what you have to."

"Oh, no, my lovely wife," he murmured against her skin. "That's not how this plays out. If you're so determined to put me to stud like a ram to a ewe, this is how it's going to be."

Fear rose to choke her, fear as crippling as the terror that had turned her to ice on their wedding night. Except as his lips and teeth teased her neck and ears, ice was the last thing she felt like. Already that throbbing weight set up in her belly, and her body softened in readiness.

She pulled away to see his face. "Hugh, you're frightening me."

Jane waited for the reliable consideration to kick in. Instead, ruthlessness hardened his features. "You'll live."

He caught her by the waist and whirled her around, until she stood behind the chair and he stood behind her. "What are you doing?"

"It's my turn to give the orders." With hard hands, he bent her over the back of the chair. He set one hand over the small of her back, pinning her in position. "Of late, you've got your own way. Put your hands flat on the seat."

She obeyed. God forgive her, despite everything, a surge of wild excitement swept through her.

"This is...odd," she said, largely for the sake of her pride.

"This way you don't have to see my face," he said in a voice like needles. "That should suit you down to the ground."

She swallowed a sob. He sounded like he hated her.

It wasn't entirely comfortable bending over the padded chair. She leaned her weight forward onto the brocade seat. He must have guessed that she wouldn't try to escape, because he stopped holding her down. She heard the rustle of his clothes, then he bundled her skirts up her legs. He'd often seen her naked, but she'd never felt as exposed as she did now, with her bare rump pointing at the ceiling.

He moved closer, and suddenly in spite of the strange position, so much that was familiar washed over her. The rich scent of his arousal. The unsteady rhythm of his breathing. His hard rod pressing between her legs in male demand.

When he leaned in and cupped her breasts, teasing the nipples through her muslin gown, she bit back a protest. In this position, her breasts tumbled into his hands as if designed for his touch.

She shivered under his bold caresses. "Hugh, this isn't..."

"Shut up, Jane." The hard, sucking kiss he placed on her neck would leave a mark. "And spread your legs."

How could she deny him? He stroked her. Now both of them knew that for all her defiance, she was hot and ready. Unforgiving hands seized her hips, and his body went taut against her back.

She couldn't restrain a yearning sob at the delay. Then a cry of satisfaction as he plunged deep inside her. With one powerful thrust, he filled her aching emptiness, and she clenched around him in help-less welcome.

He groaned against her ear, and his kiss on her neck this time expressed a longing to match hers. Even knowing that was only wishful thinking, she released another choked sob and bumped back-ward. Her wordless consent drew a low growl of satisfaction from him.

He began to move in and out, each time claiming more of what she'd tried to deny him. Soon, astonishingly soon, she began to quake with a climax that had her moaning in pleasure.

She closed her eyes and bit her lip and battled to keep some distance from him, even as every muscle quivered and tightened with rapture. She felt a great liquid surge from her womb, then Hugh thrust one last time and flooded her with every drop of his passionate heat.

Garson collapsed exhausted on Jane's back. He'd found his release, and he'd brought her to climax. He should feel triumphant, relieved, purged.

Instead he felt dirty, as though he'd desecrated something holy.

He made himself stand upright and tug down her skirts, hiding those delicious pink folds between her legs that glistened with his seed. He stepped back. Clumsy hands fastened his breeches and straightened his shirt. He felt cheap and mean. His wife deserved better of him.

"Jane, you can stand up now," he said tonelessly. "It's over."

Slowly she lifted away from the chair, so slowly that he worried if in his savagery, he might have hurt her. "Are you all right?"

When she turned, her face was flushed and her eyes were dazed. "Yes."

One trembling hand rose to her chest. The pretty dress was creased, although he took his hat off to her maid. Jane's hair remained mostly in place, apart from a few garnet tendrils clinging to the damp skin of her neck.

"Good," he said shortly.

He left her and returned to the room she'd assigned to him, where he stood in the center of the floor until he stopped shaking. Despite that massive orgasm, he felt sick and unhappy and discontented. Their encounter had been like diving into the sun, but it only proved that he wanted his wife back where she belonged. With him.

Garson didn't expect to see Jane before his departure. After all, they'd done what he came for, and she'd made it humiliatingly clear that beyond that, she had no use for him. But when he led his saddled horse out of the stable, she waited in the yard.

She'd changed into one of her old gray dresses. If she thought that might quash his desire, she was mistaken. The dress reminded him of those radiant days and nights in Salisbury, when he'd dared to believe that this marriage might lend his life purpose and joy.

For a month, regret had haunted him. Now it rose so strongly, it tasted rusty on his tongue. He regretted hurting this lovely, ardent creature, until all she offered him was this afternoon's bitter passion. He regretted that despite everything he knew of honor and goodness, his body basked in a glorious afterglow. He regretted most of all that he couldn't give his wife what she wanted, so that she trusted him to make her happy.

Garson brought Lysander to a stop. "What is it, Jane?"

He was too weary and heart-sore to be angry. He hoped like hell that she conceived soon. Too many meetings like this would finish him.

He hoped that she never conceived, because this was all she'd give him, and he couldn't bear the thought of never touching her again.

Jane looked equally wrung out. Her brief animation after her climax had faded to more of that watchful composure. "I wanted to say goodbye."

He didn't take much encouragement from that.

"Goodbye," he said curtly. But he didn't get on his horse and ride away. Not yet. "You'll write."

"Yes. Another visit may not be necessary."

"No."

She didn't move. "Has all the talk been horrid?"

What was this? A sign of some interest in his life? The brief impulse to sarcasm didn't last. He'd been here long enough to see that she was at least as unhappy with their current dilemma as he was. "The gossips have had a field day."

"That must be beastly."

"I've been through it before."

She frowned. "That makes it worse."

He shrugged, his casualness unfeigned. It was odd. When Morwenna threw him over, the public nature of his rejection had been an excruciating ordeal. When Jane left him, he hardly cared what people thought. All he cared about was how much he wanted her back and how he'd let her down so badly.

"I haven't been in London to hear most of it. I just got back from Beardsley Hall four days ago." He'd hoped returning to his estates would heal the endless ache in his soul. But without his wife by his side, the house where he'd hoped to install her as mistress had felt empty. "Susan came to see me yesterday. She wanted to know where you are."

"Did you tell her?"

"No. I assumed if you wanted to see her, you'd invite her to visit."

Susan had arrived at Half Moon Street in a state. In his opinion, her theatrics stemmed more from fear of how her sister's marital dramas might affect Lucy's prospects, than any genuine concern. But then he was biased against his sister-in-law. He'd always thought she treated Jane abominably. These days, he acknowledged that was the pot calling the kettle black.

"I don't want to see her. She hasn't spoken to me since the Oldhams' ball. If she speaks to me now, she'll only say 'I told you so,' and lecture me about people who make their own beds having to lie on them."

He winced. The mention of beds was a little too close to the bone. "I told her you needed total rest in the country, on doctor's orders."

"She wouldn't believe that."

"She didn't. She left convinced that I've strangled you and buried the body in the garden."

Jane looked startled. "Oh, no, I didn't think of that."

He gave an unamused grunt. "I assume if the magistrates take me up and charge me with murder, you'll deign to appear to prove that you're not dead."

It was her turn to wince. "Hugh, I hope you know that I don't wish you any harm."

No, even if her absence threatened to destroy him. No harm in that at all.

"How do you see this working long-term, Jane?" he asked, taking advantage of the fact that she seemed in no hurry to send him on his way.

The question surprised her, although he couldn't imagine why. "Surely I'll conceive."

"Yes," he said impatiently. "And the child might be a boy. Then you'll no longer have to suffer my distasteful advances." Perhaps after that torrid joining, his rancor at her desertion wasn't quite as exhausted as he'd thought.

Jane went pale but met his eyes. "You know your advances aren't distasteful, Hugh."

He ignored that and persisted with his questions. "Once you've had the child, who will bring it up? You? Me? Some neutral third party?"

She faltered back, although despite his hard tone, he wasn't attacking her. "I don't know. I thought perhaps we could share."

"Not the best choice for a child, to be pulled from pillar to post because his parents don't see eye to eye."

"I'm aware that all the legal power in this battle is yours."

His heart cramped in agony. "Must it be a battle?"

She looked devastated. "Hugh…"

He swung into the saddle. Either he left now, or he wouldn't leave at all. His reluctant bride would find herself tupped from the cellar to the attic of the dower house, whatever his better nature might insist upon. "What if we have a string of girls? Think about that, Jane."

She swallowed. "I assumed you were only interested in a boy."

His hands clenched on Lysander's reins, making the black sidle and snort in protest. "Then you assumed wrongly."

"You only ever mentioned an heir." She spread her hands. "I thought if we had girls you'd leave them to my care."

"I won't be a stranger to any child of mine. And as you pointed out, if it comes to a dispute, my wishes will prevail in law."

She regarded him with a touch of contempt. "I can't believe you're threatening me."

Had he fallen so low? It seemed he had. Although blackmailing her into his life and using her children against her wouldn't bring back the joy they'd shared; it would just chase it further out of reach. This damnable situation offered him no reprieves. "At the moment, the point is moot. But if there is a child…"

Her eyes narrowed on him. "You're trying to make me change my mind about my plans."

For the first time in that long, grueling day, he found himself smiling at his wife. Nastily. "What a clever girl you are."

Without waiting for her response, he dug his heels into Lysander's sides and galloped away from the house with a clatter of hooves on cobblestones.

CHAPTER THIRTY-SIX

The month before Garson's next visit to the Beeches seemed to last an eon. He retreated to Derbyshire for most of it. Gossip about his failed marriage was rife, but that wasn't the real reason he avoided society. Three and a half years ago, his life had taken a wrong turn. For so fleeting an interval that it verged on torture, the happiness he found in his marriage made him wonder if his trials were over. But that brief promise of warmth and purpose and fulfillment had soon flickered out into Stygian darkness.

Since then, every day had been a barren waste. Every day to come promised more of the same. He was back to feeling like an unwelcome intruder in his own life. Other people, even friends like Silas and Caro, scraped against him like sandpaper on wood. He was better off alone.

He had an ominous inkling that he'd be alone until he took his dying breath.

Jane's absence felt like a sin against life. Damn it, she was his wife. She should be with him.

Garson supposed he could storm and rage and demand she come back. After all, as he'd pointed out to her, he had the law on his side.

But despite his half-hearted threats at their last meeting, he despised the thought of bullying her.

Anyway, what would be the use? He didn't just want Jane back as a physical presence. He wanted their friendship. He wanted her to share her boundless sensuality with him. He wanted to know that the two of them were slowly, surely building an unbreakable bond of trust and respect and affection. He wanted the promise of family.

Insisting on his rights would wreck any chance of regaining those things. Perhaps—and he wasn't optimistic about the odds—if he gave her time to accept that she'd never have his love, she'd return, ready to try again.

Which was the only reason he'd let her call the tune so far. He couldn't risk harrying her into running beyond his reach.

Because beneath all his bluster, he understood exactly why she'd left him. After all, he was an expert on the agonies of unrequited love. Living with a man who could never respond to her love would turn her generous heart bitter and resentful. It would blight the rest of her life.

He couldn't bear to think of her vivid soul withering away in rancor and misery.

She needed to accept that some dreams could never come true, however worthy she was to have her wishes fulfilled. Because his wife was worthy. His wife was far too good for him and part of him marveled that this wonderful creature had come to love him at all. If he'd never met Morwenna…

Thinking about what might have been if he'd come to Jane with an unclaimed heart threatened to drive him insane.

After Jane's second terse note arrived, saying that their encounter at the Beeches hadn't produced a child, he rode down to Winchester once again, hiring a fresh horse at each change. This time, Jane didn't emerge onto the front steps to welcome him. She offered no hint that his visit was anything except a utilitarian solution to an awkward problem.

He stabled his mount and entered through the kitchens. As he strode through the eerily silent house, he couldn't help feeling that he wandered through Sleeping Beauty's castle. A foolish fancy, not least because the princess in this particular fairytale wouldn't let him kiss her under any circumstances.

Garson guessed she was already waiting in her bedroom. He went to the room she'd put aside for him last time. As before, there was hot water and a light luncheon set out. He paused on the threshold and surveyed the neat offerings, while his gut churned with an ocean of contrition and resentment.

When he'd left Jane last month, he'd felt tired and used, no matter how powerfully his body had relished the explosive joining. The way he felt now was worse.

With sudden determination, he turned on his heel and marched toward the neighboring room. He slammed the door open so hard that one of the landscapes on the wall crashed to the ground.

Abruptly Jane sat up from where she'd been lying on the bed. The reminder of how dutiful and frightened she'd been on their wedding night only made anger sink its teeth deeper. He'd once congratulated himself on how far they'd come since then. What a bloody fool he'd been. In this marriage, the seeds of trouble had been there from the beginning. He'd had no right to offer himself to this lovely girl unless he was able to give her his undivided allegiance.

He'd never done that. And that cheater's bargain had led to his undoing.

"Hugh!" Her gray eyes widened, as she caught sight of him. "What's the matter?"

His lips flattened. "You know what's the bloody matter," he said in a voice like gravel. "Get up and stand behind the chair. I can't bear to see your face, when I know that you hate every moment of what I'm doing."

She went ashen, although she rose from the bed. "I don't hate it," she mumbled, avoiding his glare.

"What was that?" he asked, although he'd heard her the first time.

Her eyes flashed, and he caught a fugitive glimpse of the passionate woman who had turned his nights to fire. And offered him the deceitful promise of a life he could love, even if he couldn't love her.

"I said I don't hate it." The words emerged sharp as broken glass.

She looked like a princess disdaining the advances of an over-weening courtier. He recognized with a shock that her pride far outweighed his. Perhaps there was some pique involved in her desertion after all.

"Good." He took off his hat and gloves and tossed them on a chest of drawers. "You know what to do."

Hesitantly she approached the chair and after sending him a backward glance, as if asking whether he wanted to position her, she bent over.

Lust fueled his anger. His breath emerged in tattered gasps. The sight of his wife waiting for him to service her had his cock standing up straight as a ship's mast.

He stepped behind her and tossed the frothy light blue skirts up to reveal her bare arse. Her whimper betrayed excitement and fear.

His heart pounded like a bass drum as he stared down at that luscious rump. White, smooth, perfectly curved. Her legs were splayed, ready for him to plunge inside and spend himself in shame and yearning and irresistible need. He watched her tense to accept him, and she dipped her head, so the angle of her bum became yet more brazen.

Even as his hands went to the fastenings of his breeches, he knew this wasn't what he wanted.

If he went ahead and did this now—and again and again until they made a child—he'd corrupt something precious and irreplaceable. And each time, he'd chip a little bit more off Jane's soul. What he was about to do debased the memory of the transcendent intimacies they'd shared during their first few weeks, however hellishly askew things had gone since.

God help him, he couldn't do it.

Gritting his teeth against the agonizing weight in his balls, he threw Jane's skirts down to cover her. He stepped back on shaking legs.

"Stand up," he said, his voice as flat as the Fens.

For a moment, she didn't move, and he wondered whether he

would in fact be able to resist taking her. She pushed herself up and turned, looking bewildered.

Her gaze focused on his face. He suspected he looked like thunder. Then she glanced toward the bed. "Shall I lie down?"

"No."

Her eyes widened. "Is there some other—"

With a violent gesture, he retreated a step further out of temptation's reach. "No. No other way. Not again."

Misery and confusion darkened her eyes to pewter. "I don't understand."

He hardly understood either. But he knew to the depths of his being that what they did in this room would only lead to utter devastation. "I want a wife. I want a marriage. I want a life with you. I don't want these crumbs from your table, Jane. This miserly spending of what should be gold, while we go ahead and turn everything between us into base metal. I want the whole loaf or nothing."

She spread her hands. Her expression said she thought he was losing his mind. "But what about a child?"

He bit back a string of profanities. "I don't give a tinker's damn anymore. The bloody estate can crumble into the sea, as far I'm concerned. Someone will inherit it. I'll be dead so I won't care."

"You married me to have an heir."

"And you married me to gain a home," he said with a weariness that penetrated to his bones. "If you can change your mind about what you want, why can't I?"

"So you won't…"

"No, I won't. This is my last visit to the Beeches, Jane." He folded his arms and regarded her with burning eyes. "Come home, or go your own way. It's all or nothing."

She still looked completely befuddled. "But you don't love me."

"I honor you. I want you. I believe we can create something worthwhile between us. You have to decide if that's enough." He saw her flinch, but couldn't dam the torrent of words that had been building up since the day she left him. "If not, I'll make arrangements for a generous allowance. I won't have you relying on Anthony bloody

Townsend's bounty for the food you eat." The way she'd turned to the Townsends with her troubles continued to rankle. "You're free to decide your future. But hear this—if you return to me, it's forever. No compromises, no keeping yourself from me, no half measures. You decide to be my wife, and you never waver."

She linked shaking hands at her waist. "You're asking a lot."

"I'm asking everything," he said in a flinty voice. He prowled over to collect his hat and gloves. "I await word on your decision."

He stalked away without a backward glance, even as a small voice in the corner of his mind whispered that he'd just made the biggest mistake of his life.

CHAPTER THIRTY-SEVEN

On his long ride back to London, Garson hardly registered a single mile or the inns where he stopped to change horses. All he saw was Jane's pale, shocked features as he delivered his ultimatum. An ultimatum that could result in never seeing her again.

Brilliant move, old man.

After a day and a half in the saddle, it was well after midnight when he stamped back into the house at Half Moon Street. Despite his aching exhaustion, he spent the rest of the night sitting in his library and gazing into the dark abyss of his future. He chose the brandy decanter for company, but barely touched the one glass he poured. As eyes scratchy with tiredness watched the dawn come up over London, he asked himself two questions.

How had everything gone so bloody wrong?

And was there any way to fix this damned mess?

As the day brightened into morning, he found no answers, but he finally admitted something that had been staring him in the face for weeks. He needed to swallow the few remnants of his pride and ask for help.

Garson staggered to his feet, painfully stiff after the arduous ride and hours in a chair. Still wearing shirt and breeches, he tumbled into bed and crashed into a dreamless sleep.

That afternoon, Garson knocked at Silas's shiny black door in Berkeley Square. Silas had tried to offer advice before, but Garson had been too stubborn to listen. He was ready to listen now, if his friend was willing to help him after his recent behavior had soured relations with the Nashes and their circle.

Given the way Garson's last visit to the Beeches had gone, optimism seemed like folly. But even if Silas offered a fresh perspective on the quandary, it would help. He wasn't expecting much more. Silas would need to be a miracle worker to fix the gargantuan problems in this marriage.

The butler opened the door. "Good afternoon, my lord."

"Good afternoon, Hunter. I'd like to see Lord Stone."

"His lordship has taken her ladyship and the children to the park."

Garson was so keyed up that this information sent his heart plummeting to his toes. "Oh."

Hunter smiled. "But I suspect they won't be long, as it's about to rain."

Was it? Garson had paid attention to nothing beyond his purpose. Now he glanced up at the sky and saw that the clear sunrise had deteriorated into heavy black clouds.

Hunter went on. "Would you like to wait?"

It seemed he must rein in his impatience. "Yes, please."

Hunter showed him into the drawing room. As the storm blew in, the light worsened. Garson only realized he wasn't alone when a tall, slender woman rose from a writing desk in the corner.

Hunter was surprised, too. "Mrs. Nash, I do beg your pardon. I assumed the room was empty. Lord Garson has called to see Lord Stone, but I'm sure he won't mind waiting in the library."

The butler's voice seemed to reach him through deep water.

Garson couldn't shift his gaze from the woman who had haunted him for more than four years.

Even if he'd been warned about meeting her, he'd have struggled to hide his reaction. Caught unawares, he turned to stone: dumb, unmoving, monolithic. Through the furious blood pounding in his head, he watched her walk toward him, graceful and beautiful as ever.

"No need to send Lord Garson away, Hunter. We're old friends. Perhaps you could bring tea and have the candles lit."

Her soft voice caressed his ears like music. When she passed the window, he saw her more clearly. Clearer still as his stupor faded, and he remembered to take a breath. She was so exactly like his memory of her, the moment felt unreal. Vaguely he heard Hunter leave.

"Hugh?" Morwenna cast him a concerned glance. "You don't mind keeping me company, do you?"

By God, he acted like an unmannerly lummox. He bowed and when she indicated for him to sit, he did. She took the chair opposite, her blue eyes regarding him with the solemn sincerity he'd always found irresistible.

After a humiliatingly long time, he even found the gumption to dredge out a few words. "Mrs. Nash, I didn't know you were in Town."

"Mrs. Nash?" She wrinkled her small, straight nose. "You used to call me Morwenna."

He used to call her darling and sweetheart and his love. "Morwenna, then."

"It's only a flying visit. The Admiralty want to talk to Robert about South America, although these days, he's more farmer than sailor. I doubt he'll have anything useful to say."

Garson hid a grimace at the mention of her husband. "It's a long time since I've seen you."

Over two years ago, they'd met when Silas's niece Louisa was christened. The experience had proven so grueling, he'd avoided Nash family celebrations ever since. He hadn't been alone with Morwenna since before their hideous engagement party.

"I'm glad I can offer my congratulations on your marriage. I'd love to meet your wife, if she's in Town."

Clearly Morwenna was out of touch with gossip. "Thank you," he said, "I'm afraid Jane's in the country at present."

If his last self-righteous speech hadn't sent his wife hying for Timbuctoo. Now he wished he'd stayed at the Beeches long enough to hear some response to his terms. He wasn't sorry he'd said his piece— he'd stand by every word. But he could have phrased it more as a negotiation than a final demand.

"What a pity I'll miss her. Caro says she's charming."

"She is." And lovely and troublesome and tempting, and, dear God, he wasn't sure he could live without her.

Hunter's appearance with the tea tray saved Garson from the awkward dilemma of discussing his wife with the previous candidate for the post. A footman bustled around lighting candles.

By the time he and Morwenna were alone once more, he was capable of putting two thoughts together, instead of feeling like the earth beneath his feet was about to dissolve. When he spoke, he almost sounded like a man in possession of his faculties. "How's Kerenza?"

He had fond memories of Morwenna's spirited daughter. As she passed him a cup of tea, affection softened Morwenna's smile. It made her stunningly beautiful.

His first love was beautiful. He hadn't mistaken that. But as he sat back and let her tales of an obviously happy family life in Devon wash over him, he saw he was wrong to think the years had left her unaffected.

The Morwenna he'd courted had been frail and lovely and vulnerable, wrapped in a suffocating veil of grief. She'd awoken his innate urge to heal any wounded creature, and that protective impulse had soon turned into love. Today her skin was as white as a pearl, and her eyes were as blue as the sea, and her black hair was as glossy as ever, but she'd fundamentally changed. He saw that she'd found happiness.

As he listened to her talk about her husband and children—since Robert's return, two sons had joined the family—he couldn't muster a moment's regret that she had. Which was bizarre when jealousy had tormented him for years.

Fate had reunited her with the man she'd always belonged to. Somewhere since their last meeting, Garson had gained enough distance to recognize that his presence in her life had been a mere distraction at best.

He realized a silence had fallen, and he glanced up to find Morwenna regarding him quizzically. "I apologize, Hugh. I do tend to rabbit on about the children."

He shifted uncomfortably. "I'm sorry."

She laughed. "No need." The humor drained from her face. "I'm guessing you find this meeting difficult."

Actually once his initial shock faded, he was astonished how easy it was proving. He'd devoted reams of turbulent emotion to this woman. He'd assumed if he ever had her to himself again, the drama would rival anything he could see at the Royal Opera House.

Except they were both grown-ups, and the ending of this particular melodrama was settled the moment Robert Nash returned from the dead. What was the point of accusing Morwenna of destroying his life?

At this moment, the person he'd like to blame for that was his wife. But he couldn't even do that with a clear conscience, because he was unwillingly aware that most of his present misery resulted from his blind selfishness.

"Would you rather I wait for Silas in the library?" He supposed by rights, they shouldn't be alone together, but a few minutes of private conversation in an old friend's house didn't test propriety too far.

She made a dismissive gesture. "No. I'm grateful, because it means I can apologize for how shabbily I treated you after Robert came back."

"You wrote to me. You don't need to do any more."

"Yes, I do. I hurt you, and you didn't deserve it. You behaved so beautifully, when it must have been beastly, having the whole world watching on and anticipating scandal. I can only beg your forgiveness."

"If you need my forgiveness, Morwenna—and I don't think you do —I give it to you wholeheartedly." To his astonishment, this wasn't putting a good face on something he couldn't change. He meant it. "I know you never stopped loving Robert. Everything ended up as it should."

A smile twisted her lips. "You remain the perfect gentleman, Hugh."

By God, Jane wouldn't agree. Neither she should, given how he'd behaved toward her. "I hope you'll remember our friendship with no regrets."

"I can now. Thank you, Hugh." She looked a little brighter. "And everything worked out in the end because you married Jane. If you're just a fraction as happy as Robert and I are, you'll be blessed. I wish you many wonderful years together."

Any suitable response stuck in his throat. Regret clenched his gut as he recognized that these generous wishes were unlikely to come true.

The door opened behind him, and Silas, Caro, and their four boisterous children tumbled into the room. Garson set aside his untouched tea and rose to greet his friends. He intercepted a glance between Silas and Caro that conveyed their consternation at finding him closeted with Morwenna. Clearly he hadn't been the only one expecting melodrama, should this meeting ever take place.

Within half an hour, Caro and Morwenna left for Fenella's house, and the children were safely ensconced in the nursery. Garson was at last alone with Silas in his library. With a sigh, he collapsed into a leather chair. After the long ride and months of emotional turmoil, he was exhausted, yet so jumpy, he could hardly keep still. Outside rain crashed against the windows as the storm set in.

Silas stood at the sideboard and poured two brandies without asking Garson's preference. "Here. I suspect you need this."

Garson accepted the glass and swallowed a mouthful. The liquor did little to soothe his disquiet. "Thanks."

Silas took the chair opposite and sipped his own brandy, as he eyed Garson with a doubtful expression.

"Relax," Garson said drily. "I'm not about to rampage around the house smashing the Ming vases."

Silas didn't smile. "That must be the first time you and Morwenna have been alone since she went back to Robert."

"It was." He lifted his glass to his lips. A distant corner of his mind remarked on the steadiness of his hand. So often, he'd fantasized about seeing his old love and finally getting a chance to talk to her and tell her his side of the story. Now they'd met, and in the end, the sad truth was there was nothing left to say.

"And you survived."

"I did." The churning whirlpool of emotions inside him calmed to a point where he could reflect on what had just happened. "I did," he repeated more slowly.

"Good for you."

An unexpectedly companionable silence fell. "I'm sorry I've been a stranger," he said eventually.

"You've had other things to worry about." Silas rose to refill their glasses. Garson waved him away. He didn't need liquor. He needed to make some decisions.

"Jane's left me." The bald admission should sting his pride, but he was way past the point where his pride mattered.

Silas set the decanter down without filling his glass and regarded Garson with a troubled frown. "I'm damned sad to hear that. Anthony said that she'd gone to the country for a rest."

"You didn't believe that."

"Perhaps not." Silas returned to his seat. "But I assumed any estrangement was only temporary."

Garson stared sightlessly in front of him. "I hoped so, too."

"Morwenna?"

"Yes."

"And now after all this time, you've seen her again."

"Yes."

Another silence, thornier than the last.

"Are you still in love with her?"

"Jane?"

Silas looked surprised at Garson's instinctive response. "No, Morwenna."

He prepared to deliver his usual heated declaration of eternal fealty to his first choice, then stopped before he spoke a word.

Was he still in love with Morwenna? He'd certainly loved her when he'd proposed to her. Since she'd forsaken him, he'd carried her image etched on his heart. Over the last four years, she'd been behind his every action. He'd pledged himself to her for life.

But had he? Meeting her just now had been touching and disturbing and awkward, but no overwhelming torrent of frustrated longing had risen to drown him.

She felt like someone he'd once known well and now met as almost a casual acquaintance.

While his reeling mind grappled with the prodigious change, habit shrieked that he couldn't give up his impossible love. Since she'd returned to her husband, Morwenna's absence had thwarted his every hope of happiness.

Look how his loyalty to his first love had poisoned his marriage to Jane and stopped him making a full commitment to the woman he married. At this moment, he wondered whether Jane was better off without him, after he'd caused her so much unhappiness.

A great howl of denial writhed in his belly. Not if he had anything to say about it.

So where did that leave his feelings for Morwenna? He'd pledged his love, and he'd stayed true to his word for nearly four agonizing years. But in all that time, he'd only seen her twice.

Was it possible that while the Morwenna of his dreams remained alive in his heart, the real Morwenna turned into a stranger?

"I loved her so much," he said slowly, as the babbling muddle in his head faded to allow the voice of reason to speak.

"I know you did, old chum." Silas leaned forward and linked his hands between his spread knees. "It was deuced hard watching you break your heart over her."

Garson's brows lowered, noting that they both spoke of his great love in the past tense. When the devil had that happened? "I'm not a fickle man."

Silas's snort expressed derisive amusement. "Anything but."

"She's beautiful."

"Yes."

Garson blinked to clear the haze obscuring his vision. Then he blinked again, as excruciating self-knowledge struggled up toward the light. Good God, how utterly he'd botched his life. And he didn't know if he could ever fix it. "You know, I'll always remember her fondly, but I don't think I'm in love with her anymore."

"No."

"You don't sound surprised," he said, with a hint of resentment.

Silas's gaze remained unwavering. "I think you're in love with your wife."

Garson scowled at his friend. "You just want everyone to have a happy marriage like yours. You're indulging in wishful thinking."

"Am I?"

Was he? Garson slumped back against his chair as the full magnitude of his idiocy struck him like boulders falling off a mountainside. "Oh, hell."

Silas sat back, as if he'd finally got the answer he sought. "I know Jane's in love with you."

She had been. And he was in love with her. Madly. Desperately. Forever.

It all seemed so simple, now he finally understood. For too long, he'd been blind to the truth in his heart.

Garson had loved Jane for weeks, probably since he'd married her, at least since their unconventional honeymoon. Before she left, she'd tried to get it into his thick skull that they were the perfect match. And they were. She was just the woman for him. Smart. Good. Passionate. Open-hearted. And brave. Much braver than he'd been.

How cruel he'd been to her, how thoughtless, how utterly self-centered. He cringed to recall his categorical rejection of her love, when she must have needed every ounce of courage to confess how she felt.

Devil curse him, he'd hurt her so badly. "I've made such a bloody hash of everything."

Silas sighed. "So I gather."

Guilt and despair battered him. "How can she ever forgive me?"

"No question you've been a fool. Love turns every man into a nincompoop."

At a loss about his next move, Garson stared at his friend. "What in Hades will I do if it's too late?"

Silas stood and crossed to set an encouraging hand on his shoulder. "First find out if she'll give you the time of day."

"But I've been such an utter bastard," he said bleakly.

Silas's smile was wry. "Then say you're sorry, tell her you love her, and ask her to give you another chance."

"What if she won't have me? I wouldn't blame her."

"I wouldn't either. You've been a complete dunderhead. But I'm always astounded at the generosity that lurks in the hearts of women."

His shoulders hunched in despair. "She probably won't even see me."

Silas sighed again and crossed to pick up the decanter. This time Garson didn't wave him away. "There's only one way to find out."

"Losing Morwenna nearly killed me." Garson took a gulp of brandy, but it didn't help. "It will be worse if I lose Jane." Going on without his wife by his side would curse him to an eternal darkness that would make his moping about Morwenna look like a stroll in Green Park.

"Take heart, my friend. And have courage." Silas returned to his chair and raised his glass in Garson's direction. "Sometimes love means throwing yourself off a cliff, without knowing whether a safe landing waits at the bottom."

CHAPTER THIRTY-EIGHT

$\mathcal{I}$t was a couple of hours before dawn when Garson rode up to the dower house for the third and final time. Whatever happened today, whether Jane gave him his marching orders or decided to come back to him, there would be no more visits to Hampshire to claim his conjugal rights.

In the day and a half since he'd left Silas, his heart had rocketed from hope to despair. Now he was impatient to settle his fate for good or ill. He'd wasted too many years mired in old misery. It was long past time to set a new pattern.

Jane had once loved him. Did she still? He couldn't wait any longer to find out. Every moment's delay was torture.

He threw himself off the back of the hack he'd hired at Winchester, when he'd last changed horses. Garson stumbled to the ground. London to Winchester, then back again, with this latest trip following so quickly tested any man. If his wife threw him out on his arse, he'd have to find an inn somewhere close to rest and eat before he returned to Town.

And a future as bleak as an Arctic wilderness.

He settled the horse in a stall. After he blew out the lantern, he stared grimly into the darkness. If Jane rejected him, just what the devil would he do?

He squared his shoulders. Silas had described falling in love as jumping off a cliff. Only now, as Garson teetered on the brink of elation or despair, did he comprehend quite what his friend meant. Generally he wasn't a praying man, but he prayed that his wife saw fit to give him a second chance.

"Wish me luck, old fellow." He patted the raw-boned, but surprisingly fleet bay that had carried him this far.

The horse whickered and lowered his head to the manger. No reassurance there.

Garson left the stable and walked around the house to climb the front steps. In the moonlit silence, the crash of the iron knocker resounded like the herald of doom. Soon he heard the bolt slide back, and his wife stood in the doorway, holding a candle. His heart stuttered to a stop, then began to race. His hands fisted at his sides, as he resisted the urge to sweep her up in his arms. Physical desire couldn't solve the problems between them. Only talking could. He hoped to God he found the right words.

"Hugh!" she said in shock. "What on earth are you doing here?"

It was a mild June night, and she wore one of the floaty silk peignoirs he'd bought her in Salisbury. The sweet memory of those days struck him like a blow and rendered him as tongue-tied as a nervous schoolboy in the headmaster's office. Before he could muster an answer, an older woman in a muslin nightcap fluttered up behind his wife. "My lady, who is it?"

"Don't worry, Mrs. Darrell." Jane turned to reassure her. "It's my husband, Lord Garson."

"Lawks a mercy," the woman muttered. Garson assumed Mrs. Darrell was the housekeeper. "I was afeared cutthroats turned up to murder us in our beds." She managed an awkward curtsy in her voluminous nightwear. "My lord."

"Please go back to bed," Jane said. "I'll look after his lordship."

"Very good, my lady." The woman cast him a curious glance, before she trudged back the way she'd come, leaving Garson alone with his wife.

Jane raised the candle to illuminate his face. "What is it?"

"I needed to see you."

Her silvery eyes were wide and dark. "Has something happened?"

Indeed it had. He'd discovered how much he loved her. Not before time, damn it.

But he couldn't blurt that out on the doorstep. He suddenly realized he was acting like a blasted idiot. Again. He should have waited until daylight before he came to see her, taken time to line up his arguments. Not to mention wash and put on a clean shirt and comb his hair. After those long hours in the saddle, he must look like a complete gypsy. "There's nothing to worry about, Jane."

Impatience tightened her lips. "Of course I worry when you bowl up unannounced in the middle of the night, looking like the world has ended."

"I'll come back after breakfast. I apologize for disturbing you."

To his surprise she stepped back and gestured him inside. "You may as well come in. You're here now."

"But I woke you up," he said, longing to accept her invitation, but on edge because he'd arrived with such good intentions, and already everything went to hell.

"I wasn't asleep," she said flatly.

Guilt stabbed him anew. Her unhappiness was his fault.

"You're acting like a blockhead. Stop haunting the front step and come inside and tell me what's the matter. It must be important, if it's brought you all the way back from London." Her voice hardened. "Especially as three days ago, you gave me to understand you'd never darken my door again."

"As you say, I'm a blockhead," he said uncomfortably.

What an arrogant fool he'd been, last time he saw her. He had a sinking feeling he'd been an arrogant fool from the beginning. He'd acted like his feelings were all that counted. How the hell had Jane put up with him as long as she had?

She subjected him to a thoughtful survey, then to his surprise smiled. "Not always."

Her smiles had been so rare lately that painful emotion closed his throat. He couldn't have responded, even if he wanted to. At this rate, he'd have to write her a bloody letter to tell her he loved her.

Jane turned and walked away. Without making a conscious decision, he found himself closing the door and trailing after her. His eyes clung to the subtle sway of her hips under the flowing silk. Her magnificent hair was confined in a long plait that snaked down her back.

She showed him into a drawing room. From where he stood in the center of the floor, he watched with unwavering eyes as she wandered around lighting candles. If this was the last time they were alone together, he wanted to print every detail into his memory.

At least she wasn't angry. Nor had she raised the mental barrier against him that first appeared in London and was as high as Mont Blanc by the time he visited her down here. He was too keyed up to trust his perceptions, but if he had to describe her mood, he'd say watchful.

"Please sit down," she said coolly.

He removed his hat and gloves and set them on a delicate ormolu table. "No, thank you."

"Very well." She came to a stop beside the mantelpiece and studied him. "Tell me what this is all about."

He hastened into speech. He had so much to say, so much that he needed her to know. "I saw Morwenna."

The moment the words left his mouth, he condemned himself for a sodding moron.

Jane made a faint, wounded sound and pressed back against the wall. Even in the uncertain light, he saw that she went as pale as milk. Then she gathered her defenses around her. She drew herself up to her full height, and her eyes narrowed on him. "How delightful for you."

He flinched at her sarcasm. "No, you don't understand."

"On the contrary, I understand very well. Did she proclaim her undying love?"

"She's in love with her husband. She always was."

Jane's expression turned stony. "Well, that's even better, isn't it?"

"How so?"

"Because now you've seen her, your self-pity has something fresh to feed on. You can go on pining for her as the great lost chance of your life. You don't need to engage with her as a real woman you live with day to day. She just stays on her pedestal, like a marble statue, pristine and perfect and unassailable."

Bile rose to sour his mouth as he listened to Jane pour out her bitterness. "Jane, I'm hellishly sorry that I've hurt you."

That also turned out to be the wrong thing to say. A sweep of her hand dismissed his apology as too little too late.

"What's the point of being sorry? You warned me what to expect when we married. I changed the rules of the game, not you." He could hardly bear to hear the pain fraying the edges of her voice. "Although you could have saved yourself the trouble of rushing all the way to Hampshire to inform me that your lady love is as exquisite as ever."

His brows drew together. She made him sound so cruel. Cruel and childish and selfish. Once she'd considered him a hero. He hated how he'd fallen in her esteem, which was mad when he'd also come to hate the way she thanked him for any kindness, like a beggar receiving scraps at the kitchen door.

He supposed, his queasiness sharpening, that was exactly what she felt like. By heaven, he needed to prove himself worthy of her. And he needed to tread carefully, because he was as close to losing her now as he'd ever been.

Garson inhaled and stood as straight as a soldier on parade. Before anything else, he had to clear up this matter of Morwenna, whose ghost had lingered far too long. He struggled to steady his voice. "I should have waited until a civilized hour to call on you. But when a man's been a fool for far too long, it behooves him to stop being a fool as soon he can."

Jane stared at the floor, as if she couldn't bear the sight of him. Her lush mouth turned down, and her expression was mutinous. Her arms folded over her lush bosom. "Are you saying you don't want me back after all?"

He frowned, puzzled at the question. "Were you going to come back?"

"No," she said, but after a hesitation that made him wonder if she'd considered accepting his ultimatum after all.

"I hope you will."

She raised her eyes to glare at him as if she despised him. She probably did. But like him, she wasn't a fickle person. If she'd loved him a couple of months ago, odds were she hadn't changed. Despite his blunderings.

"I won't live with you while you're in love with Morwenna Nash."

Strange how even a week ago, the mere mention of Morwenna's name had felt like someone punching a bruise. Now it only summoned a feeling of regret for all the years of futile misery.

Months ago, he should have guessed that he was falling in love with Jane. From the moment he married her, she'd occupied most of his attention. With Morwenna, he'd always acted *comme il faut*. Yet it hadn't taken Jane long to pierce his façade of the perfect gentleman, and prove he could behave as badly as any other man driven mad by love. How in Hades had he been too stupid to understand that his emotions were engaged?

"Then you can come home right now." He spoke quickly for fear she might send him away before he had a chance to tell her how he felt. "I rushed down here in such a lather to tell you that I'm not in love with Morwenna. I haven't been in love with her for a long time, although I was so used to playing the broken-hearted suitor that I couldn't see that."

He drew a deep breath. It was now or never. With a silent prayer that Silas was right, he flung himself off the edge of the cliff and into thin air. "I was once in love with Morwenna. But not anymore. Now, Jane, I'm in love with you."

CHAPTER THIRTY-NINE

*J*ane swayed as the room receded in a rush. She curled shaking fingers over the mantelpiece. Surely Hugh couldn't have just said what she thought he did. "What did you say?"

He stared into her face, his eyes blazing. "You heard me." He paused. "But I'm more than happy to say it again. I love you, Jane."

Her heart performed a dizzying cartwheel, but she'd been hurt too often to lower her guard just yet. "That seems too good to be true."

He flinched. If it was true that he loved her, her doubts would smart. The memory of how he'd dismissed her declaration of love two months ago still stung. "I've loved you since I married you."

She linked shaking hands together at her waist. Her pulse was galloping, but she couldn't trust this abrupt change. Only the fact that he'd never lied to her before prevented her from assuming this was some scheme to get her back into his bed. "Now that I really can't believe."

"Nevertheless it's true." He looked heartbreakingly sincere. The brown eyes glittered with urgency, and that telltale muscle in his cheek performed its erratic dance. "I was too buffle-headed to see it. I liked you, and wanted you, and acted like a bear with a toothache every time a man smiled at you, and I thought about nothing except you. If I had a brain in my head, I'd have understood that all adds up to love. But when I loved Morwenna, I was like Don Quixote sighing after unattainable Dulcinea. What I felt for her is nothing like the real, earthy, complicated, overwhelming passion we share. It took me too long to comprehend just what happened to me when I came looking for you in Dorset."

Jane supposed it made sense. Fenella had said something similar, that her second love was so different from her first, she'd needed time to recognize the feeling for what it was. "Are you saying you weren't Morwenna's lover?"

"I didn't even kiss her." A touch of sheepishness leavened his desperate air. "When I courted her, she was fragile and broken, and I treated her like Venetian glass."

Hugh's penchant for lame dogs raising its head again, she thought, even as relief flooded her. She'd loathed the idea of him sharing that big powerful body with his first love. Fenella had said she didn't think he'd bedded Morwenna, but now Jane knew for sure.

"I'm not Venetian glass," she said neutrally. "You don't need to rescue me, Hugh."

He shook his head. "No, and I thank God for that. You're strong enough to pull me into line and be my true partner."

She regarded him suspiciously. She so wanted to believe him, but the price of making a mistake now was utter desolation. "This change of mind still seems very convenient."

He shrugged and stepped closer. "You don't believe I'm over Morwenna?"

For a charged moment, she studied him. Did she? It was clear something momentous had happened to him since he'd ridden away in such a temper only a few days ago. A shadow had been lifted from him. She couldn't doubt that her hesitation tormented him, but despite that, he looked younger, less haunted.

Her hands stilled at her waist, and she spoke steadily. "Yes, I do."

He smiled in visible relief. "Then?"

She didn't smile back. "We both know your life will be simpler if I come back to you."

"So while you believe I'm over Morwenna, I haven't persuaded you that I love you instead?"

"Not yet."

"Kiss me, and I'll show you."

"It will take more than few kisses to convince me," she said, fearing she cut off her nose to spite her face.

His brief spark of humor faded, until he looked as austere as a Crusader knight on a tomb. "I know I've put you through hell. I've wronged you in so many ways that I can never atone for. I've been confused and destructive and bloody stupid. But, Jane, if I love you and you love me—or at least I hope you do—do you really mean to desert me and condemn us both to misery?"

She bit her lip. He sounded like he meant it. He looked like he meant it. With every word, she became more convinced that against all the odds, he had changed. She'd been agonizingly lonely and unhappy. This chance at a happy ending struck her as too unlikely.

Joy started to unfurl like a banner in her chest. But she wasn't yet ready to wave it to the skies to announce her victory. Her voice cracked. "I can't bear it if you're only being kind."

"Bloody hell!" he burst out, cutting the air with his hand. "When have I ever knowingly lied to you?"

She looked away toward the curtained window, but the image of his anguish remained burned on her eyes.

"Jane, my darling, I'll do anything to prove myself." He went on, the beautiful baritone a low rasp. "Just give me another chance."

Shocked, she glanced back at him. He looked like a man at the limits of his endurance. He looked like one word of rejection from her could destroy him.

Perhaps he did love her after all.

Joy broke free of the bonds of mistrust and past unhappiness. She swallowed. Then swallowed again as she forced out a response. "Hugh, if this turns out to be a trick, I'll put poison in your coffee."

It took him a moment to register that she'd yielded, if not in so many words. His uncertainty lingered for an instant, then the wretchedness faded. His face lit with such transcendent happiness, tears pricked at Jane's eyes. "You forgive me?"

"Mostly."

He strode forward until mere inches separated them. "And you'll come back to me?"

She tilted her chin and met his gleaming eyes. "Yes."

"And you believe I love you." It wasn't a question.

"Yes." She hadn't, until she saw his reaction to her grudging concession. Love still lit his face to brilliance. She'd never imagined Hugh would look at her like this. After the last despairing months, it beggared her understanding.

He placed his hands on her waist. "And you love me?"

She sighed. "I suppose I must."

His thick brows lowered. "Jane."

She flattened her palms on his chest. Under her touch, his heart thudded madly. The fact gradually sank in that he'd given that ardent heart over into her keeping. "Yes, I love you, Hugh."

His lips twitched, and he started to look more like himself, instead of the desperate ruffian who had arrived in such a state half an hour ago. "Say it with some enthusiasm."

She arched her eyebrows. "Don't push your luck, sir."

With a broken laugh, he gathered her up against him. "By God, I've missed your teasing."

After weeks of feeling so cold, the warmth of his embrace made her feel alive again. Their lips met in a kiss unlike any she'd known before. Because for the first time, she set her love free, and it flew to find its match in Hugh's love for her.

By the time he raised his head, tears poured down her face, and her arms curled around his neck. He regarded her with the tenderness that had always been there. Now she recognized the glow in his eyes as an abiding love that would sustain her for the rest of her life.

He caught her face between his palms. "Jane, darling, why are you crying?"

She gulped for air. "Because...because I'm happy."

He smiled. "But that's good, isn't it?"

"Yes." She blinked to clear her vision. To no avail. "And because I never thought this would happen."

Remorse darkened his eyes, and his smile faded. "I'm sorry it took me so long to see that I loved you. It's been as plain as the nose on my face for months."

"Such a noble nose, too." She choked back a soggy gurgle of laughter. "I forgive you."

This time, he didn't smile back. His gaze pierced right to her soul. "Just like that?"

"Just like that."

"When I rode here, I wasn't sure you'd have me, even after I told you I love you."

"Oh, Hugh, I'm not that proud." She kissed him softly on the lips, as gradually she accepted that against all the odds, she'd won everything she wanted. "I was almost at the point of crawling back to you anyway."

"I don't deserve you." It was his turn to kiss her, with a reverence that melted her bones to honey.

He lashed his arms about her and drew her into the shelter of his body. For a long while, she rested against him in perfect peace. They'd come so close to losing each other that she needed to come to terms with how radically her life had changed in the last few minutes. Through the silence, fear and anger and anguish drifted to oblivion, leaving only an infinity of love.

Eventually, she drew far enough away to see his beloved face. He looked made anew, too, at ease as she'd never seen him.

"What is it, my love?" he asked softly.

Wonder flooded her. "You look…happy. Truly happy."

"I am." His smile made her feel as if the sun shone just for her. "Do you love me?"

With a shock, she realized she hadn't told him. Not properly. Not so he knew how profoundly and eternally she pledged herself to him. "You know I do."

"Will you say it?"

She caressed his jaw, feeling strength beneath her fingers, while his deep, dark eyes reflected his generous heart. "I love you, Hugh," she said quietly. "I'll always love you."

He closed his eyes, as if dazzled by what he saw. When he opened them, she saw a world of love. "And I love you, Jane, my beloved wife. Can we start again? Can we go to Derbyshire and make a life where there are no more shadows between us?"

"I'd like that," she said. "Take me to Beardsley Hall, Hugh. Take me home."

EPILOGUE

Beardsley Hall, Derbyshire, March 1834

*W*hen Hugh entered the candlelit bedroom, Jane looked up from her dazed contemplation of her newborn son. She could hardly believe that she and Hugh had made this perfect little person.

"The dragon outside has at last allowed me to see you." He smiled at her from the doorway. "Are you ready for visitors?"

From where she rested against a pile of pillows in the huge four-poster bed, she discerned the signs of weariness and strain on his face. She'd been in labor most of the day, which had provided some interesting moments, but at least she'd been actively involved in events. Poor Hugh had been downstairs with nothing but his fear to keep him company. When he'd tried to see Jane before this, the midwife had given him his marching orders in no uncertain terms. Mrs. Moffatt was adamant about no men present during the delivery, well and truly earning the title of dragon.

"For you?" She smiled back. "Always."

"Thank God for that."

His clothes were rumpled, whiskers darkened his impressive jaw, and his thick hair was untidy. He looked appealingly poetic, as though he'd been battling with his inspiration all day, but she knew he wouldn't appreciate the description. "Has it been beastly?"

His lips turned down. "Vile. But nothing to compare with what you've gone through, I'm sure."

"He was worth it." Jane glanced down at the dark-haired baby, sleeping like an angel in her arms. He certainly hadn't been an angel coming into the world, although he'd been a champion when she breastfed him for the first time. "Do you plan to hover on the threshold forever? Come over and say good evening to your son."

Hugh looked sheepish and closed the door after him as he stepped into the room. "Can I kiss you?"

She laughed—very carefully. After the long, difficult labor, she was feeling fragile. "I sincerely hope you will. I've had a baby. I haven't caught some disease."

Hugh's gesture was apologetic. "After the day you've had, I mightn't be your favorite person."

"Oh, you're still that." She cuddled the warm baby against her breast. "Although you might have some competition now."

"I'll bear up," he said wryly. "How are you feeling?"

"Very proud of myself. I hope you'll feel very proud of me, too." She rearranged the baby, and extended one hand toward Hugh. "Come and meet your son, my love."

All Hugh's diffidence vanished, and he rushed forward to take Jane's hand and kiss her with the tender adoration that always turned her blood to syrup. Then he drew away to survey their child. "He doesn't look big enough to have caused this much trouble."

She smiled. "Would you like to hold him?"

"May I?"

"Of course." She released Hugh's hand and gently passed the baby across. A lot of men were hopeless with newborns, but Hugh's big hands curled around the child in perfect security. Of course they did

—he'd always provided a haven for the small and hurt and vulnerable. He was going to make an exceptional father.

"Jane, my darling," he said in awe, "did we really do this?"

"We did," she said in a choked voice. "Aren't we clever?"

"We are indeed." Hugh's expression as he observed the stirring baby was so full of love and wonder that she blinked away tears.

"He's a beautiful boy." Hugh's deep voice sounded almost as thick as hers.

The baby's cloudy blue eyes opened, and Jane waited for more of the furious wailing that had greeted his arrival into the world. But the child merely stared up at his father in fascination, as if he already knew he was in safe hands.

"Hello, lovely little man," Hugh whispered and bent to kiss the baby's forehead. The baby gave a contented sigh and closed his eyes again.

"What shall we call him?" Jane asked. They'd discussed a hundred names but had decided to wait for the baby's arrival before they reached a final decision.

"Not Amelia."

Amelia had been a possibility for a girl. Jane's lips quirked. "No, not Amelia. You favored Cedric in honor of my father."

With every moment, Hugh appeared more at home with the sleeping baby. "He doesn't look like a Cedric."

"No." She paused. "We didn't suggest this one earlier. But what about Silas?"

Hugh studied his son. "Silas?" he repeated thoughtfully, as he sat on the edge of the mattress.

"If he grows up to be half as good a man as Silas Nash, I'll be happy."

"I like it." Hugh leaned in and kissed her again, taking care not to squash the drowsing baby. "Silas Cedric. Or would you rather save Cedric for our next son?"

Jane gave a cracked laugh. "Let's not get ahead of ourselves."

Although ever since she and Hugh had set up home in beautiful, old

Beardsley Hall, she'd thought this was a house crying out to be filled with a large, happy family. Last Christmas she'd had a taste of what that would be like, when they'd hosted their closest friends, including Fenella and Anthony. Hugh had soon forgiven the Townsends for offering Jane sanctuary when she'd needed a place to nurse her broken heart.

Susan and her family also planned a stay in August. Jane didn't view that with quite such anticipation, but hopefully, the reunion would heal the lingering breach between the Norris sisters.

"Silas Cedric he shall be." Hugh's eyes glowed with love as he raised his head and stared at her. "Thank you, my beloved."

She had a horrid feeling that she looked rather smug. "Yes, I did well, didn't I?"

"Thank you for my son, and for the happiness you've brought me, and the love we share. Blessings have been showered upon my head, so many more than I deserve."

"My darling, nobody deserves them more." Oh, dear, she was choking up again. She blinked rapidly to clear the mist clouding her vision, as she reached out to touch Hugh's bristly cheek. "I love you, Hugh Rutherford."

Hugh's smile told her that he loved her, too, but she didn't mind at all when he went on to speak the words, as if he made a solemn and eternal vow. "And I love you, Jane, my beautiful wife and the light of my life."

ABOUT THE AUTHOR

ANNA CAMPBELL has written 10 multi award-winning historical romances for Grand Central Publishing and Avon HarperCollins, and her work is published in 22 languages. She has also written 21 best-selling independently published romances, including her series, The Dashing Widows and The Lairds Most Likely. Anna has won numerous awards for her Regency-set stories including Romantic Times Reviewers Choice, the Booksellers Best, the Golden Quill (three times), the Heart of Excellence (twice), the Write Touch, the Aspen Gold (twice) and the Australian Romance Readers Association's favorite historical romance (five times). Her books have three times been nominated for Romance Writers of America's prestigious RITA Award, and three times for Australia's Romantic Book of the Year. When she's not traveling the world seeking inspiration for her stories, Anna lives on the beautiful east coast of Australia.

Anna loves to hear from her readers. You can find her at:

Website: www.annacampbell.com

f facebook.com/AnnaCampbellFans

🐦 twitter.com/AnnaCampbellOz

BB bookbub.com/authors/anna-campbell

g goodreads.com/AnnaCampbell

ALSO BY ANNA CAMPBELL

Claiming the Courtesan

Untouched

Tempt the Devil

Captive of Sin

My Reckless Surrender

Midnight's Wild Passion

The Sons of Sin series:

Seven Nights in a Rogue's Bed

Days of Rakes and Roses

A Rake's Midnight Kiss

What a Duke Dares

A Scoundrel by Moonlight

Three Proposals and a Scandal

The Dashing Widows:

The Seduction of Lord Stone

Tempting Mr. Townsend

Winning Lord West

Pursuing Lord Pascal

Charming Sir Charles

Catching Captain Nash

Lord Garson's Bride

The Lairds Most Likely:

The Laird's Willful Lass

The Laird's Christmas Kiss

The Highlander's Lost Lady

Christmas Stories:

The Winter Wife

Her Christmas Earl

A Pirate for Christmas

Mistletoe and the Major

A Match Made in Mistletoe

The Christmas Stranger

Other Books:

These Haunted Hearts

Stranded with the Scottish Earl

THE SEDUCTION OF LORD STONE

(The Dashing Widows Book 1)

For this reckless widow, love is the most dangerous game of all.

Caroline, Lady Beaumont, arrives in London seeking excitement after ten dreary years of marriage and an even drearier year of mourning. That means conquering society, dancing like there's no tomorrow, and taking a lover to provide passion without promises. Promises, in this dashing widow's dictionary, equal prison. So what is an adventurous lady to do when she loses her heart to a notorious rake who, for the first time in his life, wants forever?

Devilish Silas Nash, Viscount Stone is in love at last with a beautiful, headstrong widow bent on playing the field. Worse, she's enlisted his help to set her up with his disreputable best friend. No red-blooded man takes such a challenge lying down, and Silas schemes to seduce his darling into his arms, warm, willing and besotted. But will his passionate plots come undone against a woman determined to act the mistress, but never the wife?

TEMPTING MR TOWNSEND

(The Dashing Widows Book 2)

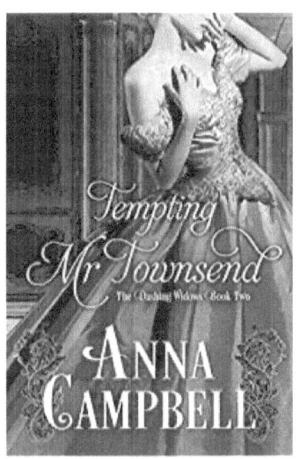

Beauty...

Fenella, Lady Deerham has rejoined society after five years of mourning her beloved husband's death at Waterloo. Now she's fêted as a diamond of the first water and London's perfect lady. But beneath her exquisite exterior, this delicate blond beauty conceals depths of courage and passion nobody has ever suspected. When her son and his school friend go missing, she vows to find them whatever it takes. Including setting off alone in the middle of the night with high-handed bear of a man, Anthony Townsend.

Will this tumultuous journey end in more tragedy? Or will the impetuous quest astonish this Dashing Widow with a breathtaking new love, and life with the last man she ever imagined?

And the Beast?

When Anthony Townsend bursts into Lady Deerham's fashionable Mayfair mansion demanding the return of his orphaned nephew, the lovely widow's beauty and spirit turn his world upside down. But surely such a refined and aristocratic creature will scorn a rough, self-made man's courtship, even if that man is now one of the richest magnates in England. Especially after he's made such a woeful first impression by barging into her house and accusing her of conniving with the runaways. But when Fenella insists on sharing the desperate search for the boys, fate offers Anthony a chance to play the hero and change her mind about him.

Will reluctant proximity convince Fenella that perhaps Mr. Townsend isn't so beastly after all? Or now that their charges are safe, will Anthony and Fenella remain forever opposites fighting their attraction?

WINNING LORD WEST

(The Dashing Widows Book 3)

All rakes are the same! Except when they're not...

Spirited Helena, Countess of Crewe, knows all about profligate rakes; she was married to one for nine years and still bears the scars. Now this Dashing Widow plans a life of glorious freedom where she does just what she wishes – and nobody will ever hurt her again.

So what is she to do when that handsome scoundrel Lord West sets out to make her his wife? Say no, of course. Which is fine, until West focuses all his sensual skills on changing her mind. And West's sensual skills are renowned far and wide as utterly irresistible...

Passionate persuasion!

Vernon Grange, Lord West, has long been estranged from his headstrong first love, Helena Nash, but he's always regretted that he didn't step in to prevent her disastrous marriage. Now Helena is free, and this time, come hell or high water, West won't let her escape him again.

His weapon of choice is seduction, and in this particular game, he's an acknowledged master. Now that he and Helena are under one roof at the year's most glamorous house party, he intends to counter her every argument with breathtaking pleasure. Could it be that Lady Crewe's dashing days are numbered?

PURSUING LORD PASCAL

(The Dashing Widows Book 4)

Golden Days...

Famous for her agricultural innovations, Amy, Lady Mowbray has never had a romantical thought in her life. Well, apart from her short-lived crush on London's handsomest man, Lord Pascal, when she was a brainless 14-year-old. She even chose her late husband because he owned the best herd of beef cattle in England!

But fate steps in and waltzes this practical widow out of her rustic retreat into the glamour of the London season. When Pascal pursues her, all her adolescent fantasies come true. Those fantasies turn disturbingly adult when grown-up desire enters the equation. Amy plunges headlong into a reckless affair that promises pleasure beyond her wildest dreams – until she discovers that this glittering world hides damaging secrets and painful revelations set to break a country girl's tender heart.

All that glitters...

Gervaise Dacre, Lord Pascal needs to marry money to save his estate, devastated after a violent storm. He's never much liked his reputation as London's handsomest man, but it certainly comes in handy when the time arrives to seek a rich bride. Unfortunately, the current crop of debutantes bores him silly, and he finds himself praying for a sensible woman with a generous dowry.

When he meets Dashing Widow Amy Mowbray, it seems all his prayers have been answered. Until he finds himself in thrall to the lovely widow, and his mercenary quest becomes dangerously complicated. Soon he's much more interested in passion than in pounds, shillings and pence. What happens if Amy discovers the sordid truth behind his whirlwind courtship? And if she does, will she see beyond his original, selfish motives to the ardent love that lies unspoken in his sinful heart?

CHARMING SIR CHARLES

(The Dashing Widows Book 5)

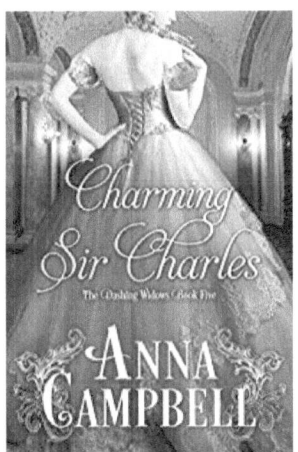

Matchmaking mayhem in Mayfair!

Sally Cowan, Countess of Norwood, spent ten miserable years married to an overbearing oaf. Now she's free, she plans to have some fun. But before she kicks her heels up, this Dashing Widow sets out to launch her pretty, headstrong niece Meg into society and find her a good husband.

When rich and charming Sir Charles Kinglake gives every sign that he can't get enough of Meg's company, Sally is delighted to play chaperone at all their meetings. Charles is everything that's desirable in a gentleman suitor. How disastrous, when over the course of the season's most elegant house party, Sally realizes that desire is precisely the name of the game. She's found her niece's perfect match—but she wants him for herself!

There are none so blind as those who will not see...

From the moment Sir Charles Kinglake meets sparkling Lady Norwood, he's smitten. He courts her as a gentleman should—dancing with her at every glittering ball, taking her to the theatre, escorting her around London. Because she's acting as chaperone to her niece, that means most times, Meg accompanies them. The lack of privacy chafes a man consumed by desire, but Charles's intentions are honorable, and he's willing to work within the rules to win the wife he wants.

However when he discovers that his careful pursuit has convinced Sally he's interested in Meg rather than her, he flings the rules out the window. When love is at stake, who cares about a little scandal? It's time for charming Sir Charles to abandon the subtle approach and play the passionate lover, not the society suitor!

Now with everything at sixes and sevens, Sir Charles risks everything to show lovely Lady Norwood they make the perfect pair!

CATCHING CAPTAIN NASH

(The Dashing Widows Book 6)

Home is the sailor, home from the sea...

Five years after he's lost off the coast of South America, presumed dead, Captain Robert Nash escapes cruel captivity, and returns to London and the bride he loves, but barely knows. When he stumbles back into the family home, he's appalled to find himself gate-crashing the party celebrating his wife's engagement to another man.

This gallant naval officer is ready to take on any challenge; but five years is a long time, and beautiful, passionate Morwenna has clearly found a life without him. Can he win back the wife who gave him a reason to survive his ordeal? Or will the woman who haunts his every thought remain eternally out of reach?

Love lost and found? Or love lost forever?

Since hearing of her beloved husband's death, Morwenna Nash has been mired in grief. After five bleak years without him, she must summon every ounce of courage and determination to become a Dashing Widow and rejoin the social whirl. She owes it to her young daughter to break free of old sorrow and find a new purpose in life, even if that means accepting a loveless marriage.

It's a miracle when Robert returns from the grave, and despite the awkward circumstances of his arrival, she's overjoyed that her husband has come back to her at last. But after years of suffering, he's not the handsome, laughing charmer she remembers. Instead he's a grim shadow of his former dashing self. He can't hide how much he still wants her—but does passion equal love?

Can Morwenna and Robert bridge the chasm of absence, suffering and mistrust, and find their way back to each other?

www.ingramcontent.com/pod-product-compliance
Lightning Source LLC
Chambersburg PA
CBHW030623110726
47901CB00002B/291